To Madeline, Nicholas, and Jennifer

rooftops

a novel

rooftops

tom lewis, 1940-

m. evans and company, inc.
new york

Nathaniel Dame 8/24/81   11·95

81-2143

Library of Congress Cataloging in Publication Data

Lewis, Tom, 1940-
  Rooftops.

  I. Title.
PS 3562.E977R6   813'.54   81-7372

ISBN 0-87131-345-6   AACR2

M. Evans and Company, Inc.
216 East 49 Street
New York, New York 10017

Design by Diane Gedymin

Manufactured in the United States of America

9 8 7 6 5 4 3 2 1

chapter one
222 east 121st street

That first night in the new apartment, a hot midsummer's night in June with the windows wide open and the sirens of the fire engines far away, William lay on his bed as though he was dreaming a new dream.

There were no blinds on the windows yet, and the freshly painted white walls and ceiling were like movie screens for lights and shadows from outside. The gray-blue glare of a streetlight filled the corner where the three angles of walls and ceiling met over William's bed. The grotesque shadow of a large bat flapped through the patch of light overhead, disappeared and returned over and over again.

William got up and walked to the window. The outside air diluted the smell of cheap fresh paint inside the room. A breeze rose from the sidewalk and gave him goose bumps. He hugged his arms around his chest and shivered, but didn't back away from the brand new night scene before him, a scene he slipped into as easily as if he'd lived here all his life. It was comfortable and familiar. Maybe he would like it here.

A streetlight hung out over the street about a floor below William's window. A moth darted and dived around the light. William watched the fuzzy shadow magnified into a bat on the walls inside his room.

Someone looking up from the sidewalk across the street would have seen a small black boy standing in his window, the dark brown skin of his arms ashen in the harsh mercury-vapor

1

light, his white tee shirt as bright as the light, his thin face open and lively, his tightly curled black hair cut short, almost to the scalp. He was eight, but they would have guessed six or seven.

The street was empty now. It was a quiet, short block of walk-up tenements and brownstones on East 123rd Street between Park and Lexington Avenues. An hour earlier, when his mother sent him to bed after the unpacking was nearly done, William had stood in this window watching a middle-aged couple drink beer from a quart bottle in a brown paper bag. They sat on the stoop of the brownstone across the street and talked quietly between themselves until the beer was gone.

The moth flew away. William went back to bed. He jumped up immediately and ran to the window again. A train was coming. It rattled up the rusted, blackened superstructure that held the elevated tracks high above Park Avenue. The tracks were level with William's room.

The trains were the best feature of the new apartment. This was a shiny aluminum commuter train with the engineer in a dark little compartment up front, like a subway, with two bright headlights shining up the rails. It made a heavy booming noise on the elevated tracks as it got closer, then steel brakes screeched as they gripped steel wheels.

William had a corner room. He ran to his other window, facing west over Park Avenue and the elevated tracks. Hot sparks, golden in the darkness, showered off the wheels of the front car as the brakes struck the wheels. The brakes released with a sharp hiss and gripped again. Some of the brake shoes glowed red with heat.

The boy clutched himself with excitement, a secret observer of Amtrak and Conrail, only thirty yards from the train. The last car passed his window. The train stopped at the 125th Street station just north of William's building. No one got on or off. The two red lamps on the last car disappeared up the tracks.

Every time a train passed that summer night, with a few solitary travelers sitting in the yellow-white light behind the moving windows, William leapt out of bed and watched. Finally his mother opened the door to his room and told him quietly it was past midnight, high time to go to sleep. There would be no more trains until morning.

2

But the boy got up once more. Out of the south window of his corner room, he could see red and green lights on a high signal tower silhouetted against the perpetual rose glow of the city's night sky. It was wonderful to see. For the first time in his life, William commanded a whole horizon.

He finally went back to bed, pulled the top sheet up tight around his shoulders, and fell asleep. For the first night in months, he slept the night through without the terror of the recurring nightmare about being trapped in the fires.

The dreams had begun the winter before, when William and his sister and mother lived in a large, yellow brick tenement in the old neighborhood just east of Madison Avenue on 115th Street.

Once freezing January night, the building next door burned. Police ran through William's building telling people to get out. His mother was quick. She stuffed a few things from the top drawer of her dresser into her purse while William and his sister dressed themselves. Then his mother wrapped them both in blankets, and they ran down the stairs to the street, the whole building in an uproar, people yelling and screaming, cops pounding on doors on the top floor and shouting *Fire! Fire! Get Out! Get Out!* William heard these words nightly in his dreams.

The real terror struck William in the street. Flames burst from every window in the building. The firemen and their trucks were covered with ice. Broken glass from the windows of the burning building was frozen under layers of ice on the sidewalk and the cars parked by the curb. Huge icicles hung from the window sills and cornices of the burning building, only inches from the heat of orange flames and black smoke.

As the little family scurried up the block past the roaring diesels of the fire engines, William heard a thin wail from high above. He stopped. Before his mother jerked him away from the sight, he saw his friend's grandmother screaming from her window on the top floor of the burning building. There were flames around her. A fireman was grasping at her from the top of a ladder. William wondered where his friend was.

Before William had run the length of another parked car, the

3

screams stopped. They ran a few more doors up the block to a building where a friend of William's mother waited for them on the sidewalk. The woman began crying and screaming thanks to God when she saw them safe, appearing before her out of smoke and noise like huddled refugees from a war.

The woman hurried them inside and upstairs. William was given warm milk and put to sleep on a couch, but he could hear his mother and her friend in the kitchen, where they had the oven on for warmth. He listened drowsily to the two women talking about the summer just past, when the junkies first appeared in large numbers on the block. They talked about abandoned buildings where the landlords just walked away because they didn't want to pay taxes or repair the buildings, or pay for fuel.

"The city lets them get away with it," said William's mother with tired anger in her voice.

"Yes, yes," said the other woman in her gospel voice, "and the city marshals come to throw you out on the street if you get behind in your rent to the vultures."

Most of the buildings on the block had no heat or hot water. Everyone who could, moved away to places in upper Harlem, or Brooklyn and Queens, which were foreign countries to William. In the abandoned buildings, junkies ripped up the wooden floors for fires to keep warm and burned the buildings down around themselves. But worse, there were arsonists, older boys who would burn a building down for fifty dollars, whether there were people living in it or not. There had already been eight or ten bad fires on the block that winter. The two women said it was lucky nobody but junkies had died.

Then their voices dropped to whispers. In the darkness of the living room, lit brightly in the boy's mind by images of the flames outside, William strained to hear the reassuring voices of his mother and her friend.

His mother said, "I think Jerome and Mrs. Jackson died in that fire tonight."

The other woman groaned deeply. Her voice rose as she told how just last Sunday the preacher at her church gave a sermon about hellfire and brimstone coming to God's people in Harlem,

4

and how the whole sinful city was going up in smoke and ashes.

William's mother said sharply, "Mrs. Jackson and her grandson weren't sinners."

William could imagine his mother wrapped in her robe and blankets, hugging her arms around her own thin body. He thought his mother was beautiful.

Then he drifted off to sleep, confused and hurt by thoughts of his friend's death. He heard his mother say that the landlord of the burning building was the same man who owned the building they lived in. Then the dream came for the first time.

After that, William woke up every night, screaming from a nightmare in which he and his sister and mother were trapped in their apartment. Sometimes the apartment was the one they lived in, and sometimes it was unfamiliar and his father was there, which made the fright worse because his father was dead.

When they went home in the morning, they saw the smoking, gutted shell of the burned building. They walked past as fast as they could. Tons of dirty ice hung from the hulk and covered the street. Their own apartment smelled bitter from smoke for months, until they moved.

The only time William regretted living in the new apartment by the train tracks was when the heavy noise of commuter trains woke him early in the gray light of school mornings. At the moment of waking, he could remember the soft quiet of mornings when he was very little, the long, peaceful mornings after his sister began kindergarten, and there was no one home but him and his mother.

But his memories were like movies. He couldn't stop them. The quiet of the old neighborhood was broken by the invasion of the junkies with their loud portable radios and screaming fights. They brought fear and endless hassles. It wasn't long before William and his sister grew afraid to play outside. The girl was eleven then and the boy seven. Most of the invaders were teenage boys and young men. They were always yelling at the girl, making invitations, terrifying the girl and the helpless little boy.

5

"Hey, yo. Bitch. Ovah heah. Come ovah heah, an' sit on mah face." And they would screech and laugh, and sometimes chase the children.

Lying in his bed, warm and cozy in the chill of a March school morning, William twisted and turned under the covers in anguish at the hateful memories. Another train rolled by, heading downtown toward the long Park Avenue tunnel that began at 97th Street and ended under Grand Central Station.

The trains rolled by one after another, with only a few minutes between them. Their noise finally silenced his memories, and his fascination with the trains and all their details took him over. He loved looking at the heavy couplings and undercarriages, the hanging pipes and hoses, the contrasts between the sleek new cars and the dirty old green cars with broken windows.

Another train rolled by William's window. He could tell it was going uptown because the brakes were grinding for the stop at 125th Street. It was time to get up and go to school. He pushed the covers back and walked the few steps to the west window overlooking the tracks. He shivered from the morning chill in the room. With two windows, it was the coldest room in the house. His mother gave him an extra blanket in the winter. He pulled it off the bed and wrapped it around himself. There was still a winter dampness in the early March mornings.

Another train went by, rolling fast downtown. The people on the train were asleep or had their faces buried in newspapers. They were nearly all white people. William saw these people every morning. He had seen them every weekday morning for nine months. He even recognized some of them. He had no idea where they lived, but he knew they worked in the tall buildings downtown.

William's mother once took him and his sister downtown on one of the trains from 125th Street to Grand Central so the kids could see where the trains went. The excursion cost much more than the subway and only lasted fifteen minutes, but William was so happy that he imagined himself a passenger on a famous overnight train to Chicago full of boxers and basketball players, singers and movie stars.

Every detail of the little trip registered on the films of his memory, especially the sudden darkness of the long tunnel and the many switches and branching tracks at the end among the platforms where there were a dozen trains parked, waiting for the afternoon rush homeward. Then there was the surprise of the huge main room of Grand Central Station, with golden stars painted in the dark blue ceiling vault high overhead.

"It's the color of the night sky," he said in wonder to his sister.

His mother laughed out loud in the middle of all the rushing people. She said, "No, honey. The night sky over this city is never that dark and clear."

The flaking blue paint and faded golden stars of Grand Central Station became the little boy's new standard. Sometimes that winter the sky was the right color, but the stars were brittle silver.

When the fast train carrying the men and women to their jobs got past his window, William could see west to the great hill in the center of Mount Morris Park, one long block away. People called it Marcus Garvey Park, too. He walked there sometimes with his sister, going under the tracks and down the block by the Hospital for Joint Diseases, with its odd open galleries on each floor looking west and south over the park and the neighboring block.

From his window, William could see the tall, open-steel framework of the bell tower at the top of Mount Morris. He wondered why they never rang the bell. The tall trees on the east side of the park were bare. Through their branches, he could see the steep rock hillside and patches of snow and ice left from the cold weather of a few days before.

This morning the sun shone brightly past William's house right down the block into the park. The snow glistened. William knew it would melt that day. Spring was on its way. His mother said they would have lunch together in warm weather in the park, little picnics, just the three of them. She was a cook at a well-known nightclub in Harlem and worked from four to midnight, sometimes later on weekends. They always had lunch together in the summer when he had no school.

7

She called him now, telling him to get washed and dressed for school. "Wear your good sweater," she said, "and your warm corduroy pants."

He walked into the dim light of the living room and around the open sofa-bed. The shades were down. His mother would go back to bed for a couple of hours of extra sleep after she fed the two children their breakfasts. William could see her standing in the kitchen in her long robe, frying bacon and eggs and making toast, the way she did late at night in the big kitchen at the back of the restaurant, with the bands and singers out front, and the people laughing and drinking.

"Hi, honey," she said, smiling at him. "How you feelin' this morning?"

"Good," said William, his voice light and quiet. "I feel good."

"That's good," she said. "Go wash up now."

He washed and went back to his room where he pulled on clean underwear and a long-sleeved polo shirt with bright yellow and red stripes. He rummaged around on the floor of his closet and found his almost new, almost clean brown corduroys and pulled them on. They were a little loose around his thin waist, but he decided not to hunt for his belt. His mother would not notice under the sweater.

Then he pulled on a thick wool ski sweater with red reindeer on a white stripe around the chest. His mother got it somewhere for Christmas, in a big store downtown. He loved the sweater. It had a funny, wet wool smell even when it was dry. No one else in his class had such a sweater. He sat down on his bed, pulled on his socks, and laced up his sneakers, a pair of ankle-high white Pro-Keds in excellent condition. He was ready for school.

"William? You ready?" His mother called from the kitchen. "Your breakfast is ready. Come on, now."

"OK, Mama. I'm coming."

He glanced out the window at another train, an old diesel yard engine belching more black smoke than an incinerator and pulling a string of filthy old cars, half of them with no lights, the passengers wearing hats and gloves, and overcoats buttoned to the neck. It was a comical sight. William laughed out loud.

He pulled the sheet and blankets up on his bed and went into the warm kitchen. His sister was already eating her breakfast.

"Over easy," his mother said. "Here's your eggs the way you like 'em, Mister William."

They ate breakfast, not talking. Their mother washed the pans in the sink and wiped the kitchen clean with the absent gestures of a skilled cook on familiar ground. She poured herself a cup of coffee and watched the children eat.

The children finished their food and went to get their coats. They kissed their mother goodbye in silence at the doorway of the little kitchen. She followed them to the apartment door, where she reminded them to come straight home from school so she could see them before the babysitter came at three-thirty.

The boy and girl walked down the short bare hallway and down the stairs to the street. The woman double locked the apartment door, went to the kitchen for her coffee cup, then to William's room to stand by his south window where she could see the streetcorner below. The day was bright, but she could feel a chill by the window. It looked as though the day might cloud up later. She pulled her robe tighter around her and held the warm coffee mug in both hands as she leaned against the window frame.

As the two children bounced out onto the front stoop, William saw that someone during the night had busted the lock on the front door and jimmied open several mailboxes in the front hall. He pointed it out to his sister, who said simply, "Tell Mama."

William understood what she meant. His sister got out of school half an hour later than he, and sometimes she didn't get home before their mother left for work.

"Look there," said William. He pointed up the street toward Lexington Avenue. The two children squinted into the morning sun. Two unfamiliar men sat on the lower steps of a stoop halfway up the block, passing a wine bottle back and forth in a brown paper bag.

"Shoot," said William's sister. "Junkies. Tell Mama."

There was an adult anger in her voice that William had never heard before. Without comment, they both knew exactly what was signified by the broken lock, the jimmied mailboxes, the two men on the stoop. Prowling junkies. The same early signs appeared in the old neighborhood only weeks before the final invasion.

This little block had been in the lee of the storm up to now. Winos and junkies were unusual, and never staked out territory on a stoop. Mostly they passed through, going from somewhere to somewhere else, usually to Mount Morris Park.

When junkies moved in, other people were already moving out. William remembered his mother saying it was like trying to stop the tide from rolling in and out. He suddenly knew what she meant. After school, he would tell her what they'd seen this morning, and what he understood.

From William's window, the woman watched her two children walk quickly to the near corner. The girl hurried because she had farther to go. Moving uptown put the family into a different school district. The girl now went to an intermediate school on Madison Avenue above 125th Street. The boy went to a school in the old district, where there was a third-grade teacher his mother knew and liked. Despite the difficult rules of the city's Board of Education, the local district superintendent was willing to overlook the family's change of address.

The girl waved her fingers at her brother and back up at the window where she knew her mother would be, then disappeared around the corner. William ran across 123rd Street to the other corner and turned to wave goodbye. His mother could see him clearly, and she waved back, thinking he could see her, but the angle of the morning sun turned the window glass into a sheet of rippling gold. William shaded his eyes from the blinding reflection and waved again, then turned and walked around the corner out of her sight.

He took the same route to school every day, down the east side of Park Avenue in the deep shadows cast by the apartment houses rising above him on his left. Across the cobblestones to his right were the dark angles of the elevated tracks. He was fascinated by the structural shapes and the way the whole thing

10

held together when the trains rolled overhead. He watched a train heading uptown. Its thunderous noise rattled around in echoes between tracks, buildings, and the dozens of cars parked in rows under the tracks.

There was no one on William's side of the avenue. Sunlight fell on a few men standing and talking in front of a Gulf station, kitty-corner across the intersection of Park and 122nd Street, over past the parked cars under the tracks. Two cars drove slowly through the intersection, then a yellow cab in a hurry. William stood in the warm sun waiting for the light to change, then ran across the street and out of the sun again.

He hurried down Park Avenue between the buildings and the tracks. He was alone on the street, and it was quiet, no trains coming and no people in sight. He knew there was an old news vendor in a little candy store at the next corner.

Halfway down the block, William passed an alley leading back between the buildings into a maze of broken chain-link fences, scruffy locust trees, and the crisscrossed patterns of clotheslines leading from building to building. Washing flapped from some of the lines.

The alley was sunlit in the morning, but it always spooked William because one of the building supers kept a savage German Shepherd that barked and snarled from behind a flimsy iron gate. The dog was bigger than William. He was afraid it would break out and bite him with its huge glistening white teeth.

William darted past the alley, happy the dog did not appear, when he heard someone close behind him call out. "Yo," said the voice. "Hey, yo."

William leapt a few more steps past the alley and turned. He saw a man wearing a purple and white stocking cap pulled tightly down over long dark hair. The cap was rolled up once to display the emblem of the Minnesota Vikings.

The man insisted, "Yo. Hey. Kid."

The dog woke up and lunged at the gate, barking and howling with single-minded purpose, toenails clicking horridly and scratching on the concrete.

The man stood in the street on the other side of a parked

11

car, having apparently crossed from the parking lot beneath the elevated tracks. He waved a piece of paper at William.

William was badly frightened by the dog and the stranger. He looked wildly around him, saw no one to help, and turned to run away. The man ran with lightning quickness between two parked cars and cut him off. The boy stopped and edged back until he could feel the rough bricks of the blank wall behind him. The bricks felt sharp and gritty.

The man made no move to grab William. Instead, he smiled at the boy and held out his hand with a piece of paper in it. *"Mira,"* he said. "Yo. *Mira* this paper, *por favor*. Please, I am lost."

The man had a thick Spanish accent, but not the familiar Puerto Rican accent of most of the Spanish-speaking children William knew from school. The boy knew what the man wanted —the Spanish words were part of the common vocabulary of the street—but William was unsure of this stranger.

The man sensed it. He looked at the drooling, growling dog and gestured for William to come down the sidewalk away from the frightening animal. William relaxed a little and walked a few yards toward the corner. The dog lost interest and padded back to its dirty lair, clicking with each step.

With the dog gone, William stepped back from the man, looking for a way to get around him. The boy looked longingly at the safe haven of the candy store and the morning sunlight in the next street, where he could turn and run for school. He was going to be late.

"I'm late for school," said William. "Let me go. I have to go."

"Please," said the man. "I do not live around here. Help me. I am trying to find this hospital."

Another train roared past overhead carrying hundreds of people to work in stores and office buildings four or five miles downtown. The little boy and the strange man stood without moving, staring at each other, locked together in the inhuman noise of the train.

William held out his hand and took the paper. It was the corner of an envelope, the return address. In official-looking blue print, it said:

Manhattan Psychiatric Center
Manhattan State Hospital
Ward's Island
New York, New York 10035

The boy gave the soiled, crumpled paper back to the smiling, patient man. William watched him put it in the breast pocket of his army field jacket, and carefully snap the pocket closed. William's father had a jacket like that. William's father was in the army when he got killed.

The man was not a junkie or a wino. He didn't look sick. He was clean.

"Where is this hospital?" asked the man. "My name is Tony. What is your name?"

William looked past the man and didn't answer. A blue and white police car came up Park Avenue, turned slowly under the tracks, and went back down the other side of the street. If the police noticed William and the man, they were careful not to betray it. The cop on the passenger's side didn't look up for a moment from his *Daily News*.

The stranger's manner was not hostile, but there was something about him the boy couldn't read quickly or easily. It was like a page missing from a book.

The man was young, about twenty, and not much taller than William's mother, who was about five and a half feet tall, William knew. The man's faded army jacket was open over a gray sweatshirt that said *New York Mets*. His khaki pants were loose and baggy. The cuffs were rolled up a couple turns over highly polished army boots. The clothes were spotless.

The man was dark-skinned, not as dark as William but darker than William's mother and sister. The man had the facial features of a Latin, but he seemed different from the Puerto Ricans William knew in school. William's mother said there were a lot of islands and countries where Latin people came from.

William suddenly began walking to the corner. Instead of blocking him, the man walked alongside.

"I have to go to school now. I think the hospital is way over there," said William, pointing east through the apartment building in the direction of the sun.

13

The man said, "The river is over there, I think, and the hospital is on a big island in the river. How far is the river?"

"I don't know. I never go there," William lied carefully. He had once walked to the river in the summer with his sister. "A long walk," he added. "Maybe ten blocks." He didn't like to lie.

When they reached the bright sunlight of the corner, the man put his hand out to touch the boy's arm. William started.

The man asked again, "What is your name?"

"William." The boy stopped walking and looked at the man carefully. The cuffs of the khaki pants were rolled almost to the tops of the shiny boots, which were laced with military precision.

"Where do you go to school?" asked the man.

"PS 7."

"Is that near the river?"

"It's on 120th Street. I have to go now. I'm late. Goodbye," said William formally.

The man touched William on the arm again. The boy drew away but did not flinch as before.

"Wait. I'll walk with you. It must be on the way."

William said, "I'm in a hurry."

The man said quickly, "I can walk fast."

Without answering, William walked away toward Lexington Avenue. The man caught up with a little jump and walked along next to the boy, who stayed carefully on the outside of the sidewalk near the curb and the parked cars.

As the two walked away from the corner, the news vendor shuffled out of his doorway and looked up the street into the sun after them. The little store was as dark as a cave, and the wizened old man had watched the exchange between William and the stranger from only a few feet away, from behind a window so dirty it might have been made of tin. With the caution of a possum, a survivor in a hostile environment, the old man did not interfere, but he watched. He could barely see them in the brilliant morning sunlight. He shaded his eyes with both hands, but all he could make out were two dark shadows moving up the block, one small and thin and bouncy, the taller one walking with a pronounced limp. The old man saw the taller shadow reach out now and then to touch the smaller shape.

Halfway down the block, William turned to watch a train

14

passing up the elevated tracks. It was the familiar string of ancient, grimy, green coaches towed by the yard engine blowing a plume of heavy black smoke into the blue sky. When the relic train rattled uptown out of sight, William asked, "Are you going to see someone?"

"Yes," said the man. "Is there a rooftop where you go sometimes where you can see the river?"

"Yes," said William. He began walking again. He had to cross Lexington, then cut down through the middle of the next block on a little street called Sylvan Place. It would take him directly to the entrance of the school on 120th Street.

"Which building is the roof?"

"It's on the way." William walked quickly. This would be the first time all year he was late for school.

"How old are you?"

"Eight. I'm in third grade."

The man offered William two quarters to show him the building with the roof. As they walked, the man held the coins out in his hand. The boy took the money and put it in his pocket.

The building was at the end of the block. It was locked. As the man tugged at the door, William looked back and saw the bent, dark figure of the old newsdealer peering up the sidewalk at them. William was sure the old man was nearly blind.

The stranger asked if there was another building. William pointed to a building on the southeast corner of 121st Street and Third Avenue. He said it was never locked.

The school crossing guard was gone from the corner of Lexington Avenue. Now William knew he was very late. He hopped from foot to foot as he waited for the light to change, then ran across. As he reached the curb, he saw the crossing guard standing in the doorway of a coffee shop, drinking coffee from a container. She smiled and waved at William, who waved back and kept running.

The stranger was running next to him but at a little distance, as though they just happened to be crossing the busy street at the same time. Despite his limp, the man was quick and agile.

At the corner of Sylvan Place, William stopped and in his formal manner, said goodbye to the stranger. They stood in the shadow of the old Harlem Courthouse. Tony thanked the boy, then offered him two more quarters to guide him to the roof of the building on the next corner.

William looked down the short block at the familiar front of PS 7. He could see people moving around inside the brightly lit classrooms. The windows of the three-story building were full of paper cutouts taped to the glass. He was very late.

"Let me see the money," he said.

The man pulled two more quarters out of his pants pocket. He said, "Help me. Show me the roof. I'm lost."

The boy scooted around the corner of the courthouse as if he were afraid of being seen from the school.

"Give me the money now," he said, "and I'll show you the building."

Tony flashed a dollar bill. "Show me the roof," he said. "I'll give you one dollar."

William agreed. The building was just half a block away, on the other side of Third Avenue. It took them only a minute to get there. William was in a desperate hurry to get the money and get to school. The front door was open, as William knew it would be.

William took the two quarters from Tony's hand and dropped them in his pocket with the first two coins. They made a little jingle. Tony gave him the dollar. William clutched it in his hand, trying to decide which pocket to put it in.

They stood just inside the outer hall of the building. The interior had the darkness of abandonment and complete neglect. Every mailbox was broken. Every tile in the floor was loose or chipped. Every pane of glass was broken. The interior door lay on the floor, glass shattered, hinges broken. Everything broken lay where it fell.

William turned to run. As he slipped past Tony, the boy felt himself gripped by the arm and around his waist harder than anyone had ever grabbed him.

Before the boy could react, the man swung him off the floor by his waist and smashed his hand over his mouth. Then William knew what was going to happen. He screamed, but the noise was trapped in his throat.

Carrying the boy in an immovable grip, the man trotted

back into the darkened first floor of the building and stopped for a moment, listening. Then he started up the stairs.

William was kicking and pounding, but the man took no notice. The man's strength was inhuman. He ran up the stairs, sometimes two at a time. He suddenly shifted his grip and clamped his thumb and forefinger over the boy's nose and his hand over the boy's mouth.

By the time they reached the fourth floor, William had fainted. The man shifted his powerful grip to the boy's throat. When the man reached the open door to the roof, seven floors above the street, the boy was mercifully dead.

chapter two
rooftop

By noon, the weather began to change. A chilly wind swept in over the East River, the sun clouded over, and the temperature dropped. A thick drizzle began to fall. By the time school let out, it was raining hard, and when William's mother began to look for her son, the rain was turning to sleet.

The boy usually got home at three-fifteen. At three-thirty when the sitter arrived, William's mother called the school. His teacher was gone, but an office aide checked the day's records and said the boy was absent.

The sitter was an old grandmother who lived alone on the first floor of the building. "Don't waste no time, honey," she said. "Call the police."

After waiting sixty rings for the emergency number at 911, William's mother was told her problem was not an emergency. She was told to call her local precinct.

"Which precinct is that?"

"It's in the phone book, lady," said the voice, and hung up.

"It's the Twenty-Eighth Precinct," said the sitter. "Says so right on the side of the cars around here."

William's mother called information and got the number. Then she called the precinct. There was no answer. On her face was the look of someone who has been told by their doctor they are going to die soon.

She dialed again. Someone answered on the third ring. "This

is Thelma Thomas," she began, "and my little boy is late from school."

She was told abruptly that the police couldn't act for twenty-four hours, but if the boy wasn't home by dinnertime, to call again. She hung up the phone with a bang.

The two women could hear the sleet washing against the windows. The sitter reached over and turned on a lamp in the dark apartment. A train clattered by. Mrs. Thomas walked to the front window in William's room. There was an inch of slush on the street. The sky was an even metallic gray. Low clouds blew hard over the rooftops. She saw the girl come around the corner, running and slipping in the slush, holding her books over her head.

"Ruth Anne and I will look for William," she said to the sitter. "You stay here and wait. Call the restaurant and tell them I'll be late."

When the girl walked in, her mother was waiting with boots and heavy coat. "Put these on, Ruth Anne," she said. "William isn't home from school. We're going to find him."

"Mama," said the girl. "Did you see the mailboxes down-stairs?"

"I know," said the mother. "I know."

It was almost four o'clock. They walked quickly along William's daily route to PS 7. He was rarely late, but now and then in bad weather, he would dawdle his way home from store to store along Lexington Avenue, then across 123rd Street to his house. They went to the school, which was dark, then traced William's alternate route home.

A few months earlier, the boy had been a little late getting home, enough to irritate his mother, who asked him sharply what took him so long. He answered simply, "I took the long-cut."

She had been disarmed and she had laughed. Now, standing in the freezing rain and snow outside her building, she remembered the moment. Tears of anger and fear came to her eyes. She turned away so the girl couldn't see.

Cars splashed by in the deepening slush. The streetlights came on, their glare softened by the wet snow. Both women were cold and wet. There was no one on the street, and this was not a cozy or comfortable neighborhood, however familiar it was to the people who lived there. Now it looked poor and deserted, and there were few lights in the windows to give warmth at the gathering end of day.

"I'm frightened, Mama," whispered the girl. She was crying.

Mrs. Thomas put her arm around her but said nothing. Then she asked, "Is that old man's store down the street still open?"

"He's always in there. He lives in the back."

They hurried, almost running down Park Avenue, tracing again the way William went in the morning. Mrs. Thomas pounded on the battered door. The old man pulled it open and peered out. An odor of cooking grease blew from the door. A candle was the only light inside. The old man was wrapped in layers of indescribable clothing. He looked steadily at the two women.

"You looking for the little boy?"

"Yes," Mrs. Thomas almost screamed. The girl drew back a step, her hand covering her mouth.

"He came by my corner like every day, but this morning he stopped to talk to a Spanish man. He come out from under the tracks. Then they talk and they go to school together."

Mrs. Thomas was gasping for breath. "To school?"

The girl said, "He didn't go to school today."

The old man looked at them. His dark eyes had the dull surface of tin, like his front window. "They stopped in the middle of the block there." He waved his arm. "I watched 'em. They was talkin' there, then they went on. I couldn't see no more in the sun." He shaded his eyes with his hand as he spoke. He answered her unspoken question. "No, ma'am. He ain't been back."

Mrs. Thomas turned on her daughter. "Ruth Anne, where would he go? Is there anyplace around here he used to go, he never told me about?"

The girl looked up at her mother. "There's an old building over on Third Avenue where he used to go up on the roof. He said you could see way downtown, and planes landing at the airport across the river." The girl was weeping. "Mama," she said, sobbing now. "Mama. He's dead."

They ran, slipping and splashing in the slush now turning to ice. They ran across Lexington Avenue and down the next block, holding hands. A woman peering out of her ground-floor window at the dismal evening saw them go by and wondered that anyone could run so fast in sleet and ice on broken sidewalks.

They ran past Sylvan Place and stopped at the corner where William had stopped seven hours earlier. Nothing but fire lights burned in the school now, an almost new school with a front of green architectural glass and rows of metal casement windows covered on the inside with the children's paper cutouts. They stared at the windows of William's classroom on the second floor, at each silhouette of flowers and Easter bunnies. Then they turned like two birds on a fence and ran past the turreted, yellow-brick Harlem Courthouse. It wasn't a courthouse anymore, but a sanitation district headquarters, a neglected monument to a past that might never have existed.

They ran across Third Avenue, dodging hand-in-hand through the heavy traffic moving slowly uptown toward the Harlem River bridges. They ran into the entrance of the old building. The girl slipped and fell on the slick wet tile floor, almost pulling her mother down with her. The girl screamed, not with pain, but anxiety and fear. The building was half-abandoned, nearly pitch dark and silent. The remaining squatters huddled in their apartments. The girl's scream was enough to freeze all activity in the standing husk of the building.

"Shush, girl," said the woman, lifting the child to her feet. "Don't be afraid. Hold my hand tight, and we'll go up and look on the rooftop."

They made their way slowly up the stairs, the woman leading, feeling her way in the dark, the girl gripping her mother's hand as tight as she could. There were faint noises in the building—a muffled voice, a TV set—the sounds of people in hiding. An ambulance made its way up Third Avenue and stopped nearby, stuck in the clot of cars and trucks at the corner outside. The siren rose and fell in a monotonous scream, then whooped and burbled. The noise was demented. There was some shouting, then the siren died away uptown.

Above them at the top of the stairs, a loose door banged and slatted in the wind. The two women could hear it as they passed

22

the third floor. They began to sense a dim, watery gray light as they neared the top floor.

There were shattered skylights in the ceiling of the top floor hallway. Every apartment on the floor was abandoned. Doors were down or hung uselessly open. Fires in some of the apartments had burned holes through the roof. Pools of slush ran into the hallway from apartments with the light of fading day in open doors. The slush was freezing to dirty ice.

The two women climbed to the roof, up rotten wooden stairs into a little cupola. The banging door they had heard below swung to and fro on its hinges in the icy wind. The rooftop looked like a battleground, with jagged holes four or five feet across, and one large hole where the ceiling of an entire apartment had fallen in, leaving broken rafters and shreds of roofing paper hanging into the rooms below.

They found the little body in the corner of the roof next to a low parapet overlooking the intersection below. They saw the ice-covered mound, blanketed by wind-blown sleet, from ten yards away across a hole in the roof.

"That's where he liked to stand and look," said the girl in a hushed voice.

The awful whine of a jet airliner landing at LaGuardia Airport across the river drowned out her mother's answer. They both looked up involuntarily and saw the big plane very low, rocking crazily in the high winds as it dropped toward the runway.

Then they got closer to the boy's body and saw what had happened. The girl collapsed to her hands and knees, sobbing so hard she couldn't breathe. The woman knelt down in perfect silence and scraped the grains of frozen slush from her son's cold corpse. He lay on his back where he had been thrown, fully clothed from the waist up, but wearing only his white knee-high basketball socks below the waist. They had green and orange stripes around the tops, and they were pulled up straight and neat. The boy's underpants, trousers, and sneakers were nearby, folded in a neat pile, frozen solid. It was a grievous and devastating sight.

William's right hand clutched a folded dollar bill. Mrs.

Thomas pulled it free, lifted it above the edge of the parapet, and let it drop away on the wind. She wrapped the boy in her coat and carried him down the dark stairs, holding his head on her shoulder the way she had when he was little. She left the cold clothing where it lay.

The girl followed carefully down the stairs, which were darker than before and slippery with water. An apartment door slammed shut on a lower floor. Loud voices shouted in Spanish, a man and a woman in a bitter quarrel. The girl held tightly to the back of her mother's old sweater as they went down step by step with the cold, stiff body of the little boy.

Lieutenant O'Malley stomped toward the front door of the station house, the clasps on his heavy rubber galoshes clinking like spurs. The desk sergeant thought the man was going to break the door.

"It's late. Son of a bitch," raged O'Malley. "Why don't these fucking people kill their fucking kids before it's time to go home?"

O'Malley slammed through the door. The desk sergeant exhaled. O'Malley's driver ran through the room, struggling into his jacket, dragging his raincoat on the floor.

The desk sergeant spoke into the telephone clutched tightly in his hand. "He's coming right now, Sergeant Rodriguez. In a black mood, too. And he's bringing his two dogs with him."

"His what?"

"Feldman and Flanagan."

"Shit," said Rodriguez very softly. "This woman needs help, not the rubber hose."

Rodriguez set the phone gently in its cradle. There was nothing he could say or do to ease the pain of the boy's mother and sister. He asked his questions and took his notes. He looked again at the three women in the room, asked again if there wasn't a minister or someone he could call, and saw the mute grief harden in their faces. He stepped out of the apartment into the hall.

A door banged downstairs. It was O'Malley, slamming the door open, and slamming it shut again.

O'Malley shouted up the stairwell. "Rodriguez? Rodriguez? Where the hell are you?"

"Fourth floor, Lieutenant."

"Jesus Christ!" O'Malley started heavily up the stairs, his galoshes clicking and clanking with every step.

Rodriguez set himself for the encounter. It was the end of his first week in the new command, and he knew already that he and his new boss were on a collision course. Rodriguez was said to be one of the best and brightest of the young blood on the force, and he knew O'Malley was widely thought to be one of the best and toughest of the old breed of homicide cops. Rodriguez was quick and street smart, having been raised in a Brooklyn ghetto, and having made it all the way up and out to a BA degree from City College. O'Malley was experienced in every way possible, having been raised in one of the old Bronx Irish ghettos, and having never spent a moment in an institution of the higher learning. Rodriguez was straight, and O'Malley was one of the old silk-stocking, Gentleman Johnny detectives for whom a gold shield was a license to buy four-hundred-dollar suits with fit hundred dollar bills.

They had one thing in common: they both hated wearing the uniform. Rodriguez had discovered it that same afternoon, when O'Malley bellowed to him in the squad room to put on his god-damn fucking uniform because all the goddamn fucking super-visors from the next shift had called in sick because of the goddamn fucking weather, the fucking pansies, and Rodriguez had just volunteered to be the patrol supervisor tonight and make some overtime.

When Rodriguez presented himself in uniform in the Lieu-tenant's office, O'Malley had glanced up and sneered, "You look pretty. You sure you got enough of those silly fucking medals they hand out every Saint Patrick's Day? Oh shit, I forgot. You're not one of us. Go find a car and a driver."

And O'Malley reached into his desk drawer and threw a handful of the little enameled metal bars out on the desk top, loose, like dice. "I've got more than you," he said, "but if you work hard, you'll catch up quick. They're easier these days."

25

Rodriguez said nothing.

"That uniform is nothing," O'Malley continued. "I hate it. I haven't worn mine for twenty years, and I'm gonna call in sick to my retirement. Any scumbag in the city can wear those rags now." There was a long pause. "Present company excepted."

O'Malley wasn't breathing hard when he reached the fourth floor, despite his bulk and two packs of Pall Malls each day. He said nothing, but he raised his eyebrows mockingly at Rodriguez, and burst into the apartment like an old bull. Rodriguez could hear Feldman and Flanagan coming up the stairs like two more bulls. Rodriguez stepped into the apartment.

O'Malley stopped in the center of the living room. His heavy, black rubber raincoat hung open and dripped on the rug. He thrust his hands into his pants pockets and stood glaring down at Mrs. Thomas, who sat on her sofa holding her daughter in her arms.

"Rodriguez, what the hell happened here? Where's the little kid?"

"On his bed in the corner bedroom there."

A train roared by. O'Malley had a rough, red Irishman's face, intelligent, capped by an unruly mess of short gray hair, but no more expressive than a piece of broken rock. He loomed over Mrs. Thomas and the girl, staring at them. He made no move to look at the body of the boy.

Feldman and Flanagan came into the room, nearly bringing the door frame with them. They were both larger than O'Malley. They moved to positions flanking him—Feldman to the left and Flanagan to the right. They looked like linebackers. The three large men stood in the center of the room and waited for some sign from Mrs. Thomas that she was guilty of something, but she was stiff with grief and rage and gave no sign of anything they cared to understand.

Another train filled the room with noise. Rodriguez was not intimidated by his colleagues, but they made him feel like an unnecessary presence in the room. He wondered what they would have done if he weren't there.

O'Malley's voice cut through the noise. "Tell me the story, Rodriguez."

Rodriguez spoke in a cop's monotone. He and his driver responded to a call to go to 121st and Third. No one was there. Then the desk sergeant sent them here. The woman, Mrs. Selma Thomas, and her daughter, Ruth Anne, had just returned home after finding the body of William, age eight, on the roof of the abandoned building at 121st and Third. Mrs. Thomas carried the boy home on foot. She left some clothing of the boy's at the scene. The boy left home for school at the normal time in the morning. He apparently never reached school. The boy and the clothes at the scene were well covered by frozen sleet, making the likely time of death sometime in the morning before the weather changed. The boy's body was badly mutilated.

When he finished, Rodriguez realized how angry he was at O'Malley for forcing him to make his recital in front of the woman and the girl. The woman held her weeping daughter and heard the story out to the end without emotion. She looked steadily back at O'Malley, perhaps wondering whether he was her accuser, or merely another white interrogator.

"My name is Thelma, not Selma," she said. "Selma is a city in Alabama."

O'Malley ignored her.

"Where's your driver, Rodriguez?"

"I sent him to secure the scene at the building where she found the body."

"Humh. You're the only one in the whole goddamn Two-Eight with any goddamn brains."

Rodriguez didn't react. After only a week in Sixth Homicide, he knew that praise from O'Malley was no more sought than blame. Contact with O'Malley was to be avoided, because he was violent and unpredictable. O'Malley was always angry, but he often got more angry.

"Who's this other woman here?" asked O'Malley with irritation, turning to look at the babysitter crying quietly in an armchair in a corner of the room. Without waiting for an answer, he asked, "She know anything about this story?"

His hard emphasis on the word *story* made it clear he didn't believe one word attributed to Mrs. Thomas, and that she was in for heavy interrogation and a terrible accusation.

"No. She's the babysitter. She lives downstairs," said Rodriguez.

"Feldman," said O'Malley.

Feldman didn't move an inch, but to Rodriguez, who already despised O'Malley's two linebackers, it appeared that he had somehow moved to front and center.

"Get her name and get her out of here," said O'Malley.

Feldman moved in front of the little old lady and pulled out his notebook as if it were a nightstick. There was a long silence.

Rodriguez knew about Feldman and Flanagan. They worked with O'Malley and no one else. Some Anglophile wit on the squad had once called them O'Malley's dogs-bodies. Now they were just O'Malley's dogs.

Horst Feldman was brutal and dumb, on the force for forty years. Sometime in the dim past, he had been assigned to homicide because he spoke German, and the Sixth Detective Division had once included the Germans of Yorkville in the East Eighties. Rodriguez admired the crude logic of it. It was not unlike assigning Puerto Ricans to Spanish-speaking neighborhoods, but Rodriguez knew Feldman had never been assigned anywhere else. Given a choice, no commander would accept Feldman.

Flanagan was an old hard-luck Irishman, once a very good cop who had moved around the city in various homicide zones and earned a lot of citations. Now he was a heavy drinker. He was also a friend of O'Malley's from one of the Bronx parishes. O'Malley protected him.

Feldman shuffled his huge feet. The old lady gave in and gave her name. She left the apartment without another word. Mrs. Thomas thanked her. Feldman closed the apartment door and returned to his position.

"Flanagan." The other flanker came to a position of slack attention. "Go look at the body." Flanagan walked into the bedroom and closed the door. Mrs. Thomas got up to follow, but O'Malley waved her back. Her face collapsed. She looked lost.

"Tell me, Mrs. Thomas. Tell me your story from the beginning. How you lost the little boy and how you found him. I want to hear it. All of it."

O'Malley's feigned politeness was spoken in a grindstone voice that cut through the noise of another passing train. He made no attempt to hide his sarcasm. Mrs. Thomas was caught between outrage and grief. She could barely speak, but she looked straight at the men looming over her and told her story again.

As she related her climb to the roof, Flanagan opened the bedroom door. His puffy drinker's face was twisted by a frozen grin. He was about to say something when O'Malley held up his hand for silence. Flanagan stood in the door, listening to the account of the discovery of the boy's body.

Rodriguez knew the grin on Flanagan's face was not arrested laughter. It was the same horror he had felt himself when he pulled down the neatly tucked blanket covering the body on the bed. When the woman finished her recitation, the girl began fresh sobbing so deep that Rodriguez was nearly moved to tears himself.

O'Malley went into the bedroom with Flanagan and closed the door. The woman held the girl and crooned to her that they would be all right, and told her not to be afraid of the policemen.

"But Mama, they think you killed William." The girl whispered the sentence in gasps.

Rodriguez couldn't contain himself. "No ma'am," he said.

Feldman stared at him in surprise. Feldman and Flanagan were O'Malley's informers and enforcers, doing exactly what O'Malley ordered, never more and never less, and reporting everything they saw and heard. Rodriguez knew he would hear about his little slip from O'Malley in the morning.

Mrs. Thomas let nothing register on her face. She had seen immediately that the lieutenant, who had not yet told her his name, was dangerous, and she was completely focused on him. Rodriguez, feeling like an accidental bystander and getting angry, knew exactly what was going on, and felt helpless to intervene. He had been watching scenes like this between white cops and brown-skinned people since he was a kid. Becoming a cop himself had changed almost nothing.

Flanagan opened the bedroom door. O'Malley's voice said, "C'mere, Rodriguez."

Rodriguez went into the room, and Flanagan closed the door. Another train roared by, filling the little room with noise. In the light of the bare overhead bulb, William's bedroom looked like a furnished room in a seedy hotel. A gray wool blanket was pulled back in a heap at the foot of the bed. The dead boy lay face up on a bedspread decorated with the names and emblems of baseball teams.

Clean, dry underpants and clean, dry blue jeans were pulled down around the boy's ankles, exposing a hideous wound between his legs. His clean pajama tops were unbuttoned. The boy's upper body had been stabbed dozens of times. His nose was broken and his mouth was cut. The room smelled of wet wool from a red, bloodstained sweater thrown incongruously onto the floor in a corner.

"They cut his little thing off," said Flanagan.

O'Malley stood at the foot of the bed with his hands in his pockets in the same belligerent pose he had struck with the boy's mother. "How'd you find this?" he asked Rodriguez.

"The boy was dressed, with the blanket tucked in neatly."

"Light on or off?"

"Off."

"Like he was sleeping," commented Flanagan from the other side of the bed.

"Shut up," said O'Malley. "What do you think, Rodriguez?"

"I believe her story."

"Yeah," said O'Malley. "That woman out there sure as hell didn't do this. Whoever killed this kid was strong as hell. They must have grabbed him from behind and clamped his nose and mouth. Then they strangled him. Look at his neck there. I'll bet he was dead before he got stabbed and bit."

"Bit?" Flanagan gagged.

"Yeah," said O'Malley, who still did not take his hands out of his pockets. "Look at the tooth marks."

Flanagan turned away. Rodriguez didn't doubt the verdict. O'Malley had seen hundreds of bodies.

"This kid was killed downstairs and carried up to the roof, stabbed and mutilated. That's it," said O'Malley with the finality of a head resident conducting a tour through the wards for interns. "Right, Rodriguez?"

Rodriguez nodded.

"Right," said Flanagan.

"Who asked you?" said O'Malley. "Rodriguez, you just caught this case. Go to the other building with Forensics and the ME. Get the kid's clothing. I'll bet you find some money in the pants he didn't have when he left here this morning. Whaddaya think, Flanagan? How much did it cost the killer to get this kid?"

"Two bits, four bits," said Flanagan in a bantering tone.

"A buck at least," said O'Malley. "Dark meat doesn't come cheap."

Rodriguez whirled, jerked the door open, and stepped into the living room. "How much money did your son have when he left home this morning?" he asked Mrs. Thomas.

"He never carried extra money," she said. "He knew better, but I always gave him twenty-five cents for after school."

"What about lunch?"

"He got free hot lunch at school."

"How did you give it to him? A quarter, or nickels and dimes?"

"I always gave him nickels and dimes, so he could make a phone call home if he had to."

Aware that O'Malley was staring at him from the bedroom, Rodriguez deliberately wrote the responses into his notebook. He said gently, "I'll be handling this investigation, Mrs. Thomas. We'll want a statement from you in the morning. Can you come in at nine?"

O'Malley slammed the bedroom door. He turned to Flanagan and said, "I'm gonna pull that spic sunnavabitch off this case. You and Feldman are gonna handle it. You two go down the street and pull in that old nigger newsdealer, and get a statement."

Flanagan said, "I'll bet it happened in the morning on the kid's way to school, that guy the woman said the newsdealer saw, the Spanish man." Flanagan's voice was shaky from lack of drink and shock at the sight on the bed.

O'Malley said, "I don't give a shit what you think, and I

31

don't care how it happened. You write that old nigger's statement for him. You say he saw a couple of young black dudes stick the kid up and trot him off down the block in the direction of that building where they found him."

"What if he wants to read the statement before he signs it?"

"Christ, Flanagan, your brain is rotten from booze. Don't show it to him. Just sign it with an X, and witness it yourself." O'Malley turned toward the window where Mrs. Thomas had stood in the morning, warming her hands around a cup of coffee and watching her two children go off to school. Flanagan pulled the blanket up over William's face. O'Malley turned back and said softly, "You and Feldman do the routine in the morning—the school, the shops. You know."

Flanagan nodded. He couldn't stop looking at the shape under the blanket.

O'Malley said, "You're not gonna find this guy—some Puerto Rican pervert running around in a black neighborhood. If it gets out that some PR killed this kid, it'll disrupt the quiet around here. This PR guy could be from anywhere, from Brooklyn or St. Mary's Park, for Chrissakes."

Flanagan smiled at the name of the park, a place in the South Bronx in what was once an Irish neighborhood, long ago when O'Malley and Flanagan were Irish children.

Another train full of home-bound commuters roared past. Despite the train, O'Malley spoke even more softly. "Flanagan, there's trouble up here. I got a call this afternoon from someone. They said someone on this squad is wired to someone downtown. I wanna know who it is."

Flanagan could hardly hear the other man over the noise of the train. He stepped forward and bent closer, then started back at the malice in O'Malley's voice.

"I wanna know who," said O'Malley. "Like I said, you're not gonna find this guy. I want this case wrapped up in two days, you get me? The paperwork. You and Feldman go over and get the shit off the roof yourselves, get a few statements, then file this case in your drawer for a couple weeks. You get it? No statement from the woman. You and Feldman are gonna look for the rat on the squad. You get me?"

Flanagan nodded dumbly. O'Malley could account for their time by saying they were assigned to the Thomas case.

O'Malley jerked the door open. The scene in the living room was like a wax tableau in a museum. Everyone was where they had been. Then two ambulance attendants and an assistant medical examiner appeared in the outer doorway. O'Malley motioned them into the bedroom.

"Tag the body, Rodriguez," he said. "Then get your driver back over here to pick you up, and get back out on the street. I forgot I promised the captain to make you shift supervisor tonight. He likes you. Feldman and Flanagan are gonna do this one. I don't need you for this."

"I'd like to do it," said Rodriguez, hearing O'Malley's lie.

"Go back to work," said O'Malley.

Rodriguez stood dumbfounded and angry, then swallowed his reaction, conscious that Mrs. Thomas was watching him closely.

O'Malley walked to the telephone as though no one else was in the room. He dialed the precinct. When the desk sergeant answered, O'Malley listened for a moment, and wrote a phone number on the back of an envelope. "Yeah," he said, "if the captain asks again, tell him it's nothing much . . . the *Daily News?* If that stiff calls again, tell him no stories today, nuthin's goin on up here, nuthin . . . you unnerstand? Not word one to the papers."

O'Malley listened to the phone for another second, the receiver two inches from his ear, his contempt and boredom radiating all over the room. "Home . . . and if I'm not there, you know where to find me." He depressed the cutoff button on the phone and dialed another number. "O'Malley," he said, listened a moment, and hung up. "Shit," he said to no one, then walked out of the apartment without another word.

Rodriguez listened to Flanagan's officious directions to the ambulance men and the ME. Flanagan looked badly shaken. Feldman looked asleep on his feet.

Rodriguez said, "It's all right, ma'am. Nothing's gonna happen to you and the girl. You want me to send the old woman back up here to sit with you?"

She nodded.

Rodriguez looked sharply at Flanagan and Feldman, and saw apprehension in Flanagan's eyes. Feldman's eyes were filled with animal stupidity, or cunning.

Mrs. Thomas said, "Sergeant Rodriguez? Thank you."

Rodriguez smiled and nodded, then walked out of the apartment and down the dreary stairs. He felt as though he were leaving a hospital ward full of people past hope, and that the mere effort of leaving drained his own day of energy and life. As he walked slowly down the stairs, he pondered the intangible costs of being a cop, and decided they were inflating out of his control, out of his ability to pay.

chapter three
junkyard dogs

"Shit," said O'Malley into the wind. He got into his car, which was warm and dry. The motor was running and the radio crackling. He snapped the radio off and said to his driver, "Go to your house first. I want the car."

The driver said in a voice heavy with sleep, "You sure you don't want to drop me at the subway? It's just a couple blocks from here."

"Naw, Frankie. I'm in no rush. Just get going."

The driver switched on the lights and wipers and turned up Park Avenue to begin the journey to the northeast Bronx. O'Malley settled back and closed his eyes. He had a problem.

His rabbi had called him twice today, once with the warning about the rat on the squad, and a second time with a message to call back. When O'Malley phoned him from the Thomas apartment, his rabbi's raspy voice said, "Be at the junkyard trailer at ten tonight," and hung up. Two calls in one day was unusual.

The night meeting didn't alarm O'Malley; it was routine for a payoff. But the first call did worry him, and that made him uneasy about the meeting, with the natural caution of paranoia.

There was more to the first call than the warning about the wired cop. The raspy smoker's voice had gone on to say, "Don't worry too much about the wire, Eddie. They're not looking for you. Just cover your ass."

O'Malley began to speculate on the identity of the rat, but

the voice had interrupted. "I got no time for bullshit this afternoon, Eddie. Don't worry about this guy, but find him, you understand? And listen. I heard a story this morning that there's another cute little outfit operating right out of the Chief's office. To look for guys like you and me. To cover the Chief's ass, Eddie. Just like you're gonna do with yours and mine if you're smart."

There was a dry gasp on the phone, which O'Malley knew was meant to be a laugh; then, "Maybe you can help the Chief out, give him a few leads, you know what I mean, Eddie?" *Gasp.* "The Chief helps those who help themselves." *Gasp. Gasp.* "Sow the seeds of confusion." There was one last, long wheeze.

"It'd be the blind leading the blind," said Eddie, "trying to confuse those bastards downtown."

The voice of O'Malley's rabbi cracked and broke up over the phone like a voice being clipped off over a radio frequency. The noises ended with another wheeze. "Listen, Eddie. You always make me laugh. But here's the bad news. The snoop who's running this little shop for the Chief is a very smart guy, a real killer, Eddie, very dangerous, very close to the Chief. There's not much I can do, you understand?" The rabbi hung up without another word.

Reflecting on the one-sided conversation, O'Malley decided it wouldn't be long before he was a blip on somebody's radar screen. That in itself didn't concern him too much, because everybody in the city was watching everybody else all the time for one reason or another, but he also understood that the steel-jacketed realities of inner police politics and external city politics made mistakes dangerous.

O'Malley had no intangible problems. His only real concern was to find ways to increase his tangible income. O'Malley knew a lot of cops who looked for quick bucks, but in his personal universe, corruption was not a matter of the easy score. It was hard work and attention to detail. He decided the phone calls were a warning. He had to work harder and pay closer attention to detail.

He opened his eyes when the snow tires hit the open-steel grating of the Madison Avenue Bridge over the Harlem River. He watched the snow fall into the river. There were fewer lights on the Bronx side than in Manhattan. O'Malley relaxed. He knew what was going on, and he knew what to do.

Frankie turned across East 138th Street into the heart of the Bronx and said, "I'm gonna stay off the Bruckner." There was no traffic. This was gypsy cab country, and the snow immobilized the gypsies with their bald tires. There were no pedestrians. Frankie drove slowly, steadily, ignoring red lights. They might have been driving through the Donner Pass.

"Yeah," said O'Malley. These old drivers had to take the odd routes. They had to show you they knew every shortcut through the maze of city streets, even when they drove you for years. O'Malley slumped deeper into his seat and closed his eyes. He didn't care how they went. He would stop at an Italian restaurant on Arthur Avenue on his way to the junkyard. He had lots of time.

He listened to the hiss of slush under the tires. They were close to where he grew up, but he hated the South Bronx because he hated the people who lived there now. He understood the Irish and Jews who once lived there, and he understood no one else. He didn't even like thinking about all the changes.

"Turn on the radio," he said. "Get WINS on AM. I want the news."

The announcer read the hourly summary of city news. Nothing about the kid. O'Malley knew his city. Nobody cared about a bad story at a bad address. O'Malley had buried the case in one hour flat. Details. One. Keep Feldman and Flanagan out of the bars and on the track of the rat. Two. Keep an eye on Rodriguez.

"Turn it off," he said. He opened his eyes again. It was beginning to rain. He rolled down his window. The air was warmer, and low clouds red with the glow of the city were scudding up from the south. The car was gliding up Southern Boulevard past blocks of low warehouses built like fortresses.

Little groups of hookers stood around fifty-five-gallon drums filled with blazing scrap lumber. They looked like 1968 in high white boots and mini-skirts. Most of them were black transvestites. Oral sex was the big thing with the truckers who passed through at three A.M. on their way into the huge produce market at Hunt's Point. No VD from TV.

37

One of the hookers stepped off the curb and into the street, trying to flag the car down. She opened her short fake-fur jacket to show huge breasts with nipples the size of thimbles, to prove she was a woman and not a TV. Frankie swerved toward her and stepped on the gas. A spray of filthy slush hit her from face to feet as she leaped back out of the way and fell on her back in the gutter.

"Good shot, Frankie-boy," shouted O'Malley.

Frankie giggled like a kid. "Fookin hoors," he said in his fifty-year-old kid's brogue.

At 9:45 that night, in a light mist, O'Malley turned his battered, dirty, dark green Dodge off the northbound side of the Major Deegan Expressway and coasted slowly up the ramp to Cedar Avenue. He was on the west edge of the middle Bronx. Across the dark sheen of the Harlem River, the heights of Fort George dropped away sharply to the flats of Inwood at the far northern tip of Manhattan.

Rain had followed the snow. Now the rain had stopped, but the streets were rivers of water. Snow clung to the stumps of pilings in the water at the river's edge. Manhattan's lights glittered on its glassy surface. The water looked as thick as oil, but O'Malley knew the surprising power of the currents in the fast suck of rising and falling tides. He had swum in this river when he was a kid.

A few clots of snow shaped the clumps of weeds and outlined the broken fences of junkyards and crumbling factories along both sides of the river. The dark hulk of an abandoned coal-fired power plant loomed on the Manhattan side of the river, and on the Bronx side, an eerie tangle of antennae and masts rose from the unused Quonset huts of the old NYU School of Aeronautical Engineering. A late commuter train rattled north.

No one turned up the ramp behind O'Malley. He watched the lights of the train curve around the river and out of sight beyond the tip of Manhattan. He stopped the car at the top of the ramp and lit a cigarette. One of the radios snapped and hissed. He turned it off in irritation. His eyes were on his rearview mirrors. Nothing was there.

He lifted his service revolver out of the holster on his right hip and snapped it open. He pulled one round from the cylinder, snapped the gun shut, and put it on the seat beside him. Carefully he scored a deep X with his penknife in the nose of the thin metal jacket covering the lead bullet. He reloaded the empty chamber and carefully turned the cylinder so the first shot would be his handmade dumdum. He settled the revolver back in the holster. Attention to detail.

He lit another cigarette and looked at his watch. A tugboat, the *Sister Mary,* pushed slowly upriver, killing time, making a high bow wave against the ebbing tide. The boat's heavy diesel engine throbbed in the misty night air. O'Malley put his car in gear and moved slowly up the street, keeping pace with the boat.

When he reached the end of the block, he cut quickly left onto Fordham Road and stepped on the gas, running a red light. He cut in front of a bus and raced across the University Heights Bridge, just before the bridge tender began to turn the bridge to let the boat through. He swerved around two cars already stopped for the red warning lights.

Back in Manhattan, he turned left onto Ninth Avenue, cutting through the line of cars stopped by the turned bridge. He could hear the bridge tender screaming at him through the PA speaker on the bridge tower. O'Malley drove slowly down the street. There was not a moving car in sight, fore or aft. He looked again at his watch, turned west to Broadway, drove around a couple blocks, and parked under the elevated IRT tracks at the corner of Tenth and Nagle Avenues. He snapped his galoshes up so they wouldn't clink, got out of his car, and locked it.

He walked east on 205th Street toward the river. The streets were deserted. This was not a neighborhood of bright lights. It was small shops, auto repair garages, walk-up tenements, little corner bars, and junkyards.

Halfway down the block, he passed thirty yards of chain-link fence twice as high as a man. The interior of the junkyard was dark. A dog growled as he passed. O'Malley waited at the corner of Exterior Street. He liked the dark here by the river. It was the hooded darkness of the past. Behind him, from the direction of the driveway of a tire shop, he heard the quack of a police radio. He stayed motionless. There was another faint burst of tinny chatter and static, then a car door closed quietly. O'Malley loosened his gun.

It was Hanratty. "Let's go in, lad," he said. "It's ten o'clock exactly." Hanratty was only a few years older than O'Malley, but he had always called the younger man *lad* because he was O'Malley's rabbi and because it made O'Malley angry. O'Malley endured it. He and Hanratty came from the same parish in the Bronx, at a time when the parish you came from was as important as the town or county your family came from in Ireland. And Deputy Chief John Hanratty was the most powerful rabbi anyone could have. Most rabbis operated in the open, guiding and protecting the careers of their protégés, but this relationship was entirely secret.

In place of the three-star uniform of a deputy chief, Hanratty wore a black raincoat over a dark suit and an immaculate white shirt with a narrow, dark knit tie. Except for the face, which rose above the dark clothes and the strip of white shirt like a mottled, dangerous fungus, he looked like a Paulist teaching brother.

They walked toward the junkyard. O'Malley lit a cigarette and looked sideways at Hanratty. They talked to each other frequently on the phone, but O'Malley hadn't seen him up close in over a year, and he was startled by the grim meanness in Hanratty's face, the look of a torturer, a killer who likes his work. O'Malley was no schoolboy, but he didn't like what he saw. There was something seriously wrong. He dropped his cigarette into a pool of water with a hiss.

"You shouldn't smoke, Eddie," rasped Hanratty. "The smartest thing I ever did was quit."

Too late, thought Eddie. Or too soon.

Hanratty reached out a gloved hand and rattled the gate in the chain-link fence. A heavy chain dragged and scraped across the asphalt of the yard. There was a low, loud growl.

"Goddamn that dog," said O'Malley.

"Shut the fuck up," said Hanratty, to both the dog and O'Malley.

The dog barked. A small boy slipped out of the shadows and unlocked the gate, then relocked it carefully after them. He picked up a baseball bat and ran at the dog, cursing it in Spanish. The dog retreated, dragging its chain under a house trailer at the back of the yard. Lights came on in the trailer, and a door opened as the men advanced across the yard. A slim shape stood in the door.

"*Buenas noches, amigos,*" said the shape.

"Who's the broad?" asked O'Malley under his breath. Hanratty said nothing. Something was off-color here, thought O'Malley. They stepped inside the trailer. The air was warm and close, and smelled of good cigars. The little boy had disappeared into the tangled metallic darkness. Ignoring the woman, O'Malley asked Hanratty, "Who's the little kid? He's got more balls than brains." Hanratty shrugged.

The door to the back room of the trailer opened. A handsome man of about forty-five stepped into the front room. He was trim and well dressed. "Mr. Hanratty," said the man. "So nice of you to come uptown on such short notice."

"Nice to see you again, Ayala. Very nice. What brings you to New York?"

"This meeting." Ayala spoke English clearly but with an unmistakable Spanish accent. O'Malley's antennae were fully extended. He had never met this man in person. They had spoken on the phone only twice in two years. Yet he was far more important to O'Malley than the Victorian Irish Catholic bureaucrats who ran the NYPD.

"Lieutenant O'Malley," said Ayala. He extended his hand with warmth and enthusiasm. "It is a pleasure to meet you at last, and to tell you in person how much I appreciate your work."

"Thank you. My pleasure," said O'Malley. He was nearly speechless with caution. Caution made him angry.

"And this is Maritza, my associate," said Ayala. They all smiled. She was a handsome woman in her early thirties, tall and well built, dressed in a tailored suit like a lawyer. She had striking red-blond hair, worn short, and her skin was a pale tan. It looked powdered, but it wasn't. O'Malley was impressed. Hanratty had the aspect of a celibate.

"Let us have a drink together," said Ayala. He motioned to Maritza, who produced a new bottle of Paddy's with clean

41

glasses and a bowl of ice. She poured. Ayala smiled graciously. He said, "In my country, we do not distill such fine whiskey. We grow only coca plants and fine marijuana. *Salud.*"

"Happy days," said Hanratty, the diplomat. They all downed the whiskey in one shot, except Maritza, who sipped hers. She poured the others a fresh shot. They sat down on metal folding chairs around a dented metal office desk. Ayala was in complete command. He was dressed in about a thousand dollars worth of custom-tailored English suiting, shirting, and shoes. He wore a .32 Beretta automatic in a little pop-up holster clipped inside the waistband of his trousers.

O'Malley let the whiskey relax him while Ayala and Hanratty mumbled pleasantries at each other, and Maritza observed. O'Malley couldn't place her in the little group. He was good at reading situations and people. She clearly wasn't Ayala's woman. She didn't defer to Ayala in any way, but there was a degree of familiarity between the two, like people who have worked together under stress.

O'Malley turned his attention to Ayala, conscious that Ayala was aware of the attention. The Beretta was not a toy. It was the kind of weapon liked by Latins and Europeans, who understood that handguns were meant for close quarters. The holster was an odd one, not a cop's holster, but neat and elegant like the man. The holster reminded O'Malley of the kid's trick; walking up to someone in school, pulling open your fly real quick and whipping out your shirttail.

While O'Malley's mind idled, his ears listened to Ayala's accent. Despite his biases, O'Malley got around. He had the concentrated power of observation and the filing-cabinet memory that went with long years as a cop.

"Lieutenant," said Ayala.

O'Malley smiled. Part of his mind began poking around in the filing cabinets. Ayala had a curious accent.

"We need your expert help more than ever, Lieutenant. My group is moving its operations over to the West Side, where there is a swarm of small-time dealers we will have to absorb or eliminate. And several other large groups are following our example. We'll put them out of business. We don't need an unpleasant war, but we don't intend to allow competition in our markets.

42

Ours is the kind of business that does well in hard times and expands rapidly in good times."

Ayala smiled at his own understanding of the crosscurrents of American economic life. Hanratty and Maritza smiled. They all looked at O'Malley. He smiled, too, and said lazily, "Where you gonna get the troops?"

"We have them," said Ayala, less gracious.

"None of your goddamn business," said Hanratty.

O'Malley shrugged. Anger rose in him like a volcano.

Ayala continued, "There are those who will attempt to do the same to us. I know others are interested in the monopoly my group enjoys as vendors of medical supplies to doctors and hospitals in upper Manhattan." Ayala smiled again, with the pride of leadership. "Your help will be invaluable, O'Malley, and essential."

O'Malley said, "Glad to hear it." He sipped his whiskey. He would be doing more of the same—covering up murders done by Ayala's men. The message would not be lost on the other side. They would know the key cop in the area was on Ayala's payroll, and they would back off enough to give Ayala the edge. Ayala would expand and pay O'Malley more money. These were the tangibles of O'Malley's universe. He looked at Hanratty and said, "I'll be moving to the West Side, I guess."

"In a month."

"No problem," said O'Malley.

"There better not be, Eddie," said Hanratty. "And you better bust your ass, too, because you're getting a big raise."

"Five thousand a month from now on," said Ayala.

Ayala's accent dropped into place in the files in the back of O'Malley's head. It was Union City, New Jersey, and Little Havana. Ayala was Cuban, not Colombian. O'Malley trusted flashes of instinct. They always led somewhere new and useful. He sensed an advantage. He set his glass down with most of the whiskey still in it. "I appreciate the raise, *Señor* Ayala. But it's not enough."

Hanratty's face turned glossy and pale pink. Ayala smiled slightly, but his body stiffened under his expensive clothes. Maritza watched.

"The five thousand makes a good monthly retainer," O'Mal-

43

ley continued, "but I want a fee for piecework on top of the retainer. Say, a thousand a job."

"You greedy mickey," mumbled Hanratty.

Ayala raised his hand for calm. "I'll consider it. You're ambitious, O'Malley, and I like that. You've done a good job so far. I'll consider it in return for a quid pro quo."

"What's that?" asked O'Malley.

"Something in return," wheezed Hanratty. "Didn't the priests teach you any Latin?"

"They didn't teach me English."

Ayala said, "I hear interesting things about this Detective Sergeant Rodriguez who works for you. They say he's smart."

"Smartass," said O'Malley.

"I want a Latin cop on my payroll," said Ayala. "I want you to bring him in."

"Jaysus," squeaked O'Malley, his vocal cords as tight as his sphincter.

"Right," said Hanratty. "That's what we want."

"That fucken spic sunnavabitch," burst out O'Malley. "That goddamn independent PR bastard. He's as straight as they come. Are you out of your goddamn minds?"

"No, my friend," said Ayala. His eyes glittered.

"You stupid fucking harp," rasped Hanratty. His pink face grew red. It looked ready to burst.

The tension was so palpable that Maritza slid her chair back a few feet with an involuntary jerk.

O'Malley broke the tension by doing something he hadn't done since parochial school: saying he was sorry.

"No offense," said Ayala, all smooth and gracious again. "I should have known better. Do you think it would be dangerous to approach Rodriguez?"

"Yes," said O'Malley.

"Then forget it. Just watch him closely. Maybe you'll spot someone else." Ayala rose to his feet. The audience was over. Maritza took a beautiful camel's-hair coat from a closet and held it for him with the air of one offering a common courtesy to a colleague. Ayala slipped into the coat like a woman putting on silk-lined mink over bare skin. *"Gracias,"* he said. "Have another drink," he said to O'Malley. "I'm afraid I have to go."

His tone was benign. "Keep in touch," he said, and left quickly. Maritza stepped outside with him. The dog's chain rattled once under the trailer, then once more, then there was no other sound.

Hanratty said, "Be careful, Eddie. You're driving too fast."

"I don't like surprises, and I don't like being jerked off. Not by him, you, or anybody else."

"What about her?"

"How the hell would you know?"

Hanratty stood up. He sighed. His face was the face of a mummy again. His voice was like a rusty file on thin metal. "Wait a couple minutes after I go. The new drop is gonna be Ryan's old bar on the corner of 106th and Amsterdam."

"Rodriguez won't play, and you know it."

"We'll see." Hanratty went out the door into the dark yard like a shadow.

Maritza came in. There was no sound of the dog under the trailer.

"What'd happen if it gets loose?" asked O'Malley.

"What?"

"The dog. That's the most vicious dog I ever saw. That chain is big enough to tow a car."

"It is."

"Is what?"

"From a tow truck." She was completely relaxed with him.

Whatever her role in the group, it was a big one, he decided. "And the dog?"

"The little boy feeds the dog every day," she said. "But the dog would kill him if it could."

"Fucking dog," said O'Malley.

"It's time for you to go," said Maritza.

O'Malley got up. He let his raincoat hang open and loosened his gun.

"Señor?"

"Huh?"

"Here is your envelope. Five thousand. It's the last time up here."

"Thanks." He stuck the thick envelope in his inside jacket pocket. He didn't like the mortuary tone in her voice. He stomped his heavy brogan on the floor. No rattle down below. He leapt through the door and down the metal steps. Light from the door lit the open space in the center of the yard. Two more jumps into the yard, and O'Malley whirled to his left. He pulled the gun loose and swept his arm up and out.

The dog leapt at him in long bounds from the darkness at the end of the trailer. One more bound and it jumped for him in a long arc. O'Malley was crouched. His first shot hit the dog square in the chest below the heavy collar. The thunk of the exploding dumdum was amplified by the slow-motion silence, then his second shot hit the dog in the left shoulder as O'Malley continued whirling to his left like a matador passing the bull. The dog was dead before it hit the ground.

O'Malley took one more whirling step, traversing his front sight across the jumbled piles of flattened auto bodies. The sight flashed past Maritza watching from the doorway and past the frightened face of the little kid standing in the shadows, still holding the end of the heavy chain. "Where's Ayala?" roared O'Malley. "Ayala, you cocksucker, where are you?"

"Here, O'Malley. Drop your gun and turn around."

O'Malley lowered the gun without dropping it and turned to face the voice. Ayala and Hanratty stepped into the light. Hanratty's hands were in his coat pockets. Ayala held his .32 at the center of O'Malley's chest.

"Listen carefully, O'Malley," said Ayala.

"Fuck you," said O'Malley. "And you too, Hanratty."

Ayala said, "You should eliminate the word 'spic' from your limited vocabulary when you're taking spic money."

O'Malley grunted. Red and yellow spots of rage flashed and exploded in his eyes.

Hanratty said, "This sharpshooter of the Chief's is gonna get turned loose one of these days. Just like that dog there. And you better be ready, Eddie, because you're out front."

Ayala said, "The Chief has his dog, and I've got mine. When we take the chain off, O'Malley, you better jump."

O'Malley's hand pointed at the dead dog lying on her side in a pool of blood that looked like dirty motor oil. The hand squeezed another shot into the carcass. The dog's body jumped.

Ayala poked his automatic into its little holster and turned to

46

Hanratty. "The retainer is fine with me, and tell Maritza to give him another thousand for his first job."

Hanratty was surprised. "What job?"

"Killing the dog." Ayala laughed. "O'Malley's meaner than a junkyard dog. I like him, Hanratty."

O'Malley squeezed another shot into the dog's body. "Like a goddamn dog, huh? We'll see about dogs."

Ayala laughed again, a clear, boyish laugh.

After the men left one by one, O'Malley richer by a thousand dollars and in a homicidal mood, Maritza and the boy wrapped the dead dog in a heavy plastic garbage bag. She sent the boy to drop the carcass into the big industrial dumpster at a nearby auto repair shop. She told the boy she would wait for him to return.

He was like one of the boys in a Dickens novel, she thought, beyond the help of any school, and older than his years in his ability to survive. He had appeared at the junkyard one day and asked for odd jobs, then became a fixture around the place; now he lived in the back of the trailer. He said he had no family. Thinking about the boy as she waited, Maritza told herself again that there was no difference between war and the grinding, invisible poverty of the truly poor, and that such poverty, to those who suffered it, justified war as their only hope for improving their lives.

When the boy returned, a bleak little figure out of the damp riverfront night, she asked him if he had food and money. Assured that he did, she left. The boy locked the junkyard gate behind her and locked himself into the trailer, bereft of the vicious junkyard dog, his only companion and protector.

Maritza walked quickly along 205th Street, intending to go up to 207th, where she could take the IRT down to the West Side where she lived. As she turned the corner onto Tenth Avenue, Ayala called her name from the back seat of his maroon Buick. He opened the door and gestured her in beside him.

"I'll drive you home," he said. "I want to talk to you. Are you hungry? We could stop to eat."

47

"No," she said. "It's very late, and I have to be at school early tomorrow morning."

Ayala spoke to the driver, then leaned back and lit a cigar as they turned up Post Avenue toward Dyckman Street. He said, "Maritza, the time has come to escalate our activities. We are going to build a base for armed action in North America. Over the next ten years, many millions of Hispanics from the Caribbean and Latin America will go north. Those people will be the sea our fish will swim in."

They were riding through Washington Heights, a solid residential area, densely built up with well-maintained apartment buildings. The driver turned into Fort Tryon Park and drove slowly along the loop around the park and the Cloisters. It was peaceful and deserted. Maritza thought of the neighborhood around the junkyard, no more than five hundred yards due east, down the steep hill from the park.

She had nothing to say to Ayala. Dealing with him was a constant struggle. He ran his operation under control from Havana and Moscow, and she ran hers in the hope of achieving freedom for the Puerto Rican people. Like many others before her, in every part of the world, she had found support from the only people who would offer it, and she took the support knowing full well it endangered the autonomy of her movement, and knowing that without it, the movement would surely fail.

"That's why I wanted you at this meeting tonight," said Ayala. "It is important for you to know Hanratty and O'Malley, and all about my side of the operation. Havana wants you to replace me if something should happen to me, or if I should be sent elsewhere."

She was silent. Now they were going to pull her all the way in. Soon she would be little more than an agent of the KGB. But she knew what would happen sooner or later if she resisted. She thought of the original leaders of the Algerian Revolution, all killed or in prison. Fighting for freedom does not mean remaining independent, she thought bitterly.

"What room is there for my point of view?" she asked. "It was only recently that I learned the money you give us comes from heroin sold to my people, and that the few weapons and explosives you supply are bought with money from the same source. This has made me an accomplice in the worst scourge of people with black and brown skins."

Ayala listened without expression. "We are not rich in raw materials like the *norteamericanos*. This is our only source of cash for operations such as yours. If you can find another source of support, you are free to go elsewhere."

"In a box," she said.

"We are not like the Russians," he said. The car was cruising slowly down the West Side Highway along the Hudson River.

"I won't run the drug business," she said.

"You might not have to," he answered quickly. "I have my eye on someone who might be able to take that over."

"Who?"

"Rodriguez."

"They are the worst," she said. "The cops."

"Hanratty and O'Malley have done valuable work."

"Scum," she said.

"This is not the nuns' school you went to when you were little."

She said nothing. She remembered the nuns trying to teach Catholic philosophy to uncomprehending little girls, and remembered one nun struggling to explain Occam's Razor—the unnecessary multiplication of explanations for something for which the actual cause was unknown.

Maritza knew Ayala and agents like him never told anyone more than they thought was necessary. They were never guilty of the philosophical sin of Occam's Razor. They doled out information as if it were scarcer than gold, which perhaps it was. Maritza only knew what she had to do in her own sphere. She closed her eyes. She had to make do with what she had. She had no choice. She felt bone weary.

"OK," she said. "Train me."

"Call me tomorrow afternoon," said Ayala.

There was a note of relief in his voice. It was the first sign of strain she had ever noticed in him. They had worked together for two years. If I don't have control of everything, she thought, I'll lose everything. I can't trust anyone but myself to do anything.

49

chapter four
2013 fifth avenue

Under the hot sun of a late April morning, a circle of men stood on the flat roof of a brownstone row house, on the east side of upper Fifth Avenue, in the short block between Mount Morris Park and 125th Street, the main street of Harlem. The block was jammed with police cars and emergency vehicles. The noise and exhaust of heavy noontime traffic rose from 125th Street. The exhaust stank. The air was windless, like midsummer. There was not a cloud in the bright blue sky above the level plain of Harlem.

Rodriguez walked to the edge of the roof and looked down into the street. They were in the very center of Harlem. There was a dead boy on the roof, and dozens of people were gathering in the street and on adjacent roofs. Soon it would be hundreds. O'Malley couldn't cover this one up.

Rodriguez walked back to the circle. The men were silent. In the center of the circle was the body of a young black boy, about the same age as William Thomas, who had lived less than three blocks away. The second boy had been murdered and mutilated the same way as the Thomas boy. This little body lay curled on its side in an attitude of awkward sleep on the dirty tar and gravel of the rooftop. A dollar bill was clenched in the boy's right fist. A few feet away, white underpants lay on neatly folded jeans. A pair of worn black high-top sneakers had been carefully placed on the clothes, as though to hold them down should the wind rise.

O'Malley was in his shirtsleeves, his hands stuck into his back pockets. He stared down at the body. This was very public trouble. It was high noon in the middle of Harlem. It was a school holiday. Every kid in the neighborhood was watching O'Malley as he stared at the body.

He murmured to Rodriguez, "He used a knife this time. The son of a bitch is a regular surgeon."

Rodriguez said, "Same guy, though. Same neighborhood."

O'Malley didn't answer. "I dunno," he finally said. "It's half the same, and half the same neighborhood. It might not be the same."

Now Rodriguez said nothing. He could see what was coming.

O'Malley asked, "What's it like on the street?"

"Crowded."

O'Malley looked around at the other roofs. "Christ, it's like the fucking *National Geographic.*" In a louder voice, he said, "Tag the body and get it outta here. Get your pictures now."

The circle broke up. One man outlined the body in heavy yellow chalk. The photographer started shooting. The man with the chalk bagged and tagged the dollar bill, then the clothes. The ambulance men stepped forward with body bag, blanket, and stretcher.

The boy's mother began to moan. She was a black woman in her late twenties, dressed in a sleeveless white blouse over green Bermuda shorts. She stood near the trap door that gave access to the roof. A skinny girl of about ten stood with her, holding a squalling tiny baby wrapped in a blanket.

Next to them stood two young boys about the same age as the victim. One held a furry little puppy in his arms. Both boys were frightened and crying. A young, black, uniformed patrolman stood behind them in a pose more protective than custodial, his face as shocked as theirs. He and his partner were the first on the scene. Rodriguez arrived a moment later. He got the story from the two boys.

The dead boy lived in an apartment on the floor just below the roof they were standing on. The two boys lived next door. They had climbed up to their roof to walk the puppy. They were afraid to go to the park, because they were afraid the junkies would take their dog. The puppy got away and jumped a low wall onto the next roof. It began running in circles and barking. The boys went to look. They thought the dog had found a dead pigeon. It was the body of their friend.

Rodriguez had forced the boys to describe the body, knowing they would block the scene after a short time and be unable to remember it. The dead boy's tee shirt had been soaked with fresh wet blood just beginning to coagulate. An awful wound gaped from the dark hollow of the pelvis. The body rested in a puddle of blood, dark red, almost brown on the black tar of the hot rooftop. There was no one else in sight. The barking dog and the screams of the boys brought the dead boy's sister up the ladder through the trap door, then the mother, then more people from the bar on the ground floor, then the police.

Rodriguez had made a fast search of the scene before too many people trampled it, but it was hopeless. If he had found anything, it would have been useless in a trial. The rooftop landscape of central Harlem was littered with evidence of fear and violence.

The ambulance men strapped the body under the blanket and passed the stretcher down the trap door. The mother wailed. Noise rose from the crowd like waves of heat from the rooftops. There were a few shouts.

Rodriguez's shirt was soaked with sweat. The heavy gold badge that tugged at his shirt pocket felt as heavy as the gun on his right hip. He was always conscious of the weight of the gun. He had never found a holster he liked. Shoulder holsters made him feel like a gunslinger.

O'Malley beckoned to him. O'Malley had no intention of pushing this case. It was his last day in the command. He was due at the precinct house on West 100th Street to take command of the Fifth Homicide Squad on the Upper West Side. Rodriguez was assigned to go with O'Malley to the West Side, and Rodriguez had no idea why. He hadn't asked for the transfer.

O'Malley called impatiently, "Rodriguez."

Rodriguez stepped over to him. They stood facing each other, quite close, the way politicians do, not looking directly at each other, but over each other's shoulders, and talking softly into each other's ears. Rodriguez's eyes were hidden behind dark sunglasses.

O'Malley's shirt was dry. He was relaxed. He said, "I wanna get outta here and get to lunch with the captain over in the Two-Four. You meet me over there later. I was gonna give this one to Feldman and Flanagan, but I just found out this morning that they're gonna come with us over to the West Side, too. That's good. Besides, I don't think this is the same as the other one last month. So you're gonna catch this one alone, and you've got about three hours to wrap it up before you report to me at the Two-Four. You unnerstand?"

They stood near the edge of the roof. Rodriguez watched the crowd in the street. It was growing larger fast, and the balance of the crowd was shifting from kids to young men and middle-aged women. It was a volatile mix.

O'Malley was having the same thoughts. "Press here yet?" he asked.

"No."

"Good. When they turn the TV lights on, this crowd'll start to act up."

Rodriguez knew that, and even as O'Malley spoke, there was a surge in the crowd as the ambulance men emerged from the building with the stretcher. The people on the other roofs pushed and shoved to see.

"I wanna get everybody outta here," said O'Malley, without stating the obvious reasons. "Right now. No canvassing, you unnerstand?" O'Malley stepped back and looked at Rodriguez. Rodriguez nodded, his guts as tight as a drum. O'Malley said, "Good. We're never gonna find this dick-biter. Jesus Christ, the kid lived right under our feet here, and nobody, not even his stupid mother, knows where he was this morning or how he got up on the roof. Don't hang around here. This case stays in this command. You write your report this afternoon, file it at the Two-Eight, and that's it. You unnerstand?"

O'Malley looked again. Rodriguez nodded again. O'Malley looked straight at him. "You're a good cop, Rodriguez. Maybe one of the best young cops I ever saw. But you work for me.

You do what I tell you. If we get along better, I can help you more. You still got a lot to learn about things."

Rodriguez looked steadily back at O'Malley, knowing the lieutenant couldn't see his eyes. Rodriguez knew what *things* meant in O'Malley's universe. Rodriguez already knew more about *things* than he wanted to know. He was a homicide detective in a city that couldn't stop murder. All he wanted to do was catch killers and put them away forever, get them off the streets. He wanted nothing to do with *things*.

"And no press," said O'Malley. "You unnerstand? I talk to reporters. Not you. Not ever."

Rodriguez nodded. There was no press to talk to. Rodriguez knew what O'Malley knew. The death of a little black kid was of small moment to the news editors in midtown.

O'Malley brushed by Rodriguez and headed for the trap door. The young black cop standing with the mother and the two kids asked him if they should clear the rooftops. O'Malley looked at him in momentary disbelief, then said in a voice loud enough to be heard on 125th Street, "Shit no, you asshole. You wanna get killed?"

O'Malley dropped down the trap door out of sight. Rodriguez walked over to the cop and said quietly, "Take the mother and the kids home, then you and your partner get going. Get off the block, you understand?"

The cop nodded and said, "Yes sir."

In two minutes, Rodriguez was standing alone on the roof. There was nothing left behind but fresh cigarette butts and the yellow outline of a small child. Rodriguez stared at the chalk. He was oblivious to the dozens of other people on the rooftops all around him. They began to edge toward him.

Ever since he had joined O'Malley's command, he supposed he had been waiting for this moment, or working toward it along a steady, inevitable curve. It began the first time they met in O'Malley's tiny, decrepit office at the Two-Eight, and O'Malley had said, "You got a hell of a reputation, Rodriguez. Too bad you're not Irish. Just remember you work for me, not the NYPD, and we'll get along fine. You unnerstand?"

Rodriguez walked to the edge of the roof and watched

O'Malley shoulder his way through the crowd in the street. He shoved a kid away from his car and got in. The siren whooped once and the car jumped at the crowd, scattering it. Rodriguez decided with sudden heat that he hated the man, that he never knew a man he hated more than O'Malley. Working for him would never get better.

A few people stepped onto the roof. Rodriguez walked past them. As he pulled the trap door down over his head, he heard dozens of feet hit the roof at once, and he heard the first bottle break.

As he walked down through the building, people surged up the steps. He pushed past them. His car was the last official car on the block, and it was surrounded. But people made way for him. He radiated such anger that the crowd instinctively made a path. When he reached his car, he thought, *What do the politicians say?* The thought stopped him with his hand on the door of the car. There was a ripple of tension in the crowd as they waited for him to make a move. Then he remembered. *Don't get mad. Get even.*

A few moments later, when Rodriguez's car disappeared around the corner of Mount Morris Park, a bottle shattered an apartment window; then, as suddenly as it had formed, the crowd broke up. In ten minutes, there were only a handful of kids and local residents on the sidewalks, and the block looked like it always did.

Mount Morris Park was an oasis, a graceful park two or three blocks square with lawns, benches, and small playgrounds around its outer edges. Shaded in summer by large trees, it offered a glimpse of what Harlem once was.

The stark steel frame of the bell tower rose on its hilltop above the foliage. Around the tower was an old-fashioned belvedere, an outlook. The killer stood at its edge, where he had gone, unnoticed, after the boy lay dead. Through a break in the trees, not yet in full leaf, he watched the boys find the body, he watched the police, and he watched the neighborhood return to normal. Then he followed the stairs and paths down the east side of the hill, where a month before, William Thomas had seen patches of glistening, unmelted snow.

The killer stopped in the dappled shade of the trees at the edge of the park. He carried fifteen thousand dollars in cocaine and good white heroin in the pockets of his field jacket, and he had four stops to make before midafternoon. He was still on time. The first was right before him. The Hospital for Joint Diseases dominated its neighborhood with the same faded elegance as the park. As careful as a soldier in a mine field, the killer stepped off the curb and walked across the street. He passed the front entrance of the hospital and went to an employee's exit on 124th Street near the back of the building. He knocked on the locked metal fire door with a sharp double rap. An orderly pushed the door open from the inside. The killer slipped him a twenty-dollar bill wrapped around two joints, then followed him down a short hall painted the ugly green that infects the back rooms of older hospitals.

At a large open hall, the orderly turned right. The killer turned left. Technicians hurried along the hall or loitered in labs and X-ray rooms. No one paid any attention to the stranger in army surplus clothing. He ducked into an X-ray lab. He found a Filipino surgeon dressed in bloodstained greens, his mask dangling around his neck, his khaki face glistening with heavy sweat. There was a quick exchange of cash for cocaine. The killer was as meticulous in his transactions as the surgeon.

As they parted, the doctor noticed a dark stain below the knee of the other man's pants leg. The doctor had never seen a speck of dirt on this man's clothing before, and he recognized it for what it was—a recent bloodstain.

"What happened?" asked the doctor, pointing.

The killer looked down. His whole body jerked once, hard, like a galvanized frog on an experimenter's table. "Nothing," he said. "I was cutting meat at the *bodega*."

The doctor nodded, shook hands with the killer, and disappeared down the hall. The killer quickly left the hospital. He had three stops to go: a Medicaid clinic on East 125th Street; the huge state psychiatric hospital on Ward's Island; and Metropolitan Hospital at 97th Street and First Avenue. He visited each of his stops two or three times a week, supplying doctors, nurses, and other hospital personnel with drugs, and through them, many patients he would never see. The mere fact of illness did nothing to diminish addiction. Heroin, in fact, was the painkiller of choice for those patients with terminal cancer who could afford the drug, obtain it, and find a cooperative nurse or relative to administer it.

At Park Avenue, the killer dodged kitty-corner through traffic to the corner of 125th Street, then walked under the elevated tracks of the 125th Street railroad station and joined the crowds of pedestrians enjoying the warm spring day. He was still on time. He was never late.

His next customer was the only man who knew the killer's entire history, but not that he was a killer. The killer liked this man—the doctor who ran the Medicaid mill on East 125th Street—and felt secure and important when he visited him there. The place was a large ground floor clinic entered through a door of heavy glass set in an unpainted concrete-block wall. There was a riot gate in a roller over the door. Inside was an open waiting area with rows of numbered orange and green plastic chairs bolted to the gray tile floor.

He never had to wait. The receptionist always led him straight back through a warren of little cubicles to the doctor's private office, where the doctor held court in the company of an old man who was his bookkeeper.

Today, as always, the killer was glad to see him. It was this doctor who had released him from the awful ward in the hospital on Ward's Island, where he had been sent for molesting a young boy. After a cursory examination, the doctor had diagnosed him as nonviolent and assigned him to an outpatient program where he was ordered to report every month. The doctor ran the outpatient clinic, too, and gave his new patient a renewable prescription for a strong tranquilizer, to be filled at the Medicaid mill owned by the doctor.

The child molester who became a killer never took the useless pills. He faithfully reported to the clinic on Ward's Island every month, filled the prescription at the Medicaid mill, and then sold the pills to the men who hung around the Dominican *bodega* at the corner of the West Side block where the killer

58

lived. The doctor was a light-skinned Cuban in his mid-forties, with a short black beard. One day he introduced his patient to an elegant fellow-Cuban. Soon the patient was a valued courier for narcotics and the doctor was a customer of his patient. The patient was selling the doctor ten thousand dollars worth of good heroin every month.

There was a little ritual to be observed with each transaction. The doctor and bookkeeper seemed to enjoy it as much as the ex-patient. The doctor took off the gown he wore over his street clothes. The bookkeeper, a paunchy, inconsequential-looking little man, closed his books. The doctor served them each a glass of orange juice with a shot of vodka in it, and they indulged themselves in a few moments of friendly chatter, much of it shoptalk about the hospital on Ward's Island. The killer, who was somewhat retarded, found the gossip soothing. He admired the order and routine of the hospital, although he didn't like being inside all day, and the other patients mystified and frightened him.

Today, the vodka and the solemn exchange of money for drugs calmed the killer to the point of forgetting the scene on the rooftop two hours before. He was able to leave the doctor's shop in good spirits. At the first bus stop, he took an M35 bus east along 125th Street, over the Triborough Bridge, and down onto Ward's Island. There he entered the hospital through the outpatient clinic. He was met by his old ward nurse, who always terrified him. She bought a small amount of heroin to resell to patients on the ward, and introduced her ex-charge to a new customer, a young woman doctor who immediately bought an ounce of cocaine and took her first snort before he could get out of the room.

He left the hospital with relief, thankful that they hadn't snared him again somehow. He walked across the footbridge to Manhattan, and down the walk along the East River to Metropolitan Hospital, where he had his last drop for the day.

The municipal and state hospitals, whatever their origins in public compassion, now existed to hide or camouflage the miseries of the city's poor, and had become places of private profit for some of their administrators and staff. Equipment and budgets were looted shamelessly. Patients, or "beds," were used as

59

mere chips in endless bargaining for state and federal reimbursement.

It was in this nether world that the ex-patient and killer spent his days, more comfortable and less threatened than anywhere else. His days were routine and his services appreciated. He was part of an enormous underground aquifer of cash, a hidden economy which only now and then sprang above the surface of the city's life.

His particular craziness made him plodding and reliable, except for the violence, which no one knew anything about except his sister, whom he lived with. His reliability made him valuable to his bosses, and they paid him for his usefulness, thus keeping him off the garbage heap of tranquilized mental patients who inhabit the city in legions.

It is not that he was a victim of society. He was not. It was others who were his victims. Perhaps if he had been victimized himself, he would not have been a killer, but his instincts for survival, which were strong enough to keep him out of Manhattan State, where he would have soon rotted like most of the others, were probably the same instincts that made him a violent murderer, a psychopath. He had no internal control over his behavior, and he was cunning and strong enough to act on impulse.

Or perhaps it was the other way around: because he was a psychopath, he was smart enough to stay out of hospitals, where he couldn't act like a psychopath without being drugged so heavily that he forgot who he was, and was put in solitary and beaten.

The end of his day came at four o'clock. Looking tired in the heavy heat, he waited in a knot of hospital workers for a crosstown bus to Amsterdam Avenue and 96th Street on the West Side. He walked up to a *bodega* on the corner of West 101st Street, where he dropped off the day's cash and accounted for it. Then he walked up to the apartment on West 109th Street where he lived with his sister.

He drank a bottle of cold beer in the kitchen and retreated into his bedroom. There he carefully unwrapped a small package of newspaper in which he had preserved the grisly souvenir of the morning's murder. He put it in a plastic sandwich bag

60

with the other penis, now dried and shriveled to half its size, and put the bag back in its hiding place under his bed. Then he took a bath, dressed in clean clothes, and ate the rice and beans his sister cooked for supper.

Later, he walked up the block to the corner of Amsterdam Avenue and watched the men playing dominoes on upended wire milk cases in front of the little Dominican *bodega*. He drank a few more beers, watched the children playing in the warm evening, watched the endless traffic, and then went home, where he watched TV and went to bed. He was a creature of habit. The people of the neighborhood, most of whom were poor illegal immigrants like himself, thought he was a harmless village idiot, and took no notice of his comings and goings.

"I'll give you a little hint, Francis. The victim had the same first name as yours. Maybe he was some relation, huh?" O'Malley winked at Rodriguez and motioned him to a chair. The lieutenant was enjoying himself, mocking a *Daily News* reporter, a rummy old hack he had known for years. Rodriguez had not realized O'Malley was a skilled mimic in addition to his basic maliciousness.

"Naw, Fran, no names. This was a kid. You know the rules." O'Malley listened to an entreaty over the phone. "Sure, Frannie, I'll give you the address. Twenty-thirteen Fifth, just above Mount Morris Park, you know? We missed you up there this morning, but I know how busy you guys are, covering all the killings at Costello's."

O'Malley sat hunched over his desk in his new office at the Two-Four. He looked like an alligator would look if someone gave it an expensive suit, a white shirt, a rep tie, and gold cuff links. The long, powerful tail was invisible because O'Malley was sitting down, but Rodriguez knew it could lash out at any moment, destroying all the furniture in the cramped room and anyone standing in the way. Rodriguez was standing in the way, at the end of his first afternoon in Fifth Homicide. He couldn't sit because the only chair on his side of the desk was piled with a winter's-worth of yellowed newspapers, topped with a pair of black rubber galoshes patched with red squares from an inner-tube repair kit. The filthy galoshes had deposited a small mound of grit and salt and probably some dog shit on the newspapers.

Rodriguez was astonished. The office looked like a time capsule. Everything in it, including the desk, chairs, coat tree, and desk litter had been moved intact from O'Malley's old office. The galoshes were in the same position on the same newspapers on the same chair.

"Fran, old buddy." O'Malley's tone was emphatic and final, the voice of the alligator about to move on to a new victim. "I got nuthin for ya. Why don't ya go up there and investigate the heinous crime yourself? Might win a Pulitzer. And when those dark folks get through dancin round on yer head, I'll send a couple boys to scrape up the pieces. It was crowded up there today, Fran. I didn't like it up there myself."

The reporter said something funny, a racial slur from the way O'Malley chuckled. "No names in your little slug, Frannie. No names at all. Keep in touch." O'Malley placed the phone in its cradle by dropping it from his outstretched hand. It bounced once. The vintage black instrument had fresh scars as though the alligator had been gnawing on the mouthpiece.

"Any witnesses up there, Danny-O?"

"None."

"How the hell do you know?" snapped O'Malley, always dangerous, even when he was in an apparently good mood. He folded his hands before him on the desk and hunched forward. His vest buttons looked ready to pop. "I thought I told you no door-to-door up there."

"I went back and talked to a couple neighbors and the old bartender in the place on the ground floor."

"So you spent half the fucking afternoon finding out what you already knew?"

"The trail's cold up there already, Lieutenant. I wanted to get what I could."

"You got nuthin." O'Malley sucked his front teeth. It sounded like the hiss of a large reptile. "The bartender give you anything?"

"Offered me a drink."

"You're not supposed to go in a licensed premise alone. You're supposed to notify a superior officer first."

"I am a superior officer," said Rodriguez.

O'Malley hunched and stared, obviously angry. But then he lit a cigarette and leaned back in his chair, lifting his feet to the top of the desk. A cardboard coffee container spilled to the floor. O'Malley watched it fall. In a relaxed tone, he said, "You're a superior smartass too, Rodriguez. You know that? When I try to be friendly and helpful, you get up on your high horse. But you're not on this case anymore. It stays over in the Sixth Division. Go home, Sergeant. See me in the morning."

As Rodriguez turned to go, O'Malley said, "Send Feldman in here."

Rodriguez walked into the squad room and motioned for Feldman. The big German propelled himself into O'Malley's office and shut the door. Flanagan was not in sight. He had undoubtedly found himself a convenient bar in the new precinct. "Off duty" meant nothing to Feldman and Flanagan. They worked for O'Malley twenty-four hours a day. When they weren't busy, they sat and drank in bars or slurped coffee in restaurants, reading the latest editions of the *Post* and *Daily News,* deep into the sports pages, deciphering the latest line. They were heavy bettors with an old bookie on East 116th Street. Their passions were the horses and basketball, but they made do with football, baseball, and even hockey when they had to.

In the month since the Thomas killing, Rodriguez had gotten to know Flanagan pretty well, but not Feldman. Flanagan was a talker when he was oiled, which was most of the time, but Feldman's jaw was wired permanently shut by stupidity and blind loyalty to O'Malley. Flanagan's loyalty seemed more conditional. Rodriguez had managed to spend an evening in an East Side bar alone with Flanagan, who had talked like a child, warning Rodriguez to be careful around O'Malley. Before he nearly passed out at the bar, Flanagan told Rodriguez about O'Malley's orders the night of the Thomas killing, repeating O'Malley's warning that someone on the squad was wired. Flanagan seemed badly frightened. Rodriguez assumed it was because he was up to his ears in O'Malley's games. It was widely thought that the lieutenant did some taking, and that Feldman and Flanagan were his bagmen. Rodriguez kept Flanagan's whiskey talk to himself. He liked the man and felt sorry for him. Rodriguez knew he had nothing to fear for himself.

Rodriguez asked around the squad room and found an empty desk in the far corner, from where he could see O'Malley's office. The building was relatively new but the place looked as dingy as the city room of a large daily newspaper. He pulled the desk around so he could tilt his chair into the corner without falling backward when he put his feet up. He pulled out each drawer and emptied it into a wastebasket. Out fell condoms, Off-Track Betting slips, newspaper clips, pencils, small change, sugar packets, and sweat-worn pocket notebooks with dozens of rubber bands wrapped around them.

Rodriguez looked at none of the debris. One of the drawers jammed. He worked his hand in and pulled out a thick handful of skin magazines. He tossed them into the wastebasket without inspection. He walked to the water cooler, moistened some paper napkins, and wiped the desk clean.

Then he went to the men's room, took a pee, and washed his hands. He remembered an old joke about the Yale man and the Princeton man at half-time in the latrine under the Yale Bowl. The Princeton man shook the dribble off, tucked himself in, zipped himself up, and started out the door. In his cultivated voice, the Yale man said, "At Yale, they teach us to wash our hands after we urinate." The Princeton man said, "At Princeton, they teach us not to piss on our hands."

Rodriguez laughed at the dumb joke. He was thinking about jokes so he wouldn't think about O'Malley. Rodriguez had never felt that way about anyone before in his life.

Back at his desk, he called the Medical Examiner's office. As he waited for someone to answer, he realized the squad room was silent. Looking up, he saw O'Malley walking toward him between the desks. Rodriguez put the phone down and waited with his hands folded before him on the desk, in deliberate imitation of O'Malley.

"I thought I told you to go home," said O'Malley.

"I have some calls to make," said Rodriguez.

O'Malley smiled with sudden charm and turned to the

hushed room. He held his arm out toward Rodriguez as though he were introducing the main speaker at a dinner of the Emerald Society. "This is Detective Sergeant Daniel Rodriguez. Some of you probably know him. I want all of you to know that I personally requested his transfer to this division from my old command. He's gonna make us all look good."

O'Malley then walked back into his office and closed the door. No one said a word. For all Rodriguez knew, O'Malley's statement was the truth. He didn't care. He picked up the telephone and dialed the ME's office again.

The Assistant ME said, "It's like the other one, Danny, except for the use of the knife on the penis."

"Weapon?" asked Rodriguez.

"A thin, short knife with a heavy haft, possibly a ground-down hunting knife. Sharp as a razor. Blade an inch wide with blood channels down each side of the blade. A real stabbing knife. This guy knows knives. He *likes* knives, you know what I mean?"

"A nut?"

"Yeah, probably, but that's a guess," said the ME.

"How much of a guess?"

"Not much. There were twenty-eight stab wounds. Bruises from the haft on almost every wound. He drove the knife in full force every time. Broke some ribs and a collarbone. He must have been in a real frenzy. There's kind of a print of the knife blade on the boy's leg, a blood smear where the guy wiped the blade clean."

"You guys ever seen mutilations like these?"

"No. Nothing like this. I'd say you got a real psychopath on your hands, Danny."

After a few more questions, Rodriguez hung up. He was disgusted. There was a psychopath loose in Harlem and no one was trying to find him. Rodriguez looked around the squad room. He saw a bunch of generally decent, competent men; mostly Irish, some Jews, a few blacks. But they were all lifers in a nineteenth-century bureaucracy that had been outrun and outflanked by the city's criminals.

Every kid in the city knew there was a five-minute lag in communications between the City Police and the Transit Police.

So if a kid snatched a purse in the subway, he ran up to the street. If he snatched it on the street, he ran into the subway. Either way, he had a five-minute head start.

Christ, thought Rodriguez, I might as well be working for the UN, for all I can do. He sat at his clean, empty desk for a few more minutes, watching the detectives at work, hearing phones ringing, typewriters clattering, and the locker-room banter of good men hard at work doing nothing.

Feldman reappeared from O'Malley's office, gave a dull look around, and picked up a phone on the first desk he came to. He dialed a number with slow precision. Rodriguez lip-read the one-sided conversation.

"Lemme speak to Detective Flanagan . . . Hughie? . . . Stay there, I'm coming over with the car . . . Eddie wants us to go to Queens . . . Yeah, what he was talking about before you left . . . Yeah . . . Bye."

Feldman lumbered out of the room. O'Malley's door was still closed. Rodriguez heard him shout for coffee. The men in the squad room ignored him. They'd soon learn that when the old alligator in his lair wanted something, he wanted it right now, and he didn't care who brought it. Rodriguez got up and left.

He walked down Amsterdam Avenue to 96th Street, where he stuck one of his credit cards between the steel lips of a cash machine welded into the side of a bank. The machine gave him fifty dollars and a warning about slow payments. He took a cab down to 72nd Street. In a place he liked, he ate a bowl of chili and drank some beers.

At nine-thirty, he stood in a light drizzle on the corner of 86th and Broadway, waiting patiently with a dozen other people for the *Daily News* truck. He bought his paper at the newsstand, then stepped aside and read quickly through the paper until he found the little box giving the day's quota of crimes not worth reporting. There was an unsigned one-inch notice of the murder of an eight-year-old Harlem boy, giving the location, but no names or details.

Rodriguez handed the paper to a surprised man next to him at the curb. The man mumbled thanks. Rodriguez walked back to the bar. He drank a few more beers, tried to pick up a lonely-looking young woman, and went home to bed alone.

The one-inch notice was bumped out of later editions of the *News*. There was no follow-up. No other paper picked it up. Radio and TV ignored it. The death of William Thomas had gone completely unremarked a month before, and now Francis Jefferson was consigned to oblivion with one inch of newsprint.

If Rodriguez had looked out the window of O'Malley's new office at about four-thirty that afternoon, he might have seen the killer limping up Amsterdam Avenue in his army fatigues.

chapter five
gray wars

Harry Nieman stood at the window waiting for the Chief to get off the phone. In the evening dusk, Nieman could see the room behind him reflected in the window more clearly than he could see the stone towers and glistening cables of the Brooklyn Bridge and the Brooklyn waterfront beyond.

Chief of Police Thomas Kinsella sat at his desk, listening intently to the voice on the phone, his left hand holding the phone, his right hand covering his other ear in the attitude of a man shutting out all distracting noises. His elbows rested on the green blotter on the desk, and as he listened, he stared down at the top page in an open file folder, lit by a pool of yellow light from an old-fashioned desk lamp with a shade of green glass. The Chief looked like a man getting bad news.

The caller was Deputy Chief John Hanratty giving the Chief the late-afternoon tally of homicides and violent assaults. Kinsella called it the body count. The memo in the file was from Nieman to the Chief and was marked "Personal and Confidential." It was the summary of a secret investigation ordered by the Chief six weeks before. Nieman suggested it and carried it out.

One of Kinsella's private mottos was *No surprises.* One of Nieman's jobs was to make sure there were none. He had come to Kinsella's attention in 1976, when Kinsella, then an assistant chief, was in charge of security for the Democratic Convention at Madison Square Garden. Nieman was a detective sergeant on the intelligence squad. Kinsella was impressed, and made him an unofficial assistant for sensitive jobs. When the new Mayor moved Kinsella up to Chief in 1978, Nieman was promoted to lieutenant.

Nieman was put out of sight. The Chief dipped into his discretionary budget to create the Police Research Office, consisting of Nieman and a part-time assistant, a young woman Nieman found in the sociology department at Columbia, who enjoyed experimenting with statistics. Now and then they produced white papers full of arcane numbers on topics such as "Random Walk Analysis of Patrol Techniques in High Crime Neighborhoods." These were filed in wastebaskets all over the department. No one ever asked Nieman what he did when he wasn't supervising his assistant.

Nieman was in his mid-thirties. Tall and angular, slouched in his rumpled suits, he might have been a college teacher. Nieman knew that Kinsella trusted him completely. Nieman did what no one else in the department could do.

The Chief hung up the phone. "Two more homicides so far today," he said, "and it isn't dark yet. A little black kid in Harlem late this morning, and an old Jewish woman in the Bronx. The kid was mutilated like the other one last month."

Nieman watched the Chief's reflection in the window against the background of the darkening sky and the lights of Brooklyn. The Chief bent over his desk, his head in his hands again, concentrating on Nieman's long memo. This was the only copy. When they finished discussing it, Nieman would take it back to his office and shred it. Nieman could have briefed his boss verbally, but Kinsella liked to see complex problems set down on paper in some kind of order as a basis for argument. Kinsella believed that an idea that wasn't worth defending wasn't much of an idea.

Kinsella sat up. He swiveled his chair around and propped his feet on the broad window sill. He unwrapped a cigar and lit it, and sat for a few minutes in silence, puffing the cigar and idly rubbing his left hand back and forth across a corner of his desk. The desk was an ancient oak monster he had salvaged from the old police headquarters on Centre Street. The scars and marks of fifty years of executive anger and boredom made it a sacred relic for Kinsella, even if it didn't fit the fluorescent sterility of the new headquarters at One Police Plaza.

Kinsella asked, "It's very simple, isn't it, Harry? Have you ever seen anything like this before?"

"Yes."

"Where?"

"They did the same thing in Southeast Asia during the war, and we did too."

"The connection between narcotics and intelligence?"

"Yep."

"What happened there?"

"Nothing. It was part of the war, and when the war ended, the connections came to an end. Most of them."

"What was the point of it?" asked Kinsella.

"There were two points," said Nieman. "The money itself was a source of off-budget funds for intelligence operations. The corruption was a tool to obtain information. And for the other side, drug addiction was a way of weakening the morale of our troops." Nieman talked in the flat tones of a briefing officer.

Kinsella said, "It worked, didn't it? I mean, for the other side."

"Christ, yes. We played right into their hands."

"And now they've taken a leaf from that book and applied it here."

"Yessir."

Kinsella pressed his intercom and said, "Bring us some tea and tell Mary I'll be home in an hour."

With that, Nieman knew he had made his case, but that Kinsella wanted to talk before he signed off on the plan.

Kinsella relit his cigar. "Are you Catholic, Harry?" he asked. "You are, aren't you?"

"Yessir, but not Irish."

Kinsella laughed. "That's too bad for a lot of reasons. But mainly because you think like a Jesuit, and they're not Catholics. I don't know what they are. You went to a Jesuit school, I'll bet."

"Fordham Prep."

"Jesus Christ, and if you'd gone to college up there, they'd have had another priest, I'll bet you too."

"That's why I went to Columbia."

Kinsella laughed. He stood up at the window next to Nieman. They were the same height, but Kinsella had the bulk of an old street cop. Nieman was thin. They were both intense, but Kinsella's intensity was deliberate. Nieman was quick and single-minded.

Kinsella said, "Now if you'd been born Irish by some happy chance, you'd have been trained by the Christian Brothers and the Paulists. Not educated, mind you, but trained, and you'd see the world in clearer terms, not these goddamn conspiracies no one but you can understand."

They had been through this before. Nieman waited. Kinsella began ticking the points off. "You say Castro's intelligence service is supporting the hard-line wing of the FALN, the Puerto Rican liberation movement."

"Yessir."

"The FALN has legitimate sympathizers here and in Puerto Rico. And this city is as much Puerto Rican as Jewish, black, Italian, or Irish. The FALN is strong here, and Cuban control or influence over the FALN would be most effective if it was established here."

"Yessir."

"The Cubans supply weapons, money, and intelligence to the terrorist wing of the FALN."

"Yessir. If they dominate the FALN in this city, they will be in effective control of the whole movement everywhere."

"And the DGI—Cuban Intelligence—has operated in this city for twenty years?"

"Yes, ever since the KGB assumed control of the DGI in 1962 and redirected Cuban intelligence priorities. You saw a report on this in 1976."

"I remember," said Kinsella, "but there was nothing in it about narcotics or the FALN." He snorted. "Besides, that was your job. I was more worried about our own Secret Service getting off the leash."

Kinsella's night secretary, a young patrolman, came in with the tea. "I called your wife, sir. She said to stop and pick up some Chinese food for yourself. She's got a meeting at the school."

72

Kinsella's wife was a schoolteacher. He waved the young man out and fished a handful of ginger snaps out of a glass jar on his desk. He began to eat them one by one between sips of tea.

"This political stuff is fascinating," said Kinsella with heavy sarcasm. "Much more fun than regular police work. Now the best part. The Cubans are supporting their operations here in New York by running a big narcotics ring. The guy who runs it is one of the DGI's top guys, and he dropped out of sight in Mexico City two years ago. Now he's here."

"I'm convinced," said Nieman. "But there's no hard evidence. Just some ambiguous informer reports."

"We don't have to take the Cubans to court, do we?"

"No."

"What do we have to do?"

"Stop them."

"Why can't the feds stop them?"

Nieman held up three fingers. "One, because they have different priorities. Two, because they can't stop anybody from doing anything these days. Three, because you don't want them on your turf."

"I think we're on the same wavelength, Harry. Now tell me what you want to do."

Nieman said, "There's more to it, sir, that's not in the memo."

"Why the hell not?" Kinsella was annoyed.

"Because I didn't want to write it down."

"Well, Christ, what is it that's so secret?"

"The Feds have a fragment of a conversation between a known FALN member in Puerto Rico and a woman they can't identify in a phone booth in New York. They were discussing information that could come only from someone familiar with NYPD operations, information that's very closely held within the department—specifically, concerning our investigation of the LaGuardia bombing in December, 1977."

Kinsella nodded. He looked out the window and sipped his tea. He was decisive, but Nieman knew he wouldn't act unless he understood each point. The Chief didn't worry about stepping on toes, but he wanted to know whose toes they were.

"Let's go back a step," said Kinsella. "You say the Cubans spotted two or three Hispanic drug rings in East Harlem and the Bronx, picked them off, consolidated them, and began to expand. They were picked not so much for profits as for their connections with corrupt law enforcement officers."

"Yessir. They probably knew it was easier to make the operations profitable than to start from scratch trying to find the right wires into this department."

"In other words, it was their way of buying into sources of high-quality information."

"They couldn't do it any other way in less than five years. The Agency had fifteen years in Vietnam, and was never more than half-successful there."

"Who knew about the LaGuardia stuff?" asked Kinsella.

"I have a list of about a dozen people, but there's no way to trace the information because everyone in the inner circle knows someone who knows someone else, and so on. Tracing leaks is fruitless, although it can give us some ideas. And besides, you can't afford the stigma of starting an internal investigation of the top cops in this department. It'd be in the *Daily News* and the *Times* tomorrow."

"True," said Kinsella.

The weight was now on Nieman's shoulders. Kinsella simply would not ask him to do what had to be done, because he could not compromise his position. Nieman had stated the problem. Kinsella had acknowledged it by uttering the one word, *true*.

Nieman said, "There's more."

"Jesus Christ, Harry," shouted Kinsella. Then he took a deep breath. "This is hard for an old nightstick man like me. I understand ordinary corruption. God knows, it's all around us. But this? How can they do this? Who the hell are they?"

Nieman stared out the window without answering. The phone rang. Kinsella's reflected image was clear against the night sky outside as he went to pick it up. He walked around the desk and sat down. It was obviously more bad news.

Outside the window was one of the great cities of the world. It took men like Kinsella out of the quiet, insular neighborhoods of the outer boroughs and gave them enormous power in the

74

larger world. Kinsella was an honest, decent man. Nieman thought him one of the best men he'd ever known, and he knew that Kinsella's moral view of himself did not include licensing a messy operation in the gray world of international intelligence. Nieman was not sure now whether he had made his case. But it would have been a serious mistake to write it all down—a dangerous mistake.

Kinsella hung up. He said crisply, "We've got to wrap this up quickly, Harry. I have to go to Queens. Hughie Flanagan was shot and killed in a bar, and his partner shot and killed the gunman. Christ Almighty, I knew Flanagan years ago. He was a good cop once, until he started drinking. Feldman's the dumbest man I ever knew, and one of the worst cops, and now I'll have to give him a medal. My God!"

Nieman knew now that his case was made, but Kinsella was not going to like it. Nieman began cautiously, "What I want to do is go in the back door quietly, by finding out who the Cubans are paying off in this department. Then maybe I can work backward toward the top."

"How?"

"One of the department's weaknesses is the way we keep records. We clear a case when an arrest is made—any arrest—without regard to the quality of the arrest or the eventual disposition of the case. We judge performance in a precinct or squad command by the clearance rate for serious crimes."

"Get to the point."

"When I located the neighborhoods where the Cubans operate, my assistant compared complaint records against clearance records for the local detective districts." Nieman's tone was as dry as chalk dust. "There were no substantial variations in clearance rates for any of the major crime squads in any of these districts. Then we looked at actual dispositions. We found that the conviction rate was also about the same for all the major crime squads in those districts, with one exception."

Kinsella sat straight up in his chair. He knew exactly what Nieman was after.

Nieman said, "We looked at dispositions going back two years, enough time to establish patterns. The exception was Sixth Homicide."

75

"Eddie O'Malley!"

"That's right."

Kinsella burst out, "I never liked the son of a bitch. There's always been a bad odor to the man. The Knapp Commission took a look at him but he was too small a fish to fry."

"That was eight years ago," said Nieman. "He's risen in the world since then. Within his district, I broke it down further. The quality of most of the arrests under his command is average or a little better, but in drug-related homicide arrests, the quality is poor. Most were thrown out for lack of evidence. There were some complaints by assistant district attorneys about bad arrests, but the turnover in the DA's office is so high that the complaints were never followed up."

"O'Malley was falling down," said Kinsella. He sounded like a judge intoning a sentence on a prisoner.

"He was clearing the books by making arrests, but he wasn't getting convictions."

"The bastard."

"There's more. On every single one of these cases, O'Malley assigned Horst Feldman and Hugh Flanagan."

"Humh," said the Chief. "Flanagan and O'Malley were pals from the old days when they were kids in the Bronx. Did you know that, Harry?"

"No."

"I'm surprised at you." Kinsella watched Nieman's profile at the window for a long moment, then seemed to relax. He leaned back and put his feet on the window sill. He said, "Tell me something, Harry. Did you know your pals in the field-associates program had Flanagan wired?"

"Yessir."

"If they got something on O'Malley, it would have screwed up your plan, right?"

"Yessir."

"I don't mean to read your mind, Harry, but am I right to assume that you believe O'Malley has a rabbi?"

"Yes."

"And if you find this rabbi, you'll be finding the traitor in our department who talks to the DGI?"

"Yessir."

"I agree. If I were this Cuban of yours, the first thing I'd do would be to get a guy like O'Malley on the payroll." Kinsella paused. "What you're suggesting, Harry, is that the shooting of Hughie Flanagan was a setup, and that Feldman was an accomplice."

There was an uneasy silence. "OK," Kinsella said at last. "Find O'Malley's ghost rabbi. I guess we're lucky, in a way. If Flanagan had burned O'Malley, we'd never find the line to the ghost, would we, Harry?"

"No."

"Christ, it's ghoulish It's like Ireland in the old days," said Kinsella. "Like my father's stories about the Black and Tans. We've got Black and Tans among the blues. God, I think it's hateful."

The agitated words were spoken without heat. Kinsella was calm. The atmosphere of the room was still and isolated. Phones rang softly in the outer office on the other side of the door. There was a ghost in the room: the ghost of O'Malley's rabbi. Or the ghost of the man Harry had been in Vietnam. Harry wasn't sure which.

Kinsella poked around in his desk and pulled out another cigar. The intercom buzzed, and he pressed the speaker button. The young patrolman's voice filled the large office. "Sir, the Mayor's on the phone."

"Where is he?"

"Gracie Mansion."

Kinsella picked up the phone without swiveling back to his desk. "Sir," he said. "Kinsella here." He listened for a moment, then said, "No leads. It looks like another goddamn off-duty barroom shooting. I'm leaving in a few minutes. Why don't I pick you up in my car? I can fill you in on the way." He listened for another moment, then hung up. He said to Nieman, "The bastard never says goodbye. He just hangs up on you when he's had the last word. He's taking his own car." Kinsella put his hands behind his head and leaned back, rolling the cigar in his mouth, talking around it, as relaxed as if he was in his own home.

"Harry, listen." Kinsella's tone was avuncular, a powerful man talking to his protégé. "There's a war in this city. Maybe more than one. This city is nothing but neighborhoods, little

77

turfs, and there were always little wars over these little territories. But now there's money to be had like never before. And there's something else."

Nieman turned to face him, but Kinsella stared out the window. "You're one of the best young guys I ever knew, Harry. But I know a couple things you don't know. I know this city is beginning a long decline. And I know this department is part of the problem. We're nothing but a conservative, Irish Catholic constabulary. We always enforced the laws, more or less, but now we're caught up in a high-speed world we just don't understand."

Kinsella turned slowly to face Nieman. "Harry, I'm charged with enforcing black and white laws in a gray world. If what you suppose is true, one of the men closest to me in this department has been corrupted by that gray world, corrupted for political reasons, not the old-fashioned reasons of money and fear. Do you know how dangerous that is? Can you imagine a force of twenty-two thousand armed men and women divided by political factions in a city that's nothing but a quilt of ethnic turfs?"

Nieman said softly, "No."

"Harry, I want O'Malley, but more than anything, I want his goddamn rabbi."

Nieman nodded.

"Harry, what do you propose to do?"

Nieman was sick inside. He had won his case, but not the way he wanted. This was the age-old question—*Who will rid me of this man?* It was the question that killed Thomas à Becket.

Nieman said, "I have to get somebody in close to O'Malley. There's a Puerto Rican detective sergeant named Daniel Rodriguez. He was already in Sixth Homicide with O'Malley."

Kinsella smiled. "I know him. He's a damn good cop. I like him. Move him over to the Fifth with O'Malley."

"Somebody already moved him."

"Who?"

"O'Malley requested his transfer, along with Flanagan and Feldman."

Kinsella said, "Maybe somebody beat you to the punch. Maybe Rodriguez is already working for the other side."

"No sir, I know him. He wouldn't."

Kinsella stood up. He pressed his intercom. "Crank up my car," he said, and released the button. "Harry, this is a war. We have to win it. You're good at the gray wars, Harry, so you fight this one. There's no one else I can count on. I'll fight the black and white wars with my boys in blue."

There was silence. Kinsella was speaking to Nieman's reflection in the glass. Nieman remained silent. There was nothing he could say. Kinsella had mousetrapped him, had seen through him. Nieman's stomach felt the way it did one morning when he was swimming in shark-infested waters off an island south of the Mekong Delta, and he stepped off a hidden ledge into deep water.

"Harry, I've always given you all the support you needed."

"Yessir."

Kinsella clipped his gun and holster to his belt on his right hip. He shrugged on his suit jacket. "But Harry, in this ugly little proxy war you're starting, you're on your own."

Rodriguez heard the news on the radio when he woke up in the morning. Flanagan had been shot in a bar in Queens the night before, and Feldman had killed the killer. Flanagan would get an inspector's funeral, and Feldman would get the first medal of his career.

The Two-Four was in an uproar when Rodriguez arrived at seven-thirty. The uniformed cops downstairs had covered their badges with black elastic. Rodriguez walked upstairs to the squad room. O'Malley was already in, and his door was closed. A button was lit on the phone on the desk outside O'Malley's office. Rodriguez decided to wait until O'Malley was off the phone. He went to scrounge a black armband from a detective he knew slightly, who was a professional mourner for dead cops.

O'Malley was listening to his rabbi. The raspy voice said, "I'm telling you for the last time, Eddie. I didn't finger Flanagan to Ayala. I don't know how Ayala found out. He won't tell me, and believe me, I'd like to know. I didn't know he had another pipeline."

"Sunnavabitch."

"Eddie, I know you're upset about your guy, but all I heard

last month was a rumor. I heard it from a guy in Internal Affairs. Eddie, you understand I can't press too hard. It looks bad."

"Sunnavabitch."

"Eddie, you're in no danger, but lay low for awhile."

"Rodriguez makes me nervous. Why did you get him transferred over here?"

"It looks fine, Eddie. Don't worry. There's a lotta spics in that neighborhood, and he's one of them. The Mayor wants to do something about crime up there, and the brass downtown is throwing darts at the board like they always do. Rodriguez is one of the darts this week."

"I don't like it. He's sharp," said O'Malley.

"Remember Lyndon Johnson, Eddie?"

"Sure, why? I'm a Democrat, aren't I?"

"Somebody asked him once why he didn't fire J. Edgar Hoover. Johnson said, 'It's better to have the bastard inside the tent pissing out, than outside the tent pissing in.'"

"What does that mean?"

"Keep an eye on the little prick. Get him inside the tent, like you were told."

"It isn't gonna work. And Ayala said to leave him alone."

"Listen, Eddie. Ayala is very pleased with the way you handled Flanagan last night on such short notice. There's a big bonus for you. But the man changed his mind. Now he wants Rodriguez in the tent. Soon, Eddie, soon. See ya at the wake."

There was a throaty rasp and a click. O'Malley threw the phone down. He had good radar. Someone was looking for him. He had to take inventory and see where he was. He had been careless. He had to find out more about this hotshot supposed to be working for the Chief. He could have asked Hanratty, who probably knew the guy, and probably knew more than he told O'Malley, but O'Malley operated on the same assumptions as Hanratty. It was better to keep some of his best cards in his own hand. O'Malley's lifetime of experience had taught him it was better to do your own dirty work. You learn more and you owe less.

He called an old pal from the old Red Squad, supposed to have been disbanded, but mostly intact in the intelligence squad —the "so-called intelligence squad," as the joke went. He made a date for lunch with the guy, who was a little nutty the way they all were on the Red Squad, but always well informed. He would buy the guy's lunch and pick his brains.

When O'Malley hung up, Rodriguez knocked once and walked in. "Sorry about Flanagan, Lieutenant. You wanted to see me this morning."

"Yeah. A woman in the Projects up the block stabbed her son last night for stealing money from her purse. He was an addict. She killed him. She's in custody, but she won't make a statement. Wrap it up in a hurry. She doesn't speak English. You're gonna get all these over here. It'll be like you're running your own little Latin detective bureau. I'm giving you responsibility, Rodriguez. Don't fuck up. Keep busy. Take the men you need. Anyone but Feldman and Flanagan."

"Flanagan?"

O'Malley looked up suddenly. His face flushed with anger. "Shit. Get the hell out and go to work."

chapter six
st. barbara

For a week after Flanagan's funeral, O'Malley was in the worst humor ever, but Rodriguez was assigned to the fatal shooting of a Columbia University law professor, and managed to avoid the old alligator most of the time. Even so, Rodriguez began to wonder what was going on that made O'Malley so crazy. He had learned to ignore the sarcasm and anger, but now he had to deal with erratic behavior—not an easy thing to live with in police work, which is based on habit and routine.

In one of his black moods, O'Malley exploded at Feldman and transferred him out of the command, back to the Sixth. Rodriguez wondered what huge favor O'Malley had promised the new commander of the Sixth in return for taking back the hulking, stupid Feldman. Rodriguez himself began to think about requesting a transfer, something he had never done. He knew it would be hard to justify and might damage his career.

The murder case was a hard one. The law professor was an elderly white man who lived in the Westchester suburbs and commuted by train to the 125th Street Station at Park Avenue. From there he took a crosstown bus on 125th Street to Amsterdam Avenue, and walked up the long hill to 116th Street and the law school. It was his daily habit.

Walking back down the hill late one afternoon, he was held up by two youths in a block of abandoned buildings, and shot. Witnesses said both boys were black. One ran away just before the shot. The killer rifled the dead man's pockets, then ran after the other boy through the yard of a public school into the upper end of Morningside Park. It was the kind of senseless, random violence that terrorized and paralyzed the city, making people prisoners in their homes, especially the elderly.

It was the kind of case Rodriguez liked, but he ran into a blank wall. He didn't know the neighborhood well enough. After a day of pointless canvassing, he went to the precinct commander, a Captain Ryan, and asked for help. Ryan loaned Rodriguez a black plainclothesman named Jack Graves from the precinct's anticrime squad.

Rodriguez and Graves covered every playground, streetcorner, and front stoop in West Harlem. They talked to playground workers and school aides. It was Rodriguez's introduction to the area. They got nowhere the first time around. "Let's shake the tree," said Graves. On their second round, in one afternoon, they hauled in twenty-eight kids for various minor weapons and drug violations. They spent half the night booking the outraged kids in Family Court. The kids knew nothing serious would happen to them, but they didn't like the hassle. When they laughed and told the cops they'd be back on their corners the next day, Rodriguez said, "So will we."

By noon the next day, Rodriguez and Graves had a name to work with. By one o'clock, they had two names, and by three o'clock, after a wild chase on foot through the paths of Morningside Park, they had two bruised thirteen-year-old boys in handcuffs in the back seat of Rodriguez's car. One was frightened, and one was unrepentant, even though he had tried to throw away a new Colt Cobra .38 in the park. The ballistics matched the flattened, bloodstained bullet Rodriguez had found at the scene of the shooting.

The state's new laws permitted adult trials for juveniles accused of murder. Rodriguez had opposed the law, but now he felt good about it, especially after the other boy told the story. The professor had no money in his pockets. He offered a bus token and said he would write the boys a check made out to cash, if they needed money so badly. In fact, he said, he would buy the gun, so the boys would get some money and not get in trouble. This simple act of charity was an insult, so the killer pulled the trigger, and the distinguished brain of a decent, humane man was sprayed all over the front of an abandoned shoe store.

After the kids were booked, O'Malley publicly praised Rodriguez in the squad room. For the first time, some of the other men came over to Rodriguez's desk, making the small talk and goofy banter that passes the time. Like O'Malley had said, Rodriguez was going to make them all look good.

The next morning was one of those bright mornings when the wind from the Atlantic washes New York City clean, and the season tilts suddenly from spring to summer. For the first time in several weeks, Rodriguez felt fresh and clear in his mind as he walked to work. He was doing what he wanted to do, and he was back in his old form. His doubts and complaints were small ones, he decided.

At seven-thirty, the tennis courts were full in the middle-class housing project at Park West Village. Farther north along Columbus Avenue was a large public housing project named the Frederick Douglass Houses. Rodriguez noted that they took up less space and housed more people than their middle class counterparts, whose balconies and tennis courts assured their occupants they were not forgotten. The public housing had benches, playgrounds, and asphalt walks crowded with people hurrying to work. The lower classes went to work every day to remind themselves that they were not on welfare even if no one else noticed.

North of the public housing was a stretch of run-down old six-story tenements, between West 106th and West 110th. In the middle of this stretch was a large public school—JHS 57, or Booker T. Washington Junior High School, or just Booker T. Behind the school, filling almost the entire square block framed by Columbus and Amsterdam Avenues and 107th and 108th Streets, was a large asphalt playground. It was here that Graves and Rodriguez got their first lead to the kid who killed the professor; and this playground was the first thing the retarded killer of two little boys saw every day when he looked out his bedroom window in the rear of the fifth floor of a building on 109th Street.

Rodriguez entered the station house on West 100th Street through the attached firehouse. The engines were out. The Dalmation slept in a patch of sun. A fireman on light duty sat in a glassed-in booth reading the paper and guarding the place. He nodded at Rodriguez, who went through a back hall and up the stairs two at a time. A scribbled note on his desk said, "See me. EOM."

In his office, O'Malley offered a chair and coffee in a clean mug. Rodriguez was surprised. Overnight, O'Malley had cleaned his office, thrown out all the old papers, thrown his galoshes behind the door, and thrown out the old coffee containers. The night before, one of the containers had held a luxuriant, hairy, pale blue mold that looked like something out of a graveyard. The floor was mopped and waxed. The window was open, the air in the room uncommonly fresh. Only the mound of butts in the large glass ashtray boosted from some Bronx bar was evidence of the everyday habits of the lieutenant in his lair.

O'Malley said, "You're doing good work, Sergeant. Like I knew you would. You make the whole squad look good, like I said. Now, I got a new assignment for you."

O'Malley's face was fresh and relaxed. His banker's pinstripe was clean and pressed. His jacket hung on a hanger on the coat tree, instead of the doorknob. The desk was clean and bare except for the black telephone and a fresh green blotter. O'Malley carefully emptied the ashtray into his wastebasket, banging the glass against the tinny metal. In the loud noise was a trace of the furious anger that normally inhabited O'Malley twenty-four hours a day.

O'Malley said, "The department is very big on community relations this year. Because the Mayor is big on community relations this year. Especially in minority neighborhoods." O'Malley pronounced the word *minority* as though it was a communicable disease. "There's always been a lot of bullshit about this stuff, but this year they're serious. The reason they're serious is the Mayor is serious."

O'Malley spoke as though reading from engraved stone. He lit a fresh Pall Mall. He was the only person Rodriguez knew who still smoked non-filter cigarettes.

"Do you know why the Mayor is serious?" O'Malley asked.

After a long pause, Rodriguez decided it wasn't a rhetorical question. "Because the Mayor has discovered this is a minority city," he answered.

For a moment, to the satisfaction of Rodriguez, it looked as though the old alligator would explode, but O'Malley checked himself. The only sign of anger was in the cigarette. O'Malley burned half an inch off the end in one drag. The end of the cigarette looked like a welding torch. He's probably thinking about the soles of my feet, thought Rodriguez.

O'Malley said, "I need a liaison from this squad with the schools. You speak good Spanish. You're gonna be my community relations."

Rodriguez couldn't speak. He stared at the spot on O'Malley's face where the bushy John L. Lewis eyebrows grew together.

"That's all," said O'Malley amiably. "Forget about the Harlem schools. Start with the district office in that elementary school down on West End and 96th. The district superintendent wants to see you. He's a big smartass spade. Then do the junior high at 108th and Columbus. They're having problems, and the principal gets in the local papers all the time."

Rodriguez forced himself to stay seated.

O'Malley said, "And first thing this morning, go to PS 165, that real big elementary school on 109th between Amsterdam and Broadway. There's some Spanish broad there, assistant principal or something, who complains to Captain Ryan downstairs that nobody here wants to talk to her. You speak the language. Go talk to her."

Rodriguez stood up to go. He stood up too fast. O'Malley smiled, knowing he had scored a direct hit. Rodriguez hadn't said a word.

"And Rodriguez. Take it easy. This is strictly nine to five, you know what I mean? You been working too hard. I'm giving you a rest. And this community relations bullshit is gonna look good for you in your record downtown."

Rodriguez stormed out of the office. O'Malley was full of shit. What looked good was lots of arrests, good ratings from superiors, and high test scores on the exams for promotion. And one of the old parishes. And a rabbi, an advisor and protector somewhere in the upper reaches of the department, an insider to shape and guide a man's career and keep him out of harm's way.

Rodriguez had everything but the rabbi and the parish. He

didn't want a rabbi. He did things on his own. Everybody thought he was Catholic because he was Puerto Rican, but his mother was a follower of half the storefront *evangelistas* in Brooklyn, and she did a lot of island *Santeria*—Cuban voodoo —with a Cuban neighbor. Maybe he ought to go home this weekend and ask his mother to ask the *orishas*—the voices— what the hell he ought to do. He decided to call Harry Nieman instead.

He and Nieman had met a few years before. Nieman was one of the few men on the force whom Rodriguez trusted enough to call for advice. Nieman said the new assignment wasn't such a bad idea. "You'll learn a lot about the neighborhood," he said. "School people know more about neighborhoods than almost anybody else." He told Rodriguez to take advantage of the assignment. "Targets of opportunity," said Nieman. "Never refuse a target of opportunity. And stay in touch, goddammit." Then Nieman asked, "You say you didn't say anything at all to O'Malley in his office?"

"I was dumbfounded," said Rodriguez.

"That's good," said Nieman. "Now go back in there and thank him for the assignment. Say you decided after all to accept it. Say you appreciate his help in your career. Smoke him out. Try a little psy-war on him. Call me back."

Taking Nieman's advice, Rodriguez went back into the alligator's lair. O'Malley was so mad that he got up and slammed the door, then cursed at Rodriguez like an old drill sergeant for even imagining he could have refused the assignment.

Rodriguez stayed cool. "I can appeal an administrative assignment. But I want it. I appreciate it. I really do."

O'Malley jerked the door open and waved Rodriguez out of the office into the squad room. The men at their desks, uncapping their coffee containers and opening their morning papers, looked up at Rodriguez in silence, like schoolboys when one of their buddies comes back from the principal's office.

Rodriguez called Nieman and reported the incident. Nieman was amused. "Good," he said. "You knocked him off balance a little bit."

They agreed to meet at Rodriguez's apartment that night for

take-out Chinese food and beer, a social evening they had promised themselves for months.

An hour later, Rodriguez walked up Amsterdam Avenue to keep an appointment with Mercedes Lopez, the assistant principal of PS 165. At 105th Street, he passed a little storefront full of religious artifacts. On a shelf in the corner of the window, where the sun struck it, was a plaster statue of St. Barbara. To his mother, this was *Chango,* one of the most powerful voices in the Yoruba pantheon, the daughter of an incestuous marriage between the Infant Jesus and another saint whose name Rodriguez could not remember. On an impulse, he went in and bought the garish statue, and had it wrapped with newspaper and tied with string.

PS 165 was a late Victorian horror. Five floors high with a gabled slate roof in bad condition, the dirty red brick building with big schoolroom windows had been constructed at the turn of the century as a high school and was now used as an elementary school. It ran through the middle of the block, with entrances on both 108th and 109th Streets, and looked to Rodriguez like one of Blake's dark, satanic mills, as it rose in an open U-shape around a barren concrete yard littered with beer and soda cans, broken glass, and dog shit.

A woman waited for him on the sidewalk in front of the main entrance in the west arm of the U, on 109th Street not far from Broadway. She was a handsome Puerto Rican woman in her early thirties, tall and well-built, with pale tan skin and short red-blond hair. She was one of the best-looking women Rodriguez had ever seen.

He already knew she was tough. When Rodriguez called for an appointment, she told him to meet her at the entrance on 109th Street because, "All the other entrances and exits are permanently locked. We can't afford security guards. We have sixteen hundred children, and a fire here would make the Triangle Shirtwaist fire look like a party."

At the entrance, Rodriguez flapped his gold badge, and Lopez introduced herself. Rodriguez felt his spirits lift when she

89

smiled at him. The two hit it off right away. By the time they began a tour of the building, which had more rooms, half-rooms, and staircases than a rabbit warren, she could not hide her pleasure at her new acquaintance. He was handsome, smart, and Spanish-speaking. She introduced him to everyone they met in the building, even the kids.

After meeting the principal, who hid from his pupils and teachers in his office, it was clear to Rodriguez that Lopez ran the school. Rodriguez guessed that there was no question of her power and influence in the large community served by the school.

As they walked Lopez talked about the school and its community. She knew everything. She had been in the school for five years. It was the largest elementary school in Manhattan. Only two-thirds to three-quarters of the sixteen hundred pupils were present on any given day. Most of the children were Hispanic, and more than half were the children of illegal aliens from the Dominican Republic.

Outside the school was an immense extended family of parents, brothers and sisters, friends and relatives that branched out all over the neighborhood. But most of them were poor and powerless. The illegal immigrants were terrified of discovery and registered their children under false names. The school had a seventy-five percent turnover of students every year. Only a small fraction of the students lasted through all six grades in this one school. This made it impossible to organize an effective parent's association, which meant in turn that the school had no organized voice to agitate for improvement.

"We reinvent the wheel every year," Lopez said. "It's a vicious circle. We're ignored by our own district office on 96th Street because we can't get more than ten or twelve parents to go to a district board meeting. Smaller schools can pack a meeting with dozens of parents. The Board of Education at One-ten Livingston Street doesn't even know we exist."

Watching her and sensing her animation at his presence, Rodriguez was self-conscious in a way he hadn't been for years.

They returned to the scruffy gym on the first floor, where they had begun. The ceilings were too low for good basketball, and none of the hoops had nets, but Rodriguez thought it didn't

90

matter much for little kids. He and Lopez stood in a swirl of two hundred kids who had just finished lunch. The noise was deafening.

Lopez gestured angrily at a large patch of peeling, water-soaked plaster in the ceiling. "We can't get routine repairs because the school is listed for a major rehabilitation. But it's been scheduled for rehab for six years, and they just took the money out of the budget again. No repairs. No rehab. Thirty kids in first grade classes. Forty in the upper grades. No education either."

She was deeply angry, not just repeating a litany for the sake of a visitor. A little flicker of corresponding anger ignited deep inside Rodriguez.

The school looked and smelled exactly like his childhood school in Brooklyn. That was a quarter-century ago, he thought. Green and brown paint covered the walls. Construction-paper cutouts hid the windows. Wire cages hung over the gym lights. A painted concrete floor. The smell of urine and disinfectant in the boys' rooms, and the faint hint of cigarette smoke. The toilets, urinals, sinks, and water fountains were set low at a child's height.

Rodriguez clutched the statue wrapped in newsprint and tied with string. Jesus, he thought, I've spent years trying to escape this. What am I doing here?

The kids looked just like the kids he grew up with. The same mothers and grandmothers hung around the front of the school and the lunchroom during lunch period. Trying to be helpful, he asked, "Why don't you ask the Board of Ed to delist the school from the rehab list?"

She answered as if she were explaining simple fractions to a slow sixth grader. "Because it took years to get this place listed for rehab on the calendars at the Board of Ed and the Board of Estimate. If we take it off, it'll never get back on; it'll just fall down faster."

Rodriguez shook his head. He heard the voices of children he hadn't seen for many years. He had tears in his eyes, but it didn't seem to matter. He heard the voice of his mother who came to school every day to take him home for lunch.

Lopez asked him something about himself. He wasn't sure

what she said. She asked again, gently. He answered, "I went to City College. I graduated, then I ran out of gas. I let the army draft me. I was an MP in Germany for two years. Then I let the PD recruit me. I was a winner in the minority sweepstakes. They promoted me fast. I'm a good cop. I'm the first *puertorriqueño* detective sergeant in homicide. That's who I am."

She took him by the arm and pulled him through the children.

He felt out of place and anxious. He remembered the sixty-year-old smiling public man in Yeats' great poem, *Among School Children.*

When they got out into the hall, and the voices of the children were muffled and distant, he realized Lopez was talking again.

"But this high turnover has one advantage for me," Lopez said, breaking the flow of his memories.

Startled, Rodriguez asked sharply, "Advantage?"

She looked at him strangely. "Yes. I know everybody between Central Park and the Hudson River, north of 96th Street and south of Columbia University—Hispanics, Haitians, people from Hong Kong and every country around the Caribbean. Or I know someone who knows them. I even know a few white people."

Rodriguez laughed. His voice echoed in the empty hall. From their room, a class of first graders looked at them with silent curiosity.

"I can help you," said Lopez.

"Help me?"

"Find what you are looking for."

"What did you say?" he asked. They stood close together. He wanted to touch her.

"I can help you find what you are looking for," she said, with the authority and finality of a promise.

He looked over her shoulder at the children in the classroom. A beautiful little girl in a white dress smiled and waved at him. Better to smile on all that smile, he thought. He asked Lopez if she was married. He was grinning with idiotic delight. She said no. He asked her to have lunch with him.

They went to the Ideal, a good Cuban restaurant on the corner of Broadway and 109th Street. They ate slowly, talking about everything they could think of. They were both late returning to work, and they agreed to meet at the restaurant for lunch the next day.

That night, Nieman told Rodriguez what O'Malley's problem was. Rodriguez also learned, to his discomfort, that he was part of the solution.

Rodriguez's apartment was in a solid old building on West 86th Street, not far from Central Park. The distant sound of night traffic from the street far below was muffled by the light hum of his air conditioner. They gorged themselves slowly on an array of Chinese food in white cartons on a low table between them. Rodriguez made extra rice, and provided bowls and chopsticks. They ate steamed dumplings, twice-fried pork, cold hacked chicken in spicy garlic sauce, and *kung pao* shrimp. They drank beer, a brand pronounced "Chafer" by Rodriguez. He spoke English with no trace of a Spanish accent, but this was by way of a private joke with Nieman, who needled him about being the only PR in New York who didn't speak PR.

Their talk wandered comfortably from baseball to politics to the department. Nieman had never talked much about himself with Rodriguez. Now he talked about his three tours in Viet nam, and the grim murderousness of it, mocking and slashing at politicians who ran for office by waving the bloody shirt of war. He felt soiled and dirtied by the war, somehow habituated to the gray world of back-alley conflict and murder. He envied Rodriguez's ability to stand out in the open and face a lawbreaker in daylight.

"You do your duty, Daniel," said Nieman. "All around us are men in high positions who lie, cheat, and steal. We're drowning in shit. You do your duty and you do it without a second thought."

Rodriguez was not embarrassed by this praise from a man he liked and respected, but he never thought of himself in this light. He tried on the image like a man trying on a new suit of clothes, not admiring himself, but turning slowly back and forth before the tailor's mirrors.

The talk turned to O'Malley. Rodriguez related the history of his time with the man, and described the murders of the two little boys. His outrage at O'Malley's indifference glowed and burned in the air in the apartment.

"If you could reopen those two cases," asked Nieman, "where would you start?"

"Do you know the cases?"

"Yes," said Nieman.

"I'd go back to that old black newsdealer down the street from the Thomas place."

"You think he was reliable?"

"Why not?" asked Rodriguez. "We're not putting him in front of a jury. All we want is information, and he's all there is."

"Why do you suppose O'Malley sat on those two cases?"

"Dunno."

"I don't know either, but he sure did sit on them." There was a long pause, then Nieman asked, "Why did he assign Feldman and Flanagan to the Thomas case? You caught it, didn't you?"

"Yeah, but I was flopping that day because there weren't enough supervisors in the precinct."

"How well did you know Flanagan and Feldman?"

"Not real well. Flanagan was OK but he should have been in AA. Feldman is one of the dumbest and most brutal men I ever met. They both licked O'Malley's hands like dogs."

Nieman shifted his slouched frame in his chair. He said, "Flanagan was wired. He was a field associate."

Rodriguez was visibly surprised. "I thought that program was dead."

"That's what everybody's supposed to think."

A silence fell, and Nieman, slouched in an expensive wing chair, glanced idly around Rodriguez's apartment. Centered on one wall was a signed print by Helen Frankenthaler. Nieman knew few people who interested him more than Rodriguez. Odd guy, thought Nieman. Interesting.

Rodriguez got up and paced around his living room. He fooled with the controls of an elaborate stereo system, snapped a cassette into a deck, turned it on, turned it off, and turned on the radio. He found an FM station playing jazz.

"What's on your mind, Harry?" he asked at last.

"I need some help."

"What kind of help?"

"You have to keep this under your hat, pal."

"Yeah, sure," said Rodriguez.

"Somebody fingered Flanagan. He had something on O'Malley, and O'Malley found out. Feldman took Flanagan drinking in a bar in Queens that hasn't had a holdup in living memory. Some young dude walked in, stuck up the bartender, and before anyone could even twitch, shot Flanagan in the back of the head. Bang, bang, bang. The dude turns and starts to run out. Feldman pulls out his gun like he was on the firing range at Rodman Neck, and drills the guy in the back with five shots. They can't identify the guy. He's an illegal immigrant, maybe Jamaican or Haitian, with no ID."

Nieman went to the kitchen and returned with two cans of fresh beer. "Now, what does that sound like to you?" he asked.

"A setup," said Rodriguez.

"I set it up," said Nieman.

"What the hell do you mean?" shouted Rodriguez. "Jesus Christ, Harry, that makes you an accomplice to first-degree murder!"

Nieman shrugged. Rodriguez stared at him. He was in his early thirties, but he often looked older, tired and undernourished, like a sick man. Tonight he looked healthy and relaxed.

"Sit down, Daniel, and let me tell you the whole story."

Nieman related the story he had told Chief Kinsella. Boiled down, it didn't take long. He ended by telling Rodriguez how he set Flanagan up.

"I called this guy Ayala and told him Flanagan was wired. I didn't tell him who I was. I said I'd call him back in a few days, and maybe we could make a deal. I figured if Ayala acted, we'd know there was a connection between him and O'Malley."

"Now you know," said Rodriguez.

"But we don't know who the connection is."

"How do you know all this shit?"

Nieman stood up and stretched. He looked like Harry Hopkins, the cadaverous gray figure who lurked in the background of wartime photographs of FDR. He said, "I work hard, pal, and I'm good at what I do. But there's a lot I don't know. You could help."

Rodriguez said, "This is a police department, not a goddamn intelligence agency. You just had a guy set up for murder to get another piece for your puzzle. I'm not gonna help you, you son of a bitch. I ought to arrest you."

Nieman smiled lazily down at Rodriguez, and said, "You and whose army?"

Rodriguez smiled back. Like magic, a snub-nosed .38 appeared in his hand, as fast as the head of a snake.

"I wouldn't need any help," he said. "Now sit down and finish your beer. There's a lot I don't understand, and I know I'm not as dumb as Feldman. You owe me some explanation."

Nieman sat down, looking simultaneously pleased and chastened.

They talked for another hour. Rodriguez asked dozens of questions. Finally, Rodriguez said he'd had enough beer for a night, and got up to make some tea.

"So you think the Cubans modeled this thing after the CIA heroin operation in Southeast Asia?" Rodriguez asked when he returned to the living room.

"Yeah," said Nieman lazily. "They want to make money and they want intelligence."

"Why New York?"

"Christ, man, this is the center of the known universe."

"Which is more important, the money or the information?"

"I can't say," said Nieman. "Both."

"Why?"

"Because intelligence services always want money that can't be traced, off-budget money. Then they can run off-budget operations."

"I don't get it."

"There's nothing mysterious about it. If Congress appropriates money to the CIA budget, then the CIA is obliged to tell Congress how they spend it. In recent years, Congress has more or less demanded to be told. But if the CIA has revenues from

96

other sources, they're under no obligation to Congress. That's partly why they set up all those proprietary corporate fronts during the early fifties."

"What about the Cubans? Does Castro know everything his own people do?"

"I doubt it."

"What about the Russians?"

"It's a known fact that the KGB runs a lot of off-budget operations, both inside and outside the Soviet Union."

"You certainly keep in touch, Harry."

"Yes, I do."

"Why don't you let the feds handle this?"

"Because they can't handle it, and if we don't do it for ourselves, we'll be standing around while a lot of people are getting hurt or killed."

"I don't like this bullshit," said Rodriguez.

"It wasn't made to like. It's *dreck*. It's paralyzing and poisoning the department. This department is as big as two full-strength army divisions, and we can't catch dopers making deals in the lobby of the Municipal Building."

Rodriguez said nothing.

"You want a career in this department?" asked Nieman. "You better help make sure it's a department to have a career in."

"I don't like informers," said Rodriguez. "I don't want to be an informer." Then, slowly: "Why was I transferred across town with O'Malley?"

Nieman said easily, "I did it."

"Why?"

"Because you're on the fast track in this department, and everybody on the fast track needs a good rabbi to watch out for them downtown. When the opportunity arose, I nominated myself to give you a helping hand."

Rodriguez was suddenly very angry. "I didn't ask for this, Harry. I was doing fine on my own. I don't like O'Malley, but I don't like these fucking games either." Rodriguez jumped up. "I'm a cop," he said, "not a narc or some goddamn CIA spook, and I'm no snoop for Internal Affairs, either. I hate informers.

97

And I don't like people fucking around with my life without asking me first. I don't give a shit about this game you and the Chief are playing."

Nieman opened his mouth to speak, but Rodriguez held up his hand. "Wait a minute, pal. You say you work for the Chief, but I can't call him up and ask him. Just which chief do you work for? Or maybe it's chiefs. Huh? How many people do you work for, Harry? You guys always work for more than one guy. Are they all here in this city? How the hell do I know? Maybe some of them are somewhere else, huh? Maybe Washington?"

Now Nieman was mad, or seemed to be. He said coldly, "I've got no defense against this bullshit, but I'll tell you plain, Danny-boy. I'm a lieutenant in the New York Police Department, and I work directly for Chief Kinsella, who you know to be an honest and decent man. I have all the authority I need to be here tonight, making this pitch to you."

"Does Kinsella know you fingered a New York City cop to a fucking slimy Cuban intelligence agent?"

"I didn't tell him in so many words."

"Oh, that's good," said Rodriguez. "That's nice. Welcome to the gray world."

"It's not a neat and tidy place we live in, Danny."

"You say that over and over. But if you can recognize good from bad, you don't need these shabby little litanies to cover your ass with."

"You sound like Kinsella," said Nieman, "but he sent me here tonight. He wants you on board."

"Tell him to go fuck himself," said Rodriguez. "If he knew you were an accomplice to murder, he'd have to arrest you, so you don't tell him in so many words, and he goes along with your polite fiction. Then you come here and tell me, knowing goddamn well I won't arrest you either."

"It's not a simple world," said Nieman, closing the argument, but without agreement from Rodriguez.

They were facing each other. Rodriguez was shorter than Nieman, under six feet, with the flat, square build of a soccer player. His hair was black. He had a handsome, regular face. His skin was a dry, light tan with a reddish cast, like a fisherman or farm worker. Until he met Rodriguez, Nieman had always wondered what the Taino Indians in the Caribbean had looked like before they were wiped out by the Spaniards.

Nieman lifted his crumpled suit jacket off the floor and fished around in one of the inside pockets. He pulled out a thin typescript and handed it to Rodriguez. It was a transcript of a telephone conversation between O'Malley and an unidentified second party, a conversation O'Malley would have remembered well. He had asked his rabbi why it was that nobody had direct dealings on the street with Italians in anything but loansharking. The raspy smoker's voice had answered the question.

"You know what a mom-and-pop store is, Eddie?"

"Sure."

"Your mom and pop ever own one?"

"Naw. My pop was a cop, like me."

"If you ever retire and buy a mom-and-pop store, Eddie, there's only two rules. One, skim off as much as you can before you pay your bills and taxes. Number two, never put anybody on the cash register except a member of the family."

"Right," said Eddie. "Or else they steal from you."

"That's exactly right, Eddie," said the voice. "This business you asked me about is like a big mom-and-pop store, only there's no moms in the business, just pops."

"Right," said Eddie in the solemn voice he used in parochial school when the parish priest undertook to illuminate him on some basic point of catechism.

The voice, now dripping with patience, said, "Loansharking is the cash register, Eddie. It's work for the family. The rest of the stuff, they hire someone else to do it for them."

"Sure," said Eddie.

"For the dirtiest stuff, like drugs, they hire niggers and spics, you understand." It was the end of the lesson. The point of the lesson was that Eddie was working at the dirty end of the stick, and should not ask stupid questions unless he already knew the answer.

"Talk to ya soon, Eddie," said the voice.

The transcript noted, "End of tape. Source T72–42–230. 12.2.72."

"What the hell is this?" asked Rodriguez. "From 1972? Who's the other voice?"

"It's the ghost rabbi," said Nieman. "It's the only trace. I found it in an old file from the Knapp Commission. They decided O'Malley wasn't worth the effort, and back then, they were right."

"It'd be nice to hear the mystery man's voice," said Rodriguez.

"The tapes were all destroyed," said Nieman, "unless they needed them for evidence."

"We keep more records than any other civilization in history, and never the right ones," Rodriguez said.

"Danny-boy, I want O'Malley's ass. But more than him, I want this ghost."

Rodriguez hesitated, then asked, "What can I do?"

"You're right there with O'Malley every day. The next time he sits on a murder investigation, I want to know about it. I want you to put pressure on him to reopen the Thomas case."

"How can I do that? The case is in another division."

"Just invent an informer on the West Side with a hot tip that the killer lives in your area."

"I don't like it."

"And hang in there," Nieman continued. "Maybe O'Malley will try to bring you on board. You speak Spanish, after all."

Rodriguez laughed curtly. "You're just like O'Malley. He's always telling me I speak Spanish, as if I didn't know. As if I learned it in college."

"I'm not like O'Malley," said Nieman.

"Why don't you bug his apartment?" asked Rodriguez. "He lives alone. Tap his office telephone. He's on the phone all the time."

"It's premature," said Nieman. "What if he sweeps his apartment? If I tap his phone at the frame, the security guys at the phone company will tell the FBI. If I tap it at the precinct, and Internal Affairs sweeps the phones, it'll scare O'Malley."

"Everybody knows O'Malley's on the pad," said Rodriguez.

"I don't want to scare him off," said Nieman. "I want him to feel secure. Then maybe he'll make a pass at you."

"I'm not gonna play," said Rodriguez.

"With him, or with me?"

"Neither one of you."

"Do me a favor, Danny, and yourself too. You don't have to say yes right now, but don't say no."

Rodriguez thought about Mercedes Lopez. He looked at the newspaper-wrapped statue lying on its back on a bookshelf.

"I'll stay in touch," he said. "But that's all."

chapter seven
m

Harry Nieman was right when he told Rodriguez the school assignment was a good one. Rodriguez worked the schools every day for a week. He was amazed at what he hadn't known about the Upper West Side, even though he lived in the middle of it. Much of the area, with its dense mixture of wealth and poverty, was familiar, but as Rodriguez walked from school to school, he saw an astonishing diversity and resilience.

There were many schools, only a few blocks apart, to meet the needs of people who lived several thousand to a block. He and Mercedes had lunch together every day at the Ideal. She illuminated and commented on what he had seen and heard since the day before. He talked to teachers, principals, parents, paraprofessionals, and kids. He heard dozens of complaints and could affect none of them, not even the few directly involving the police. What nearly overwhelmed him finally was the absurd hopelessness of people, their inability to control the circumstances of their lives. He told Mercedes that he now understood the truth of the idea that the strength of a society lies in its basic institutions—schools, police, hospitals, courts. In New York City, these institutions were in deep decay.

Mercedes knew everything and everybody. At one lunch, Rodriguez described an encounter with a Puerto Rican member of the community school board, who had cornered him at a meeting, flattering him and enlisting his help in getting new funds for a street academy for Hispanic dropouts. It was called the

Broadway Mini-School. School board funds had run out, said the man, but with a simple change in the school's charter, easily managed by the board of directors, the school could become an antidelinquency program. The man knew the police had federal funds for such programs. Could Rodriguez help? And would he serve on the board? Rodriguez had learned enough during his brief immersion in the muddy waters of the West Side to decline.

Mercedes was furious. "You *were* flattered," she said. "Admit it. Those whores! Those bastards!" The organizers of the school had gotten two hundred thousand dollars in federal funds through the local school board, which they quickly embezzled, buying new cars, taking trips to conferences in San Juan, and paying big salaries for themselves and their friends in the antipoverty crowd.

"The board refused to fund them again," she said bitterly, "but they also refused to seek an outside investigation. The white liberals on the school board went belly-up. They all have political ambitions, and these poverty parasites control Hispanic votes.

"You're a policeman," she said angrily, "and you're so naïve. You brag about how you see the worst side of life every day, but you only see the surface and you learn to ignore what the politicians will do nothing about."

Rodriguez defended himself, but she scoffed. "Law and order," she said. "You can't even keep psychopaths from murdering little boys."

"How do you know about that?" he asked sharply.

"Do you think school workers don't talk to each other? Do you think we can't add two and two?"

He told her the story, omitting any mention of Feldman, Flanagan, and Harry Nieman. She was oddly silent when he finished, and finally said, "You are a very good and decent man, Daniel, but you must be careful not to get involved in something that will only hurt and overwhelm you."

When he asked her what she meant, she brushed him off. "You're a good man," was all she'd say, "and I don't want to see you get hurt."

"You're hurting my feelings," he said, "but I can take care of myself in the streets."

At this she blushed, and tears came to her eyes. He asked her to dinner Friday night. She accepted. As they walked the half-block back to PS 165, he said he was sorry she didn't have any books for him to carry. He might as well have told her he loved her.

"Daniel, you're the best man I ever met," she said, and ran up the steps into the school. He stood on the sidewalk, confused by feelings he had forgotten, and realized foolishly that today was Friday. He had asked her to dinner tonight.

They ate at the Hunam Balcony on Broadway at 98th Street. As they ate, Rodriguez talked excitedly about his research week, as he called it. He said O'Malley had done him a favor by sending him to an advanced graduate seminar on neighborhood life. Cops saw the results of crime, not the process, not the daily work of crime, he told Mercedes. Under the surface of daily life on the West Side was a routine of crime and violence that shocked him. He had never fully understood how widespread it was, and how much a part of everyday life.

Mercedes listened with bemusement as Rodriguez told her he was re-learning, with her help, what he had known as a child. The cause of crime and violence was not sociology. It was economics. It was money. It was huge amounts of cash controlled by a handful of people. There was a cash economy on the streets, in gambling, drugs, theft, and shakedowns, that rivaled the formal economy of government and business. Rodriguez was surprised at the scale of the hidden economy.

"It's not hidden," said Mercedes, pouring his glass full of Japanese beer.

"No! You're right," he said, pouring her beer in turn. "It's completely open. Why can't we stop it?"

She shrugged.

"If you could just eliminate the street-level drug dealers and fences," he said, "you'd eliminate the cash incentive for half the violent crime, and people could use the streets again."

She nodded in agreement, amused by his innocent evangelism.

"How can we do it?" he asked. He really seemed to want an answer.

"Shoot them," she said.

Nearly shaking with excitement, they walked a few blocks down Broadway to the Thalia movie theater, where they saw *M*, Fritz Lang's 1931 classic of German expressionism. Rodriguez had seen the movie years before, as a soldier in Germany. The instant the film began, he realized why he had brought Mercedes to see it. It was the story of a psychopathic killer played by Peter Lorre, in his first great role. The killer eluded the bureaucratic police of the German city where he stalked and killed several little girls, but he was pursued and finally caught by the city's criminal underworld, which resented the disruption of its ordered existence by the police manhunt. The underworld, with its complex caste and class system, was a distorted mirror image of the official forces of law and order. Much of the movie took place in working-class and industrial neighborhoods. The killer was tried and condemned by a kangaroo court of criminals. The grainy black and white print gave the film a documentary immediacy. It was a stunning commentary on the Weimar-like world of New York City outside the doors of the Thalia.

Rodriguez and Mercedes sat through the movie, barely touching, intensely conscious of the rustle of each other's clothing, and of every breath and movement. When the movie ended, they ran to Broadway and caught a cab. Ten minutes later, without a word, they stood inside his apartment door in the dark, clinging to each other and trembling with emotion. They stripped each other naked in the hall.

In the morning, Mercedes went through his apartment room by room, asking about everything. When they came to the living room bookshelf, she asked him about the package wrapped in newspaper, remembering he had it with him the first day at PS 165. He unwrapped it and showed her the statue of St. Barbara.

She held the statue in her hands in open wonder, calling it *Chango*. She explained that in the little island village where she was born, this was the most powerful of all the voices, an intercessor for women and children in trouble. She made Rodriguez put the statue on the dresser next to his bed.

They spent the morning in bed and the afternoon wandering around the city. She bought a box of blue oratory candles and lit one before the statue as they went to bed that night.

"Don't ever let it go out," she said. "It will be very bad for both of us."

Sunday morning, they took a bus up Amsterdam Avenue to a coffee house near 111th Street, where they had breakfast. The street was quiet. A few worshippers hurried into the huge Cathedral of St. John the Divine, which dominated the neighborhood. Rodriguez had strayed into the church on Good Friday a few years before, and heard the bishop preach a sermon around the theme of a city in ashes, destroyed by arson. He never forgot the image.

He led Mercedes down 111th Street toward Broadway. It was a block of drab, large apartment houses. He told her the story of a shootout he had been in not long before, when he and a platoon of other cops had trapped a robber in the middle of the block. Thirty-six shots were fired. The robber hit no one. The cops hit him five times. Rodriguez had cut the man off on the sidewalk and emptied his gun at the man, hitting him three times.

"Who was he shooting at?" asked Mercedes.

"Me," said Rodriguez. "There were POs all over the place, and I was the only one he shot at."

"What's a PO?"

"Police officer."

He showed her the bullet scars on the rough brown bricks of the apartment buildings. They looked like streaks of silver lipstick. A car that had been hit was parked exactly where it was the afternoon of the shootout. The owner hadn't repaired it yet, and Mercedes poked at the jagged, wicked hole made by a stray bullet.

She turned to Daniel with tears streaming down her face. "What if that had hit you?"

With a little bravado he said, "It would have made a hole

107

thirty-eight hundredths of an inch in my chest, and the size of a basketball in my back. He was shooting hollow-points."

"Will you get a medal?" She was angry.

"Yes."

"You're just another *macho* Puerto Rican," she shouted, "playing with guns." She was sobbing.

He grabbed her and held her. They were trembling. He was frightened. He had been so frightened after the shootout that he had puked into the gutter, but this now was not the fright of a gunfight. It was the anxiety of the uncertain consequences of adult life. He understood in an instant how his love for Mercedes was deepening and darkening his life, coloring it so it was no longer entirely his.

"This is the only thing I know how to do for a living," he said. "I want you to know exactly what I do. I don't want you to be afraid of my job."

"There are things you don't tell me." It was not an accusation. It was a statement of fact.

"I know," said Rodriguez. "It would be violating a confidence. But if it affects you, I will tell you, I promise. You are more important to me than anything."

Even as he said it, he knew he had made a promise he couldn't keep. She looked at him with a half-smile, as if she knew it too.

As they walked back to the coffee house, they passed a decaying apartment house. Tin covered most of the windows. It was just before the corner, across from the Cathedral, and surrounded by vacant lots littered with brick and scattered garbage. The building had been occupied by squatters for ten years. It was maintained by the Cathedral as an act of charity, but the original poor families who took over the building had moved away. It was now a haven for small-time drug dealers and other petty criminals. The Cathedral still paid to heat the building in winter, but had given up maintaining it.

After the shootout, a kid on the street told Daniel that the gunman had lived in the building not long before, and Rodriguez had realized the man was running for the building when he had trapped him. The kid had told Rodriguez, in Spanish, "Robbing money, man. It's good. It's liberation."

He told this to Mercedes, who stopped and looked at the building. She said that several years before, when the diocese tried to evict the original squatters, she led a large community demonstration to prevent the police from moving into the building. She added, out of respect for fact, that it wasn't actually the Cathedral that owned the land, but a real estate trust of the Episcopal diocese. Daniel laughed and told her he had been assigned that day to mingle in the crowd and pick up information. "I remember you now," he said. "You were fantastic. Beautiful, and in control of everything."

She dropped his hand and gestured at the building. Its walls at street level were covered with fading political graffiti in Spanish. *A Free Building. A Free Puerto Rican People.*

"That is what I believe in," she said angrily. "What I can see with my own eyes. People fighting to be free. A free Puerto Rico that is not a supplier of cheap labor for the sweatshops of this city. A Puerto Rico that will be the capital of political and economic democracy for all the Caribbean."

Daniel looked at her with amazement. She looked hard back at him. "Do you understand?" she asked.

"No. I am not political. You are more important to me than painted slogans. Do you think that man who ran down this street with a gun in his hand believed in a free Puerto Rico?"

"No," she said. "Crime does not make good politics. I do not like violence." Her voice softened. They were walking to the corner again when she stopped and asked, "What happened to that man?"

"I can still quote the hospital report: Admitted in a conscious but shocked condition. A two-hour operation. Two entry wounds in his chest, an entry and exit wound in the left wrist, entry and exit wound in the left thigh, an entry wound in the left buttock, and an exit wound in the right thigh. Bullets impacted against the spine and a rib. Those were not removed."

"Where is he now?"

"Bellevue prison ward, waiting for trial."

"Will you testify?"

"Yes, of course."

"You could be dead."

"Yes, and I'd do it again," he said fiercely. "The son of a

bitch robbed a store with a gun, then ran up Broadway and down this street at five-thirty in the afternoon. If it hadn't been raining, there would have been kids all over the block. When he was warned to stop, he fired at the police."

"You were the police," she said very softly.

"Yes, goddammit, and I waited until he shot first."

"That's what you believe in?"

"Yes, that's what I believe in."

That night she stirred in bed and pulled herself close to him, fitting herself around behind him. *"Llama a la policia,"* she said.

He was almost asleep. He started, then relaxed when he realized who was speaking in his ear. "Call the police?" he asked.

"Yes. When I need you, I will call 911 and ask for the great Detective Sergeant Daniel Rodriguez."

"Those assholes. None of them speak Spanish. If you give a Spanish name, they'll hang up on you."

He could feel the blood throbbing in his cock. Her hard breasts pressed against his back, and he felt her thick pubic hair against his hip. She reached around him into his crotch, cupping him in her hand and scratching him lightly with her fingertips. He rolled over, and she pulled him on top and inside her in one motion. She was so moist and swollen open that he could barely feel himself slipping into her. They made love for the third time in an hour.

Rodriguez had been a tourist most of his adult life, with no attachments. Now he had been intercepted. Somehow, Harry Nieman and Mercedes had both gotten a grip on him at the same time. There was nothing he wanted to do about it. Under the hard surface of his professional life, there were strong remnants of Caribbean fatalism.

He was angry at Nieman for appointing himself as his rabbi, and he wasn't even sure Nieman was telling the truth about it; O'Malley had taken credit for his transfer. But he wasn't angry enough to say no to Nieman. Rodriguez was shocked by Nieman's setup of Flanagan, and by the idea that Kinsella knew

110

but wouldn't act, but he was more deeply offended by O'Malley's awful indifference to the deaths of the two children.

As he walked to work on Monday morning, with the smell and feel of Mercedes all over him, Rodriguez found it surprisingly easy to distinguish between the private wars of the police force and O'Malley's deliberate violation of a public trust. Flanagan was a grown man and could have avoided his death, had he not gotten caught up in the inner politics of private wars. It was Flanagan's own risk. But the children were innocent victims.

Rodriguez knew this was the kind of insular thinking that outsiders misunderstood, but he was a cop and couldn't avoid thinking like one. But it had gotten complicated. Harry Nieman was the only cop Rodriguez talked to as a friend, and now he was making demands Rodriguez didn't like. He might be able to explain much of this to Mercedes, but he was cautious. He didn't know her well enough. She understood easily and listened to him eagerly, but she was pulling him into deep water.

Rodriguez already knew there was an emotional link in his own mind between his separate relationships with Harry and Mercedes, but although he had actively sought involvement with Mercedes, he was simply letting events dictate what happened with Nieman.

As he walked into the station house, he was struck by an unsettling thought—in his own mind, he had named the killer of the little boys. He was calling the killer "M."

M woke up early Monday morning, before dawn. He sat on the edge of his bed and looked out the window. He had wakened from a vivid, frightening dream. A toy alligator two or three feet long, made of wood painted green and yellow with red eyes, was snapping at his toes. He was in a long, low greenhouse. He rose to the ceiling like an inflated balloon to escape the creature, but when his head bounced gently off the ceiling, he dropped low enough for the vicious ivory teeth in the clacking wooden jaws to nip him painfully.

M looked out the window for a long time. The hot colors of the dream faded as the morning sun brightened the empty gray asphalt playground across the street. Finally, all he saw was a

111

man walking slowly across the playground carrying a lunch bucket.

This was M's terrain. The leafy tops of tall sycamore trees reached up to a level just below his fifth-floor window. The trees grew in a small vest-pocket park on 108th Street just behind his building. Over the treetops and across the quiet street, the scene was dominated by the flat emptiness of the playground.

He stood at the window and watched the sidewalks on both sides of the playground slowly fill with people going to work. He nervously pulled his bent fingers through his black hair like a comb. He was nude, but there were no windows nearby with a view into his room, and the trees hid him from the street below. Only someone in the playground could have seen him, but there was no one there at this hour. His torso and neck were badly scarred from acne, his face less so. He was not ugly; he was plain. His skin was dark brown and covered with short, thick hair. The reason for his limp was obvious—the jutting, deformed hip from birth at the hands of an inexperienced midwife—a mark of poverty, a mark of the Third World. Otherwise, his body was trim and muscular, the body of a shortstop or second baseman, quick and strong.

By nine o'clock, the children would begin to appear, freed by summer vacation from school, with nowhere else to go. But at this early hour, there were no children in the playground to see M masturbating in his window.

When M got to the *bodega* at 101st Street and Amsterdam Avenue, almost directly across from the Twenty-Fourth Precinct, he learned he had nothing to do until the afternoon. It was only nine-thirty, and he decided to enjoy himself. He wrapped an eight-pack of beer in wet newspapers and put it in the bottom of a plastic shopping bag. He took a medium-size portable radio from behind the meat counter, wrapped it in a plastic bag, and put it carefully on top of the beer. He took his field jacket off and folded it on top of the radio. Now he was ready. He walked over to Broadway. In a Cuban bakery, he ate a sweet roll and drank a small cup of black coffee in which he dissolved enough sugar to make rock candy. Then he walked to a post office on 104th Street, where he bought a money order for two hundred dollars and mailed it to his mother in Santo Domingo, as requested by his sister. On Amsterdam and 107th Street, he went into a candy store and put down fifty cents six ways on the number 342, the batting average of a Dominican baseball player whose career M followed closely.

He marched under the hot sun up Amsterdam to 108th Street, where he crossed kitty-corner to the other side of the avenue. Here stood the funeral home of Frank O'Reilly and Sons, an Irish establishment that hadn't buried a person of the Irish faith in several years. Someone following M day after day through the minor variations in his routine would have discovered that he often came close to stepping in his own footsteps as he made his daily rounds.

After a quick survey of the area, M headed down the north side of 108th Street toward his favorite spot, the little park beneath his bedroom window. He passed the gaping dark entrances to two parking garages, feeling the touch of cool air. At a short ramp that led up from the sidewalk, he turned into the little park. The shade under the sycamore trees was a relief from the glare of the sun. Above the trees, the sky was cloudless and electric blue, a crystal day. The cries of children rose from the playground. The noise of heavy traffic from Amsterdam Avenue seemed muted and far away.

The little park, surrounded on three sides by the high, rough brick walls of buildings, was not much larger than a basketball court. There were benches and concrete checkers tables under the trees. Two young women with babies in strollers sat near a sandbox and swings at the far end of the park. M turned to the near end and went to his favorite bench, where he commanded a clear view of the playground across the street.

Despite the heat, M wore most of his customary uniform. His tan khaki pants were rolled up to the ankles over spit-shined army boots of black leather. He wore a sweatshirt. His only concession to the season was a bare head. In cool weather, he wore stocking caps. He kept a number of them upstairs in one of his plastic shopping bags.

He took out his radio and set it on a checkers table, then unwrapped the beer. The bottles were wet with condensation. He pulled one out of the carton, twisted off the cap, and drank

113

half the bottle in one swallow. He dropped the bottle cap into the shopping bag and set the bottle down. He tuned the radio to a Latin station. He drank the rest of the beer, dropped the bottle in the bag on top of the wet papers, opened another bottle, and settled back to watch the playground. It was jammed with a swarm of kids, big and little, running, chasing, jumping rope, playing softball and basketball, riding bikes, sitting in little groups along the perimeter fence, yelling, or standing alone in the midst of the chaos.

A small dark-skinned boy rode a little red bicycle in slow figure eights at the upper end of the playground, in the free space between a half-court basketball game and the deep outfield of a softball game. The boy seemed isolated and lonely. M watched him intently, the way a cat watches a bird out of reach across a grassy field. He took quick little sips from his beer bottle. The boy was self-absorbed as he rode his beat-up bike in careful school figures on the hot asphalt littered with bottle caps and glittering shards of broken glass.

Across the street from M was a man-sized ragged hole in the chain-link fence around the playground. Suddenly the boy rode straight for the hole. M set his bottle down with a loud smack and darted across the street. He got to the fence just before the boy, who looked up calmly at the agitated man blocking his path. The boy waited well out of arm's reach, unworried because he had an army of children at his back. He could bring them all running with one shrill scream for help.

M thought of the bigger boys with their quick cruelty and their softball bats. He caught his breath and smiled. He told the boy he admired his skill on the bicycle, and admired the red bicycle too. He asked where he could find a bike just like it for his little brother back in Brooklyn. The boy shrugged. M asked again. The boy didn't know. He said he was late getting home for lunch.

Maybe the bike was too old and too small for such a fine rider, said M. Maybe the boy should have a bike with ten gears and shiny reflectors. The boy said he had to go. Would the *señor* please move away from the hole in the fence?

M said he would buy the bike, and pay such a price that the

114

boy could buy himself a new one. The boy said he liked his bike just fine. He had to go home before his grandmother came looking for him and got angry. M said he would give the boy a quarter to meet him here after lunch to talk some more about the fine bicycle.

The boy agreed. He took the coin from M, who stepped out of the way. The boy pushed his bike through the hole in the fence and rode quickly up the gentle slope of 108th Street toward Amsterdam Avenue.

M watched the boy turn at the corner, then went back to his bench, gathered his things, and walked down 108th Street to Columbus Avenue, where there was a Dominican luncheonette he liked.

An hour later, he arrived back at his bench. The sun was high and hot. He had stopped at his apartment to shed some of his gear. Now he wore a tee shirt with the face of Billy Martin on it, and carried only a quart bottle of beer in a brown paper bag. His boots were freshly shined. They gleamed like mirrors in the sun as he walked into the park. His pants were neatly rolled almost to the tops of his boots.

A pair of uniformed cops rolled slowly by in their patrol car. M ignored them. Cops barely existed in his universe. He had carried on an illegal and dangerous activity right under their noses for several years.

The boy arrived, pedaling slowly down the sidewalk from the direction of Amsterdam Avenue. The boy saw M sitting in the shadows of the little park, but ignored him and headed for the gap in the twelve-foot fence. M left his beer on the bench and walked down the short ramp to the sidewalk. He looked cautiously up and down the street but saw nothing to make him suspicious. He called across the street to the boy.

The boy straddled his bike and walked it into the playground. M crossed the street. The boy rode slowly back along the other side of the fence and stopped. M was afraid to enter the playground. He was forced to talk to the boy through the fence.

M asked the boy again about his fine red bike, and offered

115

to trade a good ten-speed for it. The boy said nothing. He was poised, ready to flee into the crowds of noisy children on two acres of asphalt.

The boy's manner alerted M, who turned and saw an old woman watching him intently from ten yards up the sidewalk. He realized instantly it was the boy's grandmother.

"Maricone," she hissed. "What do you want with the boy?"

The boy disappeared into the playground.

M said, "Nothing. I was asking the boy about the bicycle for my little brother in Brooklyn."

The old woman was short, with skin the color of cured leather. She wore a faded green housedress and ancient leather sandals, with a bright red bandanna over her thick white hair. She walked closer to M and hissed at him again.

"I don't like the way you look. Get away from the boy. Get away from all the children here. Go back to Brooklyn. You can buy all the stolen bicycles you want for your little brother, if you have one."

M sidestepped slowly away.

"Leave the children of this *pueblo* alone," said the grandmother, now only a few feet away from him. There was real menace in her voice.

M was disturbed by her familiar accent, and by her reference to the little neighborhood in the huge city as a *pueblo*, a village. She was Dominican. She frightened him. It was like being chastised by his mother.

M said nothing more. Trying to control his limp, he crossed the street. He abandoned his beer and walked up the street past the entrances to the big garages.

The old woman watched until he disappeared around the corner. Then she walked through the fence into the playground, cutting directly through a basketball game. She re-emerged through the softball game, talking furiously to the back of her grandson, who pedaled slowly along in front of her. The ballplayers watched in silent amusement.

She threw something at the boy. It glinted silver in the sun and bounced off his back to the asphalt. After the little procession passed, the second baseman found the quarter and put it in his pocket. He watched the boy and the old woman with curiosity until someone yelled at him. "Hey. José. Wake up and die right."

The next morning, a day as bright and hot as the day before, the old woman went to PS 165 in search of Mercedes Lopez, who would know what to do about her problem, just as she had helped many others in trouble before. Lopez was not to be found at PS 165, but Mrs. Sanchez was persistent. She walked the few blocks over to Riverside Drive and 107th Street, where she found Mercedes eating lunch at the Children's Mansion, a community-controlled day-care center housed in a large, free-standing mansion overlooking Riverside Park and the Hudson River. Everyone in the neighborhood knew the place. Built by a rich Turkish importer after World War I, it was rumored to have a sealed smuggler's tunnel leading down under Riverside Drive and the park to the river. Like every other building in the area, it needed some work, and graffiti adorned its outer walls, but it was a graceful limestone house and an important landmark.

For ten years, the center had nurtured and taught nearly eighty kids a year in an atmosphere as close to family as an institution could be. It was a model for other day-care centers. Now the university had sold the building to a wealthy law professor who wanted it for a private residence. The sale meant the end of one of the most valuable social institutions in the area, and Mercedes was part of a group looking for another location for the center. Today she was eating lunch with staff and parents who were trying to define an acceptable alternative. It was a desperate search, as inflation raged at the center's austere budget and made it hard to find a decent location in the same neighborhood.

"Ah, Mrs. Sanchez," said Mercedes to the old woman. "Sit down with us. How did you find me here?"

She gave her a plate of food, and for awhile the talk returned to the possibility of occupying the Mansion by force. When the discussion broke down into angry, ritualistic denunciations of the university and the city, Mercedes said, "You are all too attached to this piece of property. True, it is a nice place with large rooms, a yard for the children to play in, and the park across the Drive. But you are afraid the Children's Mansion will fall apart if it is deprived of the structure of this aging mansion of the rich."

There were nods and frowns around the table. These people were adept at the political nuances of their situation, and there was often wild disagreement about the correct thing to do, or say, or think. Mercedes was courting an argument from several influential teachers, and she knew it, but she continued, "If you move into a new physical environment and a new neighborhood, you will be forced to adapt your teaching and your organization to new conditions. This is necessary, because conditions are changing for everyone right now, and we must adapt our work and our attitudes. *We must.*"

The argument exploded. The cadre of teachers and parents who had struggled for a decade to keep the Mansion alive in the face of official hostility and indifference considered Lopez too pragmatic, ultimately defeatist.

Mercedes turned to Mrs. Sanchez. "Now that I've started a fight, it's time to leave. The argument will go on without me." Lopez guided the old woman into the empty director's office, a small room at the front of the building, furnished with metal desks, folding chairs, and two battered filing cabinets. A bulletin board was covered with layers of yellowing memoranda from city and state agencies. The other walls were papered with the drawings of little children, some idyllic and peaceful, some fearful and violent. A large window with a burglar-proof grate looked out on the green of the park and the blue of sky and river beyond. Many of the drawings were of the same scene, as though the center was on an island.

Mrs. Sanchez asked, "You have a friend on the police, do you not?"

"Yes," laughed Mercedes. "As you have told me yourself, this neighborhood is like a little village—people who have nothing to do all day but listen to other people talking."

Mrs. Sanchez told her story, giving a careful description of the man who accosted her grandson and gave him twenty-five cents. Mercedes did not need to be told that the old woman would not talk to a policeman who was not Hispanic, and would in any event refuse to give her true identity and address.

Mercedes immediately called Rodriguez and told him the story. He agreed to meet Mrs. Sanchez at the playground, and the old woman saw Mercedes laugh and blush as he said something else that she couldn't answer in public.

Standing in the hot midafternoon sun by the hole in the fence, Rodriguez listened to Mrs. Sanchez's story. She described the man's dark face, the pockmarks, his narrow chin, a small mole on his right cheek, his clothing, his limp, and his Dominican accent. She insisted that he was Dominican. As promised by Mercedes, the description was detailed, and the old woman was sure of herself. Rodriguez didn't care about her true identity. He knew he could find her through Mercedes.

"Where is your grandson now?" he asked.

Mrs. Sanchez gestured at the playground.

"May I speak to him?"

She called in a voice that somehow reached the boy, who came riding his battered red bike through the throng of running and playing children. The boy added a few details to his grandmother's description and gave Rodriguez the sense that the man was not a stranger to the neighborhood, although neither of them had seen him before. Rodriguez sent the boy back to play, thanked the old woman, and said he would do everything he could to find the man.

He said nothing to Mrs. Sanchez then, or to Mercedes later, but as he looked at the boy on the red bicycle, a chill ran through his body. His first look at the boy, so like the other two victims, told Rodriguez he had picked up the trail of the psychopath.

In that moment, standing in the playground among many children, Rodriguez understood that M might have accosted many boys. Rodriguez wondered if the dead numbered only two. A boy's size, skin color, and behavior would form a pattern for M that triggered him to violence ending in death. It was like a dog looking at another dog.

The detective walked slowly into the playground. There

119

were three or four hundred children, almost all boys. Out of this number, only one had attracted the killer's attention, the little boy on the red bike. Did the killer search for victims? Or did he take targets of opportunity, in Harry Nieman's phrase? Rodriguez guessed that taking the money was the first step in the chain of behavior that provoked M to maniacal rage. What was the final step? Rodriguez knew that only a living survivor could describe what it was that blew the fuse in the killer's mind. And the killer's chances of finding another victim were greatly increased by the number of kids on the streets and in the playgrounds during the long hours of summer daylight.

Conventional police methods—canvassing door to door and shaking down local informers for tips—would not find this killer. Rodriguez decided to begin by writing a report of the description, disguising the old woman as an informer with a tip on a killer, and then giving the report to O'Malley. It was a variation of Nieman's suggestion to provoke O'Malley, to smoke him out, except that Rodriguez didn't have to invent the description.

This had the advantage of giving O'Malley one last try. For all the man's faults, he was an experienced homicide detective, and he might have some ideas. Rodriguez couldn't ignore any possibility.

As he walked slowly through the playground toward 107th Street, the children swirled around him like a flock of seabirds, screaming and calling, enclosing him in their midst but letting him pass. Somehow M, his victims, Harry Nieman, and Mercedes were voices in the air above the playground. Rodriguez realized with a start that he was talking out loud to himself, arguing with O'Malley.

chapter eight
chango

O'Malley spent most of his time in his new command exhuming old informants from his last tour on the West Side several years before. He found most of them, and used them to cultivate new ones with threats and promises, and a few dollars here and there. He was in and out of bars and candy stores. He stopped his car at the curb and beckoned to junkies sitting on the steps of welfare hotels. He ate free lunches and washed them down with rye and ginger in bars all over his territory. He was lord of all he surveyed.

O'Malley was shrewd and skilled, but the skills of his kind of cop were not instinctive or cerebral so much as physical and political— the skills accumulated during long years of hard experience. He knew how to use his body and his authority as weapons, and he understood very well the crude, effective commerce of favors.

One of his hangouts was a bar called the Gold Rail on Broadway just above 110th Street, a place where the owner wasn't the owner. O'Malley never took the trouble to find out who the real owner was. The pseudo-owner, who did most of the bartending, was an ex-cop fronting for someone else. O'Malley knew a lot of guys who knew this guy. O'Malley discovered quickly that this ex-cop knew his way around the West Side.

While Rodriguez met Mrs. Sanchez at the playground, O'Malley was sitting at the back of the bar, pumping the bartender and drinking rye and ginger. The bartender knew some undercover agents from Alcohol, Tobacco & Firearms who hung around West Side bars looking for gun deals. He knew who the DEA agents were, and said they were all on the take. He told O'Malley a story about a young FBI agent trying to buy a few kilos of grass from a dealer who hung around the bar. The dealer got bored and put the FBI guy together with a DEA guy who, the dealer said, was the best connection around for quality grass. The result was a week-long circle jerk before both agents realized they'd been had.

O'Malley asked about other cops. Was there a Puerto Rican cop named Rodriguez who ever came in? No there wasn't. Anybody else? Well . . . , the bartender had spotted a tall, skinny guy the night before who was in the bar for the first time. He had the look, but he didn't hang around long, and he didn't seem to be hunting anything. Maybe he just stopped in for a beer.

O'Malley couldn't pretend to himself that he wasn't concerned by this last bit of news. By the time he left the bar, when the scraggly five o'clock locals showed up on their way home, he had decided to be very careful. There was nobody unusual or suspicious hanging around his turf, and that made him nervous, knowing as he did this mysterious gunslinger working for the Chief. Whoever it was must be good. For the first time in years, O'Malley had the feeling he ought to be looking over his shoulder. Standing outside the bar, in the lee of a busy fruit stand, he watched the homeward rush from the subway exits and bus stops. He wasn't intimidated, but his permanent anger was raised to a new plateau, and he was alert.

He walked south along Broadway, past crowded supermarkets and busy bars. The remnants of old elegance, lost to most of the neighborhood, lingered in the window of a small fur store. The elderly owner was locking up. O'Malley's practiced eyes made a quick survey of alarms, locks, and gate. It would take a hand grenade to get inside the place once it was locked up, but the alarms might be hooked into the phones at the precinct or a private alarm service. O'Malley could find out. The information would be a good card to play with Ayala.

O'Malley walked slowly, his hands clasped behind his back.

Passers-by gave him a wide berth. He watched the faces closely. Jesus, he thought, all kinds live up here. Niggers, spics, illegals, Jews, and even some old Irish folks. Flotsam and jetsam. How the hell can anybody live in a neighborhood like this?

The heat was oppressive and the air unmoving in the streets. It was the tail end of the day when O'Malley got back to his office, and he was hot and thirsty, ready to call it quits. He found a message from Hanratty, a phone number with no name, but O'Malley knew the number. The time on the message was about fifteen minutes after O'Malley left the Gold Rail. Returning the call, O'Malley got a short lecture on the necessity of making a pass at Rodriguez. "Get with the program, Eddie," said Hanratty, and hung up. That told O'Malley all he needed to know about the bartender and ex-cop. It had already occurred to O'Malley that the bartender might have a connection to Ayala.

O'Malley disliked in-boxes and out-boxes because they were a visible measure of how much paperwork he did or didn't do in a day. On his desk, there was instead a litter of paper packed down like damp autumn leaves. When Rodriguez walked into the office and dropped his report on the desk, the two pieces of paper fell on top of the mound.

"Sit down, Rodriguez," said O'Malley, looking down at the paper. He hunched over, his hands folded in his lap. He read the top page. When his eyes reached the bottom of the page, one hand reached up and delicately flicked the page over. The eyes traveled to the bottom of the second page, rested for a moment on Rodriguez's signature and badge number, then rose to Rodriguez's face. O'Malley looked oddly calm, like a man who has just made a painful but necessary decision.

Keeping his voice quiet, he said, "When you make a report on a meeting with a confidential informant, you're supposed to go to the list and get an unused ID number, and you're supposed to enter the actual identity of the informant on the list next to the number. Then you use the number in your report. That's called doing it by the numbers. In my command, I like things done by the numbers."

O'Malley paused and smiled at his little joke. "In order to

do all this, you have to come to me to get the list, because I'm the boss here, and I keep the list in my locked file. When you're the boss, you can do things your way. You can tear the fucking list up in little pieces, for all I fucking care."

O'Malley hunched forward a little, with his hands still in his lap, and rocked back and forth gently.

Rodriguez said, "This isn't a long-term informant. I didn't think it was necessary to go through all the red tape."

"You didn't answer my question."

"You didn't ask a question."

"Why didn't you come to me for the list?"

"Because this isn't an informant. This is a tip."

"You disguised the identity of the person giving the description here. That's an informant."

Rodriguez shifted in his chair. He uncrossed his legs and planted both feet on the floor. O'Malley sat unmoved, like a malignant Tibetan demon, ageless and full of unmentionable rage. Rodriguez said, "I want your advice. This description matches the description the old newsdealer in the Thomas case gave to Feldman."

"How do you know?"

"Flanagan told me."

"Where is Feldman's report?"

"You know damn well what you told Feldman to do."

"I don't remember."

"I'm sure you don't."

"Get to the point."

"The old man told Feldman he saw a Spanish man with a limp."

O'Malley said, "This is not a regulation report, Rodriguez. It's useless."

Rodriguez said, "Lieutenant, this is the same guy."

O'Malley's right hand snaked up over the edge of the desk, snatched the report, and crumpled it into a little ball, working it around in his hand as though he were trying to make it small enough to eat.

Rodriguez was on his feet. O'Malley looked up at him and shouted, "How the goddamn hell can it be the same guy, Rodriguez? You know better than me that spics don't run around in

124

nigger neighborhoods. That old fucker over there didn't describe nuthin but a buncha dirty clothes runnin around on a bad leg."

O'Malley's voice got louder. "Goddammit, Rodriguez, it coulda been any old scumbag in the neighborhood. Every goddamn wino and junkie in this city has a bad leg. And that old nigger couldn't see ten feet anyway."

I'm gonna do it with a machine gun, said the loud voice in Rodriguez's brain. He forced himself to stand still. "Lieutenant, I think this could be the same guy. I want to reopen the Thomas case, now that Flanagan is dead and Feldman is off the case. I want to talk to that old man myself and see if I can find anyone else."

O'Malley said nothing.

"Lieutenant, if this is the same guy, it means he hangs around on this side of town. He might even live over here. He could kill another kid today. Lieutenant, I know this is the same guy, and I know this is an accurate description."

O'Malley stood up. His voice was now very loud. "Rodriguez, you don't know nuthin. This is a description of some spic asshole who tried to rip off some kid's bike. You wanna be flopped back on the street? You wanna look for bike thieves? Fine. But you stay off cases that aren't assigned to you. Just stay the fuck off. And if I ever hear about you working on the other side of Fifth Avenue, I'll bring you up on charges, and then I'll break your fucken legs. *Do you unnerstand me, Sergeant?*"

"*Yessir,*" shouted Rodriquez. "I understand you. I understand you don't want to find this killer."

The squad room outside O'Malley's office was crowded with men bunched around the door at a respectful distance. The men were silent. Every cop in the place was aware that every other cop always carried a gun. It had happened that confrontations like this ended in gunfire.

"And one more thing, Rodriguez. I wanna know where you are every minute of the day, even when you're up there planking that broad at the school."

How does he know? thought Rodriguez, but he put his hands on the edge of O'Malley's desk, leaned over so his face was a foot from the lieutenant's, and yelled in a drill sergeant's voice loud enough for the whole precinct to hear, *"If you ever say that again, you dumb mick son of a bitch, I'll kill you."*

O'Malley's face turned plum red. He started to say something, then stopped. He remembered the five thousand dollars in the white envelope folded in his hip pocket. He laughed and said, "Well, at least she stopped complaining to the Captain."

He said it to Rodriguez's back as he was shoving his way through the cops outside the office door. O'Malley motioned for one of the men to close the door. He lit a cigarette. After a moment, he took the balled-up report and thoughtfully smoothed it out on top of the papers on his desk. He read it again, folded it neatly, and stuck it in his hip pocket with the money. Then he called Hanratty and told him he had Rodriguez by the balls. Hanratty wheezed and gasped as though O'Malley had just told the funniest joke he ever heard.

"What's so fucking funny, Hanratty?"

"You, you dumb mick. You don't have Rodriguez by the balls. Ayala does."

"What do you mean?"

"Go take a look at that woman Lopez at PS 165 and you'll see what I mean."

Rodriguez and Mercedes Lopez lay in twilit darkness on the white bottom sheet of his bed, illuminated by the small flame of the votary candle in front of the statue of St. Barbara in her blue robes and red mantle. Rodriguez lay with his left ear on Mercedes' belly. The skin was blond and smooth, with a line of dark hair running from her bellybutton to the top of her pubic hair. He heard the soft noises of her body and felt the muscles of her stomach and pelvis jump and loosen as his fingers slipped in and out of her—two fingers, then three, then he was trying to force his whole hand inside her vagina. Her lower body began to vibrate. She cried out, and her legs jerked open, then clamped together trapping his hand in a spasm of orgasm.

He withdrew his hand and began to stroke her mound with the flat of his palm. She spread her legs, and he burrowed his face down through the thick, wet hair. His forefinger, slippery with liquid, moistened the circle of smooth skin around her anus, then he slipped his forefinger deep inside her ass and his thumb deep into her cunt.

"Ah," she gasped. "Ah, ah, ah." Her whole body leaped and arched as she struggled with the gentle grip of his hand. She grabbed wildly for him, trying to pull him on top of her on his knees, so she could take him in her mouth. She caught his left thigh from behind and hit her hand up into his crotch. He cried out with pain and surprise, and came in thick spurts across her breasts and belly, then pulled his hand loose and buried his mouth in the lips between her legs. He sucked and sponged her with his tongue until she lay motionless and flat on the bed.

Afterward, they rested side by side on the damp twisted sheet in the cool air from the open windows.

"No one has ever been so intimate with me," she said.

"There's nothing I wouldn't do to you."

"Would you hurt me?"

"Yes," he said. "Not very much, but I might. Would you like it?"

"I don't know. A little, maybe. You frighten me a little, Daniel. Not because you are mean or cruel, but because of the power of your need."

"Yes," he said. "I need you very much."

In only a few weeks, their feelings had turned to love, and deepened and darkened into permanence. He stood up and walked to the window. His body was limber and straight.

She said, "You always get up to stand at the window after we make love."

"That's because I feel good."

"Are you looking for something down on the street?"

"No," he said without turning. "Should I be?" He remembered O'Malley. *How does he know?* Rodriguez was reluctant to read minds, but he was equally hesitant to dismiss an odd sense of warning that had come to him in the last day or so. He decided O'Malley could have heard something on the station house grapevine.

"Daniel?"

"Humh?"

"You didn't answer me."

"What did you say?"

"I asked if you were afraid someone was following you."

"No. Should I be?"

"No. It's just that you don't talk about your work."

"I talk more to you than I ever have to anyone, but I want to talk about myself, not my work." He paused, and said, "I've been looking at the night lights of this city all my life. When I was little, sometimes my father took me down to the docks at night, where it was cool and quiet, and we looked at the lights of the boats."

"Was your father a dockworker?"

"Yes."

"You never told me."

"He was killed on the docks."

She said, "It was dark in my village at night. There was no electricity up in our hills. We had only the moon and the stars, but my mother always had a candle like this one burning in front of a statue of one saint or another."

"I used to think, not so long ago," he said, "that the darkness was pulling at me, or the voice of my father would call me one night out of the darkness. I was afraid I would disappear into the night. One night I was driving over the Brooklyn Bridge, coming back from my mother's house. It was very late. I wanted to drive off the bridge into the darkness of the bay, down by all the boats where my father used to take me. I knew nothing would happen to me. It was like a dream, like Hart Crane diving into the waters of the sunset."

"Who was he?"

"An Anglo poet from New York who committed suicide off a ship near Cuba many years ago."

"Daniel, why are you a cop?"

"I don't know. I told you it was all I know how to do, but that's not the reason." He sat on the bed without touching her, still looking out the window. "All those years after my father died, when I was in high school, then college, and then in Germany, I had no idea what to do. There was no one to help me. Being a cop is very hard for me, not like the schools. The schools were easy. Maybe that's why I like being a cop, because

128

it's a struggle every day with some kind of darkness in myself, and the darkness in the life of this city."

Mercedes pulled herself erect and sat up against the pillows.

"The struggle is important to me," he went on, "because it keeps my self-respect alive. If I didn't fight these things, I would die inside."

"That's why people from Puerto Rico and the other islands fight for their freedom."

Rodriguez went back to the window. For the first time, he imagined that her beliefs might be expressed in clandestine political activities of some kind. The thought appeared ridiculous; he tried to dismiss it, but couldn't.

He was unwilling to press her for information. He was a homicide cop, not a political cop. His contempt for political cops was almost boundless. He wondered about Harry Nieman.

"Sit down here," ordered Mercedes. "I want to tell you a story."

He sat cross-legged at the end of the bed, facing her. The day after he had told her about the shootout on West 111th Street, she began, she went to an old Haitian woman who had a tiny storefront on Amsterdam Avenue a few blocks down from PS 165. The old woman sold religious artifacts.

Rodriguez realized with a start that it was the shop where he bought the statue of St. Barbara, but he said nothing.

The old woman was highly regarded as a *bruja*—a witch and healer. Mercedes had never been to her before, although she remembered her mother taking her to a *bruja* when she was very little.

Mercedes asked the woman about Rodriguez. The old woman asked a few questions, and asked for a physical description of him. When Mercedes answered, she had the feeling she was telling the old woman things she already knew, and that the old woman was testing her truthfulness.

The *bruja* said the feelings between Mercedes and Rodriguez would be strong and dark, and get darker and deeper, then burst into brilliant color and light. The old woman said Rodriguez had bought a statue of *Chango* from her recently—"The day you met him for the first time."

129

Rodriguez got goose bumps as he listened to Mercedes recite the story in a small, matter-of-fact voice.

The old woman said, "You are lucky, Mercedes Lopez, to have found this man when you did. Where you are concerned, he has the strength of the supernatural and the courage of the hero. For you, he will need it."

Mercedes asked about *Chango*. The withered old *bruja* sat for a long time without speaking, pulling her shawl tightly around her. Despite the heavy afternoon traffic outside, the little storefront seemed quiet and dark. Mercedes felt as though she were somewhere far away. The *bruja* retold the story of *Orféo et Eurydiche,* partly in Spanish and partly in Haitian French, which Mercedes understood fairly well. The *bruja* concluded the story by talking about the many identities of *Eurydiche,* and by talking about Rodriguez again. *"Cet'homme,"* said the *bruja* in a near trance, "will go into a dark, deep place looking for you. I cannot tell without a sacrifice where you will be and how you will be taken there, but it will be a terrible place."

The woman concluded in a low monotone, *"Chango* is very dangerous. He, too, is more than one. When he is Saint Barbara, he is good, but when he is himself, he can destroy those who turn to him. You have been careless, and you knew better. In Haiti, *Chango* is lord of the dead under the earth, and you have awakened this power and brought it into your life by lighting the candle. I know in Cuba and Puerto Rico they do not believe this so much, but believe me now, girl. Believe what I tell you."

Mercedes sat in the tiny dark room, with the noisy sunlit street only yards away, and could not move, as though she were held down by a weight.

In his own bedroom, on the edge of his bed, watching this beautiful woman who was watching him, Rodriguez was chilled and sweating as though he had a fever.

The *bruja* said, "You gave life to this power and you cannot change it now. To try to go back along the path you have chosen would bring disaster from the terrible anger that would follow and find you. You must stay on your path until the end. You must do nothing you would not have done before, or say nothing you would not have said. I can tell you nothing more without a sacrifice, and this is not the right time. Come back again when you are ready."

"What kind of sacrifice?" asked Rodriguez.

"I don't know," said Mercedes.

Rodriguez shivered with impatience and an odd helplessness. His nerves were raw. He asked, almost shouting, "Why didn't you tell me this story before?"

"Because I didn't want to tell you the rest of the story," said Mercedes softly. "The *bruja* told me there was one more thing. She said, 'You will have a baby girl next year if you survive, and you will name it Maria, after the Mother of God, for saving you. If she saves you.'"

"Jesus," whispered Rodriguez. "How does she know?"

"She knows more than I do," said Mercedes. "You and I began sleeping together after my last period. My next one is due this week. I feel different inside, but I can't tell if it's a baby growing inside me, or what the old woman told me, or if it's my feelings for you."

"Do you believe this story?" asked Rodriguez.

"I don't know what I believe anymore." This was said in a tone of flat despair. She sat hugging herself like a small child.

Rodriguez said, "I've never heard anything like it. Is this the first of the thousand and one nights?"

She said, "I'm not Scheherazade, and you're not holding me prisoner."

"Mercedes, why did you tell me this story?" His feelings were almost numbed by its power but his mind was turning slowly. He was bothered by something, but his cop's mind couldn't find it.

She sensed his unease. She smiled and reached for him. "Because I want you to know who I am," she said. For a long time they lay quiet, then with barely a movement, they made love again and fell asleep.

All the next day, Rodriguez had a sense of foreboding. Mercedes was busy at lunchtime, so he continued his rounds of the schools. To everyone he saw, he described the man who accosted Mrs. Sanchez's grandson. No one had seen him. At his last stop of the day, he met for the first time a black man named Wilson, who was the principal of an elementary school a few blocks from PS 165. Wilson had never seen the man Rodriguez described, but asked if the inquiry had anything to do with the two boys recently murdered in central Harlem. Rodriguez lied and said no, which only increased his own unease.

He and Mercedes ate in a local Cuban–Chinese restaurant that night. Their talk was fitful. Mercedes was jumpy and preoccupied. Rodriguez was thinking about M, O'Malley, and Harry Nieman, none of whom he wanted to talk about. He couldn't tell her about Nieman, or that just before dinner, he had stopped at a pay phone and called the number Nieman had given him, leaving on a recording the work name, Robert Hemingway. If not an agreement to work for Nieman—or "with" him, as Nieman insisted—this was certainly an acceptance of Nieman's working conditions. Rodriguez knew he had crossed the line.

He learned one interesting thing from Mercedes—Wilson was an old Communist who had somehow avoided being thrown out of the public schools during the witch hunts of thirty years before, and he was an old friend of the great black singer and actor, Paul Robeson, who had died in virtual exile in Ghana. According to Mercedes, Wilson ran one of the best elementary schools in the city. She told his story with the easy sophistication of someone for whom political life was more complicated and more essential than the mere quadrennial choice of a president.

Listening to her, Rodriguez knew for certain that her own political life was very deep water. He also knew he would somehow stay with her, just as he would find the killer of the little boys. There was no particular decision to make. When he got to the line, he crossed it and kept going. Sitting at dinner in a shabby restaurant on Broadway, drinking beer and eating fried rice, Rodriguez realized that the lines he had crossed with Nieman and Mercedes that day were one and the same.

Their love-making that night was restrained and passionless, and Rodriguez was not surprised or displeased when Mercedes announced at eleven-thirty that she wanted to go home. They got dressed in near silence, and he walked her over to Broadway. When she got into the cab and tilted her cheek up for him to kiss, she inexplicably burst into tears.

As her yellow cab sped off up Broadway, Rodriguez was staggered by a wave of rage that swept over him out of nowhere. He waved down a cab and told the driver to follow the yellow cab uptown. The pursuit only lasted twenty blocks, from 86th Street to her corner at 106th Street and West End Avenue, by the tiny triangle called Straus Park, where Broadway and West End Avenue meet, or diverge, depending on whether the park is approached from uptown or downtown.

Rodriguez knew where Mercedes lived, in a good building between 106th and 107th Streets on West End Avenue, but he had never been in her apartment. He knew only that it was on the ninth floor, overlooking the little park and the busy stretch of Broadway. She had a view to the east of the upper end of Central Park, and her apartment was filled with sunlight in the morning. He didn't know why she had never invited him there, and he didn't want to know, until tonight.

He got out of his cab on the far corner of Broadway from her building, and watched her walk quickly to the door without looking around. The doorman let her in. In a few minutes, the lights in one of the apartments on the ninth floor came on. Rodriguez stepped back into the shadow of a dark doorway and waited. In ten minutes, her windows went dark again. Rodriguez waited to see if she came out again, but no one entered or left the building.

The intersection before him was really three intersections, with the park in the middle. It was almost like an open plaza in a Latin American city, except that it was not filled with people at night. The little park was a hangout for junkies and winos. At the moment there was no one in the park or on the sidewalks except a man in a phone booth on the near corner. The man turned to look at Rodriguez and hung up the phone. He was about the same height and weight as Rodriguez, and wore a dark raincoat open over a dark sweater and trousers. His hair was black, and he had the square, dark face of a *mestizo*.

133

He walked directly across the street to Rodriguez, and said in Spanish from about four feet away, "Franco Ayala would like to meet you, *Señor* Rodriguez. Please follow me."

After watching the man walk deliberately and openly across the street toward him, Rodriguez was not startled. He asked, "How do you know me?"

The man answered simply, "I have followed you for two days everywhere you went."

"Who is *Señor* Ayala?"

"He is a man who wants to meet you."

Rodriguez nodded.

"Follow me, please, but stay thirty meters behind."

The man turned and walked, nearly loping, east along 106th Street toward Amsterdam Avenue. The character of the neighborhood changed. The north side of the street was a row of substantial apartment buildings. Rodriguez knew that apartments in those buildings rented for a thousand dollars a month. On the south side, where he followed the *mestizo* at a fast clip, the buildings were smaller and poorer, mostly Hispanic, with a scattering of elderly Irish and Jewish folks, the original residents of the neighborhood. He marveled that anyone—child, adult, old man or woman—could survive the fear and deprivation of life on the south half of the street.

At Amsterdam Avenue, the *mestizo* turned south. There was still traffic on the street at this late hour, but it was mostly cabs. The storefronts were dark. Most of them had riot gates locked across the front, which discouraged only the most casual thief. During the last power blackout, looters backed their cars onto the sidewalks, looped chains from their bumpers through the gates, and pulled them down.

There were no pedestrians, even though the avenue was brightly lit by the garish glare of sodium-vapor streetlights. Without looking back, the *mestizo* dogtrotted across the avenue and up 104th Street toward Columbus Avenue. Rodriguez followed. When he rounded the corner onto the side street, he ducked into a doorway and waited. There was no tail.

The *mestizo* cut through the grounds of the Frederick Douglass Houses and crossed Columbus at 103rd Street. The neighborhood changed abruptly again, from the heavy architectural order of the public housing project, to the desolation and darkness of one of the worst DMZs in the city. At Manhattan Avenue and 102nd Street, only a short block from Central Park, the man ducked into the blank darkness of an abandoned building.

Without hesitating, Rodriguez followed. The building was the ruin of a six-story tenement, with a smell as bad as any building he had ever been in. Mixed with the urine and rot was a chemical odor, like metallic Silly-Putty, that touched Rodriguez's memory, but he couldn't label it. As he entered the doorway, he realized that every light on the street was out.

These were the factories and barracks of the drug trade. Only a swift strike by the 82nd Airborne Division could have uprooted the business from the neighborhood, and even then it would be quickly re-established a few blocks north or south. Thinking that, and remembering what it was like to be an MP with an infantry division in Germany, Rodriguez remembered what the odd smell was. It was C-4. The building was loaded with plastic explosive.

He could hear the man going up the stairs. By feel, Rodriguez went up after him. At an open door on the third floor, he turned in. There were three men in the room. The man he had followed stood by the window looking down at the street. Another man in a dark raincoat, with much the same appearance as the first, stood by the door to the hallway, not blocking it, nor threatening Rodriguez in any way, but standing there nonetheless. The third man stood in the middle of the room.

The entire apartment was bare. The walls were startlingly white, recently whitewashed. Rodriguez felt as though he had wandered through a one-way mirror. "What do you want?" he asked the man in the middle.

The man answered in Spanish, in a literate, soft accent that Rodriguez immediately placed as educated Cuban. "I did not wish to be rude or precipitous, but it seemed important that we meet tonight."

"Why?"

"Simply to make an introduction."

135

"You already know who I am," said Rodriguez, and with a sudden, sickening tightness in his guts, he thought, *You know Mercedes Lopez, too.*

"I have heard a lot about you," said Ayala. "I want you to work for me. I will pay you very well. If we achieve a working relationship, I will pay you more money than you ever dreamed of."

The offer seemed plausible enough, coming from this man. Rodriguez had heard his name a couple of times on the West Side. Ayala was said to be one of the most powerful drug dealers in Manhattan. Rodriguez didn't doubt the sincerity of the offer. Something about Ayala's appearance impressed and repelled Rodriguez at the same time. He wore a tan linen suit, a white golf shirt open at the neck, and woven leather oxfords. Standing in the barren room in a building that smelled of C-4, in a block of the city that looked like the ruins of Beirut, Ayala looked rich, healthy, and powerful.

Rodriguez said, "I'm not interested right now."

"Fine," Ayala answered. "We'll meet again. I've heard a lot about you, and I respect you. This is a standing offer. If you accept, I'll tell you anything you want to know about me."

"How can I reach you?"

Ayala smiled. "Don't call me. I'll call you, as they say in *inglés.*"

Rodriguez turned to go.

"One more thing," said Ayala. "I must caution you to forget this meeting. I know how valuable Mercedes Lopez is to you, my friend."

Rodriguez turned and said, "If you touch her, Ayala, you'll never touch another woman as long as you live."

Ayala shrugged. "There is no need to threaten me. I would rather work with you than fight you."

As Rodriguez went out the door, Ayala added, "Don't hang around here, or try to return. We are leveling this building in a minute or two."

"Taxes too high?" asked Rodriguez.

"I think we're doing the owner a favor," agreed Ayala. "Undeveloped land is taxed at a lower rate."

When Rodriguez reached the street, he ran to the corner of

102nd Street and Central Park West, where he looked up and down for a fire alarm. Seeing one a block down, he began to run, when there was a brilliant flash of light behind him, and an enormous thundering explosion. He turned and saw nothing but dust in the night air. When he reached the fire alarm, it didn't work, but he heard the sirens of the fire engines pulling out of the firehouse next to the Two-Four. They were only a few blocks away. He stepped off the curb and flagged down a gypsy cab.

"Broadway and a hunnerdansixth," he said. He felt drunk.

chapter nine
in the land of the dead

The triangle of Straus Park was no more than thirty yards on a side. A statue spilled water into a small basin. The soft noise washed out the sound of the traffic on Broadway, still fairly heavy even at one o'clock in the morning. Three winos slept on benches, and a middle-aged couple necked on another bench in the darkest part of the park. The man's hand fumbled around under the woman's sweater, and the woman's hand jerked up and down inside the man's trousers.

Rodriguez counted floors. Mercedes' windows were dark. As Rodriguez sat staring up at the windows through the palmate locust leaves of the roof of trees over the park, an odd urban peacefulness descended on him. He had planned to call her from a bar across Broadway, but he decided not to. He stood up and stretched. He would have a drink across the street, then go home.

Rodriguez saw only a rustle of clothing and the flash of a face before his head exploded. The red and white pain burst twice more across the back of his head with an audible crack. He felt the awful pain of a punch in his right kidney, then another punch.

He fell to his knees, then to his hands. He was dimly aware of a man walking nonchalantly out of the park and down Broadway, then he felt the liquid coming up in his throat. As he fell to his face, he managed to roll away from the vomit.

He did not finally pass out. No one outside the park saw

what happened. No one shouted or came running to help. By the time Rodriguez got back to his hands and knees, all the winos had disappeared. The couple from the bench were shuffling across Broadway toward 107th Street, looking fearfully back over their shoulders like Adam and Eve driven out of Eden by the angel.

Rodriguez stood. His shoulders slumped and his hands hung almost to his knees. He staggered to the nearest bench and flopped onto it, listing over on one elbow.

He forced himself to sit erect and feel the back of his head. There was a painful swelling, but none of the sharp pain of a hairline fracture. The blows had fallen on the nerves and muscles of the neck and shoulder at the base of the skull, paralyzing his right arm.

He knew he'd been hit with a sap like the one carried by many cops, a flattened, egg-shaped lead weight at the end of a short length of whippy spring steel, all wrapped in smooth leather, seamless, so no cuts were left on the victim. His right kidney throbbed with a steady ache that he knew would last for days.

A crowd was leaving the Olympia Theater on the other side of Broadway. The late show had left them laughing and happy. For a moment Rodriguez felt like one of them. He was alert and confused at the same time. The face of his attacker was familiar. He had seen him somewhere before, but the man's impassivity as he beat him was so complete that he was a blank in Rodriguez's mind.

He sat on the bench for what seemed like a long time, getting his breath, trying to decide what to do. When he realized he couldn't force his battered mind to work any faster, he relaxed, and then his mind began to clear.

He could hardly call the cops. A patrol car rolled slowly past on Broadway. Rodriguez watched it out of the corners of his eyes. He recognized the two POs, but they didn't give a second look at the man slumped over on the bench in Straus Park.

Why couldn't he call the cops? A cop *should* report a crime. But it wasn't a crime. Somehow he had asked for it and expected it.

140

"Bullshit," he said out loud.

There was a problem forming in his mind. He rolled it over slowly, elliptically, without being able to get a grip on it.

He had gone to O'Malley with a description of a man who accosted a kid only three blocks from where Rodriguez now sat. The man was the psychopath, Rodriguez was sure.

How was he sure? The idea hadn't occurred to him until he saw the grandson of Mrs. Sanchez. He wasn't even sure who she was. But they weren't standing before a judge yet. Rodriguez was looking for street truth, and he had found it. He had found the trail of the killer and O'Malley instantly recognized the implications of the report.

Rodriguez hated O'Malley, who was a brutal, bigoted, indifferent cop. As he sat on the park bench, Rodriguez tried to suspend his hatred, tried to be objective about O'Malley's reaction to the report. The report was a description of the killer, or at least a new lead. Why didn't O'Malley want to follow the lead? He was afraid of something. What was he afraid of?

Rodriguez stood up and walked slowly to the corner. His mind was reeling. He began to wonder again about Mercedes.

Was there a connection between O'Malley and Ayala and Mercedes? Rodriguez had doubted it, but now the link was a faint neon glow in his mind. Rodriguez decided to go into the bar across the street, have a drink, and call Mercedes.

The bar was called The Balcony. Before Rodriguez went in, he turned and looked back at the park and up over the trees at Mercedes' apartment. Her lights were still out. He went in and sat at a table near the door, next to the big windows on the sidewalk. The place pretended to be a sidewalk cafe. He could see her windows from his table.

He nursed a Scotch on the rocks for half an hour. The drink cleared his head a little, but gave him a sharp headache where the sap had struck. His back hurt badly. Something was wrong. His world was slipping out of joint. He reached back under his jacket to rub his cramped, bruised muscles. Only then did he realize the attacker had lifted his off-duty gun from the holster clipped inside the waistband in the small of his back.

Someone was playing with him. The sense of threat returned

with a rush. His head throbbed with redoubled pain. He put money on the table, left the bar, and walked down Broadway at a manic pace.

The stretch between 106th Street and 96th Street was one of the least hospitable sections of the Upper West Side. Muggings and rapes were common at night. It was lined with bad bars, SRO hotels, and stores that closed up early and pulled down the riot gates. For the first time in years, Rodriguez felt the fears of an ordinary citizen as he walked along the littered, broken sidewalks. The fears multiplied as he approached the 103rd Street subway entrance, which was a hangout for local hustlers.

There was no one at the corner. Rodriguez looked up 103rd Street past Amsterdam, and saw the glow of a large fire, like an early dawn. The hoods were all watching the fire. He did not need to see it to know that the building had been leveled by the explosion. He knew what well-placed *plastique* could do.

Then he thought, *These guys are pros.* He heard the soft Cuban accent. He thought of calling Nieman again, then decided to wait for the morning. He had a more urgent problem. He had to figure out how to report the loss of his off-duty gun.

He couldn't walk anymore. His legs were like rubber. He cut across Broadway and waved down a cab. When it reached the front of his building, he paid the cabby and stepped out, turning toward the street as he slammed the door. Over the roof of the cab, Rodriguez looked straight into the impassive face of the man who had led him to Ayala, then sapped him and stolen his gun. He stood in a deep doorway across the street.

As the cab pulled away, Rodriguez took off at a dead run for the man, who broke into a loping run west toward Columbus Avenue. Rodriguez changed his angle of interception to head him off, but missed him by twenty yards at the corner.

Dodging cars, they crossed Columbus and ran like two relay runners, each saving a burst of speed for the finish. At Amsterdam Avenue, they had the light. The men in the dark raincoat ran with a hard lope, the gait of a man who could run all night and day.

Rodriguez could feel his knees stiffen. His head felt like a pumpkin. With the shock of each heel on the pavement, an intense pain tore at his back. He didn't think he could get past the corner. He was slowing down. He was forty yards behind.

At 86th Street and Broadway, the man dodged a young couple and disappeared down the subway entrance. Rodriguez could hear an uptown train pulling out of the station. As he reached the entrance and slowed for the steps, a flock of five or six transvestites emerged up from the steps and walked directly into his path, chattering and gesturing among themselves in their elaborate pantomime.

They were big and husky beneath their pretty disguises. When Rodriguez burst through their group, they knocked him down as he took them down at the same time. There were cries and falsetto screams, and hoarse low curses and threats, as Rodriguez scrambled to his hands and knees, and then his feet. He knocked a hand off his arm.

There was no one but night people on the street, no cops, not even a taxi or bus. Rodriguez took a deep breath and jumped down the stairs two at a time. He stopped short. The station was silent. Instead of flashing his badge at the clerk in the booth, who barely glanced up at him from her newspaper, he dropped a token in the turnstile and walked through, like a man with time on his hands.

The platform was empty. Rodriguez walked slowly up the platform until he was out of sight of the clerk, then ran uptown to the end of the platform. He stopped and listened carefully. There was a faint crunch of gravel up the tunnel. Rodriguez listened again. There were no trains coming. At this hour, there might not be another uptown local for twenty or thirty minutes.

The tunnel here was four tracks wide, with the uptown local and uptown express tracks on one side, and the downtown local and express tracks on the other. There was a slight incline up to a spot under 93rd Street, then the tracks declined more steeply to the next station at 96th Street.

Rodriguez looked downtown. He saw the lights of the local station at 79th Street. There was no train in sight. Uptown was nothing but darkness and signal lights, changing from red to green in sequence as a train moved through the signal blocks somewhere above the 96th Street station.

There was a narrow steel ladder painted yellow at the end

of the platform. Rodriguez stepped down, grimacing with the pain in his back, and started up the tracks. In ten yards he was out of the lights of the station and in the dim twilight of the long arched tunnel.

He stopped and listened. Someone was walking quickly up the tracks a city block ahead of him. Knowing that he was silhouetted against the lights of the station, Rodriguez followed, moving as fast as he could on the greasy wooden ties. He wanted his gun back.

The tracks were separated by rows of steel columns supporting the street above. The columns were spaced apart little more than the width of a man's shoulders. From an angle, it was impossible to see from one track to another. Rodriguez decided to cross to the other side of the tunnel, to get ahead of the other man, cutting him off. With luck, the noise of passing trains would screen his movements from the almost extrasensory perceptions of the *mestizo*.

Rodriguez stepped gingerly over the third rails. He ran as fast and silently as he could, and managed almost two hundred yards before he heard the low rumble of a train coming downtown. Then he felt on his face the damp cool breeze that trains push ahead of them through the tunnels. He couldn't chance being seen by a motorman, who would call in a report of someone on the tracks. Rodriguez wanted to take care of his tormentor alone.

He stepped into the space between two columns in the gap between the local and express tracks, his ankles just inches from the exposed third rails carrying six hundred volts of direct current, enough to fry him in a second. The local topped the rise at 93rd Street. Its lights picked out the grimy details of the tunnel—the damp gray concrete walls, the thickly insulated cables, a marker with the runic message, "T32/TYY." Then the train hurtled by a foot from his face. It was hard to stand still. Rodriguez hadn't done this since he was a kid. The noise from the train was unreal. As it slowed for the 86th Street station, and the noise died away to a dull rumble, the noise of another train came from uptown. There wouldn't be two locals so close together at this hour. It must be a downtown express.

The stretch between stations here was ten blocks, the longest stretch on the West Side. Rodriguez wondered where the man was heading, then remembered there was an abandoned subway station on the uptown side at 91st Street. It was a meeting place and art gallery for graffiti gangs. There was probably an emergency exit up to the street.

Rodriguez began to run up the local tracks with the abandon of a kid. The noise of the express grew louder. Its headlights began flashing between the columns separating the tracks. It passed with a high-pitched roar that made Rodriguez wince.

The tunnel was dimly lit at intervals by signal lights and unshielded low-wattage bulbs casting a faint yellow glow. It was filthy with decades of accumulated grease and scum. Leaks from sewers, water pipes, and the street above made the tunnel permanently damp, like a limestone cave.

Rats and large cockroaches lived here, scuttling around in an ecological niche no one had ever examined very closely. And in the course of a day and night, a surprising number of human beings wandered through—workmen, bag ladies, kids in graffiti gangs, and winos. The human sociology of the tunnels depended largely on the weather. As it got colder, the bag ladies and winos moved underground seeking warmth, but Rodriguez knew there were an uncounted number of permanent residents in the subways.

By the time the noise of the express died away, he was back across the tunnel on the uptown local tracks, just a few yards below the abandoned station. A siren on the street rose and fell and vanished. Faint traffic noises filtered down to the tracks. The tunnel was just underneath Broadway. Rodriguez could hear someone moving around on the platform, but he was sure it wasn't his man. It was probably a wino making himself comfortable for the night. The smell of fresh human excrement was strong here.

Then Rodriguez heard the unmistakable scrape of a shoe on pavement and the light click of metal on metal about halfway down the platform. Far down the track behind him, a local rumbled uptown. The abandoned platform would be brightly lit by the lights of the cars as the train passed.

Rodriguez edged his way silently to the edge of the platform and climbed the ladder. The smell was nauseating. There was

145

someone at the other end of the long platform, a dim shape, a man turning round and round over a pile of rags like a dog making a bed. The uptown train was just now leaving the 86th Street station, moving slowly up the slight incline.

Rodriguez knew his adversary was here, too. He moved a few feet away from the edge of the platform. The dank breeze coming up the tunnel barely stirred the foul air. Heavy equipment boxes with huge old-fashioned padlocks lined the interior wall of the platform. Every square inch of dirty white tile on the walls was covered with layers of overlapping graffiti, the sprayed names and street numbers making a kind of impasto action painting seen only by its makers.

Rodriguez walked slowly along the platform. The train picked up speed. Its lights shone brighter and its noise grew louder. An infinitesimal noise ticked in Rodriguez's brain, the rustle of a dark raincoat. He spun on his toes, and his head exploded again in cartoon flashes of red and white stars. He cried out and fell to his knees.

A leg in dark pants appeared to his left. With his last strength, Rodriguez tackled the leg and pulled the man down on top of him. The noise of the train drowned out the grunts and shouts of combat. The edge of an open palm hit Rodriguez's face like a hammer. His nose popped and cracked with a noise louder than the train. A knee smashed into his groin. Rodriguez groaned and rolled away from the tracks. He felt the sap hit the same spot in the back of his head. He felt someone stoop over him, thrusting a hard object into his back. He rolled and his open fingers found the eyes of the man on top of him. Rodriguez dug and pulled. The man cried out in a scream Rodriguez could not hear, and fell in agony, holding his face, over the edge of the platform.

The sound of steel brakes on steel wheels filled the tunnel. A horn sounded. As Rodriguez passed out, he felt rather than heard the impact of the train against the body on the tracks.

Fifteen minutes later, Rodriguez was on a stretcher carried by two Transit Authority cops running as fast as they could along the tracks to the 96th Street station, where two ambulance attendants waited. As the cops handed the stretcher up to the platform, Rodriguez came to in a haze of red pain, and reached his hand under the small of his back. His gun was there, firmly in its holster. His gold shield was pinned to his shirt. And he knew somehow that he had been fighting two men, not one, on the abandoned platform.

"Why didn't you draw your gun?" asked Nieman. He sat on the window sill, with the unfinished north tower of the Cathedral of St. John the Divine visible in the near distance. It was the sight of the square stone tower the afternoon before that had reassured Rodriguez he was still among the living, when he woke up in his bed at St. Luke's Hospital.

Rodriguez was in a surly mood. Now Nieman was in a surly mood. O'Malley had been in a surly mood in the morning, when he visited Rodriguez with some pointed questions about being on an abandoned subway platform in the dark hours of the morning, wrestling with a man who appeared to be an illegal immigrant from South America, and who looked "like a goddamn Indian." O'Malley had viewed the battered remains in the morgue. O'Malley said, "They can send the goddamn body home in a Macy's shopping bag, except there's nobody to send it to."

"Listen, Harry," said Rodriguez, "My head hurts. Why don't you leave me alone?"

"Because I wanna know what you were doing in that tunnel, and I want you to tell me one more time what you were doing in that building on Manhattan Avenue before this guy Ayala blew it away with Vietnam surplus plastic. I want you to tell me what the hell's going on, Rodriguez, because you're in very goddamn deep water. That's why."

"I told you," said Rodriguez. "There's nothing to tell twice."

"You could lose your badge for this, Danny-boy."

"But I won't, Harry, and you know it. O'Malley assigned himself to the case, and that means he's gonna sit on it. And you assigned yourself to my case a long time ago, and as far as I'm concerned you can take a broomstick and sit on that for awhile."

Nieman slid off the window sill and sat down in a chair next

147

to the bed. He hunched over with his face near Rodriguez, and said, "You're smart, Rodriguez, and you're a smartass too, but there's a few things you don't know."

"What are they, Harry? Did someone in Washington whisper something in your ear?"

"Yes. And you better listen close, because it concerns you."

Rodriguez slumped back against his pillows. He closed his eyes. "I know what it is," he said. "It has something to do with Mercedes Lopez."

"How do you know?"

"I don't know how I know. I just do. All that stuff the other night had something to do with it, and that cocksucker O'Malley's in it, too. Someone's playing with me. I don't like it, Harry."

"I don't blame you," said Nieman. He was almost doubled over in his chair. His arm rested along the edge of the bed. It was deep water indeed. He waited for Rodriguez to talk.

In a soft, low monotone, Rodriguez repeated the story of the entire day: his meeting with Mrs. Sanchez, his confrontation with O'Malley, his Alice-in-Wonderland chase, the fight with the two look-alikes in the abandoned subway station. He told Nieman about the disappearance and reappearance of his gun.

"Jesus Christ," said Nieman at the end. "There's something about this story that makes me want to cross myself. It's like sitting around in the jungle in Laos with those mountain tribes up in the hills, listening to them tell stories about the dead."

Nieman hunched his chair a few inches across the floor toward the bed. "And just to make it all a little worse, pal, this is what I hear from the whisperers in Washington. Your friend Mercedes Lopez is on a list of people suspected of aiding and abetting the FALN."

"What does that mean?" Rodriguez's voice was no more than a sigh.

"She's at the top of a very short list. She might be a boss. She might be a member of the FALN executive committee here in the city."

"Might?" sighed Rodriguez.

"Listen. Believe me. Nobody—but nobody—has gotten inside this group. There are little bits and pieces, but nobody's got

148

nuthin on them. The FBI is looking harder for the FALN than they did for the Weathermen. The CIA is also very eager because there's a Cuban connection, but they can't make it out."

"Cuban?"

"Yeah, and let me add, Danny-boy, that for Cuban, you can read KGB."

"That guy in the haunted house the other night was an educated, upper-class Cuban." Rodriguez exhaled a long sigh, as if breathing had become difficult.

"Yeah," said Nieman. "Tell me, Danny, have you ever wondered why Lopez won't let you stay overnight at her place?"

Rodriguez lay in perfect stillness on his pile of pillows. Nieman walked to the window. When he turned around, tears were streaming down Rodriguez's face, running over and around the thick adhesive tape that held his nose in place.

M had some time to kill. He stood by the curb in front of the *bodega* for a moment, then crossed Amsterdam through a lull in traffic. To his left was a large school playground, fenced along one side by the high, windowless brick wall of a school, and along the other three sides by a partly uprooted chain-link fence. Two softball games and a half-dozen basketball games filled the playground with older kids.

To the right, on the corner of 100th Street, was a small playground with concrete benches and checkers tables under the dark shade of sycamore trees, yellow from a dry summer. Most of the benches and tables were taken by older boys resting from the games in the adjacent playground, but M spotted an empty bench and walked to it. He set his bag down, took out his radio and beer, and folded his jacket neatly into his bag. It was a very hot morning. He opened one of the beers and chugged it down. He walked a few steps and tossed the bottle into a trash basket; then he sat down, opened another beer, and turned on his radio.

There was another chain-link fence about twenty yards into the park from the sidewalk. Behind this fence was a large above-ground pool supported by an open-steel framework. It

149

was the only public pool for many blocks in any direction, and it was already full. A wide wooden walk surrounded the pool at shoulder height. The deep end under the diving board was set into the ground. Dozens of kids ran and played in the pool. Behind the pool was the wall of the Twenty-Fourth Precinct house with O'Malley's office window on the second floor overlooking the park.

Outside the fence around the pool was a kiddie playground with swings, slides, and sandboxes. It was full of younger kids with their mothers, babysitters, or older sisters. M sat with his back to the Amsterdam Avenue traffic, drinking his beer and watching the children play. The morning slid slowly by.

A bunch of little kids arrived, walking two-by-two and holding hands, with one adult for every three or four pairs. One of the women wore a tee shirt that said, "Children's Mansion," across a silk-screened print of the handsome limestone house. Once inside the playground, the little kids swarmed over the swings and slides.

There was a natural order under the apparent disorder in the park and playgrounds, and there were a number of adults watching the younger kids; but like the larger playground behind JHS 57, there were solitary children here. One of them arrived now, and M spotted him immediately.

The boy was on foot. He wandered into M's peripheral vision from uptown, and passed close by M's bench. He was black, dark, thin, and young. He wore tattered denim Bermuda shorts, a new white tee shirt, knee-high basketball socks with two green stripes at the tops, and black, low-cut Pro-Keds. He was sweating. He looked like he might have been playing basketball.

The boy poked along the fence by the pool and went to the water fountain for a long drink. He ended in the kiddie playground by the swings. One of the little day-care kids asked the boy to put her on a swing. He boosted her onto a seat, pushed her gently a few times, then wandered over to a seesaw, leaving the little girl swinging gently back and forth by herself in the deep shade under the trees.

There was no one his size to share a seesaw with, so the boy wandered back to the swings. He sat dawdling and twisting

150

slowly on one of the baby swings, the kind with a metal-backed seat and a metal bar across the front. He was still skinny enough to jam himself into the swing.

He sat for a long time, wistful and pensive, watching the smaller children around him. He had a round, pleasant face, and tight curly hair cut almost to his scalp. He might have been a first-grader, but a closer look would have shown him to be eight or nine.

As the boy sat on the swing, M drank his beer with nervous speed. He was about to move to a bench closer to the swings when a hand fell heavily on his shoulder. He looked up and saw a stocky man in a plaid flannel shirt and faded green work pants, with dark skin that looked like weathered leather, and the straight black hair of a South American Indian. In Spanish, the man said, "Get going. You'll be late."

M was badly startled. There were hidden and not-so-hidden threats contained in every instruction he received from his employers. Without looking again at the messenger, but with a quick covert glance at the boy, M gathered his things and got up to go. He crossed Amsterdam again, went into the *bodega* past a couple of men playing dominoes, and came out again a moment later with a different shopping bag, heavy with groceries.

The man in the plaid shirt waited for M to leave the *bodega*. Then he walked across Amsterdam into a dark, silent bar, empty of customers. He made two calls from a pay phone in the back. The bartender stood stone-still at the front of the bar, gazing out at the street.

Then the man walked up the block to the *bodega*. He looked like a handyman or super from one of the good apartment buildings over on West End Avenue. He spoke briefly to the two men playing dominoes on a piece of plywood set across an upended wire milk case, then went around the corner to the main entrance of the red brick building. At the top of the stoop, he opened the battered wooden door with a key. He went up the inside stairs two at a time, knocked at a door on the third floor, and was admitted. On his immediate right was a dirty bathroom. It looked like an old white-tile gas-station bathroom that hadn't been cleaned in twenty years. On his left was a dirty kitchen with a gray window onto a fire escape. Ahead was a ten-yard hall.

The man who opened the door went into the room at the end of the hall. The man in the plaid shirt followed. This room had been thinly whitewashed recently. A kitchen table and four chairs were in the center of the floor. Two dirty windows overlooked Amsterdam Avenue. There was a large alcove in the back of the room, away from the street. In it was a broken upright piano covered with twenty years of dust.

Ayala sat at the table, field-stripping and cleaning his small automatic. The gun had dark brown walnut grips, worn smooth from long use. The man in the plaid shirt stood in the doorway while Ayala wiped the parts of the gun with an oily rag, snapped the parts together, slipped in a loaded clip, and set the safety. He leaned back in his chair, stuck the gun in his waistband holster, and stood up, smoothing his shirt and tightening his tie. There was no sign of the gun. The man in the plaid shirt stepped forward.

"Can you do a job for me tonight?" asked Ayala, unrolling his shirtsleeves and fixing small gold links in the French cuffs.

"*Si, señor.*"

"You know O'Malley, who works in the station house across the street?" Ayala gestured across Amsterdam Avenue to the two-story brick building that housed the Twenty-Fourth Precinct.

"*Si, señor.*"

"I want you to do the same to him that your brother did to Rodriguez last week. Beat him badly, but do not kill him. It is a message. O'Malley was supposed to do something for me that he did not do. Be careful. And do it tonight."

chapter ten
eddie the alligator

Ayala stood in the room above the *bodega* with the phone in his left hand and a pair of binoculars in the other. He could see O'Malley across the street in his office, holding the phone to his ear and pacing around like a caged animal.

O'Malley was raging. "Ayala, you bastard. I bust my ass for you, and what do I get? You threaten me with one of your fucking goons. If you send him after me, I'll turn him inside out."

Ayala was laughing. "O'Malley, you don't understand."

"Understand what?"

"There are people in this city who are tougher and smarter than you are."

Ayala watched O'Malley throw his glass ashtray at the wall. "Shall I name them?" asked the Cuban.

There was a growl of incoherent rage.

"Me, for one," Ayala continued. "Hanratty. Mercedes Lopez—Maritza to you."

There was a roared obscenity.

"And Detective Sergeant Daniel Rodriguez."

O'Malley screamed like a woman, "I'll kill that fairy." The litter on his desk flew up, swirled around, and settled like a miniature snowstorm in a glass paperweight.

"O'Malley, you're making a mess of your office."

O'Malley stopped pacing and whirled around to his window. Ayala stepped up close to his window and waved across the street.

O'Malley breathed in a low voice into the phone, "How long have you been over there, you son of a bitch?"

"About two months."

"I'm coming right over."

Ayala hung up. There was a knock on the front door of the apartment. He went to see who it was. It was Mercedes. "You're late," said Ayala, "but it's just as well." He stepped into the kitchen, picked up a shotgun, and thrust it into Mercedes' hands. "Stand around the corner in the kitchen and hold this on O'Malley's back when he comes in. He'll be here in a moment."

Before Mercedes could protest, there was a heavy hammering on the door. She stepped back three steps as Ayala jerked the door open. O'Malley burst into the apartment, shouting.

"Ayala, you son of a bitch, if you fuck with me, I'll blow you and your whole operation outta the water."

Ayala smiled, backing slowly down the hall, drawing O'Malley into the apartment. "The next morning you would wake up without a tongue in your mouth, Lieutenant."

O'Malley's answer was to take two quick sidesteps into the kitchen, and come out holding Mercedes in one hand and the shotgun in the other. "If I wasn't a gentleman," he snarled, "I'd stuff this toy up her ass and pull the trigger."

He threw the shotgun into the kitchen with a clatter and slammed Mercedes against the hall wall. She sank to a sitting position on the floor.

There was not a trace of alarm on Ayala's face. He said, "OK, O'Malley, you've made your point. I'll call off my goons. Instead, I've got a job for you tonight."

O'Malley said, "I'm not doing any goddamn work for you tonight!"

"Shall I call Hanratty and ask him to do it?"

O'Malley shrugged and slammed the door shut behind him. He was calmer. "What's the job?"

"There will be a party tonight at the Children's Mansion to raise money. I want to deliver some cases of wine and soda to the party, and a few barrels of beer. Mercedes here will drive the delivery van. One of my men will be with her. I want you to convoy this delivery from the junkyard to the Mansion. It won't take much time."

154

"What's in these beer barrels?" asked O'Malley.

"Beer."

"Yeah," said O'Malley. "Nuthin for nuthin is my motto. Don't you have enough gorillas of your own?"

"I want you to do this job."

"What's it worth?"

"One thou."

"Up front."

Ayala beckoned to Mercedes, who got up off the floor, pulled an envelope out of her purse, counted out the money, and gave it to O'Malley, who made it disappear into his shirt pocket with the deftness of a blackjack dealer.

"I'm not gonna lay a hand on any of this stuff myself," said O'Malley.

"There'll be people at the Mansion to unload the delivery," said Ayala.

As he was leaving, O'Malley put his arm around Mercedes' shoulders in an avuncular fashion, and said, "Sweetheart, the next time you bushwhack somebody, make sure the room behind you is dark. Your shadow gave you away."

Ayala laughed. "Listen carefully, Mercedes. This is good advice from a professional."

"And one more thing," O'Malley said. "That gas-operated Remington is no good for anything but ducks. You can't swing it around fast enough at close range. A pistol is better. If you like making big holes, get yourself a cheap double-barreled shotgun, and saw it off down to the stock. But you only get two shots, and then you got nothing left. Just get yourself a good .38, honey. That's all you'll ever need."

That night about eight-thirty, as gray clouds streaked with pink-orange blew across the darkening sky behind the Palisades, a brown Chevy van rolled slowly along upper Riverside Drive. "Hillside Liquors," it said in gleaming white letters on both sides. "Fort George. We Deliver Anywhere. 888-4223."

It was going slowly, noted O'Malley from his car half a block behind, because the Drive was bumpy, and the van was riding on its axles. When the van emerged from the dense twilight of the overhanging shade trees at 135th Street onto the long viaduct that carried Riverside Drive over the valley at 125th Street, O'Malley pulled up close behind. The viaduct was four tenths of a mile long. Halfway across, O'Malley pulled in front and forced the van to the curb. He stuck the removable light on the roof of his car. It revolved slowly with a weak red blinking glare in the soft summer evening light. There was no one on the bridge, and not much traffic.

O'Malley walked back to the van. He said to Mercedes, "Don't you know there's no commercial traffic allowed on Riverside?"

She looked frightened and resigned. The man in the passenger seat stared through the windshield at the back of Grant's Tomb in the park at the far end of the bridge. The man had jet black hair and dark, reddish-brown skin. His square face was expressionless.

"Let's see what you've got in here," said O'Malley. "Open the side door."

"Ayala isn't going to like this," Mercedes protested.

"I don't give a fuck what he likes. When I'm up to my nose in shit, I like to know whose shit it is. Open up."

The other man made no move.

"Doesn't he speak English?" asked O'Malley.

"No," said Mercedes.

O'Malley reached in the open window and took her left ear between his thumb and forefinger. "Well, you better translate for me, you dumb cunt."

"Carlito, open the door," said Mercedes.

Without looking, the man reached behind his seat and unlatched the sliding side door from the inside.

O'Malley walked around the front of the van. He pulled a switchblade out of his jacket pocket. The liquor boxes looked factory sealed. He slit open the top of the first one. Inside, about twenty stun grenades nestled in white polystyrene packing beads. He slit open another box. More grenades. In the third, he found what he was looking for—thick slabs of plastic explosive wrapped in wax paper. It was like kids' modeling clay.

"You did that building on Manhattan Avenue," he said. "Ayala was supposed to warn me anytime he pulled a stunt like

156

that on my turf. He's breaking our agreements right and left. You tell that to Ayala. You understand?"

Mercedes nodded. O'Malley slit open another box. Nine small rockets were packed neatly between cardboard partitions like bottles of wine. O'Malley lifted one out of the box. Small fins surrounded its base.

"My, my," said O'Malley. "Antitank rockets. The latest model. Where are the launchers?"

Mercedes and Carlito stared through the windshield at the gathering night. O'Malley reached up and grabbed a handful of Carlito's hair. He pulled the man's head back and stuck the point of the knife under his right ear.

"Mercedes?" said O'Malley.

"Delivered last week," she said.

O'Malley let go of the hair. "This is enough for a fucking war," he said. He pulled a roll of wide packing tape out of his jacket pocket and swiftly taped the boxes shut. Before taping the last box shut, he dropped one stun grenade in each of his jacket pockets. He slammed the door shut.

"Get going," he said. "But go slow. I'll be right behind you."

By the time Mercedes parked the van halfway up on the sidewalk along the narrow service ramp in front of the Children's Mansion, it was almost night. The streetlight in front of the Mansion was broken. The corner was dark. With the help of two men from the party, they unloaded the truck and carried the boxes through the gate into a service door under the front stoop of the building.

O'Malley paid no attention to a tall skinny man walking his lap dog on a leash in the island between the service road and the Drive itself. He was wearing running shorts and a tee shirt, and to O'Malley, he looked like a fag walking his faggy little dog.

The party inside the Mansion was going full blast. Latin music racketed around the neighborhood, echoing off the surrounding buildings. People were laughing and talking in the back and side yards, and dancing in the back rooms of the basement and the first floor. The front rooms overlooking the street were dark. The smell of marijuana drifted on the breeze.

157

When the van was empty, Mercedes and Carlito emerged from the door beneath the stoop. The heavy door closed with a metallic clank and a bolt shot closed from the inside. Mercedes carried two bottles of beer. She and the *mestizo* got in the truck. She opened a bottle and drank, then put the bottle down between her thighs and started the van. Carlito drained his bottle in two gulps and dropped it to the sidewalk with a crash.

The van drove slowly off, crossing 108th Street when the light changed, and then up the service road toward 110th Street. The skinny man scooped up the little dog and jogged along behind it. The van turned east toward Broadway on 110th. About halfway along the block, Mercedes stopped and Carlito jumped out. The skinny runner with the dog under his arm turned the corner just in time to see the van speed away up Broadway. The dark-haired *mestizo* ran around the corner, heading downtown.

What the man with the dog didn't see was O'Malley cruising slowly along the service road behind him, with a thoughtful look on his face. O'Malley turned the corner, too, and parked his car in a bus stop. He slid the two grenades under the front seat and got out. He watched the skinny runner disappear around the corner onto Broadway, heading downtown.

O'Malley locked his doors, then walked quickly back down the service road toward the Children's Mansion. Something tugged at his memory. It wasn't the runner's face. It was the way he shambled when he ran.

O'Malley couldn't place the man, but he knew he had seen him somewhere, in some other costume, and he knew it would come to him sooner or later if he didn't worry at it too much.

At six the next morning, the phone by Rodriguez's bed rang. He reached across Mercedes and picked it up.

O'Malley said, "You're outta the hospital, right? You're back on duty today, right?"

"Yeah," grunted Rodriguez.

"Go down to Riverside Park below 104th Street. You know that playground way down on the lower level between the old Grand Central freight tracks and the West Side Highway?"

"Yeah."

"Some early-morning jogger found a decapitated body down

158

there. Sounds like some goddamn voodoo ritual to me, like that guy they dug out of a grave in the Bronx last year. The ME is on the way. I'm at home. It's all yours. Welcome back, asshole."

The phone clicked in Rodriguez's ear. His mind turned slowly into gear. It was Saturday morning. He had the worst headache he'd ever had in his life. He shouldn't have drunk so much. He shouldn't have drunk anything so soon after the concussion. And on top of all the beer, he had smoked at least two joints with Mercedes, maybe more, he couldn't remember. They'd gone late to the party, after she called him. He remembered flirting with half the women there, and leaving at two in the morning with Mercedes, who was very angry at him.

He had wanted to go to her house. Mercedes had refused in a rage and called him names. They had a wild argument in the middle of 107th Street, with people yelling out of windows to shut up. In the end, they took a taxi to his place, and fucked until they nearly wrecked the bed. He looked around. The room was a mess. His shirt hung from the corner of his dresser, nearly torn in half. Her clothes were all over the room.

Two weeks ago, he would have leapt out of bed at O'Malley's call. Now, he hauled himself by his elbows slowly back up onto his pillow. O'Malley sounded odd on the phone, gleeful and malicious.

The phone rang again. Rodriguez got up this time and walked around the bed. It was Nieman.

"Were you at that party last night at the Mansion?"

Rodriguez had the feeling Nieman already knew the answer. "Yes."

"I want to talk to you today."

"Call me later," said Rodriguez. "I'm on the job." Mercedes stirred and rolled over. She was out cold. She had drunk and smoked more than Rodriguez.

With a mixture of anger and regret, Rodriguez dipped into her pocketbook for her keys. He knew a locksmith on Columbus Avenue who would make copies of keys from wax impressions, no questions asked. Early in the week, while Mercedes was at work, Rodriguez would pay a surprise visit to her apartment.

She had a dozen keys on her key ring. He made careful impressions of each of them in softened candle wax, then went

back to the bedroom and quietly replaced them. In the bathroom, he took two aspirins and a codeine pill, and gratefully
stepped into a hot shower.

It was almost eight o'clock when Rodriguez arrived at the
murder scene in the park. The morning was cool. A fresh breeze
blew in from the broad estuary of the Hudson River. Small
boats sailed in a light chop. The leaves of the trees shimmered
and shook in the sun and wind. The noise of traffic came from
the highway on the other side of the high fence protecting the
playground. There was a small knot of joggers and dog walkers
at the edge of the playground in a corner littered with broken
glass and wind-blown paper.

A cop put his hand out to stop Rodriguez and said, "Hey.
No further, buddy."

"Detective Sergeant Rodriguez to you, pal," said Rodriguez,
without bothering to pull out his badge. He walked into the little
group around the covered body on the ground. There were muttered greetings. One of the ambulance attendants reached down
and pulled back the blanket.

The head had been severed almost surgically at the neck.
The anatomical details of bone, tendon, muscle, windpipe, and
throat were clean and clear. A large pool of blood and stomach
fluid had spread across the asphalt and dried. The body lay on
its back. The clothes were scuffed and torn.

"What do you think?" asked Rodriguez of another man in
plainclothes standing next to him.

"There musta been a terrific battle here. There's broken
glass ground into his arms, legs, and buttocks. His left hand and
forearm are broken, like someone stomped him, and half his
ribs are cracked. They're shattered in pieces. Somebody beat
the shit out of him."

"Any ID?"

"Nothing but subway tokens and a handful of nickels and
dimes."

Rodriguez looked down at the corpse and felt a wild anxiety
grow in the core of his stomach. He saw dark cotton pants and
black sneakers.

"Where's his head?"

In answer, the man pointed over to a nearby basketball court. The head was wedged between a backstop and the rim, like a stuck basketball. It looked as though someone had thrown it against a wall once or twice, but even in bruised and battered death, it wore a look of perfect impassivity.

When Rodriguez saw the weird sight, he thought first about the way heads were spiked on the walls of ancient cities, and bodies thrown outside the walls as carrion. He looked up at the two levels of the park rising in leafy, rock-walled tiers above him, and the tall apartment buildings rising high above Riverside Drive with the brilliant morning sun behind them. Small white clouds flew overhead like tattered flags from the parapets.

His mind wouldn't work right. He stood in silence. The others were looking at him, waiting for him to say something, give an order, make a move. He couldn't. He was paralyzed. He looked at the head severed from its body by some unknown, methodical madman, at the face wedged behind the twisted basketball hoop, and saw the faces of the men in the abandoned building on Manhattan Avenue, and in Straus Park, and in the street across from his own apartment, and in the abandoned subway station at 91st Street. They must have been twins, he thought. Rodriguez felt his whole world come unglued. Now what? He asked himself. Now what?

He turned back to the body, gave the orders, and began the most methodical, single-minded homicide investigation of his career. By ten A.M. he had the department's scientific apparatus in high gear. By noon, he had a preliminary autopsy report in his hand, fixing the time of death at sometime between nine and midnight the night before. By three he had O'Malley in a frenzy because reporters from every news outlet in town were crawling all over the story and Rodriguez was helping them. At five, unknown to Rodriguez, O'Malley's rabbi joined the frenzy.

The TV footage from the scene of the crime had the impact of a baseball bat on the heat-softened and beer-sodden brains of those citizens with the poor judgment to watch the early TV news on a summer Saturday afternoon. Outraged calls lit the switchboards of TV stations and the Mayor's office. No one liked the telephoto shots of the head.

By six, when the footage ran on the second wave of news

161

broadcasts, headquarters was calling it "The grisly ritual murder of an illegal immigrant." And O'Malley was listening to his rabbi scream over the telephone at him, "You stupid harp, what the hell are you doing at home?"

At ten o'clock, Rodriguez and Nieman huddled together in a booth in the West End, a bar on Broadway near 114th Street just below Columbia University. They were eating greasy hamburgers and French fries, and drinking beer. It was the first food Rodriguez had eaten all day.

At ten-fifteen, Rodriguez had solved the murder, and knew he would never make an arrest. Nieman told him O'Malley was the killer. "I followed the *mestizo* back down Broadway after he got out of the van," Nieman said. "When we passed 108th Street, I ran down the block to where I parked my car, threw the goddamn dog in the back seat, pulled on a warm-up suit I had in the car, locked it up, and ran after the guy again. He was just turning down 107th when I saw him. I was lucky as hell, all night."

He wiped some grease off his chin and looked sideways at the cleft in the crotch of a young woman in tight jeans who was leaning against the bar. He looked back at Rodriguez and hunched himself forward so his head almost touched the other man.

"The guy ducked into an alleyway behind the white brick building on the other corner of 107th across from the Mansion. And then I'll be goddamned if O'Malley didn't whip around the corner from Riverside a minute later, peering down over the stone fence into the backyard behind the Mansion, looking down at the party and looking in the windows of the first floor.

"I had no idea O'Malley was running around up there. It's a wonder he didn't spot me. To tell you the truth, it was Lopez I was interested in, and I wanted a good look at the Mansion."

He looked at Rodriguez, expecting a reaction, but there was none.

"As I'm standing there at the top of that little hill on 107th, wondering what the hell I'm gonna do if O'Malley recognizes me, that fucking Indian creeps across the street up behind O'Malley like a ghost and smacks him in the back of the head with a sap. He hit him three times. I could hear the crack from thirty yards away. I almost threw up."

Nieman was excited. He wiped his mouth with the back of his hand and drank half his glass of beer.

"O'Malley went down to his knees. The Indian gave him a kick in the kidney so hard it almost made me piss my pants. I had to force myself to stand there and watch. It was so bad I wanted to help O'Malley."

Nieman snickered. Rodriguez rubbed the back of his head and remembered how he pissed blood for four days.

"Then that fucking O'Malley gets up and goes after the guy, swinging a knife. The guy dodged him, but the knife caught the guy's shirt and ripped it half off. The guy took off like a shot, and O'Malley goes after him just as fast. I never saw anybody take that kind of beating and get up.

"They run along the service ramp to those steps at 106th, where that statue is, run down those steps, across the Drive, and into the park. There's nobody in the park but kids smoking dope and listening to those goddamn big radios. They don't even see these two gorillas running past. I had the feeling that Indian was loafing."

Rodriguez said, "That Indian could outrun Jesse Owens."

"They ran down that long hill," Nieman went on, "down to where that flight of stairs goes to the lower level at 90th Street, then back along the lower level through those trees and down to the bottom level by those stairs above the playground where you found the guy. Then the *mestizo* turned and waited for O'Malley."

"Were you the guy who called it in?"

"Yeah. I waited until first light at a little before five. I wanted to be sure O'Malley was home."

"What was it like?"

"I've never seen anything like it. It lasted maybe ten minutes. Those two guys just beat the shit out of each other. O'Malley must be a mess. Has anybody seen him?"

"No. He's been home all day on the phone, screaming at me for talking to reporters."

"He must be shitting bricks."

Nieman stuffed the rest of his hamburger into his mouth and

washed it down with beer. "O'Malley finally knocked the guy down and kicked him in the side of the head with his shoe. He musta stunned him, because O'Malley reached down and cut the guy's throat with one swipe of that knife. It looked like a samurai movie. Then he took his head off."

"How'd he get the head up on the hoop?"

"He overturned a trash basket and climbed up on it. He bent the rim up to hold the head in place. O'Malley is the strongest guy I've ever seen, and maybe the most dangerous."

"That's what I thought happened," said Rodriguez. "There was trash blowing around down there, and an empty basket, but it was right side up. There was a circle of broken glass and stuff below the hoop. He must have kicked most of the trash away afterward."

"Yeah," said Nieman. "That's what he did."

"Now what?"

"I don't know, pal. You tell me."

"No, Harry. You tell me."

Nieman sat up straight, wiping his fingers one by one on a shredded paper napkin. He looked around.

"OK," he said. "This place is too crowded. Let's go for a walk around Columbia, and I'll give you a quick graduate course in narcotics and terrorism."

They sat on the long flight of broad steps that dominates the open plaza of the university campus. A low-flying 727 whined its way down toward LaGuardia, two miles east. A group of students played Frisbee in the pools of light on the plaza. The campus was dark and quiet.

"No one knows what their end game is here," said Nieman. He sipped beer from a can. "We know the FALN is stockpiling sophisticated weapons in large numbers, which means they think they can command some troops when the time comes."

"Time for what?"

"No one knows. We don't know who runs the Cuban end here."

"Ayala."

"Probably."

"That's the key, isn't it?" asked Rodriguez. "And the key to

164

the key is O'Malley, and O'Malley's rabbi, this ghost you keep talking about. I think this guy went after O'Malley last night to give O'Malley a message from the Cuban godfather."

"What message?"

"That O'Malley didn't do something he was supposed to do."

"What?"

"Hire me for the godfather?"

"You're catching on," said Nieman.

"Why hasn't O'Malley himself made a pass at me?"

"He's afraid of you."

"You've made me the point man, Harry. You're playing God. I never asked for this."

Nieman said nothing.

Rodriguez stood up and stretched. He looked at the few lights in the windows around him, and felt the huge dead weight of the institution. It was all bullshit. He said, "As long as Mercedes is involved, I won't get involved. I don't give a shit about these games, Harry. They feed on themselves and use people up like candles."

Nieman's face registered loss.

"You thought you had me, Harry, but you don't. Yes, I'll sit on the case, just like O'Malley and his dogs sat on the cases of the two little boys. Just like you and the Chief sat on Flanagan's case. But I won't work for you. O'Malley and his ghost rabbi and the FALN and all that shit is all your problem."

"Mercedes Lopez is your problem," said Nieman.

"Yeah, and I'll take care of her my own way. She opens more doors for me than I ever knew existed."

Rodriguez walked away, down the stairs and through the Frisbee game. He disappeared in the direction of Broadway.

Nieman sat looking across the barren campus where years before he had been a confused and reluctant undergraduate. He could see the windows of the dormitory rooms he had lived in, and he remembered old friends, long out of touch. He looked at the squat bulk of Butler Library, with the names of great thinkers chiseled in the gray stone of its façade. Plato, Aristotle, etc.

He looked for a long time at John Jay Hall, with its long halls of single dormitory rooms. He lived alone there one semester in a room as small and spartan as an anchorite's cell. In another of those rooms, the poet Lorca lived and wrote some of the poems in *The Poet in New York* sometime in 1929 or 1930, Nieman thought. Lorca wrote about Harlem and boys like angels. In 1936, during the Spanish Civil War, the Spanish Fascists shot the poet in the back of the head and tipped him into an anonymous grave. In New York almost half a century later, the same battles were still being fought, thought Nieman, only no one knew who was who.

chapter eleven
174 west 107th street

A tall, heavy-set black man stood in his shirtsleeves on the sidewalk of 105th Street watching the children. Class by class, led by their teachers, they stood in a long line in the shade of the wide hall, inside the open doors of PS 145. To his sentimental eyes they looked like shy creatures of the woods and fields.

When their teachers released them, they burst through the doors shouting and screaming, milling around on the wide side-walk. They found their friends, mothers, older brothers and sisters, or babysitters, and moved off. Most of them waved goodbye to Mr. Wilson. He knew them all. He considered him-self lucky.

Out of the ninety-nine elementary schools in Manhattan, he was principal of one of the newer and smaller ones. He knew all his children by the time the first month of school was over, and he knew their families and their problems. He knew a good principal could make a great difference in the learning and lives of each child in an elementary school, and he began every year with the intention to make that crucial difference, to give his kids a running start in a hostile world. He ended every year with the knowledge that he had often managed to succeed.

He kept a mental list, though, of his failures. Every year the list grew a little longer. It never grew shorter, because he could never go back and undo his mistakes. He was a genuinely hum-ble man, and knew he was bound to make mistakes, but the list pained him, because the victims of his failures were children. The children of PS 145 on West 105th Street rarely got second or third chances.

A little boy walked out the door holding his teacher's hand. Here was a problem, not yet a failure. The boy smiled shyly at the big principal and waved. Wilson smiled and waved back. He boomed "Goodbye," in his loud, deep voice. He watched the little boy release his teacher's hand. The teacher, a young man Wilson was happy to have in his school, lifted hand to forehead in a mock salute to the principal, and hurried back inside.

The boy walked and bounced down the sidewalk toward Amsterdam Avenue. He walked on the balls of his feet, his lunchbox rattling with each step. Wonder what he keeps in there, thought Wilson. It sounds like pencils and loose change. In his other hand, the boy carried a thin paperback book. He's a reader, thought Wilson. I wish he wasn't so sad all the time. Wilson looked at the clean white tee shirt, loose on the thin frame, the mended blue corduroys, and the new, purple, low-cut Pro-Keds. New Pro-Keds, thought Wilson, and his eyes suddenly misted over.

He looked away. God, he whispered, I get more sentimental every year, and older too. God, keep me tough enough and smart enough to help these babies. He wiped his eyes with his fingers.

When he looked back toward Amsterdam, the boy was gone. He was a third-grader who had come into Wilson's school late in second grade, when his mother moved into a building on the corner of 107th Street and Amsterdam. She was a token clerk in the subways and worked somewhere in midtown. She had moved from somewhere uptown after a nasty divorce. The boy had obviously suffered badly. He was bright and studious, a good reader. But he was withdrawn and unhappy.

The sidewalk was empty. The children were gone from Wilson's day. He left his post and walked back into the school. As he did every single time he entered his school, he looked up at the name chiseled into the stone sill over the door. "Bloomingdale." It was the name this area of Manhattan was known by a hundred years before, when it was a village of small riverside estates and farms. As he did every day, he wished he could rename the school after Paul Robeson. There wasn't much room, thought Wilson at the end of his day, for great differences of opinion in politics, or education, or anywhere else he could think of.

Wilson's phone rang. He looked at the stacks of paperwork on his desk, sighed, and picked up the phone.

It was Mercedes Lopez, and she was nearly in hysterics. He had never heard her like this.

"Mercedes, wait," he said. "I can't understand you."

She took a deep breath and let it out slowly. Then she spoke. "Can you come up to St. Luke's right now? There's a boy up here. He's hurt badly, and I think he's one of yours."

"What do you mean?"

"The kid had a lunchbox. There was an announcement from PS 145 in it."

"Who is he?"

"You have to tell us. Hurry, Robert. The child may die."

It was the boy in the white tee shirt. When Wilson saw the slashed and battered little body on the rolling table in the hall outside the operating room, with bottles dripping fluid into the veins, he wept. He didn't break down and sob, but tears ran down his face in streams.

Mercedes Lopez stood next to him, her arm around his large waist. She looked half Wilson's size. She had known this man for years, and knew he was often in agony over his many children, but she had never seen him weep openly.

"It's him," he said. "I knew it, I knew it."

"Who?" asked Rodriguez from the other side of the table. He wore a new seersucker suit.

Wilson couldn't answer.

"Who, goddammit?" asked O'Malley. A jagged fresh scar on his face ran from his hairline down across his right eyebrow and cheekbone to a point below his right ear.

Wilson looked at him. "I'll tell you, sir, when his mother gets here, and I'm going to call her now." Wilson turned and walked down the hall.

Rodriguez looked across the table at Mercedes. It was the first time he had seen her in a month. She looked back at him,

169

then down at the boy breathing in shallow, uneven gasps. Rodriguez gestured at the nurse, who pushed the table quickly down the hall.

O'Malley moved up the hall after Wilson and cornered him by the nurse's station. "Who the hell do you think you are, mister?" said O'Malley, in a voice as loud as the hospital PA system. "When I ask you a goddamn question, I want a goddamn answer. Now, who is this kid?"

Wilson smiled at the pretty black nurse, and picked up the phone on her table. "Miss, how do I get an outside line?"

As Wilson dialed, O'Malley pressed the cut-off button on the phone. "Listen, teach. I'm gonna ask you one more time who this kid is, then I'm gonna put the cuffs on and ask you again in the station house."

Wilson knocked O'Malley's hand away from the phone. "You listen, Mr. Pó-lice-man," said Wilson. "It's Mr. Robert Wilson when you speak to me."

O'Malley stood silently, working his hands into fists.

Wilson said, "Maybe you're not familiar with Board of Education regulations, Lieutenant O'Malley, but I am. I cannot release the child's name until a positive identification is made and the parents are notified. I will ask the mother if I can release the boy's name to you for your investigation. If she agrees, I will do so." Wilson dialed a number. "I hope we catch her," he said. "She works eight to four." He covered the mouthpiece with his hand. "And another thing, Lieutenant. If this boy's wounds are of the nature described by the doctor, then there will be absolutely no publicity. It would do great harm to the boy."

"Wilson," said O'Malley. "This boy isn't gonna live long enough to suffer any psychological damage." O'Malley pronounced the word *psychological* like the name of a venereal disease.

Wilson went behind the desk at the nurse's station and pulled the phone into the corner of the alcove. He talked so quietly that O'Malley could not hear a word. Wilson hung up and thanked the nurse, then stepped into the middle of the hall, and said in the same low voice to O'Malley, "There is a very efficient grapevine around the public schools, Lieutenant O'Malley. There were two murders last year in East Harlem very similar to this one. There was no investigation of those murders worthy of the name. It's my understanding that you commanded the homicide zone over there last year, Lieutenant, at the time of those murders."

O'Malley's face was as purple as a grape.

Wilson was half a head taller than O'Malley. He stepped a little closer to the cop, close enough to smell his whiskey breath, and said, "Furthermore, I am told there is an excellent description in the hands of your department of a man who accosted a child in the playground behind JHS 57 last summer, which seems to resemble a fragmentary description of your killer from East Harlem. Am I correct?"

O'Malley shook his head no.

Wilson stepped even closer and said, "Yes."

O'Malley looked over Wilson's shoulder and saw Rodriguez standing next to Lopez.

Wilson stepped back and said, "The boy's mother agreed to let me give you her son's name. She'll be here shortly. The TA police are bringing her. She also agreed there will be absolutely no publicity on her son's case."

O'Malley said in a voice strangled with anger, "Nobody makes conditions for me, you cocksucker."

Wilson smiled and said, "Oh, yes, Lieutenant. There is one more condition. If the boy's name leaks out, if he is identified in any way, the Board of Education itself will raise questions about the other two killings. *My* Chancellor will raise the questions with *your* Mayor. Do we understand each other, O'Malley?"

O'Malley said nothing.

"I think we do," said Wilson. "The boy's name is Joseph Perry, and he lives with his mother, Eleanor Perry, in an apartment on the third floor of the building where you found him. She is a token clerk for the MTA."

"I'm gonna remember you," said O'Malley.

"Yes, you are," said Wilson. "And remember this, too. You are going to give the boy a pseudonym in all your reports."

O'Malley looked blank.

"A phony name," said Wilson, "just to be sure about leaks. And just to be sure you and I use the same phony name in our separate reports, I've picked a good one. We'll call him 'Bobby Powers.' A nice Irish name, don't you think?"

Late that night, Rodriguez asked Mercedes, "Do you remember Mrs. Sanchez saying that all the Spanish-speaking people of the *pueblo* looked up to you?"

"Yes," she said, sitting on top of him, moving herself up and down slowly with small motions so he would not slip out of her in his limp condition.

"I must be one of them, and I am looking up to you at this very moment." He was overjoyed to be with her again, after walking away from her in the middle of a terrible argument more than a month before. "And I can truthfully say that I have seen inside this woman tonight, seen what makes her tick."

Moving faster as he began to stiffen inside her, she said, "My *coño* does not tick."

Rodriguez laughed. He felt good inside her. "You do not tick with your cunt, but you think with it."

She made a face. "I do not think with my *coño*. I think with my head."

"You are doing something with your cunt right now, and it feels very much like thinking, very smooth and quick, and I like it better than talking."

Mercedes did not answer. She moved faster. Her large, darkened nipples swayed and bounced in the pale blue light of the flickering candle. Her breath came faster. Her breathing was harsh.

Rodriguez could feel the hard knob of her cervix bump against the tip of his cock as she rose and fell on him. Her face twisted in a strained grimace of pleasure as she began to come, and she stroked her hands across his belly and hers. He felt like he was in her to her throat.

He arched his back and lifted her off the bed until she had to lean back and grab his knees to keep her balance. She moved back and forth with quick short jerks, her pubic hair brushing against the root of his cock. She could not catch her breath. Rodriguez reached up and flattened her breasts against her chest with his open hands, then he came suddenly with a shudder, lifting her higher. He was so tight up inside her that he thought the semen would be trapped in his penis, but he felt her turn to liquid inside.

She cried out in gasps. "Ay, I love you very much."

He slid his hands over the sweaty skin under her arms and down her ribs around her back. Pulling her down against him, he slid his fingers up into the thick hair at the back of her head.

"I love you, too," he said softly. "Mercedes, I love you very much."

She cried out again, as she had when he entered her that night, the first time after the long absence.

Rodriguez had never said as much to any woman. How did this happen? he wondered. He was raised slightly on his pillow, and he looked down the back of the woman he was holding at her glistening skin and the spread and fold of her hips. He felt the ring of muscles in her vagina tighten and loosen around his penis. Her fingers slipped down between their bellies, and he felt the motion as she stroked herself and moved her hips again to her own rhythm. She began to come right away, almost as soon as she touched herself, and the muscles in her vagina moved of their own accord. It felt as though her fingers were inside him. The thought made him hard instantly, and she cried out again, sat up straight, and began to move against him in a frenzy. When he came again, she couldn't stop until she fell on him in exhaustion. Then she fell asleep.

Looking over her, he saw the reflection of the candle and the statue in the glass of a framed print on the wall opposite the foot of the bed. Like an old shack in a village in the islands, he thought. I should be hearing the rats in the palm thatch on the roof, the wind in the trees, the silence of clear stars in the deep darkness of the night sky. And the endless Atlantic waves phosphorescing on the beach.

Standing in the kitchen the next morning, Rodriguez asked, "Where's your diaphragm?"

Mercedes answered, "I'm pregnant."

He looked at her carefully. Trying to be flippant but sounding affectionate, he said, "I hope it's me."

173

"It is," she said firmly.

"How many months?"

"About two?"

"You're asking me?"

"No," she said. Her angular face held a look of terrible uncertainty.

He looked at her. "I know what you're thinking. You don't know whether to keep the baby or have an abortion."

"Yes," she said. "No."

"I don't know either," he said. "It's not just up to you, is it?"

"No." She paused, then said, "Yes."

Rodriguez laughed. "My God," he said, and laughed some more. "Have you ever had an abortion?"

"No."

"How many children do you have?"

"Two."

He could see the anger rising in her face. The tenderness had turned to anger before it could be fully felt. He could feel the anger rising in him, too.

He said, "You don't have two children. You lied to me."

She was wearing his robe, and she tore it open, screaming. "See these breasts? See these nipples? See how large and dark they are? Not small and perfect and pink like a young girl who has never nursed a baby at her own breasts."

She was screaming at the top of her lungs, the blood rushing to her face and neck. The soft skin between her breasts was flushed and dark. She pinched the loose skin of her belly together with her two hands and thrust herself forward at him. "See this belly? This is the belly of a woman. Are you blind? Don't you know what stretch marks are, you bastard? The child in the belly grows heavy, and the skin pulls and stretches."

She ran her fingers around her sides from her navel, along the network of tiny silvery streaks in her skin. She dropped the robe to the floor and ran her hands back onto her buttocks. "And here, too," she screamed. "Here are the marks on the skin of a woman who bore two children when she was too young."

She thrust her right hand between her legs. She lunged forward across the kitchen and grabbed his hair with her left hand,

and pulled his face down toward the dark hair between her legs. He slapped at her hand, but she had him off balance and she forced him to his knees. She screamed, "Bastard! Bastard! Bastard!" She forced his face between her legs and tried to straddle him.

"Look in there, you bastard. Open your eyes and look at what is there. See that scar that runs from my cunt to my asshole? See? See?"

Rodriguez could not fight her. He could not resist her fury.

"*See?* That scar is the mark of childbirth. Every woman has that scar, every woman who has given birth to a child."

She was beating him on the head and shoulders, squeezing his head between her legs. "Put your head in my cunt, you bastard. That is the size of the little baby. It is too big for the hole and it tears the skin."

She was hammering him, hurting him, sitting on him with all her weight, trying to force him up inside her. He pulled away, and she fell, weeping and crying.

"But your mother is dead," he said. "I know."

She sobbed. "Yes. She is dead. For three years. And my two babies, my girls, live with my sister in Puerto Rico."

"I know," he said. He was crying too. "In Puerto Rico, I saw your sister's house. I saw the girls too. They are beautiful like you. And I saw your mother's grave."

Rodriguez crawled over to Mercedes and sat cross-legged next to her. He pulled her into his lap, where she lay quietly, weeping and shivering. He dragged his robe around her. She gradually calmed herself.

He said, "I made copies of your keys, and went through your apartment one morning in late July, before I went on vacation. I didn't believe you about your daughters and your mother. Sometimes I thought you never asked me there because you had a lover. Sometimes I thought it was something else. Now I know it was something else."

Mercedes lay perfectly still, cradled in Rodriguez's lap, breathing quietly like a child hiding under the blankets.

Rodriguez said, "You are a member of the FALN."

She said nothing.

175

"You are a member of the executive committee."

She said nothing.

Rodriguez shook her by the shoulder. "Answer me, Mercedes. I know it is true, but I want you to be honest with me."

"Yes," she said, very quietly. "It is true."

"When we met, did you sleep with me because I was a cop, or because you wanted to know me?"

"Because I wanted to know you," she whispered.

"I believe you," he said. "I love you very much, Mercedes. Do you love me?"

"Yes," she said. "Yes."

"We have a serious problem," he said.

"I know," she said. "I've known that longer than you have."

She sat up and gathered the robe around her shoulders. "Daniel, I won't tell you what I do. I won't tell you any more than you already know. I'm not even sure how you know this much, since there is nothing in my apartment that would tell you anything. You must be an excellent detective, which I guess I knew all along."

Rodriguez said, "Mercedes, listen to me. I am not a child. I know what the FALN has done, and I know you had a hand in it somehow. I imagine you think it is justified."

"I want my people to be free, Daniel. They are not free now."

"Perhaps not," said Rodriguez. "I've told myself most of my life that such things aren't my concern, that there is nothing I can do one way or the other."

"There are many ways," she said.

"Listen to me," he said. "I'm a cop. Many cops are violent, but I am not. I hate violence. I hate killing. Every day in my job, I try to stop killing by taking the killers off the streets. Many killings are done by people who have done it before. It is a tiny handful of people who commit most of the worst crimes. Do you understand?"

She nodded.

"I always found it impossible to distinguish between one killing and another. People have different motives for murder, and sometimes those motives justify the killing in the eyes of the law. But for me, each killer must be dealt with by the law.

176

Not by me, because I am not the law. I am only an instrument of the law. Do you understand?"

"Yes," she said. "I am not stupid."

"Listen to me, Mercedes," he said sharply, "because what I'm saying is the way you and I are going to survive. You say you cannot tell me everything, and I say I understand. I don't want to know, because I know we cannot survive together if I know too much."

"You are doing this because of the baby," she said in a hoarse whisper.

"No," he shouted. "I am doing this for myself."

She reached out and touched him on the knee. "I'm sorry," she said. "I'm listening."

"In the last couple of months, I've overlooked two killings. I know who the killers are, and I can locate witnesses. These are airtight cases. I never dreamed I was capable of doing this."

"Why have you done it?" she asked.

"Because I want to find the killer of the little boys. Because if I go to the wall on either of these killings, which involve policemen, I will be transferred to Staten Island. And because my information is from another police officer who is after bigger game."

And because he is a threat to you, Mercedes, he continued silently.

"O'Malley," said Mercedes.

"What about him?"

"He's involved, isn't he?"

He looked at her curiously. "Involved in what?"

"In your dilemma."

"What's my dilemma?"

"A choice between two ambiguous alternatives. Whether or not to compromise yourself as a cop by protecting a member of the FALN who is pregnant with your child. And whether or not to compromise yourself as a cop by protecting O'Malley in order to pursue the killer of the little boys."

"You put it very well, Mercedes. Just when things were going well for this dumb Puerto Rican cop, they fell apart."

"Not dumb, Daniel. A very good man, which is why you have a dilemma and no solution."

He smiled weakly. "We can't solve it sitting here. We're both late for work, and I have to go to the hospital this morning to see the boy we're calling Bobby Powers."

"You never told me exactly what happened to him," Mercedes said.

Rodriguez rose stiffly to his feet and held out his hand to pull her up. "It's pretty gruesome. This psychopath got the kid up to the roof of the building the kid lives in. He's a latchkey kid. No one saw anything. I swear to God this guy is invisible. He gave the kid a dollar, because we found it tucked in the kid's clothes on the roof. A neighbor heard the kid moaning in the hallway, went out to look, and found him lying on the floor. He must have dragged himself down from the roof."

Rodriguez walked into the living room. "The kid was wearing socks and a tee shirt, nothing else. The guy took his dick off and stabbed him a few times, but not as badly as the ones who were killed."

"Yes, I know that part of it," said Mercedes softly. "I was at the hospital, remember?"

He turned and looked at her. "Yes, you were. You know, for a minute I forgot. You saw O'Malley go after Wilson, didn't you? Now you know what he's like."

She nodded.

"I won't tell you what he said about Wilson afterwards."

"What about the child?"

"He's critical, but stable. He's gonna live. I'll be able to talk to him this afternoon, but I want to talk to his mother first. She's up there now. She was there all night."

"Goddammit, Hanratty, the kid is gonna die. He was cut up very bad." O'Malley was hunched over the phone in his office. It was eight-thirty in the morning. Two untouched containers of coffee rested on the edge of his desk, and a half-eaten cheese Danish lay crumbling on top of a pile of forms.

"Where's Rodriguez?" asked the raspy voice.

"Late. I don't know where he is. He's never late."

"You're not on top of this problem, Eddie."

"What the hell do you mean?"

178

"You're attracting a lot of attention, Eddie. It's one thing to jerk off lazy reporters and the brass, but if that community blows up over this kid, certain people are gonna start looking around."

O'Malley lit a cigarette from the butt of the one he was smoking. His ashtray was piled high with stinking, crushed butts. His face was as gray as the ashtray's contents.

"Eddie, are you there?"

"Yeah, I'm here."

"The little kid is gonna live, Eddie. Did you know that?"

"What the hell do you mean? I called the hospital late last night, and they said he was worse."

"You're not on top of this, like I said. You better call them again. There was another operation in the wee hours last night, and they fixed the kid up. Now he's gonna live."

"And that noscy Rodriguez has got the case."

"You assigned him, Eddie-boy."

"That's because he's the only guy I got up here who speaks spic. Half the fucking population of Latin America lives in this city, and there aren't twenty guys with gold shields who speak the fucking language."

"Eddie, you're missing the point," said Hanratty. His rasp was getting softer and lower.

"What's that?" asked O'Malley.

"If this kid gives a description that matches the Sanchos description, you're in trouble because it means this dick-biter has been hanging around your neighborhood since last summer and you didn't find him."

"I can handle it."

"Eddie-boy, you're unusually stupid this morning. If you get in trouble and get pulled outta that command, you lose your value, you know what I mean?"

O'Malley nodded, as if his rabbi were in the room. O'Malley could feel the grayness of his face. He knew damn well what was going on, and he knew he wasn't on top of it. And he knew the consequences.

"OK," he said harshly. "Get off my back. I'm gonna take care of it."

"You better, Eddie-boy," said Hanratty. Rasp. Click. Buzz.

As O'Malley looked up from his desk, Rodriguez walked into the squad room and signed in.

"Rodriguez," bellowed O'Malley. "C'mere."

He waved Rodriguez into the chair. "Move those papers. Just throw them on the floor."

Rodriguez said, "No, thanks."

"Not friendly this morning, are we?"

"I'm in a hurry."

O'Malley said, "I want you to find the guy who nabbed this little *schwartze*. It's all yours. Night and day, baby, night and day. You unnerstand?"

"Yes," said Rodriguez evenly. "I understand."

"Well, that's good. I'll give you all the help I can." O'Malley sounded uneasy. With his hands folded on the edge of the desk in front of him, his bulk seemed less mobile than it was, fixed and Buddhalike, as he meditated on the scene before him.

"I'm gonna find him with or without your help," Rodriguez said evenly.

O'Malley looked up, his eyes bloodshot, his skin gray. He said, "Just find the cocksucker."

"Yessir," said Rodriguez, and walked out.

Rodriguez spent the morning in the most uncomfortable situation he had ever experienced as a police officer. Bobby Powers' mother was a smart, tough black woman in her early thirties, and she was angry.

Rodriguez met her at a table in the hospital cafeteria where she was eating breakfast. He had been warned by a nurse on the boy's floor that the woman blamed the police for what happened to her son, and had no intention of cooperating with the investigation.

With an indifference that chilled Rodriguez, the woman prepared to tell her story.

"Detective Rodriguez, I knew they'd send you around this morning. I'm going to tell you how I feel, and that'll be the end of the discussion."

There was nothing Rodriguez could say. He nodded, but he opened his notebook and prepared to take notes.

"Is this on the record?" she asked, surprised.

"Yes, of course," he said. "This is a major investigation."

"What I have to say to you is personal," she said.

"I understand, ma'am." He cocked his pen over the notebook.

"I don't want you to write it down."

"If I don't write it down, I won't be able to remember it accurately later, when I may need it. You might tell me something that could identify your son's assailant, something that may not make sense until days from now. I have to have it in writing." He paused, then added, "And if I ever appear in court in this case, I'll need accurate notes."

"Court?"

"Yes, of course. If we catch the assailant, and try him, or her."

"Her?" she asked. "You think a woman could have done this?"

"I'm not a psychologist, ma'am. I'm a cop. I think women can do anything men can do."

She stared across the table at him. "You bastard," she said. "You think I did it."

He looked back at her. In a surprised tone of voice, he said, "No, ma'am. I don't think anything of the sort. But it's important to have accurate records from the very beginning. What if I got pulled off this case for some reason, and some other detective was assigned to it?"

She was incredulous. She pushed her hands up across her deep brown face and massaged her scalp. She wore her hair in a short Afro. "You're threatening me. But you're being awfully nice about it. I've got an alibi, you know."

"I know where you were. I've already checked it."

"My Lord. The idea that I should say that at all!"

Rodriguez knew when to say nothing.

She looked at him. "They were awfully smart to send you. What do you want to know?"

"All I really want is permission to interview your son. I want to reassure you that there will be no publicity, for your son's sake. And I want to ask you a few questions."

She nodded her agreement, and Rodriguez began asking her

about her son's friends, his school experiences, their old uptown neighborhood, how he went to school and came home, where he played after school and on weekends, when he saw his father, where they went, and on, and on, for an hour and a half. Were there any friends in East Harlem? He read her the description given by Mrs. Sanchez, and drew a blank. Mrs. Perry had never seen such a man. Finally he stopped. She was exhausted.

She gave him little he could use, but what she told him eliminated in his mind the possibility that someone other than the psychopath had assaulted her son. Rodriguez knew the key was whether or not the boy was able to give an accurate description of his attacker. Most children the boy's age were vague about descriptions. They tended to describe people they knew, rather than the person actually involved.

They went upstairs. The doctor walked out of the boy's room as they approached, and said she was taking him off the critical list. The boy's mother leaned against the green hospital wall and began to weep in relief and exhaustion.

The boy called out, "Mama, is that you?"

The doctor put her arm around the woman's shoulders and led her into the room.

"Mama, I'm all right now," said the boy. "The doctor said so."

"This little boy has what people used to call a strong constitution," the doctor said. "And he's very brave. He really is going to be all right."

"When I peeked in here this morning," said the mother, "you were sound asleep, and I didn't want to wake you. I've been here all night and all morning."

The boy lay on his back. There were tubes in his nostrils and arms. A urine bag fed by a catheter hung from the side of the bed.

Rodriguez motioned the doctor outside the room. "How is he?"

"Well enough to talk for a few minutes. He's lightly sedated and in a little pain, but he's not in bad shape."

"What about his wounds?"

"Well, his penis is gone, but none of the stab wounds were as serious as we thought. No vital organs were hit. The problem

182

was some internal bleeding we didn't catch the first time. He'll be out of here in a week or ten days."

"Does he know?"

"Yes. He seems to take it very well. I'm no shrink, but I think this is a very healthy kid."

"The boy's principal at school thinks the kid is withdrawn."

The doctor shrugged her shoulders. She had pale skin and dark hair. Rodriguez thought she was attractive. She said, "I think this kid's in good shape."

Rodriguez went back into the room. He let the mother introduce him to the boy, then sat down and asked cautiously if the boy could describe exactly what happened.

Fifteen minutes later, Rodriguez walked out of the room. He was stunned. The boy had given him, in a calm and matter-of-fact manner, a detailed account of the assault and a complete description of the assailant. The boy was perfectly self-confident.

In nearly every way, the description matched the Sanchez description. Rodriguez was jubilant. Now they knew what the guy looked like, and Rodriguez was certain that the guy lived somewhere in the immediate neighborhood. There was only one problem. The boy had described his attacker as "white."

It was four o'clock in the afternoon and the shift was changing at the Two-Four. But no one was moving. Men in their streetclothes crowded around the foot of the stairs to the second floor. A few firemen stood in the doorway from the attached firehouse.

Captain Ryan, the uniformed precinct commander, burst in the outer doors. Someone had called him on the radio.

"What the hell's going on here?" he shouted. "Last tour, go home. Four o'clock tour, get dressed and stand in formation or I'll have every one of you on charges. *Move,* goddammit. Sergeant Bari, *get this place shaped up right now!*"

The captain forced his way through toward the stairs. "Move," he said to one man. "You're out of uniform," he said to another. "Go home," he said to a third. He pushed his way through like a cop pushing through a small mob on the street. He shoved hard and used his elbows.

The men at the head of the stairs were all detectives from the squad rooms of the detective division. This was not really Captain Ryan's turf, but the men moved quickly out of his way as he thumped up the stairs. They opened an aisle leading to O'Malley's office door.

The sounds of a violent argument came from the office.

O'Malley's voice roared, "Charges?"

The contents of the top of the desk hit the wall and floor. An ashtray bounced and shattered. "You're gonna bring charges?"

A desk chair rolled violently across the floor and shattered the glass front of a bookcase. "You fucken spic! If you bring charges against me, I'll find charges against you so bad, they'll hang you from the first fucken lamppost they find, and every other goddamn PR on this force with you."

Another chair slammed back against a wall. Rodriguez shouted, "I'm gonna kill you, you motherfucker, if you ever say the word *spic* again."

Ryan jerked the door open.

"*SPIC!*" roared O'Malley.

Ryan's right hand slammed Rodriguez into the corner of the little room. With his left foot, he kicked the desk forward, shoving it against O'Malley and pinning him to the wall. The corner of the desk caught O'Malley in the groin, and he slammed forward onto the desk top in pain.

"*Don't move!*" roared Ryan.

No one even breathed.

Ryan yelled, "Lieutenant Condello, on the double!"

A young and trim uniformed lieutenant came up the stairs three at a time.

"Yessir."

"Stand the whole goddamned precinct in formation downstairs, including these men up here." Ryan waved his hand around at the detectives.

"Yessir."

"*Now!*"

"Yessir!" Condello turned and began herding the reluctant detectives down the stairs.

Ryan said, "Rodriguez, report to me in my office immediately."

184

Rodriguez took his hand off the butt of his revolver, lifted the crumpled pages of a report from the floor, and left the room in silence.

Ryan slammed the door, pulled the desk away from O'Malley, and said in a voice loaded with anger and menace, "Now, O'Malley, what the hell's your problem? This is a police station, not a goddamned Irish saloon."

chapter twelve
charlie chopoff

    ' Mrs. Aida Harold was a teacher's aide. She stood on the sidewalk in front of PS 145 watching a group of sixth-grade boys and girls running and laughing up the sidewalk from Amsterdam Avenue. Her white blouse was soaked through with sweat. It felt like the hottest day of the year. She wiped her face and neck with a damp handkerchief and wished she'd worn her straw hat to keep the sun off her head.

    From the roof of the school three floors above came the cries of children playing after lunch. The school's only playground was a huge cage of chain-link fence with a roof of chicken wire on top of the building. It served its purpose, but it was unnerving to hear the sound of a basketball or kickball rattle against the chain links three floors up. Mrs. Harold always looked up, expecting to see a falling body, but then she always reminded herself that it was the safest playground in the neighborhood because only the pupils in the school could get into it.

    The older children—the fifth- and sixth-graders—were allowed to go two blocks up Amsterdam to play in a corner of the large playground behind Booker T. Washington Junior High School. Two or three teachers went with them, but they slipped away for a cup of coffee. Mrs. Harold covered for them by waiting in front of the school for the children to get inside.

    The children were laughing wildly as they ran for the door. They pointed and screeched at one boy walking slowly up the sidewalk from the corner. As they ran inside, the woman realized the boy was crying. She knew the boy. He was in her class. She hurried toward him down the sidewalk, saying, "Roger. Roger, honey. What's wrong? Did you get hurt? What happened?"

He was carrying something. She was nearsighted, and didn't realize what he had in his hand until she came up close to him. It was partly wrapped in a paper napkin. She clapped her hand over her mouth with horror. She thought he had cut his finger off.

She began screaming, "Mr. Wilson, Mr. Wilson." She grabbed the sobbing boy by the arm and dragged him into the hall.

Wilson came running from the office at the other end of the long hall, kept dark to save electricity. In her anxiety, she did not hear the boy saying over and over, "It's not my finger."

Wilson realized immediately what it was. He sent Mrs. Harold to his office to wait for him, and took the boy into the nurse's office down the hall. There was no nurse, nurses having been laid off several years before.

Wilson locked the door behind them, turned on the lights, and sat the boy gently down in a chair. Wilson himself kept the room clean, and kept the supplies in stock. He reached into a cabinet and took out a metal instrument pan, disengaged the object from the boy's hand, and dropped it in the pan. He covered it with a paper towel.

"Now tell me, Roger," said Mr. Wilson. "Tell me exactly where you found this."

The boy sobbed out the story. He and his classmates were playing kick-the-can in their corner of the playground.

"Which corner?" asked Wilson. "The corner nearest Amsterdam and 107th?"

The boy nodded. Some girls were jumping rope, and one of them screamed. The boys ran to see what was wrong, and then they all began to jump and scream about the man's finger on the ground.

"I knew it wasn't no finger," said the boy softly. "So I picked it up in that napkin to bring to you. Then they all began to tease me and laugh at me."

"Do you know what it is?" asked Wilson.

"Yes, sir."

"What is it?"

"A penis."

"Do you know where it came from?"

"No sir, but there's lots of voodoo men around here."

"Do the other children know what you found?"

"Yes."

"How do you know?"

"Because they calling me Doctor Pecker."

Wilson sighed. By nightfall, the entire neighborhood would know. Mrs. Perry's earnest desire to keep her son's terrible wound a secret would be a joke.

"It belongs to that little third-grader, don't it?" asked Roger.

"What third-grader?"

"You know. The one they found on the roof the day before yesterday, all cut up. He's in St. Luke's." The boy looked cautiously at the big, gentle man and added quickly, "That's what the teachers say."

Wilson said, "Yes, there is a boy from our school in St. Luke's, but I don't know if this . . ." He hesitated, annoyed with himself that he could not be forthright. Then he finished his sentence. ". . . article belongs to him."

Wilson thought in silence for a moment, then he said, "You did the right thing, Roger. In fact, you did a brave thing, to stand up to the ridicule of your classmates like you did. I'm proud of you."

The boy looked back at him, then away, stunned and disturbed by his discovery, and what it signified.

Wilson said, "I want you to do something for me. There's a very nice cop I want you to talk to. You can be a big help to him. And I want you to promise me not to talk about this to anyone but your mother and father. I'm going to give you a note to take home, asking them to call me in the morning. Will you do these things?"

"Yes."

The impact of the discovery was sinking in to both man and boy. "Why don't you come down to my office with me?" Wilson suggested. "You can spend the rest of the afternoon helping me with paperwork."

The boy nodded. Wilson was amazed at the superficial equilibrium children maintained in the face of chaos and violence, but as they walked down the hall together, Wilson put his large hand on the boy's little back. The child felt as fragile as a leaf.

There has to be a limit, thought Wilson, an end to what these little children can absorb in this dying, broken-down old neighborhood. And he knew there was no end, that the greatest burdens fell on the backs of those who could still see and hear what was going on around them.

Then a thought struck Wilson with particular force. It took him by surprise because he did not think of himself as a believer in the platitudes of religion. He thought, it's the little children who suffer most. They get a glimpse of what it must be like to be free and whole. Then the vision is taken away. No wonder they get so angry. They're treated like saints and angels when they're young, then dogs when they get older.

As they neared the end of the hall, the boy took Wilson's hand. In the darkness, it was hard to tell who was leading who.

"You found the kid's dick?" asked O'Malley, deeply amused. "In the playground?"

It was another late afternoon in O'Malley's office. A confrontation was brewing like a thunderstorm. The men in the outer office had their ears cocked.

"What were you doing in the playground, Sergeant? Jumping rope?"

Rodriguez seemed to have achieved a Zen-like level of acceptance. He sat calmly with one ankle balanced on the other knee, waiting for O'Malley to ask a question he could answer.

O'Malley imitated a faint smile. "How big was it? Was it a little black dick, or a big black cock?"

"It was the dried-out, shriveled-up little penis of an eight-year-old kid, Lieutenant."

"Can they sew it back on?"

"Of course not."

"How do they know this thing belongs to the kid?"

"Tooth marks."

O'Malley said, "I guess that's all you need to know."

"I sent it to the Medical Examiner."

O'Malley stared in disbelief, then roared with laughter. "An autopsy," he cried. "They're gonna do an autopsy on a dead dick."

Rodriguez waited patiently for the laughter to subside. Heads shook and glances were exchanged in the squad room.

"What else do you want, Rodriguez?"

"I want to move the boy to another hospital. I think the killer might make another pass at him."

O'Malley said nothing.

Rodriguez said, "Lieutenant, we now have three descriptions —the old newsdealer in the Thomas case, Mrs. Sanchez, and Bobby Powers."

O'Malley raised three fingers and bent them down one by one. "One. The newsdealer gave a lousy description. It's a description of a skinny ass in a bag of dirty clothes. You wanna chase every scumbag in Harlem? Take a vacation and do it on your own time.

"Two. Sanchez described a dark-skinned guy with a Dominican accent. You could pick up half the spics in this neighborhood with that description."

O'Malley paused like an experienced public speaker and waited for a reaction from his audience, but there was none.

"Three. This kid said the guy was white. That ain't black, and it ain't a black Dominican. So you got three different descriptions. Now get this straight, Rodriguez."

Rodriguez waited attentively for the word from the mountaintop.

"I will not alarm this neighborhood by authorizing the distribution of a description based on the words of a frightened kid. Nor will I release a description of a possibly harmless individual described by an illegal immigrant, this old lady who you refuse to identify to a superior officer."

Rodriguez stood up.

O'Malley went on. "You've got two killings and one assault, in different neighborhoods. You've got three partial and unreliable descriptions. One of which has absolutely nothing to do with the killings or the assault. We've gone through this once already. You've got some superficial similarities in MO, but you don't have one fucking witness."

Rodriguez said, "We have one living witness who gave us what I regard as an extremely reliable description. We have a very good sketch from an Identikit. And you have a neighborhood that's getting jumpy. They know someone's running around killing little boys. As you're aware, Lieutenant, there's a grapevine in the schools, and the stories of the Thomas and Jefferson killings have reached this side of town."

O'Malley said, "Let me give you a rudimentary lesson in police management, Sergeant, which I'm sure you'll be happy to know when they make you a lieutenant and give you a squad. Don't assign good dicks to bad cases."

O'Malley chuckled. Rodriguez nodded with polite appreciation.

"In other words, don't throw good money after bad," said O'Malley. "You assign the rummies and dummies to cases that aren't gonna get anywhere. You're not dumb, Rodriguez. You're the best I've got. You've got two weeks on this Bobby Powers case. Find some leads or get off the case. Go out and do some work for a change."

"Yessir," said Rodriguez, and walked out. O'Malley watched as Rodriguez walked to his desk in the far corner of the squad room and reached for his telephone.

In O'Malley's experience most sergeants liked to pretend they were lieutenants. Therefore they picked desks out of sight of the lieutenant so they could operate with the maximum possible autonomy. And that was fine with most job-wise lieutenants, because it meant the sergeants bothered them less. It now occurred to O'Malley for the first time that Sergeant Rodriguez had picked a desk in his direct line of sight, and that he had done it deliberately, to keep an eye on Lieutenant O'Malley.

For whom? O'Malley was now watching a blip closing in on his radar screen. O'Malley picked up his own phone.

"How did it go?" asked Nieman over the telephone.

Rodriguez scooted his chair into the corner and lifted

his feet to his desk. He sighted O'Malley over his shoes. He watched O'Malley dial a number, then stand up and look down through his window at the playground outside while he talked.

"He gave me two weeks on this Bobby Powers case."

"Good," said Nieman. "He's afraid to pull you off it."

"What do you want me to do?" asked Rodriguez. He was surprised at his own sense of relief at having made the decision to put himself under Nieman's direction, or rather, having the decision made for him by the assault on Bobby Powers.

Nieman said, "I want you to work twenty hours a day for the next two weeks. You've got the perfect opportunity to kill two birds with one stone. You're gonna burrow into that neighborhood like a mole to find the psychopath. At the same time, you can dig up O'Malley's connections on the Upper West Side."

"OK. OK. Don't beat me over the head with it."

"Listen, Danny, if your boss just gave you two weeks, mine just gave me two months. There is now an urgency here that didn't exist before."

Rodriguez felt a trace of annoyance. He pulled his desk calendar toward him. "I've had a sense of urgency since last winter about finding this killer," he said.

"This is different," said Nieman.

Rodriguez peered closely at the desk calendar. He put his finger on the first Tuesday in November. Two months ahead. Election Day.

"Yeah," said Rodriguez. "Anything else?"

"Keep in touch."

Rodriguez hung up. Wheels within wheels, he thought. Everybody has their own little private agenda. He decided it was time he had one, too.

At ten-thirty the next morning, a third-grader walked cautiously into the boy's room on the second floor of PS 165. These were places of harassment and danger for the smaller kids. Most of the teachers in the elementary school were women, and they never entered the boy's rooms unless there was serious trouble. Run-of-the-mill fear in the mind of an eight-year-old was not serious trouble.

It was dog-eat-dog in the boy's rooms, but this third-grader was experienced and wary. He checked it out. He made sure the hallway door was chocked open. He gave the wooden wedge under the door a light kick to be sure it was tight. He stooped down and peered along the floor under the walls between the stalls. There were no feet showing. He sniffed the air like a rabbit leaving the safety of a hedge for the dangers of the open field. There was no telltale cigarette smoke, and none of the sweetish smell of the weak joints smoked by the sixth-graders. He listened. It was silent, almost peaceful. The brown and white tile and the porcelain fixtures made it seem damp and cool in the September heat; and at this early hour, it was still clean.

The boy stuck his hall pass, a little wooden stick marked with his room number, in the back pocket of his Levis, and stepped all the way inside. He flapped the soles of his sneakers loudly as he stepped, hoping the noise would smoke out anyone hiding in the back corner. There was no response.

He stepped in further and walked to one of the low urinals. He relaxed. He unzipped his pants and began to pee. He aimed the stream around the inside of the fixture, and made bubbles in the little pool of water at the bottom.

As he zipped up and reached to flush the urinal, he heard a terrible scream behind him. He whirled in mortal terror and saw a fifth-grader with a face like a nightmare leaping at him from one of the stalls. The kid had obviously been standing on the toilet, waiting for his victim.

"Yeeaahh," screamed the tormentor. "I'm Charlie Chopoff and I'm gonna chop your little cock off."

The third-grader leapt sideways into the hall in two bounds and fled screaming. The fifth-grader fled the other way, convulsed in giggles and laughter.

That was all it took. By nightfall, the name Charlie Chopoff had reached every sidewalk and playground between 96th and 110th Streets on the West Side. The stories about the boy in the hospital and the "finger" in the playground spread everywhere, too, getting more grisly and detailed with each retelling.

Mrs. Perry heard the story on her front stoop as she arrived home from the hospital late that evening. She went upstairs and wept in her dark kitchen from anger, frustration, and fear. She knew they would have to move again.

The killer heard the story as he stood on the sidewalk of Amsterdam Avenue in front of the little Dominican *bodega* where he was watching a game of dominoes. To his ears, it was true in its essential elements. He felt a thrill of fear run through his body like an electric shock. He finished his bottle of beer and wandered away from the group, around the corner onto 109th Street, and down toward his house.

When he got there, he was afraid to go in. Someone might be there looking for him. He walked the rest of the way down the long block to Columbus Avenue, bought an eight-pack of beer, and went around the block to the little park below his bedroom window. He sat there in the dark for two hours, watching some older boys play handball in the playground by the light of a streetlight. Then he went upstairs and went to bed.

For the first time, more than a handful of cops and school officials knew there was a psychopath running around upper Manhattan. And now the killer had a terrible name that described what he did with terrible accuracy. More than anything else, it was the name that fueled the rumors and created the agitated excitement in the neighborhood streets.

The complex web of mothers and teachers—all the guardians of children in the neighborhood—began to hum and vibrate. Women took their children to school and picked them up in the afternoon. They went to the playgrounds with them and stopped sending them to the stores alone. They talked, and the talk spread. It reached the ears of various officials downtown. From downtown, phone calls began to reach back uptown.

Not surprisingly, O'Malley was able to keep a lid on the press. The city's three newspapers did very little real crime reporting anymore. It was said that the prestigious New York *Times* no longer bothered to maintain a repeater for the police department teletype in its city room. They relied instead on the public relations apparatus of the police to inform them when a major crime took place. The *Daily News* no longer had its little army of runners and legmen visiting the precincts, bearing gifts to ensure they would be the first to know when a newsworthy crime occurred. The *Post*, perfectly happy to make an ordinary murder into the crime of the year when it suited the editors, was so understaffed that it simply wasn't on the grapevine anymore.

Nonetheless, O'Malley got some calls. They were softballs and he hit them right out of the park.

"Sammy," he said to the *Times* reporter, "how would you like it if someone cut your cock off and every half-assed reporter in town began writing about it?"

"C'mon, Jerry," he said in his most oily tone to the guy from the *Post*. "You've got a couple kids yourself. Give this kid a break. His mother is dyin' inside for the poor little boy. What're you gonna do, break her heart? Ruin his life? What kind of a prick are ya?"

To his old pal from the *Daily News,* calling from his favorite bar, O'Malley said, "Frannie, did I ever steer you wrong? . . . Did I ever jerk you off? . . . So I'm tellin you, Francis, this is not a story. No one else is goin' with it, and if you do, I'm not gonna be home anymore when you call from some fucken bar and want me to write your little stories for ya. . . . OK, Frannie. You're a real sweetheart. I owe ya a big one."

And that was it. That was the end of the joke. There were no stories in the daily papers. The wire services, if they ever heard the rumors, ignored them because they didn't cover local stories, or at least, didn't cover stories local to Harlem and West 107th Street. And the radio–TV assignment editors never heard a word. For them, if it wasn't on the wires or in the papers, it didn't exist.

The mothers of the neighborhood were agitated and worried, but powerless. Without the power of journalism to illuminate and expose, not much would happen. In New York City, there were over 1700 homicides every year, about five each day. A mere assault, no matter how ugly, stood little chance of energetic investigation, and apparently no chance of attention from the Mayor or the police brass.

When O'Malley arrived at the Gold Rail at noon, he learned two things right away. One: Franco Ayala was in the bar, because his maroon Buick was parked out front on Broadway. Two: The meeting was going to be short, because the car was double-parked.

He hadn't expected to see Ayala, and the gleaming car lit a warning light in O'Malley's mind. He parked his car by a fire hydrant in the next block and walked slowly back down Broadway. He spotted one of Ayala's bodyguards across Broadway from the bar, in the shade of a restaurant awning. Ayala's driver sat upright in the Buick, alert, not half-asleep as usual. Ayala usually moved around town with no one but his driver. When he wanted more muscle, he added men in twos, for some reason. Where the hell was the third?

At the corner just above the entrance to the bar, O'Malley turned in his tracks. Number three was in the doorway of a little Oriental gift shop.

O'Malley figured three was the limit today, and he had them spotted. Five of these guys would be enough for a war. He loosened his gun.

The Gold Rail was entered through an alcove at the left of a large window. The front had the look of an old neighborhood tavern. Ayala sat inside the front door, on the bar stool by the front window, in full view of the crowded sunny street. He wore a straw Panama, a red Hawaiian shirt with white flowers printed on it, white slacks, and white shoes.

There were three empty stools to Ayala's left. He motioned with his cigar for O'Malley to sit next to him. A finger pointed at the bartender brought fresh Scotch for Ayala. O'Malley ordered vodka on the rocks.

Ayala handed O'Malley a fresh Cuban cigar, waving it under the detective's nose before he relinquished it. "Your friend Hanratty won't be here. I thought I'd come myself." Ayala was calm and pleasant as he held a lighter for O'Malley's cigar. "I thought I'd come myself because I want to impress you with the importance of what I have to say.

"First, a little theory. I'm sure you understand, Lieutenant, the principle that any organization must work with the material it has at hand."

O'Malley nodded. He thought better of saying, let's cut the

197

crap and get on with it. He puffed his cigar and sipped his taste-less drink.

"In my case, O'Malley, I have to work with you."

O'Malley's teeth gripped the cigar like the teeth of a dog trained not to break the skin of the duck.

Ayala said, "You blew it with Detective Rodriguez. I gave you a couple chances, then I was forced to make my own approach."

"You blew it, too," said O'Malley. "And half a city block with it."

"I was getting rid of an obsolete factory." Ayala had an arrogant, easy smile on his face, like an industrialist who had just closed a steel mill in Youngstown. "I've decided to be charitable," he continued. "You're a man of unquestionable talents, for which I pay you well, and which I continue to need. Is our relationship satisfactory, my friend?" inquired Ayala. His voice carried the solicitude of a KGB interrogator in a Moscow basement.

O'Malley squinted down the length of the very fine cigar. He saw the network of widely spaced veins and its unblemished, sea-green color.

"Yeah," he said. "I have no complaints."

"Good," said Ayala. "I have a job for you."

"What is it?"

"You might call this a political assassination."

O'Malley raised his eyebrows and turned on his stool to see the other man's face. "Politics is an expensive business," said O'Malley.

"You owe me something," said Ayala, "but I won't cheap you on this job. It's too important."

"How much?"

"Two thousand down. Three more on delivery."

"OK."

"The target is Mercedes Lopez."

"No," said O'Malley. "I won't do it."

"You goddamn sure will."

"No," smiled O'Malley. "Not for five thousand."

Ayala laughed and slapped O'Malley on the back. "You're

right, my friend. Politics is very expensive. Make it ten, half down and half on completion."

"Done," said O'Malley. "When?"

"By the beginning of October. That's a little more than two weeks. Take your time, and do it right."

"You don't need to tell me that," said O'Malley. He slid off his stool and dropped the expensive Cuban cigar on the floor, grinding it out with his toe. "Why all the muscle?" he asked. "Expecting trouble?"

"Not from you," said Ayala.

O'Malley was hungry. He parked in front of a Lebanese deli at 111th and Broadway and walked into the store. There was a long line of people, mostly students waiting for take-out service. O'Malley stepped to the front of the line and ordered a ham and cheese on rye with mustard, pickle, and a Coke. When the counterman handed him the order, he took the bag and walked out of the store without a word. The woman at the cash register rolled her eyes at the ceiling and said "pig" in Arabic under her breath.

O'Malley ate his lunch in his car, throwing the garbage onto the floor on the passenger side. As he ate, he thought.

There was nothing orderly or understandable about the situation. Ayala and Hanratty were in command of more information than he was, and they had their own reasons for doing things. O'Malley knew Ayala's real business was Cuban politics, not narcotics. O'Malley didn't care as long as he could make money on it.

He ate his sandwich and watched the loose breasts of young women in tee shirts. He thought the way was not clear to making much more money. He felt threatened. He felt like he was losing control. He knew exactly what the penalties were. He sat in the steaming car on the noisy street, and fixed his mind on the problem with the vise grip of the jaws of an alligator.

In O'Malley's universe, the simplest way to eliminate a threat was to eliminate the source. As he chewed, he identified the sources. First, there was the killer. O'Malley knew perfectly well that Rodriguez was right to guess the same man attacked the three boys. The existence of the killer now threatened to disrupt O'Malley's control of his turf. He was in a double bind. He hadn't wanted his dereliction in the first two murders exposed, but now he was forced to acknowledge the higher costs of letting the killer run free. If the neighborhood got out of hand, O'Malley would not be able to work for Ayala.

O'Malley slumped down in his seat behind the wheel. He reached above the visor and pulled out a stale, dried-out Dutch Masters corona. He lit it and considered the problem further.

He was faced by another threat—Rodriguez. Rodriguez was a threat because he was an independent son of a bitch and probably working for someone downtown. O'Malley had no real cause for this suspicion, but his paranoia was a highly developed instinct that had always served him well in the past.

The first problem was to eliminate the killer. The second and third problems were Rodriguez and Lopez. O'Malley could attack those problems at the same time.

They're still screwing, he knew, and then the thought occurred to him that Rodriguez was working with Lopez, not someone downtown, and that he was also involved in the Puerto Rican underground. The FALN! he thought. If I hit Lopez first, I'll have Rodriguez after me, and every crazy spic in the city.

He slumped further down behind the wheel, until only his eyes and gray hair could be seen. He puffed and chewed on the stale cigar, and wished he'd saved the good Cuban cigar Ayala gave him. I'll have to hit Rodriguez before I go after Lopez. That smart fucker Ayala knows it, too. He's getting two for one. O'Malley reached for the ignition, and cranked and kicked the beaten car into motion. He pulled into traffic and drove slowly down Broadway.

At 107th Street, he turned right and drove down the short block to the corner by the Children's Mansion. He double-parked and watched the gray-white limestone building for a few minutes. He meditated on his problems and their solutions. Then he drove back to Broadway, found a phone booth, and told his office he would be out for the afternoon.

He drove down to 105th Street and walked into an ancient, unkempt candy store where he bought a handful of fresh cigars. When he left the store, he almost ran across the sidewalk to his car. First, eliminate the killer. Second, eliminate Rodriguez. Third, hit Lopez.

chapter thirteen
bud's place

"I'm looking for a dark-skinned Hispanic male, age twenty to thirty, height five five to five ten, slender build, pock-marked face, possibly a bad limp in one leg. Wears army surplus clothing all the time. You ever seen him?"

The bartender frowned. "No," he said. "I don't think so."

O'Malley pulled a photocopied Identikit sketch out of his inner pocket. "Ever seen this guy here?" It was a sketch of the same man O'Malley had just described.

"No. Never seen this guy. Never around here."

"Well, call me if you do," said O'Malley. "He might show up." O'Malley hoisted himself onto the barstool in the dark, cool bar. "And gimme a rye and ginger, willya?"

It was the end of the afternoon. O'Malley had covered nearly every bar, candy store, *bodega,* and numbers parlor between East 116th Street and East 125th. It was an uncomfortable, muggy day, but he felt like a kid. He felt so good that he paid for the drink.

There was no one in the empty bar to talk to, so he talked to himself in his head, looking at his reflection in the darkened mirror behind the rows of bottles over the bar. He felt relaxed. He had begun his search back in his old East Harlem command, where his best sources lurked. They hadn't forgotten him. Over the years, he'd done a lot of favors for a lot of people. He held a lot of IOUs. He knew he relied too much on these obligations.

He had let his cop's skills rust and his instincts atrophy. If he had been alert, things would not have gotten out of hand. But now, for the first time in years, he was playing detective. He felt fantastic. He smiled at himself in the mirror.

By ten that night, O'Malley eliminated the possibility that an East Harlem resident had committed the murders and the assault. Knowledge of the crimes was widespread, but there were no stories on the street about any killer, no whispers, not a trace of a hint. He started looking for transients and travelers. This was the hard part, but the old alligator in action was a formidable machine.

At ten the next morning, O'Malley was back on the streets. Ten hours later, he sat in his parked car under the Park Avenue railroad tracks at East 116th Street. The noise and bustle of *La Marqueta* surrounded him. The nearby streets and the spaces under the tracks were filled with pushcarts and open-air storefronts and stalls. It was the hub of Spanish-speaking East Harlem.

It was a soft September evening at nightfall. Women shopped and talked, followed by their men and children. Most of the stores were still open.

O'Malley was eating a *pastillo*—a meat-filled pastry—and drinking ice-cold beer from a can in a brown paper bag. He was fuming with frustration and anger. The trail was cold. The scent was gone.

The hell with it, he thought suddenly. It's enough for today. He dropped the half-finished food and beer out the car window, and pulled away from the curb. He drove a few blocks over to Second Avenue and turned south.

Just past the corner, he suddenly swerved into a bus stop and slammed on his brakes with a screech. He leaned over and shouted out the passenger window, "Come over here, motherfucker, I've been looking for you all day. *Move!*"

An emaciated young man in a long-sleeved stretch shirt and skin-tight, silver and black pants walked slowly over to the car. He looked like a pretty young male dancer, but he made no effort to hide the needle marks in the veins on the backs of his hands.

He leaned in the car window with his elbows on the door.

"Lieutenant," he said, in an effeminate voice that infuriated O'Malley.

"Get in, shitface," said O'Malley.

The young man laughed. "The same old Lieutenant. He expects for free what everybody else pays for."

"Get in!"

"No." The young man looked nervously over his shoulder. His two friends had disappeared. When he looked back, he saw the dull gleam of O'Malley's gun. He shivered visibly, opened the door and got in. He was shaking like the last leaf on an autumn tree. O'Malley hit him in the face with the gun.

They cruised slowly back and forth on the side streets, weaving down through one of the worst and most abandoned neighborhoods of East Harlem.

A raw bruise showed on the young man's left forehead. In the morning, it would be the same color as the gun barrel that made it.

"Angel," said O'Malley softly.

"Si?"

"Have you ever seen this man?" O'Malley handed him the photocopy of the police sketch.

"No, never."

"Do you know about the murders of the little boys over here last spring?"

"Yes."

"Do you know who did it?"

"No. Nobody knows."

They drove in silence. O'Malley reached into his pocket and handed the young man a ten-dollar bill.

"This is the last time," said O'Malley.

Angel touched the bruise on his forehead. "You said that the last time."

"How's the dope business?"

"Rough," said Angel. "People say there will be a lot of shooting soon."

O'Malley drove very slowly along East 105th Street. Angel pointed out some social clubs in a row of abandoned brownstones. The clubs had names like *Rosita Blanca, Pacifica, Madrid.*

205

"Where are all the girls?" asked O'Malley with sudden concentration.

Angel shifted nervously toward the door. "There are no girls here. They are all fairies."

He giggled. The giggle was a mistake.

O'Malley exploded. "Fags," he screamed. He slammed on the brakes in the middle of the street. With his right hand he grabbed the back of Angel's head and slammed it forward with the momentum of the car into the dashboard.

Angel's face burst with a crunch. Blood splashed all over.

"You faggot," screamed O'Malley. "Where do they get their dope? Where do they get their fucking smack?"

Through broken teeth, Angel whimpered, "Someone from the West Side."

"Who?" screamed O'Malley, completely out of control, shaking the other man like a rag doll.

"From Manhattan Avenue. A *latino*." Angel coughed and gagged.

O'Malley reached across and opened the passenger door. He shoved Angel out and stepped on the gas. Angel screamed. The car door slammed by itself. People watched silently from doors and windows. The broken informer was as good as dead, when word spread. Some of the watchers knew O'Malley.

Now O'Malley had the first hint. A Latin runner, he thought. A spic runner from Manhattan Avenue. He drove down to East 102nd Street and through the East River Houses to a barrier at the edge of the FDR Drive at the East River. He parked and stared over the speeding traffic at the dark water. He was charged up by the violence. There were a lot of runners on the West Side, but he could narrow the choices pretty fast. One thing still puzzled him: there was little reason for any Hispanic to wander through the black neighborhoods the two boys were killed in.

He watched the glow of lights in the hundreds of windows in the huge, square-sided buildings that formed Manhattan State Hospital on Ward's Island in the middle of the river. His eyes followed the long, graceful path of the footbridge that led from Ward's Island, across the river and over the FDR Drive, ending on the Manhattan side in a double helix of pedestrian ramps in front of O'Malley's car.

He was staring at his answer. He knew the city's hospitals were hotspots for an elite narcotics trade. He formed a map of upper Manhattan in his mind. The East and West Sides were linked all the way across town by 96th, 110th, and 125th Streets. He pawed through the glove compartment of the car, through old coffee lids, crumpled napkins, lists of stolen cars, until he found a street map of the city. The upper shoulder of Manhattan was loaded with hospitals, and the Hospital for Joint Diseases was right by Mount Morris Park, one block in each direction from the homes of the first two victims.

There was one more place he could go. There was a junkie's bar called Bud's Place on the ground floor of the building on upper Fifth Avenue where the second boy was killed. O'Malley knew the bartender who owned the place. He owed O'Malley some big favors.

Over the door was a chipped tin sign that said "Bud's Place" in blue and red. It was lit by a weak incandescent bulb in an old fixture with a broken, rusted shade. It looked like a sign from an Alabama roadhouse before Prohibition.

Inside it was nearly dark except for dim lights over two small booths in the back and several weak lamps on the shelf behind the bar, which held a short line of whiskey and wine bottles. Bud's Place was a dump.

It was crowded, hot, and noisy. O'Malley walked to the back of the bar. As soon as the old black bartender could get free, he set down a shot of rye and a glass of ice water. O'Malley drank both without comment, and leaned forward.

"First Sergeant," said O'Malley. "You know anything about the kid upstairs?"

First Sergeant was the only name anybody ever called this man, although O'Malley knew his real name and a lot more. There hadn't been anyone named Bud associated with the bar in living memory.

"Not much," said First Sergeant. He set refills down in front of O'Malley, and a shot of rye and a glass of beer for himself.

"How much?" asked O'Malley.

The old man said, "They only lived here a couple months. Came here from Brooklyn, and moved back after the kid was killed. She had a boyfriend here, but he ran out. She used to come in here pretty regular. Took guys upstairs with her pretty regular, too."

"Different guys?"

"Mostly. None special. Some of them are in here tonight. You wanna talk to them?"

"Naw. What about the kid?"

"He was a kid. Came in here looking for his mama now and then, not too often. The big sister took care of the kids. You know how it is, Eddie."

O'Malley grunted and downed his second drink. He didn't flinch at the familiar use of his name. He knew First Sergeant from way back. He considered himself lucky, because First Sergeant knew as much about the street life of black East Harlem as anyone. When the old man heard something he thought O'Malley ought to know, he left a message—"Bud called."

O'Malley had no idea what motivated the man's loyalty, but over the years he'd given the cop good tips. O'Malley had stumbled into the bar for the first time one hot summer night in 1955, when he was canvassing door to door in a shooting on this same block. He sat down on the first stool by the door, ordered rye and ice water, and paid for it. It was the first time a white cop had ever paid First Sergeant for a drink in his bar. After a few more drinks and a quiet talk, First Sergeant told O'Malley that the shooter was sitting in the back booth facing the door. O'Malley agreed not to make the collar in the bar. He paid up and left.

An hour later, the shooter left the bar and walked down the block to the corner, heading for the darkness of Mount Morris Park. Before he knew what had happened, he was lying on his face in the back seat of O'Malley's car, his hands cuffed painfully behind his back. In the station house, O'Malley beat a confession out of him and closed the case.

That was the beginning of a long and fruitful relationship between First Sergeant and O'Malley. Now, as the old bartender came back down the bar after serving some customers,

O'Malley pulled out the photocopy. "Show this around, will you?" he asked. "Tell them the guy is PR or Dominican, dark-skinned, bad leg."

First Sergeant held the wrinkled page under the dim light by the cash register. When he turned back to O'Malley, he had a funny look on his dark, wrinkled face. "No need to show this around." he said. "I know this man. He comes in here now and then for a beer."

The old man looked around. "Come back in the kitchen. Nobody in here to worry about, but I don't want them to hear what I got to say to you."

The kitchen looked like it hadn't cooked a meal in the last century. "I know you a long time, Eddie, and I'm surprised at you."

"What do you mean?"

"You don't know this man?"

"Why the hell would I ask if I did?"

They were alone in the kitchen with the roaches and rats, but the old man looked around and took a step closer.

"This man works for the same man you work for . . . when you ain't working, if you get what I mean."

O'Malley was struck dumb.

"You don't have to say anything to me, but I hear things," said First Sergeant. "I hear it all. This man works for your man Ayala, that Cuban. This man comes by here every two, three, four days bringing dope to the hospitals round here. He's got a route like a milkman."

In a week of bitter fighting and tearful pleadings, Rodriguez and Mercedes had lashed themselves to the helm of the ship of their lives, as she put it one night. They would go where wind and weather took them. And there would be no abortion.

He had begun by forcing her to talk about her political beliefs, then her political work, and then the deeper politics of allegiances and enemies. He began the process, but she ended by trying to recruit him to her cause, not Ayala's. She tried to convert him from his cool Protestantism of personal salvation to a dark revolutionary Catholicism uniting beliefs and action. He

209

was reluctant. He readily abandoned the old, but stopped short of the new. He knew what happened to cops in revolutions. They became butchers, or they got killed after the victory, or the final defeat.

"Statehood means nothing but welfare for our people," she argued. "And it will give the Pentagon and the CIA a huge permanent base in the middle of the Caribbean, from which they can establish their bloody hegemony over all of Latin America. The fall of Salvador Allende will be nothing compared to what follows in Puerto Rico."

He knew she was right, and he knew she did not overlook the details of violence; she understood that good people got tortured and killed fighting for what they believed, and that bad people often found ways to survive, win, and prosper. She knew that all politics contained the seeds of violence, even the muted party politics of American democracy.

But he couldn't follow her all the way. He was still a homicide detective working for the City of New York, sworn to protect the city's citizens. He still had a killer to find.

She wanted the killer found, too. In her daytime life, she had charge of sixteen hundred children. In her nighttime life, she could not relinquish her struggle to protect and teach them. For Mercedes, the children and the conspiracy were two sides of the same coin.

It was she who finally gave Rodriguez the lead he needed. One night, she had led him back over the history of the two East Harlem murders and the assault on Bobby Powers.

"Did anyone ever question the crossing guards at PS 7?" she asked. "It's possible they saw the boy and Charlie Chopoff together that morning."

He winced at the name. He still called the killer "M."

"No," he said. "They never did, and I never thought of it."

At the end of the week, on Friday morning, Lopez called the principal of PS 7, who she knew. Off the record, she told him what she wanted, and told him there was a cop who had taken it upon himself to re-open unofficially the case of William Thomas. The principal approved and understood. He gave her the names of the crossing guards and their home addresses.

By noon on Friday, Rodriguez found the woman who had

waved at William Thomas from the shelter of the coffee shop as he ran across Lexington Avenue, late for school. She remembered the man with the limp, and from the distance of months past, gave Rodriguez a decent description. It matched all the others.

She was a very light-skinned Puerto Rican, and she described the man as black. In the ethnic melting pot of New York, nothing ever melted. She wept with despair and anger at herself when she realized she had seen the boy with his killer and had done nothing.

Rodriguez comforted her, and as she relaxed in the familiar surroundings of her own kitchen, with her own baby safe in the next room, she remembered seeing the man several more times. Always the same route, she told Rodriguez.

Rodriguez walked back along the route. When he got to the corner by the old newsdealer, he asked the old man if he had ever seen the "Spanish man" again.

"Yessir," said the old man, who was no more than sticks and rags.

"Where does he come from?"

"Up there," said the old man, pointing across Park Avenue under the black steel and shadows of the elevated railroad structure.

Rodriguez sighted along the line the old man indicated under the elevated and walked through the maze of parked cars. He heard a savage dog barking in an alleyway. Rodriguez stopped on the corner of 123rd Street and Park Avenue, by the fenced-in and guarded parking lot reserved for the staff of the Hospital for Joint Diseases.

The hospital's blank rear wall rose above the parking lot like a cliff. At the end of the next block was the sere yellow-green of Mount Morris Park. Rodriguez walked to the park and climbed the paths to the outlook at the top of the hill. The steel bell tower rose from the center of the little flagstone belvedere.

Rodriguez walked along the low wall around the outlook. It was the highest point on the broad, flat plain of Harlem. He could see from the site of the old Polo Grounds on the Harlem River in the north, to the skyscrapers south of Central Park. The trees in the park below him were yellow. It had been a dry summer. Facing north, Rodriguez looked through a gap in the trees, and saw the rooftop of the brownstone at 2013 Fifth Avenue, where the second boy was found. He turned east. There were the broken windows of the apartment of William Thomas. Dark smoke stains feathered the brick above the windows. The building was abandoned.

Rodriguez found a bench and sat down. He was shaking. Tears snaked out from under his dark glasses. He knew he had found the trail of the killer and he knew it would lead him to a confrontation with Mercedes Lopez. She would be waiting for him, expecting him, demanding him to take the route she took toward the freedom of her people. Nieman and O'Malley would be waiting too.

He walked down the hill and bought a hot dog from a push-cart. He stood in the shade of the huge sycamore trees where he could see the building at 2013 Fifth Avenue.

There was the bar on the ground floor. The chipped tin sign over the entrance said "Bud's Place" in carnival colors. An old clear glass light bulb burned in the bright sunlight over the sign. The last time Rodriguez was here, the street and the surrounding rooftops were full of sullen, silent, angry people. Now there was no one.

He walked into the bar. Except for the ancient bartender, it was empty, too. Rodriguez sat on the first stool by the door. He ordered a beer and a glass of cold water as the bartender shuffled slowly toward him, a pair of old, worn-out shoes without laces on his feet.

Rodriguez paid for the beer, then flopped his badge out. "Rodriguez," he said.

The old man said, "Everyone round here calls me First Sergeant."

"Why's that?" asked Rodriguez.

" 'Cause I was the first sergeant in a regiment of black soldiers during the war."

"Which war?"

"Number Two. The big one," said the old man. "They wouldn't send us to Africa, but they sent us all the way up the boot of Italy."

"I don't understand," said Rodriguez.

"You're not old enough," said First Sergeant. "It was because of Ethiopia. They were afraid if they sent us to Africa we'd run off and join the Arabs. They forgot it was the Arabs who invented slaves. In Italy, they figured we'd fight hard, to revenge Ethiopia, you see. Didn't make much sense. Weren't very many of us even knew where Ethiopia was."

"Yeah," said Rodriguez. "It's crystal clear now."

The old man smiled. "You've been here before. What do you want this time, sonny?"

Rodriguez produced a wrinkled photocopy of the police sketch of the killer, and handed it across the bar.

The old man glanced at it and handed it back. He smiled in a distant sort of way.

"Don't get many cops in here," he said. "But you're the second one who asked about that face. This is the one who killed the boy on the rooftop here, last spring, isn't it?"

"I think so."

"I'll tell you the same thing I told the other cop, if you'll leave me out of it."

"OK."

"I see this fella every three, four, five days. Maybe twice a week. Comes by here, down the street on his way to the old hospital over on the square there. Joint Diseases. Comes in here sometimes on hot days for a beer. In here just yesterday."

Rodriguez felt his heart pounding.

"He's a milkman," said the old man.

"Milkman?"

"In a way of speakin' that's what he is," said First Sergeant. "He delivers dope on a regular route from one hospital to the next. I think he comes down here from Sydenham, and goes on over to Manhattan State."

"You think?"

"I know. I'm an old man and I hear a lot of things. I hear everything."

"You know who I am?"

"You're Rodriguez. You was here the day the boy was killed. You work for O'Malley."

"When was he here?" asked Rodriguez. His voice betrayed him. It was harsh and angry.

213

"I didn't say he was," said the old man.

Rodriguez did something he had never done before in all his time on the force. He reached over the bar, grabbed the little old man by his scrawny chicken's neck, and dragged him half over the bar. The old man wheezed and fought feebly.

"When was he here, goddammit?"

"Las' week."

Rodriguez dropped the shaking old man. He felt almost sick with shame. He apologized.

The old man said, "That's all right. I'm trying to help. O'Malley won't do nuthin' about findin' the killer. Maybe you will. I didn't do nuthin' to hurt you, did I?"

Rodriguez shook his head in a negative.

"Then why'd you hurt me?"

"This is important," said Rodriguez, and then felt his stomach heave and roll with what he'd done and said. He had gone too far.

"Now tell me the rest," said Rodriguez.

The old man poured himself a shot of whiskey. He drew a short glass of ice water and poured the whiskey into the water. The whiskey color swirled for a moment in the glass, then the old man drank it down, and poured himself another.

"The rest of what?" The old man was sparring.

"Don't jerk me around," said Rodriguez.

Sunday night, pretending he was invisible, like a child covering his eyes, Rodriguez watched the dominoes game in silence. He was a stranger to these men, and they were strangers to him, but they had made room for him on the bench when he joined them.

When one of them got up to go across the street to the *bodega,* Rodriguez fished a wrinkled, damp dollar bill out of his pocket and chipped in for the beer.

Rodriguez sat with his back to his own precinct house. The lower half of the wall was stuccoed with cement. The upper half was brick, set with a row of metal casement windows. Heavy metal screens were welded over the windows to protect them from rocks. O'Malley's office window was directly overhead.

O'Malley sat in his car on Amsterdam Avenue, watching the *bodega* where the men from the dominoes game bought their beer. In the light rain dripping down through the trees, Rodriguez watched O'Malley watch the *bodega*.

M was in the *bodega*. O'Malley had been following M for three days, maybe longer. Rodriguez had followed O'Malley since Friday night, dozing off in doorways, sleeping on his feet or in the back of gypsy cabs.

The rule was that it took three teams of four men each to follow one man around the clock. It was often done with fewer men, but never by one man. Rodriguez promised himself he would stay on O'Malley for the weekend, then get a good night's sleep Sunday night before returning to work Monday morning. Now it was Sunday night, and Rodriguez was ill from exhaustion.

First Sergeant led him to O'Malley, and O'Malley led him to the killer. It was the perfect stalemate. It was worse than that. When Rodriguez finally forced himself to talk to Mercedes, which would be tomorrow at the latest, he would have to ask her about Franco Ayala. Then Rodriguez would have to call Nieman.

First Sergeant had told him who Ayala was. But Rodriguez wanted to know what Mercedes knew, and he wanted to know *exactly* what her connection was to this guy, who First Sergeant said was a very bad guy, one of the worst in years.

And there was more, said First Sergeant. The guy was "political." Some of the black nationalists from the early 'sixties, the real hotheads, had been infatuated with Castro at the Hotel Theresa in 1962. Some of them were still around, said First Sergeant cautiously, and they talked about a Cuban who had taken over the old pipelines from Cuba to New York.

Once upon a time, money and political advice flowed up the pipeline from Havana to Harlem. Now it was drugs, said First Sergeant. Heavy-duty stuff, he said, one of those things where there was no discussion.

"And the Italians on East 116th Street and Pleasant Avenue?" asked Rodriguez.

"They look the other way," said First Sergeant. "This is very rough stuff, maybe too rough even for them."

So Sunday night, Rodriguez sat in the rain dripping from the trees in the dark little park at the edge of Amsterdam Avenue, listening to the soft click of the dominoes. Now and then he glanced over at O'Malley's car parked at the curb by the corner. A heavy gray head was the only visible part of the man inside. The glow of a cigar and puffs of white smoke were the only sign of life.

The killer walked out the door of the brightly lit *bodega,* carrying one of his shopping bags. He headed straight up Amsterdam Avenue. O'Malley's car glided slowly in greased silence after him.

In his exhaustion, Rodriguez heard Mercedes calling for help, but there was no one there. He was hallucinating. He got up and joined the little procession uptown, mumbling his good-byes to the dominoes players.

One of the players watched him walk up the sidewalk at a pace that matched O'Malley's car. When Rodriguez was well up the block, the player got up and crossed the street to the *bodega.* He emerged a few moments later and gave a shrill, brief whistle. It rose and fell across the noise of the cars and buses in the avenue.

The dominoes players looked up. The man in front of the *bodega* motioned with his arm. Two of the players rose and walked swiftly after Rodriguez. The chase ended quickly. M turned down 109th Street toward his building, apparently unaware he was being followed. O'Malley turned down the deserted block after him and stopped a few doors up from M's building. A man ran quickly from the sidewalk to O'Malley's car and said, *"Señor* Ayala orders you to stop following this man, and tells you to do what he paid you to do."

Then the man disappeared. Enraged, O'Malley sped off down 109th Street.

Rodriguez began running when he saw the man approach O'Malley's car. At that moment, he was nothing but a cop going to the aid of another cop, but before he took ten steps, he felt the stab of a gun in his back and heard a voice say in Spanish, "Go into this doorway."

He was shoved sideways across the sidewalk into a darkened storefront. He recognized the dominoes players. He was too tired

216

to resist, and instinct warned him not to. One of the men said, "Go home now."

The short gunbarrel suddenly shot forward like the nose of a snake and struck him in the center of his stomach. Rodriguez pitched forward to his knees, feeling the puke rising in his throat. A fist like a brick struck him on the back of the head and drove him down flat on the sidewalk.

He blacked out for only an instant, but when he rose to his hands and knees, the street was empty. He stood up, bruised, sick, and filthy. His gun was gone again; and his wallet, keys, badge, and money. They had stripped him down to nothing. His playtime disguise as a wino was now complete.

On unsteady legs, he began to walk down Amsterdam Avenue toward home, twenty-three blocks away in the rain. As he stumbled along, in real pain and fear, blinded by the lights of cars heading uptown on the one-way avenue, he heard Mercedes again, calling his name, holding a baby up for him to see.

He stopped on the corner of 107th Street, sick and weak. He looked wildly around, swaying on his feet like a tapped-out Bowery bum. There was no one in sight on the sidewalks. The faces in the cars looked like fish in the aquarium, white behind thick green glass streaked with water. He held on to a light pole, praying to St. Barbara to protect Mercedes and the baby, praying to stay on his feet.

They beat him to his apartment. Upholstery and clothing was ripped and shredded. His prints hung in tatters from the walls. Books lay on the floor, their pages lolling like torn tongues. Records were bent and melted by the flame from a butane lighter, which lay discarded by the door. Crockery was smashed. Food was smeared all over the kitchen. A pile of shit lay on the kitchen floor. It was the universal mark of vandals.

Nothing was stolen. There were no messages. The kitchen and living room phones were broken, but the bedroom phone still worked. It had been kicked under the bed and forgotten. The statue of St. Barbara was untouched. Its blue offertory candle still flickered on the dresser.

Rodriguez thanked the doorman for letting him in. Rodriguez cautioned him against saying anything to anybody, but the caution wasn't necessary. The vandals had terrorized him.

When the doorman left, Rodriguez got down on his knees and reached far back under his dresser. His cache of money and spare keys was still there. He cleaned up the kitchen and living room, salvaging what he could. The numbness began to wear off. He found a bottle of uppers in the bathroom and took a couple. The drug hit him with a rush.

He picked through his clothes and found some that were overlooked. He took a shower. He shaved and took another shower, hot as a steam bath. Then he got dressed and called Harry Nieman. It was almost dawn. He told Nieman to meet him at an all-night restaurant for breakfast.

Nieman ate like a wolf. He mopped up his third poached egg with a piece of dripping toast and stuffed it in his mouth. Then he turned to a plate of home fries covered with half a bottle of ketchup. He looked thinner than ever.

He said, "There's nothing worse than losing badge and gun. But it's the best thing that ever happened to you."

Rodriguez was drinking tea and eating toast with butter and jam. He ate slowly, like a convalescent. "Bullshit," he said. "You're talking nonsense."

"No," said Nieman softly. "You're gonna just disappear."

Rodriguez watched crumbs of fried potato spray from Nieman's mouth. Nieman was not a slob, but when he was excited he forgot himself. He drank half a cup of coffee in one gulp and gave a moist whistle for the waitress.

"This isn't one of your fucking Asian spy stories," said Rodriguez. "It's Monday morning and Mercedes doesn't answer her phone. The killer is walking around the West Side, ready to kill another kid. A homicide lieutenant and a detective sergeant know who the killer is, and aren't arresting him. The lieutenant and the killer work for the same narcotics guy, and this guy is probably a Cuban commie, and he has his hooks into Mercedes somehow. And he's beat the shit out of me twice. Now he's got my badge and gun."

"Sounds like a spy story to me," said Nieman, washing down

a mouthful of potato with a cupful of coffee. Ketchup dripped from the corners of his mouth. Nieman caught Rodriguez staring at him with disgust. Nieman laughed, spraying food, and said, "Bet you never saw a werewolf eat potatoes before."

Rodriguez turned his face away and stared out the plate glass at the street. A row of yellow cabs lined the curb. Their drivers sat in a row at the counter, talking in loud voices, laughing and complaining.

He had never seen Nieman like this. The man had reverted to some earlier personality. This is what he was like in Vietnam, thought Rodriguez.

Nieman wiped his mouth and whistled for another cup of coffee. He hunched forward and said, "You don't understand, Danny. Without your badge and gun, you're nobody. The department'll put you through the wringer. You'll be goddamn lucky if they don't flop you back onto the street. At the very least, they'll take you outta that command and put you in Flatbush."

Nieman sat back with a cheerful look on his face and waited for an answer. There was none. "If you're not in that command, how are you gonna find Charlie Chopoff?"

There was no answer.

Nieman went on. "Why do you suppose O'Malley decided to look for Charlie in the first place?"

"Dunno."

"Maybe because he was gonna take Charlie out."

"I don't get it."

"You're not paranoid enough. If Charlie kills another kid up there, the neighborhood will blow up. O'Malley will be covered with shit. What use is he to Ayala then? With no freedom of movement? Maybe transferred for failure? He'll be the scapegoat for the brass."

"But why now?" asked Rodriguez. "Why did he go looking for Charlie now?"

It was the first time Rodriguez had used the name "Charlie," but he sensed it was appropriate somehow. Nieman was locked into his hunter-killer mode, thinking like an assassin, acting like he was back in Saigon. Rodriguez thought, All these guys are a bunch of loose cannons rolling around on the deck.

219

Nieman was still looking for Victor Charlie, and now Nieman had found a Charlie right in New York City.

"Maybe because he was trying to clear the decks for an important operation," replied Nieman. "He was gonna take Charlie out quietly, sorta like making sure he had a clear field of fire, cutting down the odds on surprises in the night."

"Listen to me, Harry," Rodriguez said. "You're used to this stuff. You're good at it. It's Alice-in-Wonderland. But I'm just a cop. I wanna get the guy who killed two little boys, and tried to kill a third. He is damn sure gonna kill another one soon, and I'm gonna go back uptown to the Two-Four, take my lumps, and get on with my job."

"Well, I can't stop you," said Nieman, waving his fingers at the waitress for the check. "But you haven't figured out yet what your real job is."

"Nieman was right," Rodriguez said to himself ruefully. He was at home on his ravaged sofa, smoking a joint and listening to rock and roll on a big portable radio he had bought off the shoulder of a kid on roller skates in Central Park. This was after being informed gleefully by O'Malley that he was suspended without pay pending investigation of the loss of badge and gun.

The radio was a huge Panasonic the size of a small suitcase. It was black and silver, and had a shoulder strap. It was the sort of radio Rodriguez had often wanted to shoot, as it blared down the street at two A.M. or sat on the lap of a kid sullenly sprawled on a subway bench during the rush hour.

Rodriguez sat slumped on his sofa, stupidly trying to recall how much he had paid for the ugly radio. He was dimly happy that he had some music. Fifty bucks. And the goddamn thing was hot. He was a cop. What the hell was he doing with stolen property? No. He wasn't a cop. Not anymore. He fell into a stuperous sleep.

chapter fourteen
200 west 106th street

The telephone woke him. It was dark and late. There were few lights in the windows of the buildings across the street. For a moment, Rodriguez didn't know where he was; then he remembered and stumbled into the bedroom to the phone.

It was Mercedes. She was hysterical. Tears came to his eyes when he heard her voice. She was home, she said. She had something to tell him. Where had she been? She wouldn't say. Fifteen minutes later he was in the doorway of her apartment, holding her close, and they were both crying.

"I tried to call you all day Friday and Saturday," she sobbed, "but there was no answer. I had to go to Puerto Rico."

"Puerto Rico?" he shouted into her ear. "I've been trying to call you for three days. I called the school. They said you were sick. I called here and you weren't home."

She winced and pulled away from him. She shut the apartment door with a sharp slam, and walked into her living room, patting her hair into place, turning this light off and that one on.

"Yes, I had a meeting. I called in sick long distance from San Juan."

He shrugged. "You said you had something to tell me."

"I got a terrible phone call when I got back." She looked at him oddly. "You look terrible. Where's your gun?"

He told her the story. She was aghast.

"The phone call," he insisted.

There was a gulf between them, a gap of water widening between two ships parting at sea. His heart was in his throat. He could barely talk.

"What phone call?" he shouted.

She sighed and sat down in a chair. "The phone was ringing when I walked in the door from the airport," she said.

"What time was that?" He was the cop, and she was the witness to a crime.

"About eleven."

"And?"

"It was Manny Mirabel, the man who owns the *farmacia* on the corner of 107th Street and Amsterdam. You know him?"

"I know the place."

"His nephew goes to PS 165. The boy lives with his mother on 108th Street behind the school. She's divorced. She sent the boy out for bread and milk about eight-thirty. He stopped in the *farmacia* for a visit. When they closed at nine, he left for the grocery store."

Rodriguez knew what was coming. It was thundering along like an express train. He stood helpless in its path.

"Manny lives in Yonkers. When he and his wife got home, his sister called him. She wanted to know if he had seen the' boy."

"What's the boy's name?"

"Julio Mirabel. She took back her maiden name. She's very nice," said Mercedes, "a good mother. Her husband was a pig."

"Tell me the rest," said Rodriguez.

Mercedes was crying. "She called the police. It was like the first time. There was no answer at 911. Then they answered the second time and told her it was no emergency. They told her to call the precinct and hung up on her. She called the precinct and they told her it was no emergency. They could not help her. Call back in the morning."

Now Mercedes was sobbing.

"How old is the boy?"

"Eight. He is in third grade."

"What does he look like?"

"Small for his age. Skinny. Very dark-skinned. His father was black."

"Call every politician you know," said Rodriguez. "Cash your chips. Tell them to call the Mayor, the precinct, the Chief's Office, the papers, the TV and radio. Everyone they can think of. You'll have half the PD up here in an hour, I guarantee it."

"Where are you going?" she cried.

He didn't answer. He ran out the door. Without waiting for the elevator, he ran down the fire stairs.

Rodriguez was stopped once before he got out of the neighborhood. As he stood on Broadway at 109th Street waiting for a cab going uptown, two men from the precinct narcotics squad stopped him. One of them half-recognized him. He waved them away and mumbled, "I'm on the job." They let him go, thinking he was on an undercover assignment.

Ten minutes later, Rodriguez was in a crowded Puerto Rican ballroom at Broadway and 145th Street. He pushed his way through the dancers, the lookers, the drinkers, and the smokers and snorters. He was looking for a man he knew. The place had never been so crowded. He bought a joint from a kid, and stood smoking with his back to a pillar. It was good grass. He began to relax. He found the kid and bought two more joints. The blare and beat of a Latin band lifted his spirits. When he spotted his man sitting alone at the bar, he felt lucky, better than he had in weeks.

He slid onto the barstool next to the man. They sat in silence for a few minutes. Without preamble, Rodriguez said, "Benny, my man, I need a piece."

The man looked up from his flat beer and watched Rodriguez's face in the mirror behind the bar. The glass was flecked and streaked with gold paint. It gave both men a diseased appearance in the flashing lights from the dance floor.

"How you doing, Danny? Long time."

"Good, Benny. Real good. But I don't have time to bullshit."

"I hear you're in a little trouble, Danny."

"Don't believe everything you hear."

"Danny, you setting me up?"

"No."

"I don't want heat for this."

"What do you have, Benny?"

"Ask the old man in the men's room. Tell him you wanna see the tan briefcase."

Rodriguez walked through the crowd to the men's room. It felt good to be in this place. The music and the young girls made him feel like a kid, young and clean.

The men's room was big, like one in a train station. The old man showed him to the last stall. He opened the door for Rodriguez and closed it, like a concierge. The lid on the toilet was down. On the lid was a large tan fiberglass briefcase.

Rodriguez sat down and opened the case. Inside were five guns packed in white styrofoam. Rodriguez smiled. One of them was his. He stuck it in his waistband. Three of the other guns were junk. The fourth was a brand new 9mm Browning automatic, the gun of choice on the streets of New York.

Rodriguez stuck it in his waistband next to the .38. He took the extra fourteen-shot clip for the Browning, and the box of ammunition thoughtfully provided with each gun. He closed the case and walked out of the stall, looking like a man who had just achieved peace of mind. He washed his hands and face, tipped the old man, and went back to the noisy bar.

"Good stuff, Benny. Where'd you get the .38?"

"Do I ask questions?"

"I want the badge, too, Benny."

"What's the number?"

"Forty-six twenty-eight."

Benny reached into his suit jacket and dropped a worn leather case into Rodriguez's hand. The dealer said, "I give you back your badge for nothing, but you owe me a finder's fee for the gun."

"I took the Browning, too."

"Six hundred for both."

"Make it five."

Benny sighed. "Five and a half."

Rodriguez put five hundreds, two twenties and a ten on the wet bar. He slid off the stool and stood behind the other man. "Do me a serious favor, Benny."

"What's that?"

"Tell Franco Ayala about this. Tell him I wanna see him."

The street outside was crowded with people and double-parked cars. The night air was bland. A good-looking blond woman took Rodriguez by the arm. "Danny," she said. "Where have you been?"

They were the first words spoken in English to Rodriguez in the last hour. "Hello, Sylvia," he said. "What brings you uptown?"

He hadn't seen this woman in nearly a year. For a couple of months they had made the rounds together, the jazz bars and ballrooms. She was Brazilian, and worked as a translator for her consulate at the United Nations.

"A new boyfriend," she said, pointing at a car.

"What's his name?" asked Rodriguez. "He drives a nice car."

The car was a maroon Buick, double-parked, shining clean and waxed. The driver slouched behind the wheel. He was alone in the car.

"Franco Ayala."

"Introduce me," said Rodriguez.

"He's busy," she said, rubbing against him like a cat.

"That's OK," said Rodriguez with a bright smile. "Just tell him for me that he's got sloppy seconds."

By eight-thirty the next morning, PS 165 was in an uproar. The halls were crowded with mothers and grandmothers talking about the missing boy. Anna Mirabel arrived, escorted by her brother and some neighbors. They disappeared into Mercedes' office. The mother came in the vain hope that her son had shown up at school. Several times before, without telling her, he had gone to stay with his father, who had no telephone. On those occasions, the boy simply showed up at school in the morning.

This morning, Julio Mirabel did not show up. By noon,

everyone in the neighborhood *knew* what had happened to the boy, even though no one had found the body. The first call from a reporter to the school came at nine o'clock. The reporter was tipped off by someone at police headquarters. Lopez took the call, said there was absolutely no information, told the reporter to call the Board of Education, and hung up.

Sometime after lunch, an old Irish woman in an ancient wash-worn housedress waddled down five flights of stairs in her building. She clutched her change purse and a bag of garbage. Her old dog, a hairy black mutt modeled after some kind of spaniel, followed her. When they reached the sidewalk, they discovered the garbage cans in front of the building were full. Woman and dog had lived together in the same building for years, on the south side of West 106th Street near the corner of Amsterdam Avenue, and they had a definite routine.

The woman walked slowly toward the corner to drop her garbage in the trash basket. The dog shuffled along with her. "It's hot, Milly," muttered the woman. As they passed a basement alleyway between two half-renovated buildings that had been deserted for weeks since the contractor went bankrupt, the dog stopped. She began to bark and whine at the alley.

The old woman continued slowly to the corner, dropped her small bag of garbage into the wire trash basket, and went into the corner bar, where she bought a pack of cigarettes and drank a quick rye and ginger.

Then she went back to the dog, who was still whining by the alleyway. "Milly," said the woman, "stop your noise." The woman peered uncertainly down the steps into the darkness. "There's nothing but garbage down there," she said.

Then she saw a bare leg and a child's foot in a white sock. Without making a sound, but with a face drained of blood, she ran in her old woman's shuffle back to the bar, the dark dog trotting and bouncing along behind her.

"Johnnie," she cried. "Johnnie!" Her voice was a keening sing-song. "Johnnie, there's a little body in the alley there."

The old Irish bartender grabbed a baseball bat from under the bar, shouted to an old man at the far end of the bar to take care of the place, and ran to the alley. He went down the stairs and lifted the trash off the body.

"Oh, my God," said the old woman, her hand on her heaving chest over her heart. "Call the police. This is the little Puerto Rican lad they've been searching for all night and day."

The body looked like the others. There were dozens of stab wounds through the tee shirt, which was caked with blood. The body was nude from the waist down, except for the socks. There was a hideous wound between the legs. The little face was contorted with terror and pain.

"Eddie," said the raspy voice over the telephone. "It's ten o'clock in the morning. Do you know where all your detectives are?"

"Whaddayou talkin' about?" growled O'Malley. "Hanratty, I'm in no mood for any bullshit this morning."

"Eddie, I'm talking about young Rodriguez. Do you know where he is?"

"He's around here somewhere. The bastards downtown lifted his suspension." O'Malley flattened his hand over the mouthpiece and shouted into the squad room, "Rodriguez! *Rodriguez!*"

Someone shouted back, "He's not here."

"Where the hell is he?" roared O'Malley. "Bring me the goddamn sign-out sheet."

A detective wearing his gun hung butt-down in a fancy shoulder holster hurried into O'Malley's office with a legal-size clipboard. O'Malley snatched it away.

"Son of a bitch," he muttered. "Signed out at nine-twenty. No destination."

He lifted his head again and roared through his door, *"Where is he?"*

There was no answer. Considering that there was supposed to be a major effort to find the killer of Julio Mirabel, whose body had been found the day before, there was a curious lethargy in the homicide squad room. This was due to a gathering resentment against the squad commander, his vile manner, and his lack of command. O'Malley had let things get out of hand. He knew it. And for the tenth time in two days, Hanratty was telling O'Malley that he knew it, too.

"The reason I wanna know where Rodriguez is," said Hanratty with his voice like a mill bastard file, "is because our pal wants to know where Rodriguez is. He's been getting little messages from Rodriguez. Our pal wants to talk to Rodriguez right now, Eddie. How do you think our pal is gonna feel when I tell him you don't know where Rodriguez is?"

"I don't give a fuck how he feels."

"Eddie, I'm gonna help you out. I'm gonna tell you where Rodriguez is right now. How's that?"

"Don't jerk me off, Hanratty. I'm in no mood."

"He's up at St. Luke's Hospital."

"What the hell's he doing up there?"

"Don't you know, Eddie?"

"No, goddammit, I don't!"

"Eddie, it's crystal clear that you are losing your grip on your command."

O'Malley heard the threat. Like a volcano about to blow up, O'Malley's anger rose to dangerous new temperatures inside while his outward manner froze.

"I'm in command, Hanratty. Just tell me what you know."

"A plastic surgeon is performing a minor operation on Bobby Powers this morning. Rodriguez is up there talking to the mother, and hanging around. I want to remind you, Eddie, since you forget so fast, that this kid is the only living witness to the killer and you now have another victim. Without this kid, there is not much of a case. Do you get my drift, Eddie?"

O'Malley got the drift. He sat at his desk, hunched over, his back as broad as a barrel, the black phone at his ear like a jack plugged into a socket. He was motionless, barely breathing. He was thinking.

If Rodriguez arrested Charlie Chopoff, it would draw attention to O'Malley's failure, and thus to O'Malley's clients. If Charlie was arrested, he would be guarded around the clock like Son of Sam, and hard to get at. With the kid as a witness, they had an airtight case against Charlie. Charlie might do a lot of talking about his employers.

O'Malley made a new list in his head. One. Rodriguez. Two. The kid. Three. Mercedes Lopez.

Ayala was still protecting Charlie. After following Charlie on his delivery rounds for a week, O'Malley knew why. Charlie's ability to get in and out of hospitals was worth hundreds of thousands of dollars a year to Ayala.

"Are you there, Eddie?" rasped the voice in his ear.

"I was thinking."

There was a gasp in the telephone. The cocksucker, thought O'Malley. In that dim thought, O'Malley added number three and a half to his list. *Don't get mad, get even.*

"I was hoping you'd see the necessity of that," said Hanratty.

O'Malley laughed, sort of. He said, "Shall I tell Rodriguez to ring up our pal? Since we're all so cozy now, I mean?"

The answer was a click, as Hanratty hung up his telephone.

O'Malley took a small key from his vest pocket and unlocked the bottom drawer of his old wooden desk. He pushed aside an untouched pint bottle of whiskey, and reached back into the deep drawer. He withdrew a bundle about two feet long wrapped in black oilcloth.

From the oilcloth, he took a sawed-off, gas-operated automatic shotgun, a six-shot clip, and a box of twelve-gauge shells loaded with double-O shot. He loaded the clip, snapped it into the gun, jacked a round into the chamber, and set the gun on safety.

He pawed through galoshes and rubber raincoats in the corner behind his desk and extracted a large blue gym bag with "Joan of Arc High School" printed in yellow letters on both sides. It had belonged to some hapless high school kid with the bad luck to be smoking a joint on a corner when O'Malley happened by in a bad mood.

O'Malley dumped a jumble of sweat socks and jock straps into his wastebasket. A pungent odor rose to his nose. He smiled with the pleasure of his idea. He pulled a sweatshirt out of the wastebasket and wrapped the gun in it. He wrapped the box of loose shells in a tee shirt from the wastebasket. He reached again into the back of the desk drawer. He pulled out his two stun grenades, and pulled socks over them. He packed the little arsenal in the gym bag. He shoved in more rotten gym clothes. He zipped up the bag. He smiled.

chapter fifteen
surgery

Charlie understood hospitals because he liked them, and he had been in St. Luke's so often that he could draw a map of the place. This morning he knew exactly where he was going. After hearing on the street that the boy named Bobby Powers had given a description of his attacker to the police, Charlie kept track of the boy's progress through the hospital grapevine. Charlie knew the police had a guard on the boy's room, and he had no trouble learning Bobby's room number.

St. Luke's was Charlie's first stop of the morning. He had two clients to visit. One was an emergency room nurse who paid him fifteen hundred dollars for a kilo of marijuana, shrink-wrapped. When he left her, he walked through a door into a long hall lined with examination rooms. He took an elevator marked *Doctors Only* up to the fifth floor. He walked down the hall, limping slightly, carrying his shopping bag in his left hand, invisible or anonymous under the gaze of others.

He turned into an office. A few moments later his second client hurried in, a dapper young plastic surgeon who bought large amounts of cocaine at frequent intervals for himself and his friends. He liked the risk and exoticism of masquerade. He once dressed Charlie in a set of surgical greens and took him into the scrub area of an operating room where he was working.

Charlie was no textbook psychopath. He simply had no internal controls over his behavior. His strongest instincts were for survival. He was like many normal people, predictably calm most of the time when his daily routine went well, but extraordinarily sensitive to certain stimuli, and helpless to change. Watching the surgeon at work gave Charlie the only hope of change he ever had. He wanted a new face.

When the surgeon came into the office, Charlie asked him how much a facial reconstruction would cost. They chatted for a few minutes about the techniques of such an operation, or series of operations, and the cost. Charlie handed the surgeon a plastic bag containing cocaine sealed in a number of smaller plastic bags. The surgeon went into his inner office for the money.

Charlie followed only to the door. As the surgeon put the cocaine in his desk, he said, "You would have been interested in seeing this operation I just finished. It was very unusual, an attempt to begin to reconstruct a boy's penis."

Charlie froze in panic, but the surgeon was bent over his desk and didn't notice. The surgeon said, "It's a matter of constructing the base for future operations when the boy's older."

Charlie asked, "How is the boy now?"

"Oh, he's gonna be fine. He's in recovery now, but they'll move him back to his room after lunch. This was really a minor operation."

As the surgeon talked, still bent over his desk counting money, Charlie took a set of fresh greens off a hook behind the door of the outer office, and stuffed them into his shopping bag. The surgeon walked around his desk and handed Charlie an envelope. "Twenty grand, as usual. Thank you for coming." The surgeon was surprised when Charlie stuffed the envelope into his hip pocket and walked away without another word.

Charlie entered a men's room marked *Doctors Only*. Inside, he entered one of the stalls and quickly undressed. He put his streetclothes in the shopping bag and put on the greens. As he walked out, he pushed the shopping bag into a broom closet.

He walked up a flight of stairs to the next floor, and into a wide hall. Here were the operating rooms. The hall was empty. Most of the morning's surgery was done. Only one warning light burned over a door, signaling an operation in progress.

Without hesitation, Charlie walked down the hall. The recovery room was just past a nurse's station. There was no nurse, but a uniformed cop sat in a chair behind the low counter reading a magazine. He barely glanced up. Charlie looked like a lifetime orderly. When he reached the door of the recovery room, he walked in as though he belonged there.

There were three patients in the brightly lit room. Two were adults. One was Bobby Powers. A nurse stood by one of the adults, changing a drip bottle. She was very young. She looked over her shoulder at Charlie, then back to her task. Charlie bent, as though tying his boot, and palmed the knife out of its holster. As he stepped up to the head of the boy's bed, Charlie held the knife low by his side.

The boy opened his eyes. He recognized Charlie instantly, the horrible face leaning over him as it had once before, with the bad breath of an old dog. The boy screamed. The nurse screamed and leaped at Charlie, grasping for his hand. He drove the short knife backhanded into her chest, lifting her off her feet. She fell on her back, convulsing with pain, bright red blood soaking the front of her white uniform.

Charlie turned toward the bed, then scrambled for the door when he heard the cop's yell. As the cop came through the door, drawing his gun, Charlie slammed the knife into the cop's ribcage with tremendous force. The cop staggered. With a wide sidearm swing, Charlie slammed the knife in again. The cop dropped like a felled ox. His gun clattered across the floor.

Bobby screamed and screamed. There were yells from the hall, and footsteps. Charlie gave one last look at the screaming boy, stuck the knife in his boot top, and ran out of the room, shouting, "In here."

Someone shouted at him, "Get an OR table."

"OK," he shouted back, and ducked down the stairs. On the floor below, he went into the men's room and retrieved his shopping bag. Alarms rang in bell codes on the PA system, and an amplified voice called over and over, "Trauma unit to six, please. Trauma unit to six."

People ran by him as he stood calmly waiting for the *Doctors Only* elevator. When it came, it was empty. He rode down to the ground floor and left the hospital the way he entered, through the emergency room, unchallenged in his hospital greens.

Rodriguez and the boy's mother were in the coffee shop. The cop was dead by the time they got upstairs. The cop's uniform had been sliced open and peeled back like the skin of an animal by the doctors who tried to save him, but they had failed, and now the abandoned body lay sprawled on its back in a position like drunken sleep, soaked in blood.

The nurse was still alive in an operating room across the hall. Rodriguez could hear a muffled voice shouting orders, then the voice fell silent.

Two doctors and a nurse were bent over Bobby, talking to him, trying to soothe him. He was crying and coughing. The boy's face leapt with recognition when he saw his mother.

After a moment, Rodriguez asked firmly, "Was it the same man who attacked you?"

The boy nodded.

"Where did he go?"

"Down the hall," coughed the boy.

"Was he alone?"

Nod.

"What was he wearing?"

The boy pointed to one of the doctors.

"A green suit?" asked Rodriguez.

The boy nodded, then vomited.

"Don't leave him alone," said Rodriguez to the doctors and the nurse as he left.

By the time the description of the killer went over the police radio, the green hospital suit was in the bottom of a black plastic bag full of paper towels and other bathroom trash in a men's room on the first floor of a Columbia University dormitory across the street from St. Luke's. Charlie lifted the plastic bag out of the trash can, knotted the top of it, and dropped it in a corner, where it looked like it was forgotten by a lazy janitor.

Charlie gave his hands another wash, dried them carefully, checked his pants cuffs, and walked out of the building past two bored university guards.

Nieman sat in the back of the Chief's car with Kinsella. The Deputy Commissioner for Public Information sat in the front seat with the driver. The deputy was an ex-reporter who affected a gun in a shoulder holster now that he was a pseudo-cop. He had one of the car's radio telephones in one ear and his finger in the other. He had long ago learned that he didn't want to hear what was said in the back seat of this car. It made it harder to lie to reporters.

When he hung up the telephone, Kinsella leaned forward and poked him. "No comment on the condition of the kid in the hospital except to say he's well," the Chief ordered. "No comment on the Mirabel case except there are a dozen detectives assigned. Make sure nobody connects these cases to the other two in Harlem. Deny the connection if you have to, but not on the record. You might not even have to mention the kid in St. Luke's. Just say the dead cop was guarding a material witness, then work the press privately to make them understand the mother doesn't want any publicity. Got it?"

The deputy nodded. He had the ruined face of an alcoholic reporter, which is what he had been. No one liked him much because he pretended to be a cop when he was with cops, and a reporter when he was with reporters, but it was his pretensions that made him good at his job. He could blow smoke better than anyone else in the city. He picked up the car phone again and dialed the number of the *Times*.

Nieman handed the Chief a long white envelope, wrinkled and frayed from days in Nieman's pocket. On the back were fourteen names written in pencil. Thirteen were crossed off. The survivor was Deputy Chief John Hanratty, Chief of Detectives.

The car was racing fast up the inside lane of the FDR Drive, through the dark tunnel under the United Nations. Kinsella looked at the list for a long time. He handed it back to Nieman.

Nieman said, "It was a process of triangulation and elimination. It took us three weeks of going through personnel records, duty records, and case files."

Kinsella stared blankly at the road ahead. He looked sick, like a cardinal who had just learned one of his bishops was married.

Nieman leaned toward Kinsella to make himself heard above the chatter of the radios in the front. "I called an old pal in DC last night," said Nieman. "They were overjoyed to locate Ayala again. Points for us."

"Rodriguez is the one who found him," said Kinsella.

"Or the other way around," said Nieman.

"Yeah. What else?"

"My pal emphasized that they were doing me a personal favor by giving me the hit on Hanratty in Walnut."

"Walnut?"

"Their Big Brother computer, their Prince of Darkness. It's the one that knows everything about everybody."

Kinsella sighed.

Nieman said, "Hanratty has a long record of doing business on the side with the Agency. He's an important informant for them. He gives them dirt on New York politicians and high rollers. Who's on the take, who's fucking who, who's boozing; stuff like that."

Kinsella's eyes were closed.

"Here's the good part," said Nieman. "During the days of King Richard, when the Plumbers were in the saddle, Hanratty was their guide to the back rooms of this department. Among other things, he steered them to a few cops who were willing to do odd jobs for the White House. The cops were all retired but one."

"O'Malley."

"Good hit."

"I don't like this cute shit," said Kinsella, with sudden anger at Nieman. "Those bastards in Washington must be glad to have their hooks back into you again. What'd this cost us?"

"They want to have lunch with me real soon."

Kinsella sat in silence for a few long minutes. They were passing 72nd Street. "I guess that's not too much."

The driver interrupted. "Sir, there's a message on the radio. Mr. Hopkins should call his office right away."

Kinsella said, "When you get off the Drive at 97th Street, find a phone booth."

When Nieman returned to the car from the phone booth, the deputy was giving Kinsella a quick press briefing. "I don't think we're gonna have any problems," he was saying. "No surprises. They're not looking for a press conference and we're not gonna give 'em one. Just a routine statement by your office that I'll give them verbally when I get to the hospital. No pictures of anything. TV sure as hell won't run head and shoulders shots of me talking to a reporter with a mike, so they've got nothing to show. We're in good shape."

"Who's up there?" asked Kinsella.

"Three channels, but there's a fire in midtown and they might all be gone by the time I get to St. Luke's. It's a good thing the Mayor didn't go to the hospital."

"I'm sorry he didn't," snapped Kinsella.

"Sir?"

"If the cop had lived, the Mayor would have gone to see him."

"Yessir. Let's see what else. No problems with the *Daily News* or the *Times*. They see it as nothing more than a cop killing. The *Post* wants a statement by you, but I'll phone it in later."

"OK, Howie. Good job. Keep it low key."

The car was crossing Central Park on the 97th Street Transverse. The deputy picked up the phone again and stuck his finger in his other ear.

Nieman said, "It was Rodriguez. He and O'Malley had an argument. O'Malley took him off the cop killing, and told him to go back to the squad room. Rodriguez says it was Charlie who killed the cop. Charlie was trying for the boy."

"Where is Rodriguez now?"

"When I told him we were on our way to the Two-Four, he told me to stuff it. He wants Charlie off the streets, and he's gonna go find him, he says."

"He's AWOL," said Kinsella.

"Let him go," said Nieman. "Let him find Charlie."

"What the hell is going on?"

Nieman shrugged. He poked the driver. "Let me out here," said Nieman.

"What about Hanratty?" asked Kinsella.

"Leave him to me. I think we've stumbled on the last few pieces in the puzzle. We still don't know exactly what they're doing."

"I suppose it's a good thing we can't torture and pillage like the goddamn Brits in Ulster," said Kinsella. "The temptation would be too strong."

"Sir?" said the driver.

Kinsella looked up.

"The radio says Hanratty'll be at the meeting at the Two-Four. That's the whole list you asked for."

"I guess I'd better be there too," said Kinsella. He turned to Nieman and said, "Every son of a bitch in this mess has his own agenda. It's nothing but loose wires. You keep in touch, goddammit. Remember who you work for. You work for me, Harry, not those bastards in Washington."

Hanratty stood in the door of the Twenty-Fourth Precinct, waiting for Kinsella. He wanted to tell Kinsella there would be a demonstration in the morning in front of the precinct to protest police inaction on the killings of the little boys. The press had dropped the ball and failed to connect the killings, but the people in the neighborhood knew what was going on, and they were frightened and mad. Kinsella was late, but Hanratty waited patiently. He wanted to see Kinsella for a moment alone, to take a reading of the Chief's mood. Hanratty was worried.

At five-thirty that morning, he had been awakened by a phone call.

The voice on the phone said, "Hanratty?"

"Speaking."

"Listen carefully. This is an old friend. Do you recognize the voice?"

"Yes."

"Someone scored a hit on your name in Walnut late yesterday. There's no way to tell who it was, but we thought you might want to know someone pulled your file."

The line went dead.

Hanratty didn't believe for a moment that there was no list of Walnut users, with times, access codes, and station locations on a printout in a safe in Langley, but he appreciated the warning. They owed him some favors, and he was more useful where he was than somewhere else. It was all a matter of where you sat at the table.

When Kinsella arrived, he listened to Hanratty's information, then brushed by. The two weren't friends, but they had worked together for years. Hanratty knew Kinsella had a hard time disguising his feelings, and Hanratty felt the chill.

Like most good executives, Hanratty was good at cutting his losses. As he pondered the problem of how to do it, the desk sergeant called him to the phone.

It was Ayala. He said, "I'm on 109th Street, you know where I mean?"

"Yes."

"Mr. Charlie has flown the coop. You know what that means?"

"Yes."

"Where's Rodriguez?" asked Ayala.

"No one knows. He and O'Malley got into it when O'Malley pulled him off the cop killing this morning."

"Where's O'Malley?"

"Upstairs at a meeting. They're looking for Charlie, too."

"Tell him to do what I told him, and tell him to do it tonight."

The line went dead. No one was saying goodbye this morning.

Hanratty knew what it meant. He knew it was all coming apart. Pretty soon everyone would be scrambling for the back door. He had a few back doors of his own, but he had been in the game too long to join an undignified scramble. He wanted to retire in one piece. He walked out to the sidewalk and stood in the warm sun. Like a good executive, he began to enumerate his options.

He could stick with Ayala, but Ayala was in so deep he couldn't get out, and Ayala's clients in Havana and Moscow were vindictive. They punished failure and Ayala had failed.

He could try to work things out with Kinsella, who couldn't afford a scandal in the department in an election year. Unless Kinsella's hand was forced, he couldn't do anything but let Hanratty retire quietly. Hanratty had friends on the force who would help, but there were obstacles.

Hanratty listed them. Rodriguez was a loose wire. Ayala was the keystone. He had to go. The Chief's gunslinger was the spring in the works, turning all the other wheels so Harry Nieman had to go. O'Malley was a threat. And Lopez. She was a problem, but she was also an opportunity.

It was simple. It was a Mexican stand-off. They all had the drop on each other already. At the first shot, they would all blaze away. He would provoke the first shot. It would be a fine distraction, and Hanratty would slip away.

The sun on the sidewalk warmed Hanratty. He felt chilly even on hot days.

Howie Patterson jumped out of the Chief's car and trotted up the steps of the station house. Hanratty hated the public relations man, but held the door for him.

"Thanks, Chief," said Patterson.

"Hiya, Howie."

"See ya," said Patterson. Hanratty grabbed his arm and pulled him aside. "I gotta get up there and see the Chief," said Patterson, then fell silent under the flat stare of Hanratty.

"I'm waiting for someone," said Hanratty. "I wonder if you've seen him."

"Whozzat?"

"The guy you came up with in the Chief's car."

"Oh, you mean that guy Nieman? We dropped him off at 96th and Amsterdam. I don't know where the hell he is. I gotta go now."

Hanratty let him go. Hanratty had his plan. He would set O'Malley loose on Rodriguez. That would occupy the two of them. Then Hanratty would snatch Lopez. She was more useful alive than dead. It wasn't a matter of hiding anything, so much as neutralizing the opposition, making it unprofitable for them to act. If Hanratty had Lopez, they would all have to come to him, and he would know where they were and what they wanted. Then it would be easy to pit them against each other. Then Hanratty would make another plan, choosing from more options as they became available. Hanratty intended to be standing on his feet at the end.

The meeting broke up. When Kinsella got downstairs and saw Hanratty still standing by the door, he walked over to him and pulled him aside.

"I want this Charlie Chopoff found, Hanratty. You better shake the tree."

Hanratty nodded.

"Let me tell you a story," said Kinsella. "One of my kids gave me a lovely tie for Christmas last year. It was one of those rep ties, and I wore it all the time, standing on TV with the Mayor, and that sort of thing. I liked the tie. Then I found out the tie belonged to an English regiment that tortured and burned its way all across Ireland in the old days, and I burned the fucking tie in the kitchen sink. My wife thought I'd gone around the bend, but no, I hadn't. I wasn't crazy at all, was I?"

Kinsella turned on his heel and slammed through the doors to the sidewalk, yelling for his driver, leaving a gang of puzzled top cops in his wake. They looked at Hanratty. He shrugged. He headed upstairs to talk to O'Malley.

"You're losing your grip," he told O'Malley. "I'm bringing in the Manhattan homicide commando squad on this case. You better not get in their way, Eddie. Our pal is looking for Charlie, too, and nobody cares who finds him."

O'Malley said, "That fucking Rodriguez. If you hadn't sent him over here, none of this would have happened."

Hanratty said, "No, Eddie. You fucked up."

O'Malley said, "Don't ever say that to me again, Hanratty. I'm sick of your shit."

Hanratty smiled. "That fucking Rodriguez is your problem now, Eddie. I just talked to Ayala. This problem is all yours. You better take care of your problems, Eddie. Then you won't be a problem yourself."

Hanratty smiled. The smile looked like it would split the skin on his necrotic face.

Rodriguez had patched up his apartment, but he couldn't avoid the knot of anger in his belly every time he unlocked his door and walked in. It was like living with someone he hated.

He opened a beer. He slapped a sandwich together and ate it in gulps, furious with himself, and furious with the dead cop who Rodriguez had ordered not to let anyone into the recovery room without identification by the nurse. If you want it done right, do it yourself. That was a hell of a motto for a department the size of two Army divisions.

He left the remains of the sandwich and walked into the bedroom. A votary candle burned with a still, small flame before the statue. He missed Mercedes terribly. Events were driving them apart with the force of a hurricane. Mercedes was pregnant with his child, but Rodriguez could think of no way to cross the gulf between them.

He looked at the statue. On the wall above it, hung a poster from an exhibit of Franz Kline's paintings. The poster was patched with Scotch tape. Rodriguez reached up and swept it off the wall into the corner. The fuckers! He was hunting a killer from an island so primitive that it was outside the realm of his experience. Tribes of Cold Warriors with computers and nuclear weapons were in the bushes with the Caribbean crazies. And there was O'Malley, feeding off the carrion.

On the television news that morning, and in the *Times,* the world was presented in a clear, rational order. Everything, no matter how horrible or how trivial, was neatly ranked and superficially connected to everything else. Yet fifty blocks north of midtown Manhattan and the electronic navel of the world, Rodriguez inhabited a world of dark violence and primitive belief that was invisible to journalism and its practitioners and customers.

Rodriguez was not part of that dark world, or equipped for it, and he knew it, but he wanted revenge, and that was enough. He was going to get Charlie Chopoff, then O'Malley. He was going to do it for the sake of Mercedes and the unborn child, and perhaps himself. Then they would figure out what to do next. He was ready to go back to the Caribbean with her, if that was what she wanted.

He set his beer can in front of the statue and began to change his clothes. Over a black cotton tee shirt, he pulled an elastic band as broad as his open hand, and smoothed it in place around his middle. Part of the band was double thickness to form a large, tight pouch. He tugged the band around until the pouch was under his left arm.

He took the 9mm Browning out of a drawer, checked the load, and fit the gun into the pouch. The gun was snug and invisible. He had worn this apparatus on undercover assignments. The tee shirt soaked up sweat. It also matched the color of the band, so the band wouldn't show as an outline through the fabric of a shirt or sweater.

He put on khaki pants and a loose pullover sweater. He tied double knots in the laces of his running shoes. He put on a tan golf jacket. The outside pockets had flaps with buttons. In one pocket, he dropped two speed-loaders for his .38. In the other, he put his badge. He took his sunglasses out of a narrow inside pocket of the jacket and replaced them with the loaded extra clip for the Browning. He clipped his service revolver into the waistband holster in the small of his back.

He checked himself in the broken mirror on the back of his closet door. He looked like a man going to the museum on a pleasant autumn afternoon. He had it both ways now. He had the tools and the authority of a cop, and the hardware and the freedom of the outlaw.

He knew Nieman had told him almost nothing, and had manipulated and misled him, and it had made him mad, but he didn't care now. He had advantages in this game that Nieman didn't have—the freedom of the streets and a standing offer from Ayala. Nieman was trapped in his games, thought Rodriguez. Rodriguez had a back door.

He lit another votary candle and left it burning beside the first one. He made one more check. His handcuffs in their worn leather case sat on the dresser. He left them there. They were dead weight. He wasn't taking prisoners. He wasn't a cop anymore.

chapter sixteen
dmz

The people of 109th Street had decided to beautify their neighborhood by painting the fronts of their buildings with free paint supplied by the city parks department, using funds in turn supplied by the federal government. It was a program that generously substituted buckets of pink, blue, yellow, and white paint for jobs. The result was that the south half of the block of 109th Street between Amsterdam and Columbus Avenues had taken on the peeling, motley appearance of a Caribbean waterfront, without the charm of the sea and the warmth of the tropics.

The north side of the street was unpainted brown and gray, the natural colors of the four- and five-story brownstone houses that lined the block. Rodriguez stood in the afternoon shadows beside the stoop of one of these, and studied Charlie's building. It was blue with red trim. He crossed the street and went inside.

He went from door to door, flashing his badge. People were angry. They were more angry at him because he was Puerto Rican. What the hell was he doing here *now?* Where the hell had he been? Every door in the building had been knocked on ten times by ignorant cops who didn't speak Spanish, or spoke enough to be rude. And earlier today, there was one last, awful man, a brute, who cursed and yelled at them as if the murders were their fault.

They all knew who Charlie Chopoff was. Had they seen

him? asked Rodriguez with his cop's poker-faced patience. No, of course not. He was probably back in Santo Domingo by now, with his sister and mother. Rodriguez wondered if Charlie was leading him to O'Malley, or if O'Malley would get to Charlie first.

The door of the top rear apartment was locked. Rodriguez gave a perfunctory knock, then kicked the door off its hinges with two hard kicks. The place had been overturned in a frenzy. Charlie's spartan room was in the back, overlooking the playground. Tee shirts and sweatshirts were thrown all over. The mattress and the seat of a chair were slit open.

Rodriguez walked into the kitchen, knowing he would find a pile of day-old feces. Sure enough. "Kaka," he said out loud. He walked back to the bedroom. In the corner was a small voodoo shrine on an upturned plastic milk case. The shrine was curiously untouched. Ayala's *mestizos* were probably afraid of it. Perhaps Ayala himself was a respecter of shrines, if not afraid. On the case, which was covered by a white cloth, sat St. Barbara in her robes. Small saucers held the stubs of candles of various colors. Rodriguez wondered if Charlie was a member of a local *santeria* sect, or just wanted to keep in touch on his own with the gods. He squatted in front of the shrine and lifted the cloth. In a brown manila envelope taped to the underside of the top of the case, he found a small plastic bag and a white envelope. In the plastic bag were two small dried penises. In the white envelope were ten thousand dollars in hundred-dollar bills.

Rodriguez put the bag and the envelope in his pocket. He replaced the cloth and, on an impulse, lit one of the candles and stuck it upright on its saucer.

The noise of two hundred children seemed louder and shriller than usual to Rodriguez as he approached the playground behind JHS 57. There were more adults than usual, standing and talking in small groups. They watched Rodriguez suspiciously as he questioned the older boys in the softball and basketball games, asking them if they had seen Charlie.

He knew that a lot of the neighborhood kids were saying

they knew who Charlie was, and where he lived. Rodriguez now discovered this was true, and the knowledge of it shook him. If he had stuck to his original intention to find the killer, and had approached the case in the normal way, and not let himself be sidetracked by his vendetta against O'Malley, he might have found the killer sooner. He might have prevented the assault on Bobby Powers, the deaths of the cop and the nurse in St. Luke's, and the death of the Mirabel boy.

The kids on the playground gave Rodriguez different answers, but there was general agreement that Charlie Chopoff was a retarded Dominican who walked with a limp and lived on 109th Street. No one had seen him for several days.

It was getting late in the afternoon. Rodriguez worked his way around the playground, asking the same questions and getting the same answers. Now and then, he got the scent of O'Malley. When he got back to the hole in the fence on 108th Street, Rodriguez looked up at Charlie's window. He saw a fleeting shadow. He wanted to run around the block and up to the apartment, but he couldn't move. He felt weak and inexplicably discouraged. He had to lean against the fence.

He wished he could talk to Mercedes, but he couldn't approach her. He didn't know how to talk to her. He looked up at the apartment again. There was the shadow again. Rodriguez suddenly buckled to his knees. He felt a wave of hostility and anger sweep over him, directed at him, and then a sense of Mercedes' presence in his life, and a sense of danger.

He was tempted to go to a phone and call her, but he forced himself to sit still, resting on the ground by the fence, conscious that people were staring curiously at him. He had to clear his head. He had to believe that Charlie would continue to hang around this neighborhood, that he had nowhere else to go. If he left the neighborhood, no one would ever find him. In New York City, finding someone out of his neighborhood was like looking for a needle in a haystack. There was no point in trying.

Rodriguez pulled himself to his feet. He remembered a doctor telling him the symptoms of concussion could return if he was under strain. He decided to get a bowl of soup and a cup of coffee, then try the *bodegas*, the bars, and the corners. He was still afraid to call Mercedes. He didn't know what to say if she answered, or what to do if she didn't.

As Rodriguez crossed Amsterdam Avenue on his way to Broadway to find a place to eat, he saw the *botanica,* the little shop where he bought the statue of St. Barbara. He remembered Mercedes' story about the old Haitian woman. He walked in.

The place was empty and dark, lit only by the light from the street. Rodriguez called out, and a young man in a white shirt came out from a curtain hung across the door to the back.

"Oui?" he said.

"Is the old woman here?" asked Rodriguez in Spanish.

The young man called into the back, *"Maman."*

The old woman shuffled out to the counter, took one look at Rodriguez, and sent the young man out to the sidewalk. She motioned Rodriguez to follow her into the back.

"Your woman never came back to me for the sacrifice," she said. "She is in great danger now."

Rodriguez put the white envelope and the plastic bag on the table.

"I do not want your money," she said. "Put it away. If it is not yours, give it to those who need it. This money smells of blood."

"Do you know what these are?" he asked.

"Yes. Where did you get them?"

He told her.

She said, "There is good voodoo and bad voodoo. These are powerful juju for bad voodoo. They are no good to anyone who does not take them himself. They can raise the dead, and protect the one who calls the dead to life. This is food for the dead, just as chickens and goats are food for the gods in good voodoo. If someone calls on the gods of the dead and does not offer them their favorite food, the gods get angry and take the person who calls them."

She looked steadily at Rodriguez. She said, "Even so, these juju can bring harm to the one who possesses them. You are looking for the man who did this?"

"Yes."

248

"Good," she said. "I will help you. I will keep these juju here because I know what to do with them, and you do not."

"These cannot harm you?" he asked.

She laughed, with a dry cackle like an old hen. "No," she said. "I am strong. You are strong, too, but not this way."

He hesitated.

"Hurry," she commanded. "If you are brave, you will find your woman safe before the end of the day."

"Where is she?"

"I am not sure. But soon it will be dark all around her, and you must finish this other search before you can look for her. Go. You are wasting time."

When he left the *botanica*, Rodriguez went straight to a pay phone and called the Gold Rail. He asked for Ayala.

The bartender answered, "Never heard of him."

"This is Rodriguez."

"Oh, yeah. He's been looking for you. He'll be back in a few minutes."

"Tell him I'll be there."

Rodriguez stood at the bar in the cool, dim light of late afternoon, watching the crowds on the sidewalks. He drank Coke. He listened to the jukebox and the clatter of the kitchen. As he waited for Ayala, he turned the whole problem over in his mind.

The legal case against Charlie was weak. The dried penises were impossible evidence. There were no witnesses to the first two killings. Bobby Powers would make a superb witness in his own assault case, but felonious assault was not murder. The charge would be plea-bargained down a step or two and might not go to trial because Bobby's mother was adamantly opposed to letting her son testify in court.

The cop killing and the murder of the nurse were equally impossible. The boy had been heavily sedated after his operation, and there was no other way to place Charlie at the scene. Even an inexperienced, court-appointed lawyer would have an easy defense. That left the Mirabel killing. Again, there was no witness.

249

That left nothing. Here was a man who committed five murders and one violent assault with the same weapon in six months, and he was not culpable before the law. The law would say, arrest him. Bring him before the process of the law, and let the law decide. But Rodriguez knew that if he arrested Charlie, and read him his rights, and turned him over to the criminal justice system for trial, the probability was that Charlie would be declared legally insane. Sooner or later, the killer would be released by the leaky system, which was not really a system at all. It was a jury-rigged hulk lashed together by politics and expediency. Worse criminals than Charlie were put back on the street every day, declared to be rehabilitated.

Four police officers—O'Malley, Nieman, Kinsella, and himself—knew Charlie was the killer, yet Charlie was out there walking around. They had all taken the same oath. They were all what the law, with its own mumbo-jumbo, liked to call sworn officers of the law.

Rodriguez shook with anger and frustration. He felt like a twelve-year-old kid cornered by a bunch of bigger kids, knowing they could do anything to him they wanted to do, and that they were going to do it. For a moment, Rodriguez felt the fear of the four little boys. He was ready to kill someone.

Ayala walked into the bar, quick and brusque. "In the back," he said, and led the way to a back booth, dark and private. One of his *mestizos* sat in the shadows of another booth, watching with a look two thousand years old.

"You left a message," said Ayala.

"Here's my deal," said Rodriguez. "You take Charlie off the streets, and I go to work for you. I want the bastard stuffed in a trash can on Broadway and 106th Street, so everybody in this neighborhood knows it's safe to send their kids outside again."

"What's in it for me?"

"Me."

Ayala said, "I was interested in you, Rodriguez, but you waited too long."

"That's the carrot," said Rodriguez. "Here's the stick. If I find him before his boss does, I'll come looking for his boss, too."

Ayala smiled softly, almost sadly, and said, "I wanted you to work for me, but such a deal is not the way."

"That's my best offer."

"In my business," said Ayala, "One should never admit weakness, but I will admit to you, my friend, that I have no idea where Charlie is right now."

"Perhaps O'Malley can tell you."

"Yes, perhaps he can." Ayala was thoughtful. "Why don't you call back here in an hour or so."

"OK," said Rodriguez. "I'll do that."

Ayala smiled softly again. Rodriguez got up and walked out.

An hour later, with the same *mestizo* watching, Ayala slid a black and white photo across the table in the booth to O'Malley. Ayala was smooth, in a shirt so white it glowed. His suit coat hung on a hook by the booth.

"You know this guy?" asked Ayala.

A file opened in O'Malley's memory. This was the shambling runner outside the Children's Mansion. *This was the Chief's gunslinger!*

"Yeah. It's a cop named Harry Nieman."

"Find him and take him out tonight. Tonight. You understand? Same price as Lopez."

"What about Lopez?"

"She'll keep."

"Not for long."

"No, not for long," agreed Ayala. "Eddie, I've got no use for people who can't deliver. She didn't deliver. Neither did you."

He spoke so softly that O'Malley had to lean forward to hear him. "But she's not a junkyard dog like you. You fucked up everything, Eddie. Now you better unfuck."

Ayala left the photo on the table and walked out. O'Malley slapped his left hand to his right biceps and shot his right fist in the air at Ayala's back. The *mestizo* smiled.

O'Malley turned the photo over. A stamp on the back read, "NYPD Photo Lab." This was Hanratty's work: that fucking mummy was an old hand at the game of Let's You and Him Fight. O'Malley could feel the doors closing behind him. He de-

251

cided not to tell Ayala that Charlie Chopoff was lying trussed up on his side in an abandoned apartment only a block away. Charlie had just lost all his value as a hostage.

Just as it was getting dark, Rodriguez found the place where the trails of Charlie and O'Malley intersected. It was a little Dominican lunch counter on Columbus Avenue. The owner was badly shaken. He told Rodriguez that a terrible man, a cop with a gold badge like *señor's,* a big man with a temper like an alligator, had pulled one of his customers out of the store kicking and screaming in the middle of the afternoon.

Who was this customer? asked Rodriguez. The owner said the man was a harmless local idiot who ate in the place nearly every day. Where did they go? The owner didn't know. The policeman said he would destroy the store if the owner followed him outside. The owner believed him.

Rodriguez reassured the man, thanked him, then called the Gold Rail. Ayala was gone. Rodriguez called Nieman's office. No answer. He called Nieman's answer service and left a message asking for a meeting that night. He called Mercedes. There was no answer, and the bottom dropped out of his world. O'Malley had Charlie, and Mercedes was gone.

Mercedes hated to be late for anything, and she disliked waiting for others. The only exception was her obstetrician, who was a good doctor, but was always behind schedule by late afternoon, the only time Mercedes could go. By the time Mercedes got out of the doctor's office, it was after six. She had to be at the Children's Mansion by seven for a vote on whether or not to sit in at the Mansion after the closing date for the sale of the building to its new owner.

When she got home she forced herself to eat. There was no time to change clothes. She wanted to be at the Mansion early, to have time to talk to the others before the meeting. She grabbed a light raincoat and ran out of her apartment. Downstairs, she darted up West End Avenue and turned left into

107th Street. This was a short block of brownstones, with a little hill in the middle of the block, and a sharp drop down to the service ramp of Riverside Drive. The Children's Mansion was at the end of the block, on the ramp.

Mercedes relaxed and slowed down. She had time. There were a few faint streaks of blue in the western sky over the Hudson River, and streaks of flame in the gray clouds. She loved the clear weather and odd restlessness of autumn.

At the top of the little hill, someone in a dark raincoat stepped out of a car parked by the curb. She was startled. The man turned directly in front of her and said, "Excuse me, miss." She smiled and side-stepped to avoid the open door.

Then she saw the rotted face. In a moment of awful terror, it loomed at her like a face in a dream. She tried to flee but her knees weakened. Like a dream, her feet had no weight but would not move. The man's hand slapped over her nose and mouth. He pinched an artery in her neck. She thought she was drowning. The blue and orange of the sky grew and filled her vision. The gray night clouds roared in her head. The man's breath stank like garbage. She tried to struggle, then stopped as the gray of evening turned to fiery red dawn behind her eyes.

When she woke up she was in total darkness, and the air was dank and cool. She could hear the faint rumble of traffic overhead. She was bound with tape, and gagged. There was no need for a blindfold. She could hear the drip of water and the rustle of rats. She knew the rats would not bother her as long as she stayed awake. She knew exactly where she was.

Nieman found two messages at his office—one from Rodriguez asking for a meeting at the Gold Rail, and one from Hemingway asking to meet at the Straus Park Cafe, a few blocks south of the Gold Rail. It was a pleasant bar and restaurant between 107th and 108th Streets, with a good view of the intersection and the little park, but it was glassed in, and quite open to view. Nieman wondered why Rodriguez chose the place, and wondered who it was who called himself Rodriguez and wanted to meet at the Gold Rail.

Nieman decided to take his second gun, a light-weight Beretta .38 automatic. He liked the gun because it had almost no recoil. He pulled the gun and its shoulder holster out of a drawer, checked it, and put it on. He opened a box of fresh ammunition. He filled two speed-loaders for his service revolver, and two clips for the Beretta. He dropped them in the pocket of his suit jacket hung over the back of his chair.

The phone rang.

"Hello," said Nieman.

"Harry? It's Bobby."

"Hey, how are ya?" Bobby was a pal from Vietnam days, and now a supervisor at Alcohol, Tobacco & Firearms.

"Good, Harry, real good. I still owe ya that lunch. Listen, I heard something tonight you need to know."

"Yeah?"

"You know a bar on Broadway called the Gold Rail?"

"Yeah."

"I shoulda told you this before, you never know, but we've got a gal in there. Works as a waitress. We think there's some very heavy gun-dealing in there."

"No shit?"

"Yeah, the bartender is an ex-cop and we think he's wired to Noraid and the IRA."

"No shit?"

"You pulling my leg, Harry?"

"No, no. I'm surprised, is all."

"Yeah, well, this gal picked up a photograph off a table that had just been vacated by a cop, one of your guys, goes in there all the time, named O'Malley."

"Who was he talking to?"

"Guy goes by the name of Ayala. We think he's a big dealer, scrap, not smack, you know what I mean?"

"Yeah."

"We think he's got a big deal going down to sell a lot of hardware."

"Who's in the picture?" asked Nieman.

"You."

"Doing what?"

"Staring at the camera. It looks like a long telephoto."

Nieman said nothing. When Bobby said nothing, Nieman said, "Thanks, Bobby. I owe you one."

"That's OK. The print is stamped NYPD. This mean anything, Harry?"

"I'll let you know."

"Yeah, sure. Ha, ha. Listen, Harry, one more thing. Another guy of yours, named Rodriguez maybe? He was in the bar earlier talking to Ayala. You guys got something going up there? We don't want to muddy your water."

"It's OK, Bobby. This is real good stuff. Listen, lemme ask you one question."

"Yeah, shoot."

"Who's buying this hardware?"

"We thought maybe you guys were."

"Can you keep this under your hat, Bobby?"

"Sure."

"We are. Can you stay away from it?"

"Sure, if you cut us in on the bust."

"It's a deal, Bobby. Listen, when did your gal pick this photo up?"

"Maybe thirty minutes ago."

"How'd you do the ID so fast?"

"She's not an informer. She's an agent, real good, one of the best. She knew them right away."

"OK, Bobby. Thanks."

Nieman stared out his window at the empty plaza behind the Municipal Building. It was a small world. It was a goldfish bowl. Everybody knew what everybody was doing all the time. They just didn't know why.

It wasn't secrecy that allowed everyone to continue in their rotten little businesses. It was deals and power, the kind of power that made you untouchable and invisible, even if your name was in every computer in the world.

But now and then something went wrong with the game. The computers went out to lunch. Everybody thought they knew what was happening, but they were all groping in the dark. All the invisible guys were closing in on all the other invisible guys.

255

At the first bump in the dark, the shooting would start. This was the night Nieman had been waiting for. He stood up and pulled his jacket on. It was time to saddle up.

In his long, shambling gait, Nieman covered the whole neighborhood in the vicinity of Broadway and 108th Street, near the Straus Park Cafe, in quick time. He saw nothing to make him suspicious but he hadn't expected anything. He went in and ordered a beer and a rare hamburger at the bar. It was exactly seven o'clock.

The bartender was a young woman. She looked at him carefully and asked, "Are you Mr. Hopkins?"

"Hopkins is my name."

"Mr. Hemingway says he'll be late, but he'll call you soon if you can wait."

"Thanks," said Nieman. "Waiting's my game."

She flashed a wary smile, and went back to the kitchen with the order. Nieman sat in the pleasant bar waiting for Rodriguez to call, and watching the people on Broadway. It was a warm, hazy night. The sidewalks were crowded. It reminded him of evenings in the same neighborhood twenty years before, and of evenings in Saigon fifteen years before. Someone was setting him up. He wondered who it was. He wondered if it was Hanratty. Maybe Rodriguez had gone over to the other side. Nieman relaxed as a sense of the familiar settled over him. All the players were in motion. There was nothing to do but wait.

Rodriguez wandered around the neighborhood, trying to puzzle out where O'Malley might have taken Charlie. Every time Rodriguez passed a pay phone, he called the Gold Rail, asking for Ayala, but Ayala wasn't there. He grew afraid that Ayala was going to keep his end of the bargain, and then Rodriguez was going to have to keep his. As he passed the stores and bars of the neighborhood, full of ordinary people going about their ordinary business, the idea of working for Ayala seemed less attractive.

It was seven o'clock. He had to call Nieman at the Straus

Park Cafe, but he didn't know what to tell him. He wasn't sure he wanted Nieman's help now. He stopped at the corner of 109th Street and Amsterdam Avenue. He was caught again in a dilemma, a choice between two unsatisfactory alternatives.

He decided to force the issue. He called the Gold Rail. When the bartender told him again that Ayala wasn't there, Rodriguez said, "Tell the son of a bitch to forget the carrot. Tell him he better start thinking about the stick."

Then he headed down 109th Street toward Broadway and the Straus Park Cafe. He'd see if Nieman wanted to join the hunt. As Rodriguez walked past PS 165, which looked like a medieval ruin in the half-light of early night, he heard someone calling him.

"Mistah. Hey, mistah. Yo, mistah."

Rodriguez turned and saw a boy riding his bike wildly up the sidewalk after him, calling and waving. "Mistah, wait for me."

Rodriguez waited. The kid stopped short ten yards away. Rodriguez recognized him as one of the kids he had questioned in the playground that afternoon.

The boy spoke in Spanish. He knew where Charlie Chopoff was, he said. Why didn't the boy call the police? asked Rodriguez. Because the boy was afraid of the big detective. Who was this detective? The boy didn't know his name, but he was big and mean, and he yelled at all the kids in the playground that afternoon, before the *senor* came around.

Where was Charlie Chopoff? The boy hesitated a moment in palpable fear, then said the big detective had him. Where? The big detective took Charlie into the squatters' building on Amsterdam Avenue across from the big church. When? Late in the afternoon. "Thank you," said Rodriguez. "You are very brave." The boy said they were in the apartment on the third floor in the back of the building. How did the boy know this? He followed them. "You are very foolish," said Rodriguez. Why did the boy do this? He didn't know. Maybe he wanted to be a cop when he grew up. Rodriguez was moved. He said, "If you ever need help, you or your family, you call me, Detective Sergeant Daniel Rodriguez, and wherever I am, I will help you. Now go home and keep this a secret between you and me, OK?"

"OK," said the boy, and he pedaled away down the street

257

to a building where an old woman stood anxiously watching from a stoop. For all she knows, thought Rodriguez, I'm Charlie Chopoff. He turned back to Amsterdam Avenue and the pay phone.

The phone in the Straus Park Cafe rang. A waiter answered. He turned and said to the bar, "Is Mr. Hopkins here?"

Nieman took the phone. Rodriguez said, "Charlie's in an apartment in the squatters' building at 111th and Amsterdam. O'Malley took him there maybe two hours ago, maybe three. That son of a bitch Ayala knew all along."

"What do you mean?"

"I'll tell you later. There's a pizza place on Amsterdam just above 110th. Meet me there. I've gotta have some food."

Nieman hung up and dropped a ten-dollar bill on the bar. He stepped out onto the sidewalk as if he were stepping onto a sheet of ice. Just as he left, the pay phone rang again. A waitress answered it. "Is Mr. Nieman here?" she called. The bartender said, "I think that was him who just left." The waiter said, "No, that was Mr. Hopkins." The waitress said into the phone, "Whoever he was, he just left," but the phone was dead.

258

chapter seventeen
the children's mansion

Rodriguez stood in the shadows of a bus stop on Amsterdam Avenue, across from the pizzeria. He devoured two slices of pizza mashed together into an oily, dripping sandwich. He threw the crusts into the gutter, wiped his fingers on a paper napkin, dropped it in the gutter, and picked up an open can of Coke from the sidewalk by his feet. He drained the can and dropped it on the street with a clatter. He wiped his mouth with the back of his hand and burped.

Nieman came around the corner from 110th Street. He gave no sign of seeing Rodriguez. He walked up the block to 111th Street and ducked around the corner out of sight. Several minutes passed before he reappeared at the corner. Rodriguez saw no one following, and crossed the street to meet him. They moved back around the corner and stood in the dark entrance of an apartment building across the street from the squatters' building.

There were no fewer streetlights here than anywhere else, but the vacant lots around the squatters' building, and the empty grounds around the cathedral, made the area seem dark. Half the windows of the squatters' building were tinned up. Some of the rest were lit, but every window on the third floor was dark. Going into the building would be like going into a coal mine.

In the empty lot next to the building, the squatters had shoved the rubble around to make a garden with walks of salvaged brick, garden plots, and a little goldfish pool. Rodriguez

259

thought this was what Germany had looked like in 1945—a pinched, desperate life sprouting out of the ruins.

He asked Nieman, "Do you know the building?"

"Just the back on the outside. I've seen it from 112th Street through the vacant lot."

"There's no way off the roof, and only two ways out the back—a back door to the basement, and a fire escape that's broken off below the second floor, with a two-floor drop to the back alleyway."

"The third floor is all dark."

"I looked around before you got here," said Rodriguez. "The third-floor rear isn't boarded up."

"Do you want me to take the back?"

Rodriguez thought for a moment. "No," he said. "Let's both go in the front. This guy's very dangerous. If you're out back, and he takes me out, he'll be gone and you won't know it."

"Are we taking prisoners?"

"No."

"OK," said Nieman. "It's your show."

"No, Harry. I'm just the hired help."

As they crossed the street, Rodriguez said, "If Charlie runs, it'll be out the back. The alleyway goes the whole interior length of the block on different levels behind each building, with a lot of walls and fences. Once he gets back in there, he's trapped. The only way out is to go the whole length of the block, and through the basement of 545, that big building on the corner of Broadway. You know the one?" Rodriguez waved down the block at a huge ten-floor building, lit up like the *Titanic* at sea.

Nieman grunted.

"If he gets in there, he can go up through the building to the street, or up to the roof. There must be six or eight fire escapes down the back and sides, or he can cross to the building behind. We'll have to keep him out of there."

As they stood in the dark porch of the squatters' building, Nieman asked, "What about O'Malley?"

"What about him?"

"He must be around here, too."

"I hope so," said Rodriguez.

Inside the building, both men gagged. The smell was the worst Rodriguez had ever experienced. It wasn't just urine. It was the smell of excrement and death. There were no cooking smells. People didn't live in this building. They died here.

There were no lights on the first floor, but the dark hall was dimly lit by light from the street. Rodriguez motioned at a stairwell in the back. They walked quietly along the hall. A dog growled behind a door. There was a vicious thud. The dog shut up. There was no other noise.

Rodriguez went up the stairs fast, two at a time, his revolver muzzle up in his hand. Nieman went up slowly, listening for noises behind them. A low-watt bulb glowed in a ceiling socket near the front of the second-floor hallway. The stairwell above the second floor was pitch dark. A streak of light under one of the doors on the second floor went out. It was as though the entire building sensed their presence and was shutting itself off.

The once pearly mosaic tiles in the hall floor were chipped and loose. The walls and floor were filthy. There was no color except smeared gray-brown. There was no noise.

Rodriguez went up the next flight of stairs faster than the first, without a sound. Nieman went slowly again, his gun in his hand, too, barrel up, the ball of his first finger on the trigger. Bright light glowed under the door of the rear apartment on the third floor. They stood silently by the door. There was a rustling noise from inside.

"Rats," whispered Rodriguez. "The place is full of rats. We've been set up, but we've gotta go in."

Nieman whispered, "I've got hard shoes. I'll kick the door and go to the left."

Rodriguez stepped back. Nieman gently tried the doorknob with his left hand.

"It's open," he shouted. He slammed the door open and went in low to his left. Rodriguez went to the right. Chirping and squealing, a gray-brown mass of rats fled the intruders. The rats moved like shallow dirty water across the floor in all directions. They were gone in an instant.

Propped in the corner of the bare room was the nude body of Charlie Chopoff, his clothes and the contents of two shopping bags scattered in a heap on the floor. The pile of clothes wiggled. A lone rat the size of a cat darted out and ran for the door.

The body was battered and broken. Blood was splattered and smeared all over the room. There were dents in the plaster wall where the body had been smashed. It had been flung about like a rag doll. The throat was cut from ear to ear. A black-handled knife stuck straight out of the chest like a switch. Charlie's penis was stuck in the corner of his mouth like an exploded trick cigar. The small gash between his legs was neat and surgical.

Nieman was warily watching the door. "You're the homicide cop," he said. "What do you think?"

Rodriguez bent over and flexed one of the arms. It was broken in three or four places, and wobbled oddly. "The rat bites aren't too bad," said Rodriguez. "They probably didn't show up until dark, but the corpse is getting stiff. Maybe late afternoon."

They looked at each other. "O'Malley," said Rodriguez. "The kid was right."

They both moved out of the line of sight of the window.

O'Malley waited a decent interval after Rodriguez and Nieman entered the squatters' building, then stepped out of the shadows and picked his way carefully through the bricks and debris of the vacant lot. He felt good. He was in control again. He had worked like a dog all afternoon to drive things ahead to this point. Sending the kid after Rodriguez and keeping track of Nieman had been easy. Now here they were together, in one nice package.

In the dark alleyway filled with rubble, below the window of the apartment where Charlie lay, O'Malley opened the gym bag. He pulled out a dark blue nylon raincoat and put it on. He took the stun grenades out of the socks and dropped the grenades in the pockets of the raincoat. He assembled the shotgun and snapped the clip in place. He filled the pockets of his suit jacket with shotgun shells. He heaved the gym bag into the vacant lot.

When he heard the door slam open on the third floor, he stepped quietly into the basement of the building, flicked on a small pocket flashlight, and started cautiously up the stairs from the basement to the first floor.

Rodriguez said quietly, "There's hardly any blood from the throat. He must have beat the guy to death before he cut his throat."

"Who's worse? Charlie or O'Malley?"

"Dead is dead," said Rodriguez.

"If O'Malley's hanging around, let's take him now."

"Let's do it right."

"Let's do it my way," said Nieman. He stepped out of the apartment and started down the stairs. Rodriguez said, "Fuck you, Harry," at Nieman's back, and followed.

The building was silent. There was no rat noise, no dog noise, and no human noise but the slip of grit under their own feet on the steps.

They passed the second floor. Halfway down the steps to the first floor, Nieman lurched back at Rodriguez, literally picked him off his feet and carried him in two jumps back up to the second floor.

"Grenade!" he screamed, and threw Rodriguez and himself halfway down the hallway.

It was like a lightning bolt. There was a flash of red yellow white light and a noise like the end of the world. The whole building shook. The floor under Rodriguez rippled like foam rubber. The concussion felt like sledgehammers on the soles of his feet. Every door on the floor burst open. He saw Nieman's mouth shouting something in the split second before the lone light bulb blew out, but he heard nothing.

Nieman was on his feet, running for the back apartment. Rodriguez scrambled up and followed. He was stone deaf. Nieman peered out the rear window of the apartment, shoved his gun in his holster, climbed out the window, and dropped off the fire escape to the ground. Rodriguez followed.

O'Malley was running down the alleyway with amazing agility. A dark raincoat billowed out behind him like a cloak. Nieman fired two shots that sounded to Rodriguez like the distant clicks of a door lock. O'Malley didn't miss a step.

Rodriguez screamed, "Take the sidewalk!"

Nieman turned and scrambled up a pile of rubble toward the front of the building. Rodriguez took off after O'Malley. He got three buildings down the block, over cement-block walls and through rotted wooden fences, before he lost sight of the dark shape.

Rodriguez stopped. Every light in every window was on. He knew he couldn't hear right, but the faint sound of sirens came to his ears. He crept forward. He was in the middle of the block. There were three or four more buildings ahead, and then 545. From here on, there was a high chain-link fence down the center line of the alley. O'Malley couldn't climb it without being seen. Rodriguez moved as fast as he could through the dark shadows of the back yards, careful not to trip over garbage and litter.

His hearing faded out completely, and for a moment, he felt like he was underwater, gliding silently past the hulls of sunken wooden ships. He stopped and pulled out his gun. He wondered if he had somehow passed O'Malley. He turned around to look back.

Something furry brushed past him. It gave him an awful start. It was a cat, followed by another cat streaking away in terror. Rodriguez leapt aside. There was a white muzzle blast no more than ten yards from his face, and another, and another. He felt the hot blasts rush by. He heard the faint rattle of shot on the fence behind him.

He lay a moment where he fell, forcing himself not to shoot. His own muzzle blast would give him away in the shadows where he lay. He heard sirens, louder now, and the call of someone from a window above. He heard a large shape moving away. As he stood up, O'Malley went over the last low fence into the concrete-paved courtyard of 545. Rodriguez snapped off one shot but heard it smack the building wall.

When Rodriguez cleared the last fence, he knew O'Malley had gotten into the building. The basement door was broken inward off its hinges. Rodriguez ran to the door and stopped short. He could hear sirens all around, and the shouts of cops up on the street. He took his badge out of his pocket and pinned it on his jacket. There were almost as many cops killed in New York by other cops as by anyone else.

Inside the door was a long, well-lit hall with whitewashed walls and a sloping gray concrete floor that glistened like oil. Rodriguez reloaded the empty chamber of his gun and ran for a door twenty yards down. There was silence. The next stop was an alcove ten yards down the other side of the hall, then the hall opened into a wide basement mostly hidden from Rodriguez's view.

He ran for the alcove, firing wildly down the hall as he went. There was a double blast from O'Malley's shotgun. The buckshot raked the walls. The shots came from the basement. Rodriguez slid into the alcove. He's got an automatic, he thought. He's blasting the bushes. He doesn't want a fight. He wants to get away. Rodriguez reloaded his gun again. Heavy feet ran up the metal staircase from the basement to the lobby. Rodriguez sprinted after.

The door at the head of the stairs slammed open and shut on its heavy spring. The stairs were narrow and steep. Rodriguez took them three at a time. He burst through the door, skidding into the lobby, nearly trampling a young woman pushing a child in a stroller. She began to scream. The doorman ran to help her.

There were two flights of stairs leading up out of the lobby. Nieman shouted at the doorman, who was very frightened, "Which stairs?"

"No," said the doorman. "I no see heem."

"Asshole," screamed Rodriguez in Spanish. "The man with the gun."

"Upstairs," said the doorman.

Rodriguez was already on one flight of stairs. Nieman headed for the other. The street was filled with patrol cars, their lights flashing through the lobby doors. Cops were running toward the other end of the block.

Both flights of stairs went up the same end of the building, separated by an ell in the structure. At each landing, Nieman and Rodriguez could see each other. They could hear O'Malley moving up the stairs ahead of them, heading for the roof.

265

At the tenth floor, Rodriguez and Nieman came together again, breathing so hard they could barely speak. Rodriguez pointed to the staircase to the roof. They crept up into the darkness of a rooftop shed. The heavy door onto the roof was closed, but the hook that locked it from the inside hung loose.

Rodriguez took a deep breath and said, "The roof is shaped like a big E. We're at the foot. There are standpipes and ventilation fans all over, and a big water tank on legs in the middle. There's a chest-high wall all around the roof, and fire escapes, but he won't use them now. Right behind this shed is a six-foot wall up to the roof of the next building, with barbed wire on top, but kids climb it all the time. It won't stop him."

Rodriguez sucked in another breath, and said, "We'll go out about ten yards. I'll cover you. You go down the roof to the other end along the back wall and flush him back toward me. He'll have to go for this door or the other roof behind us."

"OK. Now!" said Nieman. He pulled the door open. Rodriguez scuttled out and crouched beside the shed. It had begun to drizzle. The only light on the flat, black-tarred roof came from the windows of a few taller buildings in the vicinity. It was very dark in the shadows cast by the parapet. There was loud noise on the streets below—sirens, the crackle of radios, the hubbub of a crowd.

Nieman came through the door in a crouch. He moved around the corner of the shed and into the shadow of the rear parapet. He moved ten yards and waited. Rodriguez followed him, feeling as though he was moving nightmarishly slow. They stopped where they could see the whole roof.

Neither man could see the dark shape lying on top of the flat metal roof of the shed. O'Malley could not hear their whispers, but he knew what they were doing because it was exactly what he would have done. He was trapped unless he got them both and got away over the next roof. Down on the street, his badge would be all the protection he needed.

He shifted slightly on the metal roof. He had managed to reload the clip in the few seconds before the two had come up the last steps below him, but he hadn't been able to cock the gun by jacking the new round into the chamber. They would have heard. He would have to roll, cock, and shoot in the same motion, but they were perfect targets. He knew he could take them both.

"Maybe he already went over the other roof," said Rodriguez.

"He didn't have time."

"Where the hell is he?"

Nieman held his hand up for silence. There was the faint whuppa-whuppa noise of a helicopter flying low up the edge of Manhattan. There might soon be a powerful searchlight overhead. "It sounds like Tet," said Nieman.

O'Malley heard the helicopter, too. He tensed, ready to roll.

"He's not up here," said Rodriguez.

"He's here," said Nieman.

In that moment, they both heard a guttural growl—*"Cocksuckers,"* said the voice—and the sharp metallic clack-clack of the action of a shotgun. Nieman dove flat out across the roof, Rodriguez straight toward the voice. There was a bright flash and a stuttered explosion from the roof of the shed. Rodriguez slammed head-and-shoulders-first into the door of the shed. He fell half inside.

He could hear himself screaming as he tore the Browning out of the elastic under his shirt. O'Malley started to roll off the shed roof and drop down. There were fifteen rounds in the Browning. Tracking O'Malley's black silhouette, Rodriguez emptied his gun. The Browning sounded like a machine gun. All fifteen shots hit. O'Malley landed on the rooftop like a sack of cement. He hand jerked, and the last round in his shotgun exploded. The shot tore past Rodriguez's face and took out a jagged hole in the roof of the shed.

There was only a moment's silence. Nieman yelled, "Search him quick."

As Rodriguez stripped the pockets of the devastated O'Malley, Nieman stood stiffly and walked over. He said, "I thought he got you for sure."

"A pack of smack, an envelope full of money, and a grenade," said Rodriguez. "He musta took the smack off Charlie."

"Give it all to me and let's go," said Nieman.

"Are you nuts?" shouted Rodriguez. "Isn't this the end?"

"Hanratty," said Nieman. "And Ayala. And you still don't know where Mercedes is. Then that's the end."

They could hear the heavy footsteps of cops pounding up the stairs below them. They went up the wall to the next roof like a couple of neighborhood kids. Rodriguez pulled Nieman up after him, tearing Nieman's clothes on the barbed wire. When they got down to the lobby, a security guard blocked their way. "Who do you think you are?" he said.

"Police."

The guard did not move.

"*Police, motherfucker,*" shouted Rodriguez. "Don't you know a gold badge when you see one?"

"Looks just like mine," said the guard as he stepped back out of the way.

Out on the sidewalk, Nieman said, "Ayala has enough hardware stashed around the city to start a war."

"Where is this stuff?"

"Here and there."

"Where, goddammit?" Rodriguez snatched Nieman by the shirt. "No more games, or I'll drop you right here."

"The Children's Mansion." Nieman thought for a moment, then asked, "Who's the only person not heard from today?"

"Hanratty."

"Call Ayala at the Gold Rail. If he's not there, tell the bartender to thank him for delivering Charlie and O'Malley in one package, and to tell Ayala you have some stuff from O'Malley's pockets that he might be looking for. Tell him you'll call back in ten minutes with a location to meet."

Rodriguez went to the phone and came back. "Now what?"

"Let's stay out of sight," said Nieman. "There are too goddamn many cops around here."

At ten precisely, Ayala's maroon Buick glided up to the bus stop in front of Columbia at 116th Street and Broadway. Rodriguez was waiting. To Ayala's surprise, a tall man in a shabby suit, carrying an old shopping bag in one hand, insisted on getting into the back seat with Ayala and Rodriguez.

"Hey," shouted Ayala. "Who's this?"

"Shut up," said Rodriguez, his gun in Ayala's ribs.

Nieman's gun was in the driver's ear.

Rodriguez said, "Go to Grant's Tomb and find a parking spot. We have the stuff from Charlie and O'Malley, but we need to talk first."

"Let me see it," said Ayala.

"Never mind," said Nieman. "It's in the shopping bag. Money and shit."

Ayala spoke to the driver. They rode slowly up Broadway in the dark stretch between Columbia and Barnard. Ayala asked innocently, "What happened?"

"We bumped into O'Malley in a dark stairwell," said Nieman. "I guess we were kind of looking for each other."

"I think we can make a deal, Mr. Nieman," said Ayala.

"Yeah?"

"Tell us about Charlie," said Rodriguez.

"He worked for me," said Ayala. "He was an errand boy."

"Just helping out behind the counter?" asked Nieman.

"How long did you know about the little boys?" asked Rodriguez.

"From the beginning," said Ayala. "Do you understand what he was doing?"

"No," said Rodriguez. "Tell me. I thought he was crazy, especially when I found the dried-up penises."

"You don't know much about voodoo," said Ayala.

"Some," said Rodriguez. "My mother is a *bruja*."

"A Puerto Rican witch," said Ayala with contempt. He winced as Rodriguez drove the gun muzzle into his ribs. "Or a healer, if she's any good. But it's not the same. Voodoo is another universe. In Cuba, in Haiti, in the *Republica Dominicana* where this boy Charlie came from, they still do it back in the hills and little villages, and in the slums. They do the old, powerful voodoo, the stuff that can raise the dead and bury the living."

"This is bullshit," said Nieman. He poked the driver in the ear with his gun. "Hurry up."

269

"Oh, no," said Ayala. "Believe me. I've seen it right here in Manhattan. And where this boy came from, those dried-up little dicks are a very powerful juju. You didn't understand this, or you could have found him sooner."

Rodriguez had an aching sadness in his chest. He had to start all over. He wanted Mercedes. He could hear her voice calling him.

They turned onto West 120th Street, driving slowly through the quiet square formed by Barnard, the Interfaith Center, Union Theological Seminary, and Riverside Church.

"I'll tell you something else," said Ayala. Rodriguez could feel the Cuban relaxing. He had to be careful. If they were going to find Mercedes, they had to do this step by step.

"What's that?"

"If you know where to go, even in this most civilized city of Christians and Jews, you can buy such jujus for a price, if you don't want to make them for yourself."

"Was Charlie selling them?"

"No. Didn't you see the shrine in his room?"

Rodriguez could only nod. His voice was gone. He felt the terrible fear and pain of the little boys.

"Oh, yes," said Ayala. "Mr. Chopoff wasn't murdering those little boys. There was nothing I could do. He was *sacrificing* them."

"Oh, my God," said Rodriguez. Tears leaked from his eyes. "My God."

"Horseshit," said Nieman. "Stop here."

Ayala mumbled to the driver. The driver parked the car. The road glistened with light rain. Before them, a half-mile up Riverside Drive, was the broad estuary of the Hudson River. To their left was Grant's Tomb, and to their right, just over the curb, a steep hill overgrown with trees and underbrush. It was a quiet, peaceful place.

Nieman shot the driver in the back of the head. Rodriguez's ears began ringing again. He could smell Ayala's fear.

Nieman said, "Keep an eye on Ayala while I roll this dead Indian into the underbrush." He fumbled with the door. "Ayala, how do you work these goddamn door locks?"

"A switch under the cigar lighter."

Nieman reached a long arm forward and moved the switch. All four door locks bumped. Ayala opened his door and lunged. He was very fast, but Rodriguez was faster. He brought his gun butt down hard at the bottom of Ayala's spine. Ayala screamed with pain and sagged to the street, only half out of the car. Rodriguez dragged him back.

Nieman searched the driver, relieved the body of a few items, and rolled the body over the hill. Nieman got into the driver's seat and busied himself for a few moments with something below the level of the back of the seat. Ayala craned his neck to see, but Rodriguez pulled him back.

"Lie down on the floor," said Rodriguez. "Put your hands behind your back. Then we'll talk."

Ayala complied. Rodriguez handcuffed him with Nieman's cuffs.

"Now," said Nieman. "Where is Mercedes Lopez?"

"I don't know," said Ayala.

"That's your first and last lie," said Nieman. "I'm gonna teach you a little trick we used in Vietnam. I'm gonna make you an instant heroin addict."

Ayala snorted.

"Don't scoff," said Nieman. "It always works. On the way to the bus stop, I stopped in a friendly drugstore and bought a big syringe and some Sterno. Now I'm gonna cook up some of Charlie's smack."

In a few moments, the smell of jellied gas and melting heroin filled the car. Nieman leaned over the seat. His hand held a full syringe. Without ceremony, he jabbed it into the back of Ayala's thigh through the worsted fabric of the fine suit. Nieman emptied the syringe.

Ayala squirmed and screamed in terror. "No-o-o-o," he wailed. Rodriguez held him down with his feet.

"A small dose of your own medicine," said Nieman. "You'll feel it right away. You're gonna love it. But one more load, and you'll OD, right here on the dirty floor of your beautiful car. That's a sorry way to go, for one of Havana's master spies."

Nieman was watching his watch. He tapped Rodriguez, who asked again, "Where's Lopez?"

Ayala hesitated. Nieman lit the Sterno can again, with a faint whoosh of flame. "More?" asked Nieman.

His words already slurring, Ayala said, "The Children's Mansion."

"Who with?" asked Rodriguez.

"Hanratty."

"How do you know?"

"Hanratty called me. He did it on his own."

"Why?"

"I don't know."

"Where in the Mansion?"

"The tunnel."

"With all the hardware?" asked Nieman.

"*Si.*" It was a whisper.

"Who takes over when you drop out?" asked Nieman.

There was no answer.

Rodriguez felt the pulse in Ayala's neck. "It's very slow."

"Fuck him," said Nieman. "We got what we wanted. If he lives, we can trade him to the CIA for a year's supply of money. The trick to a good, quick interrogation," added Nieman, in a professorial tone, "is never to lie to the guy about what you're gonna do to him."

Rodriguez double-parked the Buick on 107th Street, looking down the little hill at the back corner of the Mansion. The building was dark.

"Someone must be in there," said Rodriguez. "The fire lights are out."

"Describe the place," said Nieman.

"The basement has a big back room, a couple small rooms in the middle, and the boiler room in the front. The steel service door under the front stoop opens into the boiler room. The old smuggler's tunnel is under the stoop. There's a heavy iron door. The tunnel runs down toward the river."

"How far?"

"I don't know."

"Go on."

"The first floor has the office and a classroom in the front, a large central hall with the staircase, and a classroom and kitchen in the back. The second floor is all classrooms. The third floor is a big open garret. There's a flight of back stairs from the basement to the kitchen to the second floor."

"Entrances?"

"The service door under the stoop, side and back doors into the basement, and the main front door on the first floor."

Nieman said, "One of the keys we took off Ayala ought to fit one of the doors."

"We gotta be careful, Harry. I want Mercedes out in one piece."

"Sure, Danny. And where did Ayala get his keys?"

Rodriguez fell silent. Nieman added, unnecessarily, "You're a consenting adult, Rodriguez. You didn't have to play."

"I did it to protect Mercedes."

"That's nice."

At the sound of the sarcasm in Nieman's voice, a wave of nausea hit Rodriguez, then violent anger, then nothing. He felt nothing at all.

"OK," he said. "Let's do it."

Hanratty prowled around the huge old house from room to room like a ghost in the darkness. While the meeting ran on and on earlier in the evening, with loud voices rising and falling from the rear classroom on the first floor, Hanratty roamed through the basement and the rooms on the second and third floors, going up and down the back stairs. He poked into closets and drawers and peered out each window. Several times, he had gone up the back stairs to the second floor, then down the great front stairs to the director's office off the main hall on the first floor. Ayala was supposed to be here by now. There was nothing to do but wait.

It was nearly midnight when the meeting broke up and the last person left, locking the front door behind her. Hanratty made one last tour of the place. He set his defensive traps, then retired to the third floor, which had windows all around where he could wait and watch.

He saw Rodriguez go over the wall and drop into the back

yard. He heard the side door into the basement open, and heard the artfully placed toy truck clatter when the opening door struck it. A few long moments later, the soda bottle at the foot of the basement stairs fell and broke. That meant Rodriguez was coming upstairs instead of heading for the tunnel door. Then the basket of plastic building blocks was kicked across the front hall with a rattle like dozens of dice. Rodriguez was coming up the main staircase.

Hanratty started slowly down the stairs from the third floor, hugging the wall to keep the old wooden treads from squeaking. He heard the light scuff of a footstep on a marble tread below. Hanratty didn't hesitate. Though he looked like a dead man, he had the skills of years of experience. He went quickly and soundlessly down the stairs.

The interior of the building was not completely dark. Streaks of light from streetlights and the surrounding buildings shone in the windows and cast oblongs of light on the floors and walls. There was a kind of twilight in the great central hall. Hanratty crept along the bannister on the second floor above the broad central stairs. He froze. Rodriguez was coming up the stairs very slowly, one by one, gun in hand, listening for noise from above and below, looking from the dark at the top of the stairs to the shadows below. Hanratty moved without a sound. In his black raincoat, he was a shadow. He backed away from the bannister and waited.

Nieman squatted on both heels like a Vietnamese peasant in the pitch-black shadows at the head of the back stairs on the second floor. He had a clear view down the hall. Hanratty was in his sights. Trapping him was easy. Rodriguez was good bait. But Nieman was worried about Hanratty's booby traps. There might be worse traps than Tonka trucks.

Rodriguez was almost at the top of the stairs. He looked pale and scared. His head and torso were exposed above the bannister. Hanratty raised his gun and pointed it. In a shaft of light from a window, the gun appeared to be floating in air.

"Police! Freeze, Hanratty!" screamed Nieman.

Rodriguez ducked and rolled. There were two shots. One hit

the marble wall along the staircase and shattered, sending splinters of lead and stone flying like shrapnel. Then there was a soft smack like a melon breaking. Hanratty toppled to the floor, his clothes rustling softly, his gun clattering. Then silence.

Then Rodriguez said softly, "Shit."

Nieman said, without moving, "He must be alone. I was afraid some of the Indians might be here."

"They never work with anyone but Ayala," said Rodriguez, walking slowly up the stairs, wiping little streaks of blood off the side of his face. "Frisk him," said Rodriguez. "There's no time."

Nieman rolled the body over and poked through the pockets. "More keys," he said.

They ran back down the back stairs to the basement, the way Nieman had come up. There was just enough light to see by. Nieman handed the keys to Rodriguez.

"Let me go first," said Nieman. He squatted down on his heels and duckwalked slowly forward, gently moving his hands outward along the floor from his feet to the walls, up the walls to head height, back to his face, then down to his feet. "I wish I had a bayonet," he said.

At the door to the boiler room, he felt over the sill and all around the frame, then stood up. There were no sounds. They both jerked back when the boiler turned on.

"Fuck it," said Rodriguez. He reached around the door frame and snapped on the boiler-room light.

"No," screamed Nieman.

There was a light *ping,* and the unmistakable sound of a hand grenade bouncing and rolling across the concrete floor. They both watched, horrified. The boiler room floor was two steps down. The grenade rolled to a stop against the bottom step. A thin wire dangled loose from the light switch. Hanratty had pulled the pin from the grenade, then threaded the end of the wire through the pin hole, and slowly and delicately released the grenade's handle, so the thin wire kept the handle in place. He then set the grenade on its base on the concrete floor below the light switch, and tied the fine wire around the switch, perfectly taut to the grenade below. When Rodriguez snapped on the switch, the weight of the grenade held it steady while the wire slipped out of the hole, releasing the handle, and igniting the fuse.

Nieman shoved Rodriguez back up the hall and lunged after him. The explosion was a huge roar, followed by an enormous slap of concussion. Windows broke all over the basement. There was a light, hard rattle like rain on a tin roof. Nieman groaned softly.

Rodriguez leapt up and stumbled over Nieman. He jumped across the boiler room to the tunnel door. A heavy hiss of steam escaped the ruptured boiler. Fuel oil ran from a broken line and began to burn. The dull red light from the spreading fire gave Rodriguez enough light to see. Nieman groaned behind him, slumping against the door frame.

The fifth key fit. Rodriguez heaved the heavy door open. A flight of crumbling brick stairs led down to a landing, then down underneath the street. He found a light switch, hesitated a moment, and flicked it on. A row of naked bulbs strung along the ceiling lit a steep, broad tunnel carved out of the gray Manhattan rock. The tunnel was lined with cases of arms and ammunition.

On the first landing, Mercedes Lopez lay on her side, trussed like a chicken. Her eyes blinked uncontrollably in the bright light. Her head rested at an odd angle on the edge of a step.

Rodriguez jumped wildly down the steps to her side. Her eyes rolled with fear, but she did not move. She was rigid. Rodriguez reached for her face. He said, "God. Thank God."

In a ghastly voice, with a moist rattle, Nieman shouted, "No, no, Rodriguez. Don't touch her. She's booby-trapped."

Rodriguez froze. Then he saw it. There was a grenade under Mercedes' neck.

Nieman wheezed, "I can't come down there. Go down a few steps on the other side of her. Do what I tell you."

Rodriguez stepped over Mercedes and crouched down.

"Is the pin out?"

Rodriguez put his face close to Mercedes to see. "Yes," he whispered. If she moved, the grenade would explode.

"Run your hands around under her very slowly and carefully. Feel for wires."

Rodriguez did it. The touch of Mercedes was like electricity. "There's nothing," said Rodriguez.

"Hold her head steady by the hair, and put your hand slowly but firmly around the grenade. Hold that handle down."

Rodriguez held Mercedes' head with his left hand and took the grenade with his right hand. He pulled the grenade out and set her head gently down. The grenade was heavy and cold.

"Give it to me," said Nieman.

Rodriguez stood up and handed the grenade to Nieman, who held it in two hands in his lap. He was bleeding heavily from a bad wound in his throat. He was the color of plaster. The fire from the leaking fuel line flared up. "Get her out of here," said Nieman.

Rodriguez pulled the gag out of Mercedes' mouth. "Daniel," she sobbed. "Mother of God."

He picked her up and started up the stairs. There was a loud hiss and another flare-up of the fire.

"The fuel tank," wheezed Nieman. "Run."

Rodriguez leapt over Nieman's legs and across the boiler room. As they reached the door to the basement, the fuel tank exploded with a soft suck of air.

"Run," cried Nieman, then he screamed with pain.

Rodriguez ran, carrying Mercedes toward the side door out of the basement, the way he had entered. Mercedes lay in his arms, saying over and over, "Daniel, Daniel, Daniel."

He was at the door when the grenade exploded. He ran into the yard and threw Mercedes under a heavy wooden picnic table at the edge of the yard, and flattened himself on top of her.

There was another loud explosion, and another, then a noise that split the night. The tunnel was like a huge cannon, and the explosion of the ammunition roared out of the mouth of the tunnel with enormous force into the boiler room and the basement, breaking walls and masonry columns.

As the columns cracked, the heavy marble floors above began to settle, collapsing in toward the center of the old building. Joists cracked, then roof beams, as the great weight of the limestone walls leaned inward.

The ground around the building began to shake and flex

like an earthquake. With an inhuman rumble that seemed endless, and a choking dense explosion of dust and mortar, the beautiful old building fell into the basement as neatly as a child's toy, leaving the living observers dirty but unhurt under their picnic table.

This novel is emphatically not journalism, nor is it thinly fiction-alized local history. It is fiction in every sense. The characters are, without exception, the inventions of fiction. Having said that, I must say that *Rooftops* is based very loosely on murders that actually took place in 1972 and 1973 in the neighborhoods described in the novel. The killer was never found. The fourth victim of the killer was a boy named Luis Ortiz, who was a schoolmate of my son at PS 165. On the door of a closet in the principal's office, there is a small brass plaque commemorating the dead child.

Kinderhook
February, 1981